CHILD OF DESTINY
Shadows of the Sun

Book Two

By
Mina Ambrose

Full Quiver Publishing
Pakenham, ON

Child of Destiny
Shadows of the Sun #2
Copyright 2021 Mina Ambrose

Published by
Full Quiver Publishing
PO Box 244
Pakenham, Ontario K0A 2X0
www.fullquiverpublishing.com

ISBN: 978-1-987970-25-8
Printed and bound in the USA
Cover design: James Hrkach
Cover photo: Zeferli iStock

NATIONAL LIBRARY OF CANADA
CATALOGUING IN PUBLICATION

Published by FQ Publishing
A Division of Innate Productions

"Look at the stars! Look, look up at the skies!
O look at all the fire-folk sitting in the air!
The bright boroughs, the circle-citadels there!
Down in dim woods the diamond delves! the elves-eyes."
Gerard Manley Hopkins

Part I: An Ancient Prophecy Unveiled

The Prophecy

Deep underground, there sprawled a labyrinth, formed in ancient times — not only by the forces of nature, it was said, but by deep magic as well — for some long-forgotten dark purpose. A vast network of narrow winding passages at several levels connected many chambers, large and small. Some of these lay empty, not abandoned, just dormant until their time should come. A goodly number served as storehouses for vast treasures gathered throughout the ages: heaps upon heaps of arms and armor, as well as cups, plates, and images cast in precious metals and adorned with gems; countless chests overflowed with jewels of every kind, and coins of gold and silver.

Another smaller chamber served as a study. In its center was a table on which lay maps and charts marked with hastily scrawled notes, figures and equations; a pen and inkpot; and a large tome lying open beside a small oil lamp. One entire wall was covered with shelves, some filled with books and scrolls, others, a clutter of musical instruments and various scientific devices, including an astrolabe, and finally, a row of human skulls, displayed like trophies. More maps and charts were tacked to another wall; every remaining wall space was hung with weapons, mostly of medieval or ancient origin.

The largest and most splendid chamber of all was known as the Great Hall. This was the throne room of the master, Charon, lord of the darkest creatures of the night. Yet for all its splendor, the Great Hall was grim and forbidding as the ruins of a war-ravaged cathedral with every vestige of light and beauty blasted from it. Here the master gathered round him the Vampire Brotherhood, minions, and mortal guests as well — for he was easily bored and ever hungry. And, though the most powerful of them all, he alone was confined to the Underground, night as well as day.

When the Prince, his favorite, had defected a year ago this past spring, and their old lair beneath the caverns of California was compromised, they'd had to swiftly relocate. This new haven lay halfway across the continent to the east, where an obscure arm of the vast subterranean network known as the Mammoth Caves surfaced near the town of Sylvan, in southern Illinois. A perfect haven hidden from both the rays of the sun and the eyes of mortal men. Equally important, for the master's purposes, was its geographical location: it lay within that narrow strip extending from Oregon to Virginia, where the predicted solar eclipse of 2017 would cast its umbra. And failing that, yet another slated for 2024, according to the master's calculations.

The Great Hall was, like the master, magnificent, yet wrong, somehow, falling just short of beautiful. Vaulted ceilings curved inelegantly above. Along the walls, archways gaped like hungry maws, as though to swallow whosoever should enter there. In actuality, they were merely passages to other chambers or stairways, some descending to the depths, others rising to the Upperworld where night skies beckoned to the thrill of the hunt — for all but the master. His domain here below was gloomy as Hades' realm, but for the torches affixed high up on the walls the entire length of the Great Hall; even these emitted only a feeble light, their guttering flames struggling to survive the dance with shadow. Reeking smoke spiraled up toward the ceiling, while black streams of melted pitch crept down the walls of stone, almost as if the very Earth was bleeding.

Whispers and murmurs echoed through the Great Hall. The flutter and snap of black cloaks stirred up the smell of blood and death, though that mattered not to any of those present. Only to a mortal, had any been there. Little would have been visible to him in the feeble light, however. Nothing but a pale glimmer of faces and hands suspended in blackness like a sinister mime show. He would likely have shivered from an eerie chill, not of the natural kind. But on this particular night, there were no mortals here.

Only vampires.

The one concession to light and beauty in this grim bleakness was the tall and imposing throne of the master. Carved of fiery orange alabaster, it was adorned with ivory and jade inlaid with gold. Its many precious stones sparkled with a brilliance unnatural in the feeble light of the torches, like eyes glowing in the dark. Two spiral columns, delicately carved, thrust upward from the back of the magnificent ornate chair to support a crown of spikes, upon which were affixed human heads. Though somewhat obscured by the drifting smoke from the torches, it was a gruesome display: some were whited skulls, others in various stages of decomposition. All except one. This one remained lovely and serene (even after over a hundred years) as though merely asleep.

The crowd continued to gather. Faces gleamed in the light of the torches; a sea of faces, and like the sea, never still. Not at the moment. Faces dead white, eyes dead black, except when they flared with an unholy light. An eerie sight, for most of them wore the long black cloak that made a vampire invisible in the night. Fangs flashed, and hisses protested the jostle and press of the crowd. Nervous expectation filled the Hall; the very air crackled with it. Snarls and murmurs increased as time dragged. A summons with no explanation was not to their liking, but they dared not defy the master.

"What he want of us?" one of them said, a tall vampire in a tattered cloak. "So close to—" Here he halted, just short of saying that hated word. *Christmas.*

"Yes, why does he call us here, now?" growled the craggy-faced one. "You. Rojo. You must know."

Rojo, short, wiry, with flowing red hair, rasped, "I know nothing, Genie. I was about to go on one last binge before, um, you know. Then I got the summons."

The quiet one with the long brown curls, known as Blue Boy, spoke up. "We were already outside when they called."

"And I had plans!" pouted the curly-haired blonde clinging to his arm. She was called Pinkie. Someone once thought these two resembled the sweet children in the famous paintings, and the names stuck.

"Did they tell you why?" The tall thin one's words rushed out in accents of old Mexico. "It is not because it is almost— that comes every year."

"Why is your eye twitching? And your cloak so ill-kept?" Rojo said rudely. The thin one's glare stopped him in his tracks, but not for long. He went on. "Do I know you? Hey, turn your head, just so. From this angle you—"

"They were so insistent." Pinkie frowned. "Don't tell me there's a solar eclipse again so soon!"

"I take no notice of such things," said the thin one, momentarily distracted from Rojo's unwelcome attention. "But maybe that is it. Just like up north that time."

"Hey, ugly!" Rojo shrieked, unreasonably.

"Calm down," the Genie said. He turned to the thin one. "So? What is your name? Are you new?"

"Where you been? I am Will. I, too, was up north." He turned his one fierce eye on Rojo. "You hear of that big battle out west last year? I was there. I do not recall seeing you. So. You say nothing about my eye. Nada. Okay?"

The redhead scowled and subsided ungraciously, though he continued to cast speculative glances toward the other.

"Ah. Now I recall," the Genie rumbled. "Sweet William. It's the damage to your face. You used to be pretty." He gave a short laugh. "Well, better than losing your head altogether."

Will's one good eye pierced the Genie with all its intensity. "Right. I almost lose it that time. But I drink the blood of the Huntress. I am healing. Soon I will be like new."

Silence followed this remark. Huntress. That name was one to strike fear into all their hearts. Throughout the centuries, whenever the creatures of the night grew strong enough to become a serious threat to the human race, a mortal female child known as the Huntress was born to rise up and subdue them. She was not an ordinary mortal but had special immunity to their demonic powers; she was created to hunt and kill vampires. This she did whenever they intruded too boldly on the mortal domain. As a general rule, mortals were easy prey. She was not. Most vampires wisely tried to steer clear of her.

The Genie regarded Will with new respect. "I hear you. Been there myself a time or two, never liked it much. Love the blood, but no. I prefer to keep my head."

The red-haired one spoke again, in a calmer tone. "Ah, Will, I remember you now. You were there the time we nearly got her, before that battle you speak of. But when we took that other Huntress up north a hundred years ago, I had a hand in that. With her own arrow, I brought her down," he boasted.

The tall thin one inclined his head. "If only I had been there, but I was too new then, Nyx said, and she hid me away. As for *la chica*, I never want to face her again, ever!" He shook his head. "She don't look like much, but ¡ay! So many of us did not return."

"We might have taken her head last year — we were so close! If not for —" The redhead broke off. "Um, you know; you were there."

"Right. If not for the Prince —" Will halted in confusion. "Forget I say that name. It just slip out. Forget it, okay?"

The others shifted their feet and glanced away; that name was anathema in this company.

"One thing is certain," said Pinkie, attempting a safer topic, "The Huntress won't find us here tonight. Would she think to search under a haunted house or a mausoleum? Hah! She'd get lost in the maze soon enough if she did."

Rojo cast a scornful glance her way. *Dumb blonde*, it said. "A Huntress can sense our kind anywhere; it's how she is."

"But Charon has released the Dog. No mortal can get past that beast," Pinkie insisted defensively.

"Hey. You don't know her," he scoffed.

Pinkie flicked an indifferent glance his way and clutched Blue Boy's arm as she turned to scan the Great Hall again.

"Huntresses can be killed, even so," the Genie said. "But if she shows, I'm out of here. I'll leave her to you heroes."

"Let's hope that don't happen," Will said. "The master will be *loco* if he has to move again so soon."

"Look over there." Pinkie's curls bobbed as she stood on her toes to peer over the heads of the crowd. "He's coming."

All faces turned toward the far end of the Great Hall. All fell silent as their attention focused on the figures emerging from one of the archways. One of them stood out from the rest. His tall and imposing stature, his striking air, commanded the crowd's undivided attention at once, though he had said no word. It was the master, Charon. He fit this name he had chosen long ago, for he too had ferried many a mortal across the River of Death (though, of course, he took his toll in blood rather than coin). But he was feared by all, not just mortals; he was known to blast from existence vampires, who had the misfortune to displease him as well.

Smoke-orange light glinted off angular lines of his brow and jaw. Deeply shadowed eyes narrowed to slits as he gazed imperiously down his aquiline nose; his scarlet lips, slightly parted, revealed sharp white teeth; his dark hair was a lustrous mane hanging to his waist. The long black cloak concealed his form but not the sheer power of his being. He was keenly aware of his own magnificence.

With a faint rustling and a flutter of his cloak, he ascended the throne and seated himself in regal dignity, impassive as a marble statue as he surveyed the crowded hall. His long pale hands snaked out to grip the carven arms of the chair, their restless fingering of the ornate bosses and the tap-tapping of his nails the only sign of his excitement.

His current favorites, sometimes referred to as the elite, flowed into their accustomed places at the base of his throne:

At Charon's right stood Nyx. Her black cloak was spangled with stars, distinctive among this company, as were the harem pants and black boots she was fond of wearing. Wild hair, like black rays, framed a heart-shaped face irresistibly lovely, but pale and cold as Grecian marble. She regarded the crowd with an air of possessiveness and superiority, as well she might. Despite her dainty youthful appearance, she was the most ancient of them all, her powers far exceeding those of the entire crowd.

Next to her was Styx, her hood thrown back to reveal long, crinkled moon-bright tresses. Her sweet pixie face that appeared so lovely and fair but for the deep purple shadows around those cornflower eyes was, upon closer inspection, hard and sharp as glass. The ethereal black cloak that fell in graceful folds to her dainty toes was her only attire and barely concealed her perfect form; every movement revealed tantalizing glimpses of alabaster skin. Her woeful gaze darted over the crowd, searching in vain for that one elusive face.

A little apart from the rest stood Bellatrix, tall and regal, her long, shining black hair hanging past her waist. Her face was as though sculpted of olive-tinted marble, its high cheekbones, prominent nose, and the shining hoops at her ears loudly proclaiming her Iberian origins. Her black cloak seemed more of a fashion statement than a practical necessity, a finishing touch to her elegant velvet-and-satin gown strewn with precious gems. After a cursory scan of the crowd, she fixed her adoring gaze upon the master.

The Sandman, a slight figure in a black trench coat, was nearest on Charon's left. His perpetual half-smile and tousled sandy hair were those of a winsome mischief-maker, but his pale blue eyes were cruel and cold. He directed a snide comment toward the slender, dark-haired, elegant Rocket, who cowered, half-hidden behind him. The Rocket responded with a quick glance from hot black eyes and a sneer, forgetting for the moment his precarious position of disfavor. Fortunately for him, their ongoing rivalry was old news; the master did not condescend to notice.

The Rocket still dared to maintain his undying ambition, which was to one day stand at Charon's right hand. For now, he kept a low profile, but when the moment presented itself, he intended to be ready; to grovel at Charon's feet, if necessary. He would regain his position of favor and more. He'd remind the master of his speed and agility. He was still of great use, and the master would see that. He may have failed to turn the Huntress's friend, as the master had ordered. But it wasn't his fault. It was the master's vaunted Prince, who, after rejecting them in favor of a human –the Huntress, no less, whom he claimed to love – had stolen his prey and foiled his plan.

The Rocket had remained in hiding for almost a year, regenerating after the master had blasted him. Now he was ready, waiting for an opportunity to redeem himself in the master's eyes. The master's anger should be aimed at the Prince, not him. He was loyal, always had been, and yet he'd suffered the full brunt of the master's wrath for his failure—when it was the Prince's fault! No excuses were accepted, no explanations allowed. Just that instant blast of fury, of fire, and the sound of his own shrieking ringing in his ears as he was dragged away.

He whimpered at the memory of coming to, lying on the floor outside the Great Hall where they had thrown him. Pungent odors of singed hair and charred flesh had recalled to him Charon's nightmare glare and the red-hot flame.

But for Nyx, he wouldn't have survived the ordeal. She and the Sandman were all that had stood between him and annihilation, he recalled now with a rush of shame. He'd shaken off their hands and crawled painfully away, down the winding passage to the crypt, where he'd crept into his niche and slept until he regenerated.

Time had healed him. Now he was ready for vengeance!

Malice burned inside him. The Prince, how he hated him!

From the first, he had envied him, wanted to be him. He wanted that number one position.

The Prince was now fallen; he would have his chance. If not for the Sandman, who'd dared to step into the breach during the Rocket's regeneration, to take that number one place, he would already be... at that thought, he could feel the worms of hate and envy eating at him from the inside. That the Sandman had interceded for him with Charon only added fuel to the fire.

One thing only had sustained him: the thought of revenge. The Prince must pay.

Nyx had turned the Rocket, once upon a time, and favored her own "children" above all others (though she often neglected them, depending on her mood). She was able to save the Rocket this time because the master listened to her as to no one else. Charon was hers, too, it was said; she was the one who had transformed him into the all-powerful master, the most wonderful being on the face of the Earth.

Then came the Prince. It was said that five-hundred years ago, when Nyx brought him home, Charon was furious. He had expressly commanded that she kill that entire family, and yet she'd dared—! The master had been about to blast this reminder of his shame from existence when something gave him pause. He'd tasted and was intrigued.

Charon had sensed something beyond the ordinary in the Prince, perhaps, and a brilliant idea struck him. He would take this son of his ancient enemy and make of him a vampire par excellence, superior to all (save himself, of course). Thus would vengeance be his. And he would thereby prove his equality with God. (So he told himself, and all of them.) As his Adversary had breathed life into a creature of clay (he announced), making man in His image and likeness, just so would Charon, having no breath, blast this newly made creature with his own blood and power, making what had once been a man into his image and likeness. And so he did — he made him into a perfect monster, like himself.

And so, the Prince became Charon's favorite.

The Rocket had not come on the scene for another two-hundred years, but he had heard the story too many times to count. Ad nauseam. If only the master had blasted the Prince into oblivion. But he had not.

Of course, if he had known then what was to come, he surely would have.

But who could have guessed that this masterpiece he had created would one day repudiate him and go over to the Enemy? How like his Adversary to resort to underhanded methods! The Prince was his! (Thus he raged.) His own! Proud Charon was blind to the fact that he was nothing like God; he could not create, but only took what God had created and ruined it. For that was all he could do. God had only taken back that which was His in the first place. (They all knew that but, of course, they dared not say it.)

Of late, it had begun to be whispered that the Prince's defection was only the beginning of the rain of heavenly fire, the Wrath of God, upon Charon's rebellious head. He was not daunted. Instead, like Lucifer, he shook a fist at the heavens and swore vengeance. If he could not reach the master, he would make her, the Huntress, His handmaid, pay.

Charon had then sent out the Rocket to turn one of her friends, on the chance that that would perhaps entice the Huntress herself to confront him, whence she should meet her doom. But alas, the Rocket had proved himself unworthy of the task in the master's eyes, and instead of receiving the highest favor, he had burned.

But now — now, it seemed, his time had come.

In the center of the Great Hall, the gathering throng was abuzz with uneasy questions. The din gradually built to a crescendo until Charon growled, a deep, menacing sound easily heard throughout the Hall with no apparent effort on his part. At once, silence again fell. All eyes turned to him and were ensnared by his hypnotic gaze. There was no escape; his cold eyes transfixed each one of them, to search the very core of their being. After a long, tense moment, he released them. Though there could be no sigh, the relief was almost palpable.

He then began to speak in a pleasant tone. "You wonder why I have called you here. We come to a crisis. It is, simply, a matter of life or death. For us. You are thinking that is nothing new. No, this time is different. In a way never before seen, the seed of our victory or our destruction is imminent. Whatever has gone before is nothing. Rituals, sacrifices, omens, celestial signs – all that promised everything and yet came to naught were only a prelude. The fulfillment of that ancient prophecy is now at hand. This being, this terrible instrument of our destruction, is about to appear. We must deal with him now or be destroyed."

He reached inside his cloak, drew out an ancient scroll of parchment, and lifted it up for all to see. A low questioning murmur rippled through the crowd. They were not often privileged to share in the results of his incessant study. In silent expectation, they watched as his long nails untied the cord that bound the scroll. The yellowed parchment rattled as he unrolled it. His eyes swept the throng; its rapt attention was fully upon him. When at last he began to speak, his deep voice carried effortlessly to every corner of the Great Hall.

"Listen to me, all you who would live forever, and heed these words of prophecy!" He lowered his voice to amend, "A poor translation, I know, but sufficient for our purpose." Then he cast his gaze down to the scroll and began to read:

"We, who once were men but men no more
Will rule the Earth when blood-red star
And darkened sun doth signify
A virgin's blood shall satisfy.
The sacred spear shall lead the way
To pierce the power of Sun's bright ray
Victory to him who wears the ring
To sacrifice the blood of a king.
But hold! The era's end shall thus portend
That sting of death for us, not men
The moon twice blue shall be the sign
Of light to foil our scheme malign.
Upon her brow the twelve-starr'd crown
She who rules has mark'd her own
Above the blade a key of gold
Her shield of virtue he shall hold.
Beware that spawn of night and day
Whose deeds his own kin shall betray
Beware ye, who prey on men of Earth
A radiant moon reveals his birth."

The echo of his voice died away. He rolled up the scroll and retied it. Like magic, it vanished within his cloak, and he lifted his gaze once more to the faces before him, his eyes aglow with incandescent malice. The crowd shrank back, but then they saw that the look was not directed at them, and their tension eased.

After a long moment, he spoke again. "So there you have it, briefly. Or, you find it obscure, perhaps? What does it mean? you ask. It means we shall rule the world. We will have our time in the sun." Murmurs of astonishment arose from the crowd. To them, the sun meant fiery destruction. The master raised his hand for silence. "What concerns us now is that on this night of the moon's perigee, the radiant moon of prophecy, a child shall be born, the spawn of night and day. That is, a child born of one of us and one of them." His lip curled in scorn at the concept.

A din erupted, and a great stir of agitation rippled through the throng. "That's impossible!" voices cried.

The master fixed his black gaze on them, and silence fell once more. "It is not possible, I grant you, but nevertheless it is so. This child is the Consecrated One told of in ancient legend. He is the Destroyer, destined to crush us, to wipe us off the face of the Earth. If we take him now, while he is a mere babe, we may yet foil that ancient prophecy. It is said that the blood of kings flows through his veins. If he will share it, well and good. If not, we take it. Then shall we walk in daylight and the world will be ours! Go. Bring the child to me."

With that, the Great Hall erupted into chaos.

"How can we?"

"Not now, Master!"

"It's almost, you know, C-Christmas!" Some bold creature dared to voice that terrible word. All felt the constraints caused by the birthday celebration of the Light of the World, during which they must remain hidden underground.

At the master's menacing growl, the uproar subsided. "Fear not. Christmas is yet two days away. I want the babe now, this very night. Go, at once. Its birth is imminent. Sandman, you are in charge of this expedition."

There was a general movement toward complying with these orders. The Rocket saw his chance; he crept over to the feet of Charon. "Please, Master, may I have the honor of bringing the child, once captured, to you? For I am fastest and will certainly be back before dawn, whereas no other —"

At once, there were cries from the crowd. "No, I shall!" "No, Master, choose me!" For all knew that whoever brought in the child would gain great favor with the master.

But the Sandman outshouted them all. "Master, I am in charge here. I, myself, shall bring him to you."

Charon swept them all with his gaze before bringing it to rest on the Rocket. "True, you are the fastest. Yes, you must bring him to me.

Sandman, see to it."

No one dared grumble once the master had spoken. Even the Sandman, though he shot the Rocket a furious glare.

"The child shall be mine!" Nyx hissed, her eyes alight with unholy fire. "I will see to that shield of virtue!"

Charon turned an indulgent glance upon her. "He is yours, then, Nyx. And vengeance will be mine." His gaze shifted to the throng. "I have spoken. Go now. Bring the moonchild to me." His voice, like thunder, echoed through the labyrinth.

Dark forms spewed forth from the depths like cinders wafted up from the fires of hell, boiling up into the night sky, blotting out stars as they clustered and swarmed. Then they shot out like a dark, deadly flight of arrows toward the western horizon.

Time passed, but not too much time by human reckoning. The shadowy figures clustered once more, obscuring the pristine silvery disc of the moon. Then they dropped down, out of the night sky, to converge on a small town in southern California.

A Child is Born

Archangel, California, the eleventh hour

Christmas lights dimmed, and the tinny sounds of sleigh bells and carols in downtown Archangel were abruptly muffled as dark figures circled and were sucked downward like leaves in a whirlwind, toward a tall edifice in the old part of town. A dry wind whipped around ancient red brick corners, whistled through eaves, and rattled rusted downspouts that stretched from top to bottom of the four-story building. Streaks of lightning illuminated the gables; wind-lashed branches scraped the darkened windows of the old hospital. Thunder cracked overhead and rumbled into the distance. Wind gusted intermittently. A discarded plastic bag slapped against the wrought-iron fence; odd bits of paper rattled out the gate and down the dimly lit street.

A shadowy form materialized beside a Joshua tree, its pale face turned upward, its eyes on the thin vertical line of light that shone beside the drawn shade of a second-story window. More dark figures were gathered on the roof and clinging to surrounding trees. Others glided over the fence to take up positions on the lawn. Hollow eyes fixed intently on the lone sliver of light. Black cloaks fluttered in the wind. In silence, they waited.

Inside, patients were settled in for the night, the silence interrupted only by the beeping of monitors. On each floor, nurses were at their desks, taking advantage of the quiet to catch up on reports and fill in patients' charts. The emergency room was calm and brightened by the small Christmas tree in the lobby.

Only on the second floor, in the delivery room, was there a flurry of activity, as babies come when they will. Sister Rafaela, a nursing sister of the Carmelite order, bustled into the room to check the monitors. A young mother, who seemed hardly more than a child herself, lay on the bed and moaned softly at intervals as the pangs of childbirth came and went. Beside the bed stood her husband. His pale brow furrowed with concern as he smoothed the damp tendrils of blond hair away from her forehead. Her blue eyes opened and met his black ones.

He appeared anxious but attempted a smile. "It should be okay, this close to Christmas."

She touched his hand. "Just don't leave me." She closed her eyes. A tear slid down her cheek.

"Never!" He leaned over to kiss her forehead, then spoke very softly into her ear. "I'll be by your side every minute, watching over you in your hour of need. Just concentrate on having our baby—it's all you must think about now. I am here. Never shall the minions of hell take you from me, my love."

The young nurse briskly began to make final preparations for the impending birth, wondering, why this sense of danger? What had the young man meant by that odd remark about Christmas, and… she wasn't sure, he spoke so softly, but—minions of hell? What could he mean? She touched the crucifix beneath her apron top and prayed.

Soon Doctor Luke Papaianou entered, a short, stocky man dressed in greens, accompanied by Edna, a tall, gray-haired nurse.

"Hello, dear little mother," said the doctor cheerily, though his expressive black brows wore a slight frown as his quick dark eyes warned Sister Rafaela to be prepared for an emergency. She understood that nothing must be said; Edna wasn't privy to the secret. He saw the father's anxiety and added lightly, "Don't go fainting on us now, Dad."

This drew no response, other than a somber glance.

They proceeded with the delivery. Sister Rafaela stood by to assist, with words of encouragement to the mother. The father's haunted expression stirred her to compassion. "It'll be fine," she reassured him, smiling. "Mothers have had babies since time began."

His piercing gaze met hers for a moment. His eyes—so strangely compelling and attractive! She caught herself at that disturbing thought and flushed. But he'd turned away to comfort his wife. The nurse could not help noticing that now and again, he gave a start at some untoward sound, glancing around the room as though he, too, sensed danger. It kept her on edge and praying.

Soon a loud squalling announced the baby's entry into the world. "There's nothing wrong with those lungs," the doctor declared heartily. "You have a fine boy!"

Sister Rafaela glanced at the clock. "11:47. Just under the wire for the twenty-second. That's cutting it close, little man."

Edna clamped and cut the umbilical cord. The doctor handed the wailing baby to Sister Rafaela, who gently placed the child in his mother's arms; he quieted at once. The nurse smiled at the father's beaming face as he gazed down at his wife and child. He appeared to have forgotten his anxiety for the moment.

"Oh, my darling," he said in an awed tone. "What have I ever done to deserve this?"

The young mother's face was radiant, her eyes on the baby, who was making squeaky little sounds of contentment. After a long moment, she smiled up at her husband.

"He's beautiful," she murmured, "like you."

"Like you," he said at the same time.

Exhausted, the young mother closed her eyes. Sister Rafaela reached out for the baby. "Come, little one, let's get you weighed and dressed while mother gets settled in." She touched the father's shoulder and was startled by how cold he was; she barely managed not to shiver. "Sir, you're welcome to lie down in the waiting room for a bit of rest, if you like. When mother and baby are ready, we'll let you know."

"I will stay," he said with an anxious glance around. "My wife wishes it." Then his expression softened, and he managed a faint smile. "Just take care of our little boy."

Of course, that's my job. What is going on here tonight? The young nurse brushed off an unaccountable foreboding. She wrapped the baby in a soft flannel blanket and carried him from the room.

Downstairs in the emergency ward, the scratching of a pen sounded loud in the stillness as Sarah, the night nurse, scribbled away at her reports. The faint but regular sounds of several snoring patients alternated with the beeping monitors. All was normal, aside from the lack of after-hours accident and mugging victims.

Sarah reached up a freckled hand to tuck her unruly red hair behind her ears, and at the sight of the colored lights on the little Christmas tree, she had to smile. Such a cheery touch in the bleak old hospital! She returned to her writing.

The lights dimmed momentarily. She glanced up. Not another power failure! But no, they were steady and bright again. For no apparent reason, she shivered, and the hair on the back of her neck stood up. She thought she glimpsed a shadowy figure from the corner of her eye, but when she turned, nothing was there. She shrugged and was about to attend to another chart when she heard the outside door close.

She frowned and got up to investigate, her shoes squeaking on the tile floor as she went to look around the corner. There was no one near the door; the corridor was empty. No sound of footsteps, either, but the tinsel on the tree was shimmering as from a slight draft. So the door had closed; it wasn't her imagination. She had seen someone. Or maybe she was working too many late shifts. She shook her head as she returned to her desk and picked up her pen once more.

Then came a faint, but definitely alien, sound. Now her nerves were on edge; she had to stop writing every few seconds to listen. There it was again, almost like the flapping of wings. She glanced up. *There!* Another shadowy figure disappearing down the corridor. This time she was sure of it.

"Excuse me," she called, getting up to start down the hall. There was no answer, only the echo of her own voice and footsteps. No one was in sight. "I must be imagining things," she muttered as she turned to go back to her desk. "Oh!" she exclaimed, taken by surprise as she nearly bumped into someone.

He cut a trim figure in his black trench coat, though his sandy hair was mussed as though he'd just climbed out of bed. In a face ghastly pale, red lips smiled, but the black eyes did not. A hideous effect.

"May I help you?" she forced herself to say in her most confident tone, though she quaked inside. He wasn't there a moment ago, she was sure. It was eerie, almost as though he had materialized out of thin air. He made no answer, only stared. "Are you in need of medical attention?" she asked then, buying time as she tried to edge past him toward her desk and the alarm. Then she couldn't tear her gaze away from those unblinking black eyes like flat black pebbles, reflecting nothing. They seemed to ripple, and she felt dizzy, as though she might fall into them. At that moment, a dark figure flitted past, breaking the spell. She shook her head to clear it and saw three more shadows glide past in quick succession. "Excuse me, sir!" she called after the disappearing figures, "I'm afraid you can't—visiting hours are over. Sir?" They paid no heed. Exasperated, she moved briskly toward the desk and the alarm button.

There was a sudden rush of wind, and the stranger's slender hand clamped down on hers. "No," he said softly, still with that little smile. "You don't want to do that."

She shivered at the icy coldness of his grip and trembled at the sight of that terrible face with the dead eyes, but managed a firm tone. "Sir, let go of my hand." He withdrew his hand slowly, gently dragging his claws across her forearm. It made her skin crawl. She thought of screaming for help but got the eerie feeling it would be the last move she'd ever make. A beeper sounded. The stranger flinched, his smile fading. Sarah looked at the flashing monitor and breathed again. "My patient. I need to check on him."

The flat black eyes narrowed, and white teeth glinted. At that moment,

Janet, her partner in Emerge, appeared, carrying a steaming cup of coffee. Her sturdy white shoes squeaked on the tile floor, injecting some sort of normalcy into the surreal scene. "I figured you needed an eye-opener this time of night," she said, cheerfully unaware of the little drama at the desk. "This coffee should hit the spot."

Sarah had no time to breathe a word of warning. In the blink of an eye, the stranger had Janet by the throat with one hand, his face only inches from hers. His tongue darted out against her cheek, and she promptly fainted. He flung her away, left her lying on the floor in the pool of spilled coffee, and turned back to confront Sarah again, all before she could move to sound the alarm.

This had to be something out of a nightmare. Still disbelieving, she stumbled back against the filing cabinet. In that instant, the thing was crouched on her desk, red lips drawn back from terrible teeth, eyes fixed on her.

Sister Rafaela hummed softly as she sponged off the baby and dried him with a warm towel. As she turned him on his stomach, she noticed a spot just above his right shoulder blade that hadn't washed off; a golden brown mark that stood out against his fair skin. A birthmark. Oddly shaped, though. It resembled a familiar symbol she couldn't quite place, precise as though drawn with a fine pen whose ink had bled and softened the edges a bit. Struck by the thought that there was more to this than met the eye, she wondered: what was the significance of this tiny scrap of humanity and this pang of apprehension she felt? She glanced around quickly and held him close, as though to protect him. From what, she did not know.

With an effort, she forced herself back to her task. She weighed him, put him back on the change table, and brushed his hair, so fine, like silk. His cheeks crinkled as he opened one eye and protested in his creaky, newborn voice. He began sucking on his fists.

"So you're hungry now, are you, little boy?" She smiled and tickled his cheek. "Let's get you dressed."

She put a white nightgown on him, then fished a Miraculous Medal from her apron pocket. She kissed the embossed metal oval depicting the Blessed Virgin on one side and the crown of twelve stars on the other, then tied it by a narrow blue satin ribbon around the baby's neck. Once she had him bundled securely in a warm white blanket, she gave him a kiss and tucked him into bed.

"I'll take you to see your mommy soon." She traced the Sign of the Cross on his forehead and breathed a silent prayer, asking his guardian angel to protect him. She did this for every baby entrusted to her care but had a feeling that there was urgent need for this one. Quietly she closed the door.

Her footsteps echoed in the corridor, loud in the quiet of the night. She shivered. It seemed that a faint sound like the flapping of wings came from behind her, so real that she turned, then scolded herself for being silly. *Or, was that a dark shadow streaking past? No, how could it be?* But she felt a sharp premonition of danger. She reached for her crucifix and pushed open the delivery room door, heart pounding.

Edna glanced up. "You're just in time. We're ready to move her now."

The young mother was covered with a warm blanket; her eyes were closed. All seemed normal. Then Sister Rafaela caught the husband's anxious glance as he hovered near the bed and was suddenly afraid.

"Your little boy is fine," she said, trying to sound more reassuring than she felt.

He neither replied to her comment nor relaxed his watchfulness. As the two nurses pushed the bed toward the door, he somehow got there first and quickly scanned the corridor in both directions. Then he preceded them, his alert dark eyes peering into each doorway. The wheels on the bed sounded loud in the night as they trundled along.

Funny how the man seemed to glide rather than walk and made no sound at all, Sister Rafaela was thinking, when she heard that eerie sound of flapping wings again. She glanced at Edna, but the older nurse gave no sign that she had noticed. *Maybe I'm losing it.* No, the baby's father had glanced around quickly as though he had heard it too. And as they approached the room, he rushed ahead to the door to search every corner of it, it seemed, from floor to ceiling, before they could enter.

"No one else is in here," Edna said, sounding annoyed. "We've given her a room by herself, as you requested."

He did not take offense, just seemed preoccupied as he stood back to let them through the doorway. The young mother opened her eyes as the two nurses transferred her to the bed and settled her in, then she drifted off to sleep again. The father pulled up a chair and sat beside the bed as the nurses started to wheel the other bed out the door.

"She's sleeping now. You might want to get some rest, too," Edna said, more kindly. "It's been a long night."

"Thank you. You are very kind," he said agreeably but stayed where he was.

Sister Rafaela spoke softly. "I'll see if I can round up a little snack. She'll be hungry when she wakes up." She smiled. "There's a reason why it's called labor."

"Yes, I see that." He seemed about to continue but paused and glanced at Edna, then back to Sister Rafaela.

She took the hint, and as she helped Edna push the bed through the doorway, she said to her, "You go ahead. I'll catch up." When Edna had gone, she turned back to the baby's father. "Is there something else I can get you? A sandwich, maybe? You're certainly welcome to a snack."

In an instant, he was across the room, so close, she was startled. He spoke in a low tone. "Could you bring our baby here? And call Father Michael right away, please?"

She saw the distraught face, the dark shadows beneath his eyes, and recalled her own odd feeling of impending disaster. Absurd, of course. "Certainly," she said, more calmly than she felt. "Don't worry, the baby's fine. Everything is fine."

Despite her reassurances, he was as watchful as ever as he resumed his position at the bedside. The dim light shone on his waxen profile, outlining the striking classic features. Only the dark shadows around his eyes marred his extraordinarily good looks. Sister Rafaela glanced toward the peacefully sleeping mother. *Lovely. No wonder the child looks like an angel.* She went to join Edna in the corridor, and together they pushed the empty bed back to the delivery room.

"A strange man," Edna commented. "He seems overly possessive of his wife. She looks so young."

"He's concerned about her. They must love each other very much," Sister Rafaela said generously; she always tried to discourage gossip. "Anyway, he looks about the same age." Or does he? Upon reflection, she couldn't be sure; he appeared young, but there was something ageless about him. An odd thought, really. "Anyway, it's okay if he wants to doze in the chair."

What was with the hidden undercurrents here tonight? She was unable to express her uneasiness to Edna. *I can't very well ask her if she hears bats!* She tried in vain to laugh at herself. With a feeling of misgiving, she glanced over her shoulder and shivered. She couldn't think why; the old hospital was like a second home to her. And it had very good security.

Why would the young man ask for Father Mike at such an hour?

Edna was back at her desk, writing up her reports when Sister Rafaela paged the chaplain and found he was still in the building despite the late hour. Then she went to the snack room and gathered sandwiches, cookies, orange juice, and some wonderful-smelling coffee on a tray; two of everything, in case the father was hungry after all.

As she came out into the corridor, a shadow seemed to streak out of sight. It gave her a jolt. Was she imagining things? She heard a faint rustling sound, and now there was an odd smell, too. With a quick glance toward the nurses' station, she saw Edna sitting at the desk, writing as before.

"The baby!" she whispered, with no idea why she was suddenly anxious, or why she was afraid of being overheard or by whom. Edna glanced up and stared after her in puzzlement as she hastened down the corridor toward the nursery, but she had no time to try to explain. She regarded each doorway she passed with trepidation, and her feeling of dread increased the nearer she drew to the nursery. "Angel of God, my guardian dear… " she prayed, clutching at her crucifix as she peered through the window into the nursery. All seemed well; the babies were asleep. She couldn't resist a quick glance around as she set the tray on a cart outside the door, but all seemed as usual. She entered the nursery and saw that the newest one was awake, after all. He had worked himself out of the covers and, with pitiful little sounds, jammed his fists into his mouth.

She smiled as she straightened his gown and tucked him into his blanket once more. He gazed up at her with blue eyes so bright they almost seemed to glow. "You're hungry, little man?" she murmured, smoothing his hair. "Let's go see Dad. And maybe Mommy will wake up to feed you." She picked him up and pushed open the door.

As she stepped into the corridor and took the tray from the cart, she felt a cold chill. There was Edna, at the far end of the hall, in the bright light of her desk lamp, busy at her reports as though nothing was amiss. But the empty corridor seemed a mile long, like something out of a nightmare. *This is the same hospital I've worked in for the past how many years*, she told herself resolutely. Nothing like this ever—what is happening here tonight? She glanced down at the infant on her arm; his trusting gaze was on her face.

"You're fine. It'll be okay," she whispered.

She held the baby on one arm, balanced the tray on the other hand, and with an anxious glance around, hurried down the corridor to the young mother's room. She still had that odd feeling of being watched. Had the curtain across the way moved? *No, of course not; that room is empty. Anyway, this is silly.*

The baby's father stood up as she rushed into the room. His anxious look did nothing to ease her fears.

"I'm sorry it took so long," she said with forced calm as she set the tray on the bedside table. "I called Father. He'll be here soon. Um, let's have some light." She switched on the lamp.

The soft light shone on the baby. His eyes seemed to glow (of course they didn't really, that was impossible) as he fixed them on his father's face. The man regarded his child with an expression of wonder and reached out to touch its fine hair, golden as a halo in the lamplight. For the first time, the nurse noticed how long and tapered and white were the young man's hands, how oddly gleaming were those nails.

"He's so tiny, like a doll," he said, glancing up. "It's hard to believe he's real."

Startled out of her preoccupation with his appearance, she stammered, "Er, oh, yes. Yes, he's real enough, as you'll find when he keeps you awake nights," she laughed a little to cover her confusion. The father's expression changed at that; something dark seemed to pass behind his eyes. She suddenly felt that she had seen something personal and private, and quickly added, "Would you like to hold him?"

He nodded, and a little anxiously settled the infant in the crook of his arm.

"Don't worry," she smiled, "He won't break. Babies are tough."

"Especially our baby," came a quiet voice from the bed. The young mother had awakened and now cast a fond look upon her husband and son. Her blond hair was disheveled against the pillow, but she seemed revitalized, curiously no longer showing any sign of exhaustion.

"I've brought you something to eat." Sister Rafaela began moving the adjustable table nearer to the bed.

"Thanks. I'm starving," the girl said.

By the time the table was in place, the young mother had donned a terry bathrobe and was sitting on the edge of the bed, smiling upon the infant in the arms of his father. Lunch was spread before her, and she fell to it with gusto, rather at odds with her delicate appearance. The nurse tried not to stare. Soon the girl had finished both sandwiches, all the cookies, orange juice, and both cups of coffee without offering any to her husband. By then, the child was fretting in earnest. She gathered him into her arms.

Sister Rafaela managed a smile. "Baby knows it's lunchtime."

The little family was content for the moment. Sister Rafaela decided to allow them some privacy. On her way out of the room, she breathed a prayer.

Enter Sandman

Time seemed to stand still. Downstairs in the emergency room, Sarah was petrified with fear. Pressed against the filing cabinet, she faced the intruder. A terrible thought struck her: *this thing is not human!* The way those terrible eyes fixed on her, exactly the way a cat looks at a bird, with hungry eyes. Those teeth, so sharp, and he was so strong and fast; even the way he moved wasn't natural.

But monsters weren't real (were they?). And he wasn't even very big, only about her height. So why did she feel so helpless? Or, had she fallen asleep at her desk, and this was a nightmare? *Help me, God*, she prayed, for the first time in years.

Shadowy figures glided past, down the corridor. At once, distracted, the creature glanced at them. When he turned back to her, that comparatively friendly half-smile was on his face once more. Sarah sagged against the cabinet, weak with relief, momentarily. The cold, pale blue eyes made her shiver, and a thought struck her: *Weren't they black, just a second ago?*

The stranger jumped down from the desk, abandoning his predatory crouch for a more human upright stance. With the claw of his forefinger, he lifted her chin; her sense of relief fled. Her breaths became ragged gasps. His eyes fixed on her throat, and his tongue whipped out, unnaturally long and snake-like. She recoiled and shivered at his cold touch. *Omigosh, what is it?*

He laughed, an unpleasant rasping sound. "I am the Sandman. So sorry I can't stay to play with you tonight, little girl," he said in a regretful tone. Then his smile faded. "Be warned. Mind your work and leave us to ours, and you'll not be hurt. No one has to die tonight—your choice." With that, he vanished down the corridor after the others.

Sarah sagged against the desk, trying to recover from the shock. For a moment, she contemplated pressing the alarm button but thought of what the little monster had said. It had sounded like a threat. He wasn't human, despite his resemblance to a man. Couldn't be. But what was he? Maybe she ought to call someone. But who would believe her? She wouldn't, if she hadn't seen it herself. Was this old building haunted, as some said? Or had something been slipped into her coffee? *Don't be silly, Sarah.*

Coffee! She recalled Janet and got up to look. Afraid. But there was Janet sitting on the floor, groggily looking around. Alive. Dark blotches stained her white uniform. Blood? Sarah's breath caught for a moment; then she realized it was only coffee. *Get ahold of yourself, girl!*

"Oh, my head," Janet moaned. "What happened?"

Sarah rushed over to help her to her feet. "Don't you remember that strange—" She burst out crying. "Oh, sorry." She managed to get herself under control. Took a deep breath. "Looks like you… um, here, let me help you up." She dabbed at the stains on her friend's uniform with a Kleenex as Janet stood there, a little unsteadily. "Maybe sit in my chair, and I'll have a look at that bump on your head. Gosh. That's a real goose egg. You must have slipped on a wet spot." *Of course, that must be it.*

Janet winced. "It's a bit tender when you touch it, but I'm all right."

"You just sit there a minute. I'll clean that up before someone else falls."

The corridor was quiet and empty, but even so, shivers ran up her spine as she got the mop and cleaned up the coffee. When Sarah returned, Janet was leaning her head on her hand, her eyes closed. The light was still flashing on the monitor, so Sarah shook off her qualms and hurried down the hall to attend to her patient. She couldn't help glancing over her shoulder a time or two, but there was nothing out of the ordinary. When she returned to her desk, Janet had a bit of color in her cheeks again.

"I think I'll get a coffee. I seem to have spilled it," Janet said cheerfully, as though determined to prove she was fine. "Would you like me to get you one, too?"

"No, thanks. Later, maybe," Sarah managed. *A good stiff drink is what I need!* Soon she was alone at her desk once more. She picked up the papers lying scattered on the floor. Evidence of a scuffle, proof that she hadn't imagined it.

Still puzzled, she resumed her work. Once she thought she heard a step, but a quick glance assured her that the corridor was empty. Her eyes slid to the alarm button. *Maybe I should… No. Who would believe me? A monster with pointy teeth that moves so fast it's just a blur? And that tongue!* She shuddered. A vampire? *But they aren't real; everyone knows that. What am I thinking? It's not even Halloween! Maybe I did imagine it.* Her hands were trembling. That was certainly real enough. *No, I have to make that call.*

She reached for the telephone and pressed the buttons quickly before her courage failed her. "Hello, Edna. Sarah here, in ER. How's everything on second floor? … It's pretty quiet here, too. Unusually quiet, I'd say, for this close to Christmas. You'd think with all the celebrating, we'd have a few accidents and beatings. You know, the usual. Not tonight, though. Any new babies? … Just one? … Well, all right." She stifled a sob. "Actually, it's a bit too quiet around here. … Okay, see you. No, wait! You, uh, haven't had any visitors, tonight, then? Like to see that new baby? Sure, okay."

She could have kicked herself. Edna would think she was losing it for sure now. Visitors, this time of night? She glanced at her watch. Past midnight. As if that thing meant to visit anyone, much less a newborn child. What was it doing here? A name popped into her head: King Herod. A chill went up her spine. *No, that's ridiculous. Must be going crazy.* Nevertheless, however she tried, she couldn't dispel the multitude of disturbing thoughts clamoring for attention. Then she noticed that she was still on the telephone. "Uh, okay, Edna, be careful, will you? Bye."

She replaced the receiver and glanced uneasily down the corridor. The silence screamed at her. Resolutely, she reached for the telephone again and pressed the buttons.

"Hello, security. Sarah from ER here." She nearly lost her resolve as a smooth male voice answered. She quickly went on, "Yes, okay, hi, Chuck. There's something strange going on. Could you please check it out?"

He'd sounded agreeable enough. *Be one sec*, he'd said. She hung up with a sigh. *Now I've done it!* She tried not to think of the monster's implied threat. At the moment, it was Chuck she dreaded. True to his word, he was there, Johnny-on-the-spot. She glanced up as the muscular young man with a blond brush-cut rounded the corner. The few times she had seen him in the year he'd worked here, she had always hoped it was the last.

He smiled, his small blue eyes sweeping over her in a way she didn't like. "Got a problem here?"

"Yes, as a matter of fact." She took a firm tone. *Gosh, I don't even know the guy, really.* Might as well give him the benefit of the doubt. She plunged on. "Some creep came in a few minutes ago, but he took off that way." She gestured toward the corridor. "A short, wiry guy in a trench coat, with messy blond hair. And some of his pals, I'm pretty sure; though they moved so fast I couldn't see—"

"So, they went thataway, did they?" Chuck cut in, shaking his head. "Okay, babe, if it'll make you feel better, I'll check it out." He winked at her and ambled off down the corridor.

Sarah scowled. *I hope he finds the creep;* then see how smug he looks. Annoyed, she went back to her reports. A short time later, she heard the echo of footsteps in the corridor. She tensed, but it was only Chuck. As he drew near her desk, he caught her questioning glance and grinned.

"Nothing. Just as I thought, you girls get lonely down here at night and just want some company." He sat on the corner of her desk with a leer and a wink. "Well, here's ol' Chuck, at your service, babe."

She glared daggers at him. "There was someone here. You couldn't have searched very far; you weren't gone that long. Maybe he went upstairs.

Now could you please remove your—er, yourself from my desk?"

Chuck grinned bigger. "Or what? You'll call security?" He laughed but got off her desk. "Okay, okay. I'll go have another look-see. A guy could get frostbite around here." He started down the corridor, then turned to look back. "Don't worry, babe. Ol' Chuck'll get the boogeyman for you."

Chuck is the boogeyman, she thought. Then she recalled the creature and shivered. *No, Chuck is nothing like that thing.*

Back at her desk on the second floor, Sister Rafaela waited for Father Mike, her mind still not completely at ease. The feeling that something was wrong lingered, but her frequent glances down the corridor revealed nothing out of the ordinary. No rustling sounds or black streaks now. It probably had been her imagination. Still, she prayed; couldn't help feeling the need to be watchful. For what, she had no idea.

Edna got off the telephone. "That was Sarah, asking if I'd seen anything unusual."

"Unusual?" Sister Rafaela was suddenly alert.

"Odd, really. She said it was quiet but asked about visitors. She seemed nervous."

"Sarah?" Sister Rafaela frowned. "It takes a lot to rattle her."

The sound of the elevator doors opening startled them into silence. When Father Mike emerged and strode toward them, they unconsciously breathed sighs of relief. Father Michael O'Donovan was tall and imposing in a traditional black cassock and Roman collar, with a crucifix tucked in his belt, but his face was kind. In one hand, he carried a black case containing his emergency kit.

"Thank God it's you, Father," Sister Rafaela said.

He smiled. "You expected someone else?"

The young nurse felt suddenly self-conscious about her fears. Now that Father Mike was here, they seemed silly and childish, like imagining monsters in the closet or under the bed. She smiled ruefully. "It's a bit too quiet around here, I guess. You know how it is sometimes, in the middle of the night."

"Old Scratch hasn't been up to his old tricks, has he?" the priest chuckled. "Okay, I won't tease you on a grim night like this." He grew serious. "What's the emergency?"

Edna raised her eyebrows at Sister Rafaela as if to say, *you explain this one.* She didn't think it proper to call the priest at such an hour except in a life-or-death situation, which, in her opinion, this was not. She returned to writing reports.

Sister Rafaela felt the sting of disapproval. Her confidence shaken, she turned to the priest. "Yes, Father. A baby was born here tonight, and his father asked that I call you. He didn't explain, but I understood that—"

"A rather strange man," Edna said without looking up.

"He appeared overly anxious, even for a new father," said Sister Rafaela, then added in his defense, "I assumed he had a reason, though I had no idea—" She paused as she noted the dawn of understanding and concern on the priest's face.

"I know them. Show me the way. Quickly."

Relieved to have Father Mike in charge, she led him down the corridor. His outward calm failed to dispel her misgivings. She had glimpsed apprehension in his eyes. She said a Hail Mary under her breath. A feeling of terror struck her suddenly, as though the hounds of hell were on their heels. She glanced around, but nothing was there. Nothing visible. She thought she heard an eerie wailing in the distance. But no, it had to be a—maybe a siren? As she reached the young couple's room, she shivered. Forced herself to stop and take a deep breath. No, the door was ajar, just as she had left it.

She knocked gently and stood aside for the priest to enter. Her heart pounded as she followed him into the room, not knowing what to expect. What she found was an oasis of calm that took her by surprise. The young mother was still sitting on the edge of the bed, her golden hair now neatly combed, sweet as a Madonna with her baby asleep in her arms. Her husband stood nearby, protectively, which seemed odd in surroundings so serene.

Father Mike strode over to the bedside. With a friendly greeting, he reached out to the young man, who shook his hand, though at the same time seemed to draw back. The priest then turned to the girl, took her slender hand, and searched her eyes. "And how are you, my child?"

She met his gaze, tears welling up as she attempted to smile. "I'm fine. My baby... " Her voice caught. "You said... "

Father Mike looked down at the infant sleeping in her arms. "Wonderful," he said gently. "A great gift from God. Children are our hope for the future – this one in particular. May I see?" As the young mother began to unwrap the baby's blanket, the priest glanced at the nurse. "You attended the birth, Sister. Did you notice anything out of the ordinary? A birthmark, perhaps?"

"Yes," she said slowly. "Yes, I did. The baby had an unusual birthmark on his back. But many people have birthmarks. Not a matter of concern," she hastened to add, then wondered at his faint change of expression. "Is it of significance?" Even as she voiced the thought, she realized how ridiculous it sounded.

"I believe so," he said calmly, to her surprise. "Let's have a look." The young mother removed the baby's blanket and turned him on his stomach. Sister Rafaela untied the gown and drew it back to reveal the birthmark. "So, it's true," the priest murmured. "Born December twenty-second. Full moon in perigee."

"What is it?" asked the child's mother.

"It has been said—I hardly knew whether to believe and yet... " He traced the shape with his finger. "Here, the tau, or T-shaped cross, also known as the hammer. There. You see? The mark of Our Lady's Hammer, the one destined to save mankind from a rising darkness." The baby awoke and began to squirm, with little noises of protest. Sister Rafaela smoothed his silky hair. "And you see here the attached circle forming the *crux ansata*, the ancient symbol of eternal life. The Key of Life, symbol of resurrection, commonly known as the ankh symbol. It's the sign of one destined to shed his innocent blood for others. A savior."

"What does it mean, Father?" The mother spoke up. "Not that—not that he must... "

"I shouldn't have put it quite that way, I suppose; these things are often ambiguous. It's better not to read too much into them. Only after the fact will we truly understand. You see how bright the full moon is tonight, or maybe not; you were a little busy in here. That too is one of the signs pointing to the birth of this child." He opened his case. "Not to worry. But I'm glad you remembered to call me right away," he said with a quick glance at the child's father. "We do what we can and trust in God for the rest. There isn't much time, I'm afraid. The first thing is to baptize the child. Once he's sealed with the mark of the Holy Spirit, Satan and his minions have no power over him. Otherwise... well, we must do this now, while we still can, for they will attempt to turn him to their evil purpose." All shifted uneasily at the urgency of his tone.

"But he's just a baby!" the mother cried in anxious wonder. "And he's so significant to the fate of the world?"

"So it is said." The priest donned his purple stole and began the ritual. "What name do you give your child?"

"Michael," replied the mother, who then glanced apologetically at her husband. "Okay, honey? I know it wasn't on our list. It just came to me out of the blue."

All eyes turned to him. His gaze shifted uneasily, but he nodded agreement. "Yes, it is a good, strong name."

Just as the priest was about to continue, she added, "And Jude, for the patron of impossible cases. Isn't that what this is?" Her eyes lifted to her husband again.

He nodded, though he seemed distracted.

"Right. A good choice," Father Mike assured them. "St. Jude was very close to Our Lord, a cousin, in fact. And I've always been partial to St. Michael the Archangel myself." Despite his attempt at levity, he seemed tense. "This child may yet need the protection of a powerful warrior," he added under his breath. Then he continued, "And what do you ask of our Holy Mother Church for Michael Jude?"

"Baptism," the parents replied in unison.

The nurse started and glanced up; she'd heard again that eerie fluttering sound. The baby's father had moved to the doorway, where he stood as though on guard. Tense, watchful. With an effort, she turned back to the business at hand.

Father Mike took out a small vial from his case and anointed the baby with holy oil. He continued with the prayers of exorcism in a calm voice. Sister Rafaela stood in as godmother, answering in the child's place along with the mother. They made the profession of faith for him. The priest then reached for another small vial. While pouring a few drops of holy water on the child's head three times, he spoke the words of baptism. "Michael Jude, I baptize you in the name of the Father, and of the Son, and of the Holy Spirit, Amen." After praying the intercessory prayers, he concluded the ritual. "Michael Jude, I claim you now for Christ, our Savior."

The child had fallen asleep. The nurse helped the young mother secure his clothing and blankets once more.

The father turned in the doorway. "They're coming." His voice was harsh; *almost a growl*, Sister Rafaela thought.

A sound like rushing wings drew nearer, this time accompanied by muttering and high-pitched squeaking. The nurse shivered; she felt a little faint. *What is going on here?*

"Hurry, Father," said the young mother.

The priest spoke calmly. "We'll now consecrate him to Our Lady. Pray with me now." Together they made the Sign of the Cross and said the prayers of consecration to Mary (Father Mike completely focused, the two young women somewhat distracted). He then blessed the child and placed a brown scapular over its head. The nurse tucked the woolen squares beneath the white flannel gown. Father Mike spoke softly. "Be not afraid. Our Lady will protect this little one whom she has chosen for her own."

Sister Rafaela straightened the baby's clothing and wrapped him securely in the blanket once more. He awoke and opened his eyes. His fine hair shone in the lamplight. "You are a very special little boy," she said softly as she handed him back to his mother.

The priest went toward the doorway. "They're here. Beware, they dare not leave without the child."

The unnatural sounds were louder now. The child's father drew back as the priest neared him, eyeing the crucifix with an odd mix of doubt and fear (it seemed to Sister Rafaela). He went to his wife, and as a look passed between them, they seemed to come to an understanding. He turned to the nurse. "They're coming. Will you help us?"

She was astonished, not only by his strange remark, but also that he should ask a favor of her, a near stranger. "Yes, of course. What must I—um, who's coming?"

He didn't reply, but with a look of anguish, gently took the baby from its mother's arms, kissed it, and held it out to her. "Here, Godmother, keep him safe for us."

She stepped back in confusion. "But I—but how can I—?"

Then all was pandemonium. As though borne by a sudden whirlwind roaring down the corridor, black shadowy forms swooped toward the door, rushing to pour into the room. But there they seemed to run up against a rock. The intrepid Father Mike stood in the doorway, his feet planted and his crucifix held high. His eyes were closed, and his lips moved in prayer. The bat-like squeaking turned to shrieks of pain and fury as the maelstrom of evil was confronted by the image of Christ on the cross.

The front line of unholy beasts fell back, howling, but fear of their master fueled the desperate determination of those behind them. The next wave forged ahead, pressing the vanguard before them. Eyes aglow and teeth glinting, they hissed and screeched and snarled in terror and pain and fury. They surged forward, knocking the crucifix from the priest's hand, thus opening the way for the deluge. With a great howling, the mass of vampires poured through the doorway and into the room.

Many years had passed since the occasional Saturday night donnybrook when Father Mike had stood beside his brothers against the O'Malleys and the Clenaghans, but now, as then, he did not mean to go down without a fight. His long arms shot out; his big fists slammed foes to the floor. Despite his best efforts, they soon overran him and down he went beneath the onrush. Dark forms surged into the room amid shrieks and snarls and the gnashing of teeth. White faces shone eerily in the glow of the bedside lamp, and flat black eyes, empty and dead.

"Father!" cried Sister Rafaela. Her voice was lost in the din as the roaring force flung her against the bed. With her hands over her ears, she turned toward the young mother, fearing for the safety of her patient.

She was astounded to see that the girl had leaped up and into a fighting stance, all signs of weakness gone. Now she looked fierce, her expression set, and her hair swirling about her like a golden cloud. Her hands and feet blurred as her kicks and punches, with lightning speed, sent the terrible foe spinning in every direction.

Sister Rafaela stared. The enemy kept coming, but the girl seemed oddly undaunted. At last, the vanguard paused, dark cloaks whipping around them as they fell back to regroup, snarling and hissing threats and blasphemies. The girl stood panting, yet alert for their next move, her eyes hard as sapphires and fixed on them with deadly intent.

From out of chaos, it seemed, the father thrust the child into Sister Rafaela's arms. "Take him!" he hissed. "Take him to the chapel, now!" He propelled her toward the door.

There was no resisting him. That terrible voice was not the soft-spoken one that had heretofore come out of his mouth. Sister Rafaela stared in shock as his eyes flared red, and he turned a glowing gaze upon the intruders. Lightning shot from his eyes, and those before him were gone— poof! into a cloud of dust. Then he opened wide his mouth, and with an inhuman shriek, sprang into the fray.

Taken

Her blood ran cold. *The child's father a vampire? A vampire! But they weren't real! Couldn't be. But what were those things, if not vampires? No, impossible.* With an effort, she tore her disbelieving gaze from the whirlwind of chaos, clutched the baby to her breast, and flung herself out the door. *My Jesus, Blessed Mother, angels, and saints, help me*! A vampire? How can it be? And—and if vampires are real, they're evil. The father, a vampire? No… no…

As she ran down the corridor, she could hear the battle only dimly now. Was it real? Had to be; she could hear Father Mike, as though from a great distance, urging her to flee. She hesitated and gazed down at the child in her arms. What was it? No, it was innocent, whatever else. To the chapel, the father had said. Of course, the baby would be safe there. She ran to the nurses' station.

Edna stared, astonished. "What are you doing? The baby—is something wrong, Sister?" She seemed confused, or maybe disbelieving? Surely, she could hear the tumult?

"Just pray," Sister Rafaela panted. "Please pray."

She thought she heard a flutter of wings from down the hall to her left and froze as a figure appeared at the stairway door. The tousled sandy hair gave him a boyish look, quickly dispelled as he moved toward her with an odd inhuman glide. Those eyes! They were like black holes in the dead-white mask of a face. The blood-red lips smiled slightly. *Dear God. Fangs.* He wasn't a human, though at first glance, he did resemble one.

A vampire! And he was blocking the way to the stairs! She turned and ran for the elevator. The door stood open. She flung herself inside and hit the button for the main floor. But the creature was quick; he slipped inside just as the door closed.

With quaking heart, she turned her back on him to shield the baby. *Hail Mary, full of grace, the Lord is with thee. Blessed art thou among women and blessed is the fruit of thy womb, Jesus.* She prayed silently, desperately, as the elevator began moving downward. The sudden grip of claws on her shoulder was like a vise; with inhuman ease, he turned her to face him.

"Give me the child, and you may go free!" he rasped.

She shut her eyes—couldn't look at those terrible teeth or endure that hypnotic stare—and held the baby close. So sure he'd tear the baby from her arms...but he didn't (she couldn't begin to guess why). Overcome by terror, she concluded her prayer aloud. "Holy Mary, Mother of God, pray for us sinners now and at the hour of our death. Amen."

He fell back, hissing as though her words burned him, but quickly recovered and drew her into his embrace. *Cold, so cold, and that smell of death... God, help me.*

The baby awoke and began to wail. At once distracted, the vampire relaxed his grip and his mouth curved into that half-smile again; long fingers crept toward the child. In desperation, Sister Rafaela glanced around for escape, but the thing had her trapped in the corner. She watched in helpless fascination as a talon touched the baby's cheek, and the vampire said softly, "Come to me, little one." He leaned in, mouth opening wide.

Sister Rafaela cried out in alarm, and the thing started; his eyes crackled, and his mouth snapped shut. With a longing look, he laid hold of the baby, as though to rip him from her arms. *Sweet Jesus, help*, she prayed; and recalled the crucifix beneath her apron top. She drew it out and shoved it into the vampire's face.

With a piercing shriek, he flung himself away, to the far corner of the elevator, where he crouched, shielding his eyes.

She sobbed with relief as she soothed the wailing baby.

Blinking lights and the sound of a chime indicated that the elevator had reached the first floor. A long, tense moment passed before the elevator shuddered to a halt, and the doors opened, so slowly, it seemed. Then she was out the door and running, holding her crucifix like a shield over the baby. In the stillness of the night, her footsteps echoed loudly through the corridor.

She heard a roar of rage behind her. Her heart leaped into her throat, and she put on a burst of speed. *St. Michael, help me!* She rounded the corner, and there, at the far end of the hall, was the sign indicating the hospital chapel. *Sanctuary!* Hope renewed, she pounded down the home stretch. Her lungs were near to bursting when she heard a hideous shriek behind her, and a sound like the flapping of wings.

She dared not glance back. The sound of her heartbeat filled her ears. She willed her feet to move faster. Her lungs burned. The end of the corridor seemed so far, never-ending, like in a nightmare. And the vampire was so fast. A figure appeared just then, outside the chapel door. A big blond young man in a blue security uniform. *Thank God, someone to help.* Her legs felt like lead. "Help me," she gasped. "Help..."

She heard scrabbling on the tiles behind her. The thing was gaining. A chill ran down her spine. *Don't look back*! That flapping sound, like the fluttering of bats' wings, was louder now. An eerie high-pitched squeaking grew and grew until it seemed to pierce her brain with shattering intensity. It reached its crescendo in a deafening shriek, and she wanted to drop everything to cover her ears but dared not.

The baby! She had to save the baby. She sobbed in terror as a great shadow loomed over her and lifted pleading eyes to the man standing at the chapel door. *Why is he smiling like that? And looking, just looking. Am I the only one who sees the monster? Or, maybe he didn't hear me.* "Help," she croaked.

Then, abrupt silence. A shadow descended upon her like a shroud, dark and suffocating. A white hand, long and thin, materialized out of the blackness and reached for the child in her arms. It touched the crucifix, and with a snap and a flash and a hideous shriek, the vampire was thrown back. Claws raked the side of her face, but he was gone, cowering against the wall.

Pain seared across her cheek, but she ran again toward the chapel and sanctuary. She had nearly reached her goal when the security officer stepped forward. She thought he meant to open the door for her, and she sobbed in relief.

He smiled, his eyes like blue chips of ice as he reached out with big ham hands. "I'll take that," he said and plucked the baby from her arms.

With a rush of wind, the child was gone. Chuck, the security man, was still standing there, but the baby had vanished right before her eyes. How had that happened? One moment he was there, and the next, not. She looked around, bewildered. Something wasn't right. Chuck still had that smile on his face. She had seen him take the baby, but he didn't have it now. She stared in disbelief.

No, no. She *had* been holding the baby. Then Chuck reached out and... *oh, no.* The father had entrusted his child to her, and she had failed him. Failed. Oh, what had happened to the baby? How could she explain? Or had she just imagined — then where was the child? With a cry, she dashed back to the elevator, but a quick scan of the inside told the tale. It was empty. No baby. Frantic, she ran as fast as she could back to the chapel. The vampire she had last seen crouching against the wall was nowhere to be seen. He was gone, and with him the babe, she realized now.

Chuck met her as she rounded the corner once more. He said something she didn't catch, like wondering what she was doing. She blinked, confused, and glanced past him, but the corridor was empty. Silent, except for the monitors beeping, machines humming, the snoring of a patient, and an occasional moan. No flapping wings, no vampires.

"Where's the baby?" she asked him, her voice failing at the last.

He gave her a peculiar smile and turned away. She flushed red for some reason. And put him out of her mind at once. She had to figure this out. Was she dreaming? Or losing it? Maybe she'd find the baby in the chapel, safe and sound, after all. She opened the door and surveyed the hushed, dimly lit room. It smelled faintly of burning beeswax; the vigil lamp indicating the Presence of Jesus glowed red. No one was here. She threw herself onto her knees and poured out her troubles.

She recalled very clearly that the father had given her his child for safekeeping. And though he himself had turned out to be a vampire (no, that couldn't be true, could it?), he, oddly enough, had told her to flee to the chapel.

She had almost made it. She wasn't quite sure even now what had happened, except that they had taken the baby. Whatever *they* were. The look of that tiny, innocent face so fair and delicate, so fragile, those lovely blue eyes, haunted her now.

God, forgive me, I was supposed to save him. She felt for the rosary at her waist and began to pray for the protection of that poor babe now in their hands.

Tears stung her cheek. She tried to brush them away, but that set the side of her face on fire. She jerked her hand away and looked down at it. Red smeared her fingers.

This Means War!

Dead silence. What the—? Mara stood panting in the center of the hospital room, holding her stance as she stared around in disbelief. All vampires had vanished—the enemy, that is. She turned to the Prince, and as her gaze met his, realization dawned.

The baby! It's not me they want—they're after the baby!

In the same instant, she saw the Prince's eyes flare. He whipped around as lightning shot from them; scorch marks appeared on the far wall and acrid smoke spiraled up to the ceiling. He opened wide his mouth and howled; an inhuman, long, drawn-out, absolutely terrifying sound that soared to an ear-shattering shriek and petrified every mortal within hearing.

Including Mara. For a split second, she shook, then caught herself. *What's this…?* She was not afraid of vampires, like ordinary mortals. But the Prince!? She'd never seen him revert to type, ever! Well, not since his transformation, that is. Never wanted to; that thought made her shiver.

"No-oo-ooo! Prince, wait!"

There was no reply; he, too, had vanished. The baby—had they taken it?

Filled with dread, Mara leaped out of the room and sped down the hall, past the startled nurse Edna. The Prince was nowhere to be seen. She hit the stairs running, down, down, to the landing and through the door onto the main floor. She glanced both ways; the halls were empty… no one lying hurt—or dead, thank God. Even now, that was her main concern.

At the nurses' station were three nurses in a huddle. They looked at her wide-eyed, faces ashen, as though just coming alive after having been struck by the White Witch's wand and turned to stone.

"Did you see anyone—" she began. The red-haired nurse pointed to the doors. Mara slammed through them and ran outside.

She scanned the night. *No Prince.* She couldn't get even a faint sense of his presence. *Jesus, help me find him, and the baby, safe and sound.*

Her feet suddenly felt cold. Oh. She'd forgotten she was barefoot and wearing only a gown and terry robe. She wrapped her arms around herself and shivered as she surveyed the night, including the sky. Especially the sky. Empty. No vampires, anywhere. But the chill she felt wasn't from the cold. Where had the Prince gone, and… oh dear, what was he going to do? She felt suddenly afraid for him.

Or… would he find the baby? *Poor sweet baby…*

She dashed away tears—no time for that now—turned and went back inside. The nurses were still at the station, one observing as the redhead applied a bandage to the cheek of the third, who was seated on a chair. Nothing serious, it appeared, though her cheeks were streaked with tears.

Mara then realized that the injured one was the delivery room nurse.

"My baby? You got him safely away?" she choked out, despite herself; she already knew the answer. What had Father Mike said about the vampires? They dare not leave without the child. And they were gone! Tears flooded her eyes again. *Why didn't I listen?*

The nurse blanched. "Oh, it's you! I'm so sorry. I—I—couldn't— They took the baby before I could— And—and—oh, I couldn't save him!"

"Not your fault," Mara managed. *No, it's mine. I should have known. Oh, God, help me!*

With some difficulty—Sister Rafaela, wasn't it?—pulled herself together and attempted to dry her tears as she reverted to nurse mode once more. "But… you should be resting. You've just had a baby!"

At that, Mara only just managed to fight back her own tears. *My baby— but he's gone!* Of course, the nurse had no way of knowing of her capability to recover more rapidly than ordinary mortals from injury or stress on the body. But she had no time to explain, even if she'd wanted to.

My clothes! She ran for the stairs, taking them two at a time to the second floor. The nurse Edna gave her a deer-in-the-headlights look as she ran past, down the hall to her room.

She grabbed her clothes from the locker and whipped off her robe. At that moment, she heard a groan. Glanced over and saw Father Mike lying on the floor behind an overturned chair. He was slowly trying to sit up while holding his head.

"Father, are you okay?" Mara rushed over and helped him onto the chair, which she had set upright. "My goodness, your face! Father, have you been brawling again?" She tried to laugh but instead burst into tears.

"You should see the other guy!" he quipped, then, "I'm sorry, that was ill-timed."

"Oh, Father, they've taken our baby! And I don't know what to do—the Prince is gone! Just flown away, I don't know what he's thinking!"

"There, there. Don't cry." He patted her shoulder. "I'm sorry, I—"

"Life was so wonderful, and then everything just fell apart. Oh, I'm so afraid—what will the Prince do? And—and—my sweet little boy is stolen away!" she wailed. "What will they do to him? Oh, what am I to do?

"First, you may want to get dressed. Then we'll go down to the chapel and ask Our Lord for assistance in this matter."

She took his advice as usual and soon reappeared from the bathroom wearing her own clothes, her face freshly washed. "Sorry, Father, I didn't wait for your answer. You look a little the worse for wear; are you okay?'

He got up from the chair, wincing. "I believe I'll live. It's been a few years. Tomorrow, I'll be feeling it, sure."

They went to the chapel and prayed a rosary. Halfway through, Sister Rafaela joined them, weeping silently.

Through the rest of the night, and the nights following, Mara searched the town and all possible haunts of vampires and such but found no sign of the Prince or any other vampires. What was he doing? Where had he gone? Maybe he had an idea where they'd take the baby? A faint hope, but — *oh, if only he'd come back!* They could figure this out together.

Mara began to worry that the Prince had fallen prey to despair and would never return, and her heart bled. During those bleak days and black nights, she was never without tears, and spent long hours in prayer. Would life ever be right again? Father Mike was her bulwark; God was her lifeline. But she needed the Prince — was desolate without him. Had they killed him? No, she would have felt something. Wouldn't she?

Or — horror of horrors — had he become that monster once again, the one she'd fought in the church that first night they'd met? With that thought, she fell into a pit of darkness.

Christmas came and went; she found no joy in it, though her parents, friends, and Father Mike did what they could. She was grateful for that. She spent much of her time before the tabernacle, placing her troubles and hopes at the feet of the Lord, gaining there the strength to go on. Each night she went out patrolling, as always. This was her life; she had to do this. Oh, where was the Prince? They had to find the baby.

After what seemed an eternity of dark and empty nights on the verge of despair, she walked out of the church one night to begin her usual rounds. As the great door softly closed behind her, she scanned her surroundings, as always. The night was clear, and the stars sparkled like diamonds in the black silk sky; the frosty streets glittered like shattered crystal in the light of the streetlamps. Beauty, cold and devoid of joy. She breathed deeply of the night air, the familiar odors of fried food from the café just down the street, a whiff of exhaust as a car slowly cruised by, its tires crunching, its motor rumbling. Yet would anything ever be the same again?

She heard a slight sound, like a flutter of wings. Vampire? If so, it was the first one to manifest since that fateful night just before Christmas. She paused, holding her breath. Yes, it was! *At last, something to kill!* They'd taken her baby! It was time to dispense justice, and she was ready for them! She narrowed her eyes and assumed her fighting stance.

"Come out, come out, wherever you are! I know you're there!" she challenged. They should know they couldn't sneak up on her. *So, would it run? Just give me another hint, and you're dead!*

Then she saw a tall form materialize halfway down the block. She tensed. But… that white face, the black cloak with the flash of a jeweled clasp at his throat… it was the Prince! A lump formed in her throat, tears welled up in her eyes. Why did he just stand there?

"Prince?" she said tentatively.

In a blur of movement, he was right in front of her. And she was in his arms, weeping.

He hadn't found the baby. Every vampire he'd met was no more. Most had fled, but a few had thought to have a last feast before Christmas forced them underground. Very few managed to accomplish their designs before he caught them, and for those that did, it was their last. But none of them could tell him where the baby was, only that the Rocket had taken him. He'd picked up the scent, or sense, of them and followed, but the Rocket was too fast. Eventually, the trail had faded to nothing, and search as he might, he was unable to pick it up again.

Mara clung to him, unable to let him go. The baby had vanished. What if she lost the Prince too? But now he was oddly silent. Beyond his grief at the loss of the baby, something else disturbed him. He was so still.

"What is it? Prince, tell me," she said finally, with a sense of foreboding. She tried to look into his face, his eyes, but he cast them down.

And finally he came out with it. "You'll want to kill me now, I know. I've failed to protect our baby, could not find him. I should have known they were after him. Father Mike warned us, but I thought I… knew. And, Mara—" His voice broke. "Oh, Mara. I felt myself falling into the pit again. After I lost the trail, I—"

Mara felt a jolt of horror. "You— tell me you didn't break your oath!"

He cast his eyes down in shame. "I found a willing victim—of course, she couldn't help herself—and—oh, Mara! At the last possible moment, I looked into her eyes and saw yours! That stopped me. But I was so close— so close! Please, Mara, I beg you, release me from this curse!"

"Don't say such things! Only God has the right to—" she stifled a sob. "I love you—need you! And you just left me! Alone—to try to figure this all out! Don't ever do that to me again!" She angrily dashed away tears.

"I'm sorry, I didn't realize… It was my fault, and I thought you'd hate me—thought you'd want to kill me."

"I'll never hate you! And I can't kill you—you should know that, after… Anyway, it wasn't your fault, it was mine. I didn't listen to Father Mike either, and I should know from past experience the consequences of that. And now our precious baby is gone," she moaned, then took a deep breath. "No. No, we'll figure this out together. With God's help, we—"

"The baby—what Charon will do to him—" here he halted, his face twisted with anguish. He pressed her close, weeping tearlessly.

"We'll find him," she murmured into his cloak, her cheek against his cold, still heart. "If I have to search for the rest of my life, we will find him and save him from them. Our Lady is watching over him, Father Mike says. He's baptized and also consecrated to the Blessed Mother. She will keep him safe and show us the way to him. She has to!" She stifled a sob.

The Prince was silent for a long while, just held her close. "After the miracle granted to me, how can I doubt?" he said, finally. "We'll figure this out, somehow. Together."

Mara stepped back and tugged at his hand. "Let's patrol," she said, drying her tears with her sleeve. "Enough moping; I can't just sit around lamenting, when our baby's future—his very life—is at stake. We have work to do." They set off down the street. "So, while you were gone, my group of friends weren't about to abandon me to despair—thank God!"

"I'm sorry," the Prince murmured. "I shouldn't have left you so long."

She squeezed his hand. "Well, the future does seem brighter and more hopeful now that you're back. It was pretty black there for a while. But George never let me forget how you worked with him on that vampire-tracking software of his; he was so certain now that he's got it up and running, you'd be back to help him fine-tune it. Josh, of course, has that talent for designing awesome weapons for this kind of work. But now it turns out that he has this hidden genius for strategy too. He said, 'Mara, they took your baby. I know you're the expert on vampires, but I gotta tell you—this is war. Let's go find your baby. Let's take the war to them!' And he actually had some great ideas I'd never thought of. Seems I'm no longer alone in this, and it's not just you and me. Maggie's declared herself willing to help in any way she can, and Timmy's still raring to kill vampires; he's volunteered to test out the new weapons. I think he's still too young and hotheaded, but with a few more years of training— And Prince, even Father Mike's onboard!"

The Prince raised an eyebrow. "What exactly are you planning, my dear?"

"We're going to build an army!"

Fallen Star

December 23, 1999

A dark streak shot up from the town of Archangel, momentarily tarnishing the silver dollar moon, then vanished into the night sky. The Rocket glanced back once, saw the lights of the town far below whirl away out of sight. There was no sign of pursuit, which didn't surprise him, given his speed. He reveled in the rush of wind against his pale cheeks, the ruffling of his black hair and cloak as he sliced like an arrow through the night sky.

He thought little of the bundle he carried, except that it was something the master coveted, and therefore his own ticket to honor and glory. Then the precious bundle moved inside his cloak; he felt its warmth and clutched it tighter to his chest. Far from stirring his cold heart to tenderness — for there was nothing of love in it; he loved no one, could not recall ever loving anyone — instead, it awakened an instinct more savage, a thirst for blood.

With increasing intensity, he felt the pulsing through its veins. His hunger rose, sharp and demanding. He plucked the blanket back from the little face and gazed with longing eyes. He shook off the temptation and flew faster. The rush of cold air cleared his head somewhat, and he recalled the master's orders. They were explicit: this all-important child was to be retrieved this very night, intact. To taste would be fatal, he knew. Charon had many fine qualities, but mercy was not one of them.

The Rocket's speed was unmatched within the Brotherhood. While the others battled, the Sandman had snatched the baby, and the Rocket made his getaway with it. Many were certain to be annihilated in the process — that was only to be expected — but Charon must have this child of destiny, this spawn of the Huntress and that Betrayer, the Prince, who once was the master's favorite. Now, tonight. That was all that mattered.

The Rocket flew fast and hard, northeast, true as a homing pigeon.

Almost there. But something seemed not quite right. A barely perceptible lightening of the sky had appeared in the east. Fear jolted him. Dawn! He put on a burst of speed. *I can make it. I must. He said tonight! I must not fail. If I hug the tops of the trees…*

It was all the Sandman's fault. If he hadn't taken time to toy with the mortals, or... that nurse and her crucifix! A near-disaster, she had almost reached that chapel. Luckily a minion was there to help. *The master will hear of this; then the Sandman will no longer be his favorite. I will.*

The Rocket could have found a place to hide out for the day, to resume his journey at sunset. But the master had said... anyway, such a delay was fraught with a host of perils that had not occurred to him when he volunteered for this task. What if the child came to harm, or vanished while he slept? A horrifying thought.

His primary motive in undertaking this dangerous endeavor was personal glory. He still felt the sting of how swiftly the Sandman had stepped into the number one position vacated due to the Prince's defection. How he hated the Sandman; almost as much as he hated the Prince! The Sandman would not have succeeded in snatching the child if not for the Prince's one fatal error: he had assumed that their primary target was the Huntress. It was said that the priest tried to warn him, but the Prince, proud as ever, did not listen. He would pay for it now. An unpleasant smile stole over the Rocket's face. He had the Prince's child. At last, he'd found a way to hurt him! The thought exhilarated him.

All of a sudden, a powerful lassitude overcame him, jolting him out of his gloating reverie and into reality. The dawn! How had he let himself forget? He glanced up anxiously to see the inexorable lightening of the sky. *Must hurry. Must stay low.*

His arm tightened around the tiny warm bundle as he skimmed just above the trees in the shadow of the hills. The little thing began to squirm and to make small sounds of protest, a perilous distraction. His black eyes riveted on the child; his hand seemed to acquire a will of its own, tugging the blanket back. Hunger stirred once more; his tongue darted out against the warm skin. The baby opened its eyes and gazed at him solemnly for a moment, then began to cry. Its face reddened; the rush of blood just beneath the skin caused full-fledged hunger to explode within him.

He snagged the edge of the blanket and drew it back to expose the child's throat. *One little nibble won't hurt.* With bared teeth, he leaned in.

In that instant, the rushing wind whipped the scapular out of the baby's clothing, and the small woolen square with the image of Our Lady of Mount Carmel struck the Rocket in the eye. He flung himself back with a squeal to claw at his face, and as a consequence, lost his grip on the child. Quickly he snatched at the infant. The blanket loosened, the wind whipped the scapular off over the baby's head and wrapped it around the Rocket's throat. He clutched at the strangling thing. His shriek of terror choked off as the strings tightened around his neck and the small woolen squares fluttered out behind.

He released his grip on the baby, tore the fearsome object from around his neck and, with a whimper, flung it away. He heard a gasp and realized that the unthinkable had happened. He had dropped the baby! The terrifying reality of Charon's wrath filled his mind. In a panic, he shot downward to intercept it as it fell toward Earth. Almost to the tops of the trees, he stretched out his arms with a final burst of speed and flung himself at the baby. One claw snagged its gown; he clutched it to his chest once more and realized he must halt his downward plunge. A crash would be fatal to his prize and perhaps damaging to himself. He shot upward like the rocket for which he was named, his usual method of escape, and flew directly into the first rays of the sun shooting out over the tops of the hills. He flung one arm up to shield his eyes, the other outward in a vain attempt to stop his headlong rush to destruction. The baby flew from his grasp just as he was engulfed in flames. With a piercing scream, he plunged to Earth like a meteor.

The baby dropped out of the sky. His blanket fell away, and he gasped as the cold air touched him. With a wail of distress, he plunged downward.

Be not afraid, a soft voice soothed, and gentle hands caught him. *I am with you always.*

The baby quieted; he gazed up into the face of a Lady in Blue. She wrapped him in his blanket once more and tucked her mantle around him. Her sweet song lulled him to sleep, so that he was blissfully unaware when a slender branch of a dogwood tree snagged the blue mantle and cradled him above the snow-covered hillside, under the morning sun.

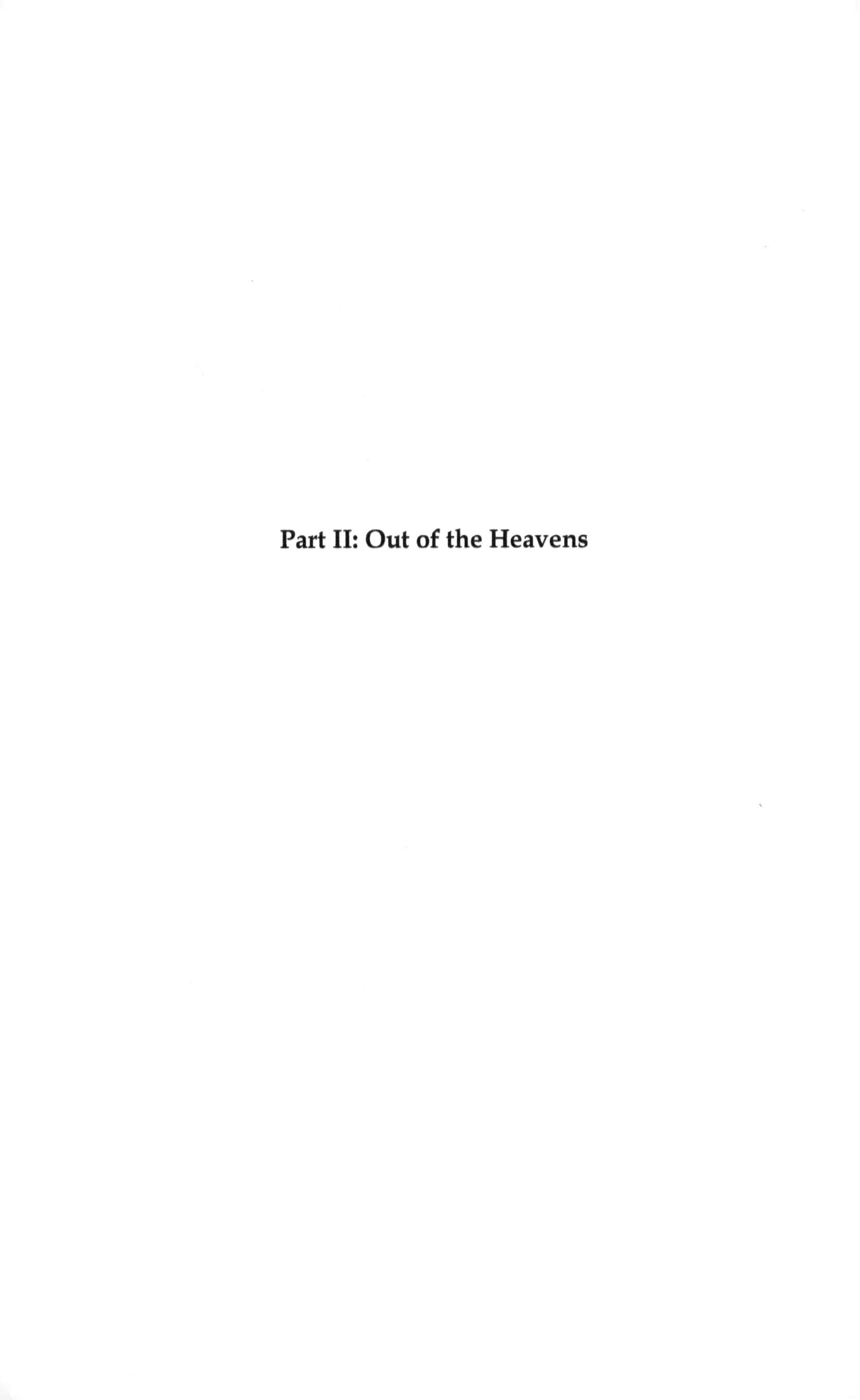

Part II: Out of the Heavens

Fireball

Hanna, Oklahoma. December 23, 1999

Thomas Martel was out by dawn, bringing in an armload of wood when he heard the scream. He glanced up just in time to see a fireball drop out of the sky. It was screaming. An oath escaped him as he ducked, certain the thing was coming down on his head. But the light winked out beyond the trees; the scream abruptly cut off.

Thomas was a man not easily ruffled, but now he stood shaking and breathless, his heart in his throat, as the silence stretched out. It was as though the world had gone dead. There was no chirping of morning birds or wind rattling winter-bare branches, not even the usual waking-up sounds of the sheep and goats and chickens.

No sound, no movement, anywhere. The early morning mist hung motionless over the creek; the white puffs of the animals' breath dissipated into the chill morning air above the corral. Even the rank barnyard and chicken house odors seemed oddly muted. Only Thomas's red plaid mackinaw emitted its usual smell of damp wool. At least that was normal.

After what seemed an eternity, he heard a faint whisper of sound. His head snapped around; his heart slammed into overdrive. But it was only deer. Two silent, graceful shadows bounced into view, out across a patch of snow behind the barn, to melt into the copse beyond. A doe and a half-grown fawn. Frightened of something. Something not far away, from the look of it.

He marked point zero fifty-some yards upslope from the mass of redbuds on the other side of the creek, then frowned and continued walking toward the house. A shiver went up his spine for some inexplicable reason.

First things first. It would never do to let the fire die.

Once inside, he dropped his armload of wood into the woodbox and bent to stir the coals in the kitchen stove. Anyhow, it would be better to wait until full daylight to check it out. Not that he was scared—just common sense.

Mamie appeared in the doorway of the bedroom, tying the sash of her housecoat, her waist-length hair tousled from sleep, spreading over her shoulders and down her back like a dark, silver-streaked veil.

"Did you hear that, Thomas?" Her voice was dull; dark circles ringed her eyes. "I thought I heard a scream."

"Go back to bed, dear, till the house warms up. I'll check it out."

To see her like this filled him with sadness. She had always been the strong and cheerful one, buoying him up when things went wrong. Especially in those early years. Back then, nothing ever got her down.

It was her faith that kept them going, for he had none. He had become accustomed to her way of clinging to the icons of her childhood; they seemed to sustain her when things got rough. That small, worn statue of the Madonna on the kitchen windowsill, the faded Infant of Prague on the corner shelf, and others. He knew their names by now, even though he didn't understand them. Or believe. The statue of a man with a flame on top of his head, and wearing a green robe, had come later after a dozen doctors and specialists had told her she would never be able to have a child. St. Jude, she'd said he was, the patron of impossible cases.

Well, whatever made her happy was fine by him.

But then everything had changed. She'd finally got her miracle, after so many years of waiting and praying. It took long enough, he'd thought grudgingly; they were both well past forty-five. Then he'd chided himself for being ungrateful. Mamie was happy; he wouldn't quibble. She believed her prayers had been answered, and no amount of logical argument would persuade her otherwise.

Despite himself, a shadow of doubt had been cast upon his steadfastly held skepticism; upon his lifelong disbelief in anything that could not be proven scientifically. Could this granting of their dearest wish have been due to the intercession of St. Jude, as she insisted? For a short while, he caught himself regarding with new respect that image of the saint who had apparently been instrumental in the performing of this miracle (if there were such things).

Everything had gone well throughout the nine months. Then, just before her time, the storm blew in. An unprecedented cold spell and continuous snowfall with drifts that obliterated roads and fences. To drive anywhere was impossible. Thomas had delivered the baby at home in mid-December. The child squalled a protest at his first sight of a frozen world. They'd named him Aaron.

For a few days, everything had been fine. The snow stopped falling, though the cold hung on. The skies cleared at night, driving the temperature down, down, but the woodshed was full of dry pine. A fire crackled in the stove and the hearth, radiating heat during the day, fending off the chill at night. Despite featherbeds, goose-down quilts, and a fire in the hearth, the child had sickened, and one morning was cold in his bed. Dead. They were stunned. Disbelieving. But there was nothing they could do.

Mamie was devastated. How could this be? She had been so certain of the miracle. This was the answer to her prayers. How could God have recalled His gift? No, the baby couldn't really be dead. She held him close, wrapped in thick woolen blankets to warm him, but it wasn't enough. Thomas had tried to console her, but she only glanced at him with grieving, reddened eyes, and went back to her rocking. Even after he'd built a small pine casket, she continued to rock the baby, unwilling to allow him to be consigned to the cold earth.

Finally, she realized it was time to let go. She dressed the child in tear-stained garments lovingly made by her own hands and, at last, allowed Thomas to take him from her arms. When he laid him in the box, she cast a reproachful glance at the little green-robed statue of St. Jude. He saw that look, and his heart was sorely wounded that anyone should hurt her.

They had buried the child Aaron and their dreams with him. Mamie sank into a great abyss of despair where Thomas could not reach her. She sat in the rocking chair with her back to the statue she could not bear to look at. Her eyes, once so bright with hope and cheer, were now dull with sorrow. She sat rocking, rocking, with no baby to sing to sleep; only a cold lap and empty arms.

He feared what she might do. Careful never to leave her alone for long, he kept his own grief inside and talked of practical things. If only she could hold to her belief that suicide was out of the question, that it would separate them forever, then she could weather this storm, too. Just as they had survived every other. Together.

So Thomas had not only his own grief to contend with in the following days, but also the frustration of helplessness to remedy the matter. Just the sight of the green-robed statue was like a dagger, stabbing him to the heart. The saint had failed Mamie after she had so trusted him. It struck Thomas as unfair.

That evening, as he hung up his coat on the peg beside the back door, Mamie was still sitting by the hearth, lost in her world of grief. She seemed so tired, so beaten. After all these years of yearning for a child, to finally get one, only to have it cruelly snatched away. What kind of a God would do that? *Oh, right, there is no God.* But there was that statue, standing there smug and useless.

In a sudden fit of rage, he threw his hat. The statue hit the floor with a crash. His instant of satisfaction was quickly replaced by remorse. He glanced at Mamie. This was the image of one of her favorite saints. She would surely reproach him for his show of temper. And rightly so.

She didn't even glance up. Though his heart sank at this further evidence of her despondency, he felt some small relief that he hadn't been caught. He crossed the room to assess the damage. It didn't look too bad; only the head and one hand were broken off, easily mended. He picked up the pieces and laid them on the countertop. The sweet face looked at him benignly, and he thought of the many years Mamie had prayed with unshakable faith only to have her hopes crushed forever. He suddenly couldn't look at the broken thing. With a furtive look around, he swept the pieces into a drawer, out of sight, then put on his coat and went outside. He gazed upward, beyond the stars, and shook his fist at the sky. *Do You even care? She believed in You, and this is how You reward her?* There was no answer. *Are You even there?* He cried out in his heart. With a shuddering sigh, he bowed his head and wept.

Those five days had passed under a dark cloud, figuratively as well as literally. Mamie rocked and groaned with sorrow and pain, holding a bundle of tear-soaked blankets to her breast, unable to fathom the loss. Thomas prepared meals and tried to coax her to eat.

"You must regain your strength," he'd repeatedly told her. "It'll help if you eat, to feel better. You know that."

She knew, but a few bites were all she could manage. "I'm sorry, Thomas. This is unfair to you, but I'm afraid my heart has turned to stone."

Meanwhile, he kept his face composed, despite the turmoil inside, for he believed that eventually, her grief would be exhausted. He had to be strong for both of them. "You'll be fine," he tried to reassure her, his heart breaking.

This brought on another spate of weeping, for which he could give no comfort. It seemed as though nothing in the world would ever be right again.

The thought of Christmas drove the dagger deeper. They had already made presents for the child and had found the perfect tree, which Thomas was to bring in shortly. They had so looked forward to celebrating their baby's first Christmas and the decorating; they had even considered visiting with neighbors over cups of cider and Christmas cake, a new trend for them. Because of the baby, they had begun to see the world differently, felt the need to reach out to others for his sake. Now all that was gone. They had only each other to lean on, and it was not enough. The world seemed so desolate now that they had lost the child, that wondrous answer to their hopes and dreams.

He'd tucked a quilt around Mamie's knees as she sat rocking before the crackling fire, smoothed her hair (how tired and sad she looked!), and put on a reassuring smile as best he could. She had no one but him now, and even he could not fill the void left by the loss of the baby. Only time could mend such a wound, however imperfectly, and it would. Surely.

He'd forced himself to go on with some semblance of normality, for Mamie's sake. By nature, he had always been calm, practical, always keeping a steady hand on the helm, no matter the fierce gales that threatened to disrupt or destroy, keeping his little family safe from the elements. But this blow had taxed every last bit of his strength. Too much, too much, and nowhere to turn. *Okay, get ahold of yourself, man,* he'd told himself, then. Christmas is coming; it's past time to get a tree. With that, he'd walked outside into the bleak sunlight, crunching through the snow to the woodshed for the ax.

Was that only yesterday?

Mamie had her faith in God to sustain her. For him, there was no turning to God. He wanted to curse God, except he didn't believe in Him. How could he hate something that wasn't there? All these years had Mamie believed in a lie, after all? It had begun to seem a good thing—he had almost come to believe, just a little. The feeling that the rug had been pulled from under his feet must mean that something had been there and now was not. But no, just as he had always thought, he was on his own.

Okay, the tree.

He'd unlatched the woodshed door (how mournfully it had creaked as he opened it) and saw what he'd come for: a long-handled ax embedded in the chopping block just inside on a scattering of wood shavings. He glanced around and saw the wood stacked to the eaves of the little shed. All that work, he thought dejectedly. And for what?

With one determined stride, he'd reached for the ax, yanked it from the chopping block, and gripped it in both hands. Rage surged in him; for the first time in his life, he wanted to destroy, to kill, and he glared upward. But what was the good of that? There was no God. Pointless, pointless. At once, his rage melted into grief, for he was not a violent man. He sat down heavily on the block of wood, leaned on the ax, and wept bitter tears, the Christmas tree forgotten.

When at last he'd returned to the house, Mamie was still sitting before the hearth, rocking. Even at the sound of his step, she hadn't glanced up. He'd dreaded the look of disappointment when she saw that he had no tree, but this apathy was worse. Neither had she climbed into the loft to bring down the Christmas decorations, as she had assured him she would when he had announced that he would get the tree. He hadn't really expected her to, he realized. He moved numbly to stoke the fire and to get on with his daily tasks until nightfall. Through the long sleepless night, they mourned, dry-eyed, for they had no more tears.

Their world was empty and dead.

They couldn't have known what the next morning would bring, after that black night of despair. Thomas was up before dawn, as usual. He'd gone out to start his daily round of chores. The blue of the night sky was fading; a few stars still glittered above.

The first pink rays had just peeped over the hill when that shrieking fireball dropped out of the sky and changed everything, forever.

The fire was stoked in stove and hearth, and the first rays of the sun brightened the windowpanes. Thomas took a deep breath. *Okay, time to check out that scream.* His heart skipped a beat at the thought, and he felt a chill. But he had to know. With one last look over his shoulder at Mamie in the rocking chair, he put on his hat and went outside to investigate.

Little Herald — Out of the Mouth of Babes

A good piece down the road from the Martels' gate lived their nearest neighbors, the Aldens. Ten-year-old Daisy Alden shivered in the early morning chill as she stood at the window of their old farmhouse, holding her baby brother Beau. They watched their father and elder brother Arlie tromp through the snow to the barn to milk the cows.

Daisy sighed happily. She loved Christmas, with the snow glistening so brightly outside and the soft glow of colored lights on the perfect pine in the dark living room. The smell of frying bacon drifted in from the kitchen; Daisy could see Mama through the doorway, tending the stove. The Christmas music playing on the radio filled the air with the spirit of the season. Daisy felt a rush of warmth and hugged two-year-old Beau a little tighter.

When Daddy and Arlie disappeared inside the barn, the two children at the window turned their faces upward. The stars had already begun to fade as the deep blue of the night sky washed out to turquoise, blending like watered silk into the pink band behind the dark, jagged silhouette of the distant pinewoods. They watched in silent wonder the coming of the dawn.

Suddenly, a bright flash lit up the night as a ball of fire fell out of the sky, trailing flame. Daisy stared open-mouthed as it plunged to Earth behind the pine-covered hill.

"Beebee, beebee!" shrilled Beau, pointing skyward.

"No, no, sweet pea — that's a shooting star," Daisy corrected him, then yelled, "Mama, did you see? A real big shooting star! It fell straight down out of the sky. Over toward Coon Hollow, I bet!"

She was so excited that she hardly noticed Beau's continuing refrain. "Beebee, beebee!" he shouted, as he hopped up and down in her arms.

Lizzie glanced up from tending the grits and bacon. "Calm down, girl. What did you say?"

"Hush, Beau!" Daisy patted his mouth to quiet his strident cries. "A huge ball of fire, Mama — it come down out of the sky! Close, Mama, real close!"

"Fiddlesticks! They always look closer than they are," grumbled Lizzie, who had not yet had her morning cup of coffee.

Six-year-old Alyssa came into the room, groggily rubbing her eyes.

"What's that, Daisy?"

"A huge flash of light! A shooting star or something. My goodness, John Beauregard, honey, would you set still, and just hush up a minute?"

"What's he saying, Daisy?" Lizzie frowned. "He's trying to tell you something."

"Sounds like he's saying — oh, I don't know — beebee, or something. Why would he — Beau, what are you saying? Baby?"

Alyssa pushed her way to the window. "I don't see nothing."

The little boy ceased leaping about and nodded, his large, earnest eyes fixed on his big sister's face. "Beebee."

"Sure, Beau. If you say so." Daisy wasn't sure at all what a shooting star had to do with a baby.

"Hurry and set the table, Daisy," Lizzie said. "I hear Daddy and Arlie on the stoop already. My, that was quick."

Daisy set Beau down and rushed to do her mama's bidding. Her father and brother came in with a cloud of vapor and a blast of winter cold. Daisy shivered as she set the table, glad when they shut the door. They brought in the foaming buckets of milk and set about straining it. Before she could burst out with the news, they were already talking.

"It was the biggest shooting star I ever seen!" shouted Arlie. "Just glanced up from milking, and there it was, clear as all get-out! A-coming down out of the sky like — man, oh man! It was a sight to see!"

"Me and Beau seen it too!" Daisy cried. "We was looking out the window and —"

"It was so cool!" Arlie was agog. "It come right down over there, into them trees. Daddy says it's sure to 'a' landed nigh Coon Hollow, on Martel's hill."

"See, Mama? What did I tell you? Can we go look, Daddy?"

"Won't nobody be looking anytime soon," Zach replied gruffly without turning from his work of pouring the milk through the strainer. "'Less'n it's Martel hisself. I reckon they're still snowed in over there, anyhow."

"I sure hope they're all right," Lizzie said. "You and Arlie better hike in there later and check up on them. Mamie's due to have her baby any time, and I ain't seen hide nor hair of them since mid-November."

"If I get time. I need to brace up the sheep shed roof; it's sagging so bad, what with all this snow. Least till I can fix it proper," said Zach. Lizzie gave him a look, and he added in a tone of complaint, "You know how the Martels are about prying neighbors. I don't like to go poking my nose in where it don't belong."

"Mamie ain't no spring chicken anymore. That's what's got me worried,"

Lizzie interrupted, her hands on her hips. He refused to look up from rinsing out the buckets, so the effect was lost. She turned back to the stove. "You could take some Christmas baking and a jar of our raspberry jam. I'll wrap them up real pretty. And you could invite them to dinner. They ain't got no family around here." She flipped the bacon. It sizzled and spat. "That turkey we got out there is big enough for all of us, and them, too."

He gave in. "Oh, all right, Liz. Arlie and me'll take the old pickup; with chains on, I reckon we can make it." There was no getting out of it once Lizzie got an idea in her head, but he couldn't give in too easily. "After we get that sheep shed propped up."

"Well, don't be long about it." She softened her frown with a tender look. "Tomorrow's Christmas Eve already."

The Foundling

The snow gleamed pinkish in the dawn light as Thomas trudged across the barnyard; it brightened the way toward the grove of trees where the star had gone down. He crossed the ice-encrusted creek, stepping from rock to rock, went through the cottonwoods, and followed the trail that led up the hill. The snow was sparse under the trees, making his passage easier. The sky gradually brightened as dawn spread across the snow-white horizon; he could see better now. Once through the oak grove and the patches of redbud, he figured, a short climb through the stand of pines should bring him to the spot where he guessed the star had landed.

Unless it was further than he had thought. He frowned.

No, he was pretty certain. He continued on, intrigued by the fresh sign of deer and rabbit tracks fanning out from point zero, as though running scared, fleeing from whatever it was.

The only sound was the crunch of his boots in the snow as he pressed on up the slope...until a piercing wail brought him to an abrupt halt. It sounded like (*no, it couldn't be!*) a newborn child! He shook his head. Wishful thinking. A rabbit in a snare, more likely. Except he hadn't set any up this way.

He listened. There, again the cry. He pinpointed the direction, off to his left, downslope a bit. No, he was not imagining it. The cry was real – sharp and clear in the crisp dawn. He turned toward the sound, regretfully veering from the track of his original objective. Well, he could find the meteor later. It wasn't going anywhere.

Snow fell into his boots from the brush and drifts as he pushed through, grumbling to himself. Stark gray twigs and branches clawed at his clothing, his eyes, his beard, but he elbowed them aside. Now, where had that sound come from? He halted. All was quiet again. He parted some branches and was trying to get his bearings when he was suddenly brought up short.

He stared. Just ahead was a dogwood, one of several scattered among the redbuds, but this one was blooming! In the middle of winter?! He shook his head to clear it. Rubbed his eyes, but there it was. No doubt about it.

He moved ahead for a closer look. Unbelievable. The whole tree was covered with blooms. Not just a few strays from last fall, withered and gray. Hundreds of fresh, pearl-white bracts. *This couldn't be real.* But it was. He gazed in wonder. Why were none of the other trees blooming, then?

As he stared in astonishment, something caught his eye among the branches. He went nearer. There, almost hidden within the mass of snowy blossoms, was something blue. A bundle, it looked like, caught in the tree, hanging from a branch. He reached out, careful not to damage the flowers, which seemed a kind of miracle (if he'd believed in such things). The atmosphere, for some reason, demanded reverence, as though he was in one of those cathedrals. Even he, the skeptic, was awed by the display.

His heart pounded with excitement. His breath made little puffs of white vapor in the chill of the morning. He touched the mysterious blue thing. It was cloth, in which was enclosed something about the size of a good-sized winter squash. Soft, and not heavy; the slender branch did not bow down much under its weight. He supported it easily with one hand as he gently unhooked it from the tree.

The bundle moved. He started back and nearly dropped it. He stared as the knot loosened and seemed to separate of its own accord. The cloth fell open, revealing fine hair and a little face with eyes wide and looking at him. It was a newborn baby!

Eyes startling blue as the summer sky flashed in the dawn light like the finest crystal. How piercing for such a little one! They met his gaze and seemed to look into his soul as though weighing his merits in some inexplicable way. At once, the baby seemed to smile, just a little. A wonderful thing.

Disturbed, he glanced around. "Hello! Is someone there?"

There was no reply, no sound at all. There must be someone. But who would leave a baby hanging from a branch, even if they were nearby? He lifted up his eyes to the tree, and his mind whirled. A newborn baby? It was very new, so tiny. It was like a dream, like a fairy tale come true. But he didn't believe in fairy tales any more than miracles. Still, there was the flowering dogwood in the middle of winter. And the child was certainly real.

It squirmed in his arms and made a creaky noise with its newborn's voice. He glanced down apprehensively. The child was now gazing up at him with pleading eyes. It jammed a tiny fist into its mouth and made loud sucking noises. He was at a loss; he had no experience with babies. It let out another wail, its eyes on him, reproachfully, it seemed to him. It wanted something, but there was no one here to hand it to.

"Shh, shh. Are you cold, little one?" He covered its head with the blanket. "Is anyone here?" he called again. He wouldn't want to run off with someone's baby. On the other hand, Mamie would know what to do.

He peered through the trees. Who would bring their baby out in the woods so early in the morning, in this cold with no cap or hood? He rocked the baby in his arms, and it quieted. He surveyed the expanse of snow around him. There were tracks of deer, rabbits, squirrels, and birds, but no human ones except his. How could the baby have come to be hanging in the tree? He frowned and glanced around uncertainly.

Did this have something to do with that falling star? But how? No, impossible. That was Superman. Still, the fact remained that there was a baby, and he was holding it. He must do something; find out whose it was.

The baby wailed again. He held it close and patted it. "Shh, shh, it's okay. You lost your mama?"

He thought of Mamie back at the house, rocking; her empty arms, her lost hope. No, the baby belonged to someone. It would be cruel to tease her with it, only to have it taken away. He scanned the area again, puzzled at the lack of sign, and listened. There was only the twittering of chickadees returning to normal after their fright.

Well, he had to do something with the baby. He couldn't carry it around all day, and he had to check out the falling star. But that dogwood blooming out of season, what could it mean? Maybe it would be okay to let Mamie take care of the baby until he found the parents. It might lift her spirits just enough to ease her through the blackness of her grief, help her regain a small sliver of hope in the possibility of happiness.

He started back down the hill, one arm shielding the child against branches. He waded through the snow, across meadow and creek, through the barnyard to the house. He stomped his boots on the porch to rid them of snow before removing them in the entryway and crossed the kitchen in his sock feet. He lifted the corner of the blue cloth. The baby was sleeping again.

Stepping softly, he neared the hearth where Mamie sat rocking listlessly, the quilt over her knees. She must have heard him come in, but she did not look up. This grieved him, and he questioned the wisdom of what he was about to do. Still, he had to do something.

"Look, dear, see what I've found."

Slowly she turned her head, trying to feign interest, but it took an effort, he could tell. Her sad, dark eyes lit on the bundle in his arms. He drew back the corner of the blanket. The baby started awake and let out a thin wail.

She stared. "Oh my goodness, a baby! My baby? Aaron?" Then her voice broke, and her face sagged. "No, it can't be."

"No, it's not Aaron. But it's a baby, crying for its mama." He held the noisy, squirming bundle out to her. "I figure you'll know what to do."

"Of course." She touched the tiny cheek. "A baby," she said in wonder, but still disbelieving. Then her eyes lit up. "It is. Oh, Thomas, it's real."

He put the baby in her arms, but a little frown of concern furrowed his brow. "I found it in the woods. I don't know whose it is, but I think it's hungry."

"Yes, my little one," she crooned to the baby. "Mama will take care of that."

Thomas stood by uncertainly at first, seemingly forgotten as the baby's wails ceased, replaced by sounds of contentment as it suckled. The rocker creaked on the wooden floor. The fire crackled in the hearth. The sweet strains of a lullaby filled the room. He marveled, for he had never thought to hear her sing again.

Outside he went once more; his eyes turned toward the hill above the redbuds. The first rays of dawn painted the tops of the trees pink and gold. He took the trail up the hillside and circled, looking for tracks, occasionally pausing to listen. He tightened his circle. There were no tracks, except those of fleeing forest creatures. But what was this? The trees, the ground, seemed different here.

He wrinkled his nose at a faint unpleasant smell, narrowed his eyes against the glare of the snow in the brightening dawn, and halted. He spotted a windfall with a bare patch in its cap of snow, as though something had brushed it off, or been dragged across it. He went closer. On the weathered gray bark was a glistening brownish-black smear.

A stench caught him suddenly in the throat, choking. He recoiled, heart pounding. With a shudder of loathing, he forced himself to lean down for a closer look. Another wave hit him. He gagged and pulled out a handkerchief to hold over his nose as he leaned closer to try to identify the smear. It looked like blood, but was more black than red, and shining as though wet and fresh.

Once again, he scanned his surroundings and finally saw something of a trail. He followed the sign up the slope. The ground was scored as though by fine sharp blades, through patches of snow, up to a jumble of broken rock. Some of these had similar smears on them, but then the trail ended abruptly. Thomas scratched his head, more puzzled than ever, for the track was gone; there was no more sign. Unless he was mistaken, and the thing had landed here and gone downhill. No, the sign said otherwise.

He turned and followed the trail back down the hill, past the smeared log where he had begun. He kept his eye to the ground but did not relax his vigilance. He couldn't quite dispel the feeling that something might drop out of the trees or leap from the bushes at him. As often as he had hunted these woods, he had never felt this eerie chill of evil. This was not the trail of any animal he had ever tracked. Nor could he say it was human.

A slight gust of wind set bare winter branches tap-tapping. Thomas stopped and stood for a moment, gazing downhill at the woods beyond. The single flowering dogwood stood out bright as springtime amidst leafless winter redbuds and snow-covered evergreens. Then the breeze slammed him with the choking stench, stronger than ever, carried up from below. He bent double, retching. *Hell!* Yes, hell was what it was, that stink of a burning, rotting carcass, and sulfur.

With the handkerchief to his nose, he steeled himself and plunged downhill. The smell grew stronger until even through the cloth, it was overpowering. His eyes watered, but he kept on. Then he found it. He stopped and stared, aghast, bile rising in his throat. Here, in a hollow among the trees were drifts deeper than those ragged patches around it, one of the areas that he would have skirted so as not to wallow through waist-deep snow.

The center of the drift was no more. It was gone, completely melted away. Brush and trees around it were charred and blackened as though something had burned near them, white-hot. The falling star! But that stench?

He nearly gagged as his lungs tried to draw a breath and repel the fetid air at the same time. He studied the ground for some sign of—what? A meteor? Some cosmic bit of rock? Shouldn't there be a crater, at least? It didn't look right. There was no crater. Just the ground, torn-up in a circular area as though with sharp edges of some kind. Blades, or claws? No, that was absurd.

After a thorough examination of the area, he still had no idea. The signs and trail made no sense. They resembled nothing in his experience made by human or animal. The word alien came to mind, but no, he was a skeptic when it came to science fiction, too.

He retraced his steps, still holding the handkerchief to his nose. He followed the track through the grove and up the hill again until he came to the pile of broken boulders once more. The trail really had come to a dead stop. There was nothing to explain how or why. Or was there? He moved closer to the final smear and scoring on the flat side of a large stone. Here was something he hadn't noticed before. A fissure angled away to the right, cutting into the side of the hill. It was narrow, but deep. He peered into it. Sure enough, the smear went over the edge and into the crack.

What is this thing? It had to be much too large to crawl into a crack only inches wide, if the sign was any indication of its size. Impossible, for anything natural, at least. Thomas shivered, but not from the cold. He thought of Mamie back at the house alone with the foundling; he thought of the infant's strange flashing blue eyes. They seemed sinister, all of a sudden, in his imagination. A demon child? No, that could not be. Surely.

God, help us!

He plunged downhill, heedless of the underbrush clawing at his coat, tearing at his overalls, plucking his hat from his head. He left the hat without a thought, barked his shin on a windfall and took a tumble, scrambled to his feet, and rushed on. He ducked under low-hanging branches, crossed the meadow, and ran through the grove. He leaped from rock to rock across the creek, over the fence, and into the barnyard. Sheep and goats scattered. Chickens squawked and fluttered in every direction.

With a final burst of energy, Thomas cleared the fence into the yard (he hadn't managed that for years!), ran up the back steps, and opened the door to the enclosed porch. His breath gone, he kicked off his boots and fought panic. Everything seemed to be as he had left it. In a cold sweat, he reached for the door to the kitchen. It opened silently, and he slipped inside, and heard the fire crackling merrily in the hearth.

He peered through the doorway into the living room, and his heart stood still. The rocking chair was empty.

"Mamie?" His voice was tight with dread.

"In here," she called from the bedroom.

He breathed again. She appeared in the doorway with the baby against her shoulder, her expression unreadable.

"How is everything?" He was unable to breathe easily just yet. Everything seemed fine, but he took a good long look, unsure even now. What had he expected?

"Um, all's fine." She said with a quizzical glance. "I'm glad you're here. Could you help me with this?" She gestured toward the bedroom. "I wanted to move the cradle out by the fire but can't manage it myself. The bedroom's too cold for the baby."

He exhaled in relief. "Of course, I can do that." Within a few minutes, he had the cradle next to the hearth.

She tucked the baby in with a thick crocheted blanket she had made. Velvet hair blazed red-gold in the firelight, and long lashes rested on pale cheeks that seemed almost translucent. Thomas couldn't help but note how unlike their own child this one was; it was like comparing an angel with a child of Earth.

He wanted to tell Mamie about the flowering dogwood and the results of his investigation but was afraid of the rest of the story, the part about the trail and the stench. He didn't want to frighten her. And yet, Mamie would want to see the dogwood. She would say it was a miracle. And that would be okay by him.

All at once, he noticed that she must have said something. Did she just call the baby Aaron? "Er, Mamie, um, this isn't Aaron," he said before he thought. Still, it would do her no good to persist in fantasy.

Her face fell. "Oh. Yes, I know. It's just that—" She turned her gaze to the baby, a tear sliding down her cheek.

He put his arms around her. "It's okay," he soothed. "When you're ready, tomorrow or next day, I'll show you where I found him, er, or her? You won't believe—"

"After this, I'd believe anything. And yes, it's a boy. Oh, my dear, if only you could believe too."

"Yes, well. After this, I don't know. Some things are hard to explain, I have to admit. A newborn child sleeping in a dogwood tree, no tracks to indicate how it got there—it's like the fairies brought it—and Mamie, the tree is blooming in the dead of winter!"

She dabbed at her tears with her sleeve. "You're serious. But it's a miracle, not fairies. Only God could have the power to bring us joy this Christmas."

"If you say so." He smoothed her hair, lines of worry creasing his brow. "All I know is, the baby was alone and crying for its mama." And Mama's bound to come looking, sooner or later. But we'll worry about that when the time comes. Meanwhile, healing could begin. Maybe it would be enough. He'd ask around; keep his eyes open for whoever had—well, that was only fair. Still, it wouldn't hurt to wait until after Christmas. Just until after Christmas.

"You said there are no tracks. There you go. The angels must have brought him. They meant him to be ours."

He held her close. "For now. Just for a little while."

"Look at him, Thomas. He's so beautiful, he must be one of their own."

He regarded the infant sleeping in the cradle. "Yes, he is, isn't he?" He noticed that she was trembling. "A penny for your thoughts, dear."

"Oh, nothing. No, that's not true." She took a deep breath. "I changed his clothes, put away those he was wearing, and dressed him in the ones I made." With a look of resignation, she got up and went into the bedroom.

After a moment, she came out with a small bundle, which she set on the table and unfolded. "I wasn't sure what to make of these blankets, or the nightgown and this hospital ID band I cut from his ankle." The words seemed to stick in her throat; she glanced toward the fireplace.

So she had been tempted to throw the evidence into the fire. Then who would ever know? Thomas studied the nightgown and the white blanket. Standard hospital issue. Nothing unusual about them. Except his reluctance to examine them closely. What if they were marked? Would that lead them to the baby's rightful parents? How could he do that now? How could he not? He flicked a glance toward Mamie, and his heart gave a painful lurch. If only she had destroyed the evidence. But no, that wouldn't be right.

He picked up the items, each in turn. Blanket, nightgown; each was marked, but so faded or damaged that he honestly could not make them out. He left the plastic identification bracelet until last, sure that it would give everything away. Finally, with a feeling of dread, he forced himself to pick it up.

It, too, was damaged. The edges were blackened. Fire? He smelled the acrid odor of smoke and burnt plastic. He pressed it flat. The part that was legible read: boy Sperl… Dec. 22, 1999, 11:47 PM…angel CA.

California? he wondered, but no—something was odd about this. Then it dawned on him. He shook his head. "There must be some mistake. The baby can't have been born in California last night at just about midnight and be here in Oklahoma by dawn."

"Of course not," Mamie agreed. "It says it right here on the band: angel. I told you the angels brought him."

"There's got to be an explanation," Thomas muttered, as though she hadn't spoken. "What would 'CA' mean, if not California? Unless—I'll have to check around." At that, a flash of fear crossed her face, and he quickly added, "Discreetly, of course." Already she thought of the baby as theirs; it would be too cruel to take it from her. Yet they could not in good conscience keep the child of another. Still, he would let no one take the baby without sufficient proof. "But look, it's been burnt. Is the baby injured?"

"No, I checked. Just a few scorch marks on the nightie and this flannel blanket. The baby's fine. Not a burn or scratch or bruise anywhere." Mamie folded the nightgown and white blanket and put them in a shoebox with the identification bracelet. Then she picked up the blue cloth and pressed it to her cheek. "And no damage on this blue blanket, at all. Look, Thomas, how light and soft it is. It has no hospital stamp or tag, though.

Maybe those others are secondhand things."

He took the blue cloth in his big, rough hands. "What is this stuff?" The feel of it was like nothing he had ever known. Baffled, he bent to examine it, even got a magnifying glass, and brought it nearer the light. "Strange. It's fine as silk, but it's not silk; I've never seen the like."

"There you go," said Mamie triumphantly. "It's from heaven. The angels did bring him. God took pity on us this Christmas."

Why would angels need hand-me-downs? Thomas said to himself but decided against mentioning that. He handed her the cloth, which she took almost reverently.

"There's got to be an explanation," he muttered. His gaze flicked to the sweet-faced babe sleeping peacefully in the cradle by the hearth.

Those lovely winter blooms! How did they fit in with the stinking trail? Sulfur and smoke and rotting corpses had more to do with devils than angels, to his knowledge. And where did the falling star come into it? He could have sworn he'd felt a chill on that hillside, not of the natural kind, of something dark and evil. He did not believe in such things, of course. He watched Mamie with a little frown of concern as she folded the cloth and put it in the box with the other items.

"What are you doing with those?"

"I'm putting them away. When he's older, we can explain to him. We have enough of our own blankets. He won't need these." Under his scrutiny, she finished lamely, "He may want them for keepsakes one day." Of course, they were only putting off the inevitable, and yet, what harm was there in this temporary deception? For a little while. She got up, went to the cradle and drew back a corner of the blanket. "See, he's wearing a Miraculous Medal." Sure enough, a medal was attached to a blue satin ribbon around the baby's neck. "Someone put him under the Blessed Mother's protection."

Superstition, he thought, but would never hurt her by saying so. Let her think what she liked if it was a consolation to her.

"I'll get the tree now," he said.

"Yes, we'd better get to it," she said, with a fond glance at the peacefully sleeping child. "Tomorrow's Christmas Eve already. I'll get the ornaments down from the attic."

Thomas went out, with spirits elevated, to the woodshed. He plucked the ax from the chopping block, hefted it to his shoulder, and headed into the woods. After a laborious hike, trying to avoid the deepest snowdrifts, he finally found the tree he had remarked upon last summer as the perfect

Christmas tree. It stood in a little clearing, dwarfed by taller evergreens roundabout, but would look big enough in their living room.

As he started across the clearing, movement caught his eye. Not a bird or squirrel, but something inanimate, caught in a thicket and fluttering in the breeze. He tromped over to investigate; it at first appeared to be a loop of brown ribbon. Puzzled, he untangled it from the twigs and held it up to examine it. Then he saw that small squares of brown woolen material were attached to each end of two strands of ribbon; one of the squares was imprinted with a religious picture and the other with writing. Probably some Catholic thing; Mamie might know what it was. But how had it come to be here? It wasn't weather-beaten or snow-covered, so it was obviously recent. He searched the area but saw no tracks or other sign, aside from that of the usual wildlife.

Odd, these things happening, one after another. The fireball. The baby. The blooming dogwood. There was no accounting for any of it. It was the dead of winter, with the weather this past month especially fierce, and now this. A little thing, and yet... he frowned at the object in his hand, then shrugged and stuffed it into his pocket.

He chopped down the little pine and set out for home. Mamie had the ornaments out and the decorating of the house well begun by the time he arrived. She was pleased with the tree he had chosen.

Christmas Eve. The tree stood in the corner of the living room; the star on top almost touched the ceiling. Ornaments and tinsel icicles glittered in the glow of the fire in the hearth. The scent of pine permeated the house. Strings of popcorn and cranberries draped the walls. On the mantel stood a small nativity scene, one of Mamie's childhood traditions. Without a crib, she said, Christmas would not be Christmas. It was all the same to Thomas, but he was glad to see her happy again.

The baby slept in his cradle in front of a crackling fire while Thomas did his chores, and Mamie caught up on housework that had been neglected while she lay sunk in the morass of grief. They wanted to watch the child every minute, worrying unduly because of the shocking swiftness with which their own infant had been taken, but he seemed healthy. He slept most of the time, as newborns do, waking only to be changed or fed, and had suffered no apparent ill effects from his mysterious adventure.

On the table was a small branch from the dogwood tree, smelling fresh and sweet of the outdoors, and glorious with blooms; each set of four showy two-inch petal-like white bracts notched on their outer edge surrounded a greenish central boss of minute true, four-petaled flowers. Thomas had picked it for Mamie; she wasn't ready to venture out herself, much less to expose the baby to the winter weather. Mamie would dry the flowers and put them in the shoebox with the other keepsakes.

Thomas pulled out of his pocket the object that had been hanging on the bush in the clearing. "Here's something I found out in the woods. Figured you might know what it is."

"Oh, of course. It's a scapular! I used to have one when I was a girl. Where did you find this?"

"Up on the far hill, near where I got our Christmas tree. Like the baby, it appears to have come out of nowhere. No tracks. But it's light; a breeze might have blown it there." He shrugged. "It was quite a ways from where I found him, but I couldn't help wondering if there's a connection."

"He was wearing a Miraculous Medal. Someone wanted Our Lady to protect him. A scapular would be logical."

Logical, was Thomas's reflexive sardonic thought, then he silently berated himself. It seemed a betrayal, almost, after the recent bombardment of what appeared to be miracles and other signs of the supernatural, so blatant as to shake his hardcore cynicism. "Maybe you're right," he conceded. "There's a lot more here than meets the eye."

"Some things are meant to remain a mystery, but this makes sense," Mamie said. "I'll save it for him too."

Thomas had brought out the broken statue earlier and confessed his guilt. More afraid that he had offended Mamie than St. Jude, he was relieved when she assured him that he was forgiven, as long as he repaired it, she added with a smile. (How glad he was to see her smile again!) All afternoon he sat at the kitchen table working on it. He glued it together with painstaking care, then touched it up with paint and set it to dry.

Mamie suggested they name the baby Jude, after the beloved saint. She was certain it was through his intercession that an angel was sent to console them in their grief. Thomas nodded. Whatever made her happy.

"And Michael could be his middle name since the angels brought him. Unless you have a better idea, Daddy," she added with a smile.

Daddy. That jolted him. He was a daddy, after all. He had a son who would one day call him Daddy! After he'd resigned himself, thinking he'd lost his one chance when he'd buried their child. The thought pleased him.

Later in the afternoon, he went out to gather the eggs; he was on his way back to the house when he thought he heard sleigh bells. *What next? Was Santa real, too?* No, he must have imagined it. He halted to listen and heard the rumbling of a motor laboring up the drive, accompanied by that rhythmic clanking. *Ah. Chains.* He caught a flash of red through the trees. That had to be the Aldens.

The Aldens were, in Thomas's opinion, the perfect neighbors: they were friendly and helpful but didn't intrude. Also, they had occasionally hired him when he was in need of a buck.

Now his heart quickened. What if they found out about the child? He was so fair; he didn't resemble either of them in the slightest. Would anyone believe he was theirs? But if they said he was, who would argue? After all, it was common knowledge that they were expecting a baby. No one knew their baby had already been born, died, and was buried. Because of the snowstorm, they hadn't been out, nor had they seen anyone through the month of December. No one needed to know.

Still, he was an honest man; the guilt was sure to show in his face. He wasn't ready to brave the public or to baldly assert that the child was theirs. Nor was he willing to risk Mamie's health and perhaps sanity by revealing the truth. It was too soon. Her state was too fragile just yet for such a blow.

But here they came. Zach and his thirteen-year-old son, Arlie, were climbing out of the pickup. They had already seen him. His mouth went dry as he called a greeting.

"Merry Christmas, Thomas," Zach called back. "How are you this fine day?" As Thomas fumbled for words, Zach went on cheerily, "I can see you're busy, but Liz sent along some baking and raspberry jam. Kind of a Christmas present."

"That's very kind," Thomas managed.

"She wanted me to invite you and the missus over for Christmas dinner tomorrow," Zach said in a hearty tone as he reached into the pickup and brought out a box wrapped in red and green paper, tied with a ribbon. He noted Thomas's discomfort and added, "If you don't already have other plans, that is."

Thomas tried to smile with equal heartiness but did not succeed; he was no good at faking it. "Er—" His glance flicked toward the house. "Thank you very much for the invitation, but, er, Mamie's just had the, uh, baby, and she's not feeling up to going out just yet and, er, taking the baby out in this weather."

"What the heck?" Zach burst out. "Congratulations! We had no idea!" He turned to the boy. "Won't Mama be up in the air about that!" He faced Thomas again. "You made it out of Coon Hollow? When was this? I didn't see no tracks when I come in, so I figured you got snowed in, too."

"Yes, we did get snowed in. I delivered the child myself." He couldn't prevent his gaze from shifting, wary as he was of revealing his guilt by a word or expression.

Zach shook his head and grinned. "Ain't that something! Never woulda thought."

Thomas steered the conversation to the weather, which they discussed for a while. Meanwhile, he tried to think of how to get them to leave without being impolite before he inadvertently let the cat out of the bag. "Well, uh, I'll tell Mamie you came. Er, unless you'd like to come in for coffee."

Zach seemed to sense that this wasn't a good time to accept the offer of hospitality. "Some other time, I reckon. We got to get back. There's still a lot to be done. You know, getting ready for Santa and all that. But I'll tell Lizzie about the baby. By the way, is it a boy or a girl? She's sure to ask."

Thomas managed what he hoped was a suitably proud grin. "It's a boy."

"Well, if that don't beat all! So when you get a chance, stop by, will you?"

"Sure," said Thomas with forced heartiness. "We'll have to take a run into town to register the baby one of these first days. Maybe then."

"You're more than welcome anytime, Thomas," Zach assured him. "Here's your box of goodies. I can pack it up to the house for you, if you like."

"No, that's fine, Zach. I can manage." He took the box on one arm and was surprised to find the bucket of eggs in his other hand. He nodded once in reply to their cheerful shouts of Merry Christmas as they drove away.

Full of apprehension (for he knew confrontations with other people could not be put off forever), his steps dragged as he went toward the house.

Little Visitor

Daisy would never forget the day the Martels finally came to visit. It was January, on an afternoon of a day of baking. Mama was stirring up another batch of cookies. At the sound of a knock at the door, she started to yell at someone to answer it. But Daisy was up to her elbows in flour, kneading the bread dough, Daddy and Arlie were out in the barn, Alyssa was licking the icing bowl (with sticky hands), and Beau was too little. Mama dusted flour off her apron and went to open the door herself, wooden spoon in hand. There stood Mr. Martel, his grizzled beard neatly trimmed for a change.

"You wanted to see the baby," he said diffidently. Daisy thought he ought to sound more excited. He didn't seem to notice that his hands were crushing his old cap.

"Oh, you brought your family, did you, Thomas?" said Mama warmly. "Tell Mamie to come right on in. There's coffee brewing and cinnamon rolls in the oven. We're itching to see that little tyke of yours."

Daisy hastily slapped the dough into a big, fat ball, put it back into the bowl, covered it with a dishtowel, and set it near the stove to rise. By the time the Martels came inside, she had hung her apron on its peg and washed her hands. Mama shook her head, but with a smile; she knew how much Daisy liked babies.

Miz Martel looked rather peaked, to Daisy's mind, but was beaming as she turned back the patchwork quilt so they could see the baby. Mama offered her the rocking chair. Once seated, Miz Martel unwrapped the quilt further, then the thick woolen blanket underneath. Still, another blanket remained. Daisy giggled, reminded of the set of Russian dolls Aunt Sally had sent her for Christmas one year, those that nestled one inside the other. It seemed you could go on opening them forever, and there would still be another smaller one inside.

When the baby's face was finally revealed, Daisy gasped. It was fair as that of an angel child. Daisy peeped over Miz Martel's shoulder, wishing she could hold the baby but not daring to ask. Miz Martel told them the baby's name was Jude Michael. Mama asked if the baby was called Jude because the Martels were Beatles fans, but Miz Martel said no, he was named after St. Jude.

Just then, Alyssa came rushing over. "Don't you touch anything till you wash your hands, young lady!" Mama scolded as she steered the little girl toward the sink.

Daisy was thankful for the interruption. Everyone knew that Miz Martel used to be Catholic. She still had a lot of pagan notions, even if she never went to church (as far as Daisy knew, anyhow). Mama was very opinionated on the subject, so it was best not to let her get started. Daisy watched, fascinated, as Miz Martel undid the tie under the baby's chin and removed his cap. He slept soundly through it all.

"What a sweet little thing!" Mama exclaimed.

"Oh, ain't he cute!" cried Daisy at the same time, certain she would never be satisfied with a doll again. She gazed down at him, rapt. Next thing she knew, Mama was holding him. Daisy stood close at her elbow.

"Dear child," laughed Mama. "I'm sure Miz Martel won't mind if you take a turn holding him."

Daisy flushed and shyly ducked her head.

"That's all right, Daisy," said Miz Martel kindly. "I've always loved babies too. They're so precious. You certainly may hold him, if your mama wants to give him up."

"Set down on that chair, Daisy," Mama said. "Then I'll hand him to you. There you go, girl. Be careful now. We haven't had one this tiny around for a while." She cast a fond eye on her curly-haired two-year-old placidly eating a cookie, chocolate smeared on his cherub face. She turned to Mr. Martel. "Thomas, you just set in that chair right there, and I'll pour us all some coffee. The rolls will be out of the oven in a jiffy."

Daisy felt a rush of joy bubbling up inside her as she gazed down at the child sleeping in her arms. She had always loved babies but felt especially drawn to this one. He was so beautiful she wanted to cry. With hair finer than a kitten's, dark gold in the winter light, and cheeks pale and almost translucent, like flower petals. Like those roses Mama grew in the garden, the white ones with just a tinge of pink on the edges. Tiny perfect fingers gripped the edge of the blanket. He had not stirred, even with the jostling. "I want one, Mama."

"Dear child!" declared Mama in a tone that sounded like she actually meant foolish child, and Daisy flushed to the roots of her hair at the realization that she had spoken her thought aloud. "I'm sure you'll have your own someday, but you have to grow up and get married first." Mama reached for the coffeepot and changed the subject. "Zach was wondering if you had time in the next week or so to help him repair the sheep shed, Thomas," Mama said as she poured the steaming coffee into a mug and handed it to him. "But I suppose he already mentioned it. After that snowstorm last month, the whole roof was like to cave in. My goodness, I never did see a storm like that. I tell you —"

The door slammed, and Daddy cursed the wind under his breath. Mama had turned back to dropping spoonfuls of batter onto a cookie sheet and pretended not to hear, while Mr. Martel greeted Daddy, and Miz Martel sipped her coffee. Conversation resumed, with talk of the weather. Then the men began discussing the repairing of sheds and old pickups; the women turned to the subject of children and new recipes. Daisy feasted her eyes on the baby, happy to have him to herself.

Alyssa came over, holding out her hands so everyone could see that they were clean. No one scolded, so she gingerly touched the baby's hair.

"Careful, Liss, don't wake him," whispered Daisy.

"Ain't he the cutest thing?" Alyssa whispered back. "Can I hold him when you're done?"

"I ain't done yet. Anyhow, you got to ask Mama."

She caught the word "fireball" from the muddle of adult conversation, and her ears pricked up.

"I seen it on the news too," Daddy was saying. "People called the TV station about it. Did you see that news report?"

"We don't have a TV, but I believe there was some mention of it on the radio," Mr. Martel said.

"They talked like it was one of them meteorites," said Mama. "Some was going on about UFOs, but that's hogwash. Zach seen it go down over Coon Hollow."

"So, you saw it yourself?" Mr. Martel said to Daddy.

"Yup, sure did. Me and Arlie was milking. We heard this scream, took a gander at the sky, and there it was. It flared up for a second or two and then went down, like this." With an expansive gesture, he demonstrated. "Like Liz says, it disappeared behind the trees, over yonder." He stirred his coffee, oblivious to the look that passed between the two guests.

Mama noticed (she always saw everything), even while she stirred raisins into the cookie batter. Daisy lowered her eyes as both Martels glanced her way. They seemed awful quiet all of a sudden.

"You don't say." Mr. Martel drank some coffee. It seemed to Daisy as though he was trying not to appear concerned, meanwhile thinking hard.

"Ol' Tom seen it too," Daddy went on. "Same thing. He done heard a scream, and this ball of fire dropped right out of the sky." Daddy took a bite of cinnamon roll and a gulp of the steaming coffee. "Ow, hot. Anyhow, me and Arlie reckoned it was a big cat 'til we seen that flash. You sure you didn't see nothing?" he added regretfully. "You was closest, I'll wager."

Thomas shrugged. "Yeah. But these things always seem closer than they are, and the exact location tends to be elusive, like the pot of gold at the end of the rainbow."

"You're probably right. Anyhow, ol' Tom, he's up on all this talk about alien abductions and such like, so he called Ned and Ira, and Tremayne with his dogs, wanting all of them to go up there together, armed to the teeth."

"And did they?" Mr. Martel's tone was soft.

"Ira told him they wouldn't make it ten foot off the road, what with the snow and all." Daddy shook his head, grinning. "Crazy old fool. Aliens!" he snorted.

"Well, I believe he knows where the boundary lies," said Mr. Martel, his tone full of meaning. Most of his neighbors knew to respect his property line.

"I reckon that was what was in Ira's mind," Daddy said. "But that old Tom, he's got a screw loose, anyhow."

Mr. Martel nodded. "A little too much of that special recipe of his, no doubt."

Daisy took a peek from under her lashes, wondering if Mama or Daddy would mention that she and Beau had seen the shooting star, too, and the cute thing Beau had said. Daddy reached for another roll. Mama started greasing another cookie sheet. It didn't seem like they were going to say anything. Daisy tried to catch Mama's eye.

"Mama!" she said urgently, under her breath. Shy as she was, she felt if she couldn't tell the Martels, she'd burst. Mama was intent on her work and didn't notice. Daisy saw Miz Martel glance at her, and she blurted out, "I seen it, too. Me and Beau did."

"Oh?" said Miz Martel with a forced little smile. "You were up so early in the morning?"

"I'm always up early. Beau's my alarm clock. He's my little sweet pea." She smiled fondly at him and his chubby face creased with a chocolaty grin. "He was so cute, pointing at the shooting star and yelling 'Beebee! Beebee!' That's how he says baby," she added by way of explanation.

Miz Martel's face froze, just for an instant, but then she managed another smile. "That is…cute. But why would he say that?"

"I reckon 'cause he knew Jesus was coming down from heaven," Daisy grinned. "It was just before Christmas."

"Oh, yes, of course." Miz Martel sounded relieved. She gave Beau a strange look, but he just grinned, basking in the attention.

"Well, I reckon now the snow's about gone, you'll be checking it out," Daddy said. "I coulda sworn it landed somewhere on your property. My hunch is, you'll maybe get visitors one of these days, now that it's on the news and all."

"I despise media hounds," Mr. Martel said with a hard look. "They'll heed my 'no trespassing' signs, if they know what's good for them. There's no meteorite on my land. I already checked."

"Nary a crater, neither?" Daddy said tentatively, sounding a bit disappointed.

"No crater. Nope, there's nothing for them to see."

Daddy raised an eyebrow. He wasn't as argumentative as Mama and hesitated to press the matter. But he'd seen, and others had, too. Cross-checking by interested parties would pinpoint the spot; it was only a matter of time. "Yeah, I don't take kindly to strangers tramping all over my land, neither." After a lengthy pause, he spoke again. "So you heard it, too?"

"Sure did. But aliens?" Mr. Martel shook his head.

Daddy gave a short laugh. "Not aliens, no. Still, it didn't seem natural, to my way of thinking." He paused, but Mr. Martel seemed to be studying his coffee. "Like ol' Tom says, right gives a man the shivers," Daddy ventured. After another long silence, and a general preoccupation with coffee and cinnamon rolls, he made one last try. "So I reckon whatever signs are there'll be too old to read by now, what with the snow and all?"

Mr. Martel shrugged and reached for another roll. He wasn't taking the hint; he didn't mean to invite Daddy to have a closer look.

"What my husband ain't saying, Thomas," Mama interjected into the lull in the conversation, jabbing the air with the sugar spoon, "Is that I says to him, 'You stay away from there, Zach Alden!' Sounds like it's of the devil, if you ask me."

"Oh, Lizzie," Daddy cut in. "There's got to be a natural explanation."

"There always is," agreed Mr. Martel, too mildly.

Mama looked at him askance but remembered her manners. "The sheriff mighta got to the bottom of it by now if ol' Tom wasn't afraid he'd be sniffing around his still next," she grumbled.

"Like I said, there's nothing to see," Mr. Martel said as he stirred his coffee. "No cougar sign, or bear, no spaceship, not even a meteorite."

"What did I tell you?" Mama said to no one in particular. "It's likely over on that old moonshiner property yonder, where them monks call up the devil night and day. When the wind's just so, I can hear their chanting from here. Right gives you the chills, and that's a fact. The place is cursed, I tell you."

Daisy shuddered. That was something she didn't want to think about. Not when she sometimes had to walk home from school by herself, or go outside in the yard after dark to shut the chicken house door. The baby stirred just then, and the voices faded into the background along with all thought of screaming, the devil, and such. She gazed at the child in wonder as he squirmed and stretched. His eyes opened, and his bright gaze met hers.

A grin spread across her face. "Ain't you the sweetest, little chinquapin?" she murmured (assigning him this pet name, not because the tree was remarkable, but because to her, it sounded cute, just as Beau was her little sweet pea). The baby smiled, his sapphire eyes aglow. *No, it had to be a trick of the light; peoples' eyes didn't glow.* "Oh, look, Mama, he's smiling. I declare, he has the prettiest blue eyes."

Miz Martel glanced over with a pleased expression. "Yes, he smiles already. And he's a sweet baby. Never any trouble. He's been a perfect angel right from day one."

Mama leaned across the table to have a look. "Clearest blue eyes I ever seen on such a young'un. What day did you say he was born?"

For some reason, Miz Martel looked flustered, her dark eyes flicking to her husband momentarily as though with a plea for help. He was lost in conversation with Daddy, however. With an effort, she composed herself. Mama seemed completely engrossed in spooning cookie batter onto the pan, but Daisy knew better. Mama never missed a thing.

When Miz Martel spoke, she seemed calm enough, and Daisy decided she must have been imagining things again. "December twenty-second." At Mama's speculative look, Miz Martel rushed on, "Without a doubt, our best Christmas present ever."

Mama wasn't about to be diverted by talk of Christmas presents. "I do declare—I never seen quite that shade of blue before. They almost glow, don't they? And the both of you with brown eyes. Ain't that precious?" Everything went quiet all of a sudden. Mama hurried on. "Now that I think on it, I never seen a baby that pretty, not even my own. No doubt about it, he's going to be a heartbreaker someday."

Daddy was talking about the weather again. Mama put the pan in the oven. Alyssa started to whine about holding the baby. Daisy tried to shush her, but Mama noticed. "Let Alyssa hold him, now that he's awake," she said, in a tone that brooked no argument. "Just set there on the couch,

Alyssa. He's such a little one."

Daisy felt a pang of jealousy as Mama put the baby in Alyssa's arms. It seemed her little sister eyed him greedily, as though he were a new toy. Daisy glared from behind Mama's back.

"Ain't he sweet, Alyssa?" said Mama, hovering.

"Yeah, cute as my baby doll," said Alyssa. She sighed. "Heavier, though."

"Not as heavy as Beau, and you're always packing him around," Daisy put in. Alyssa glared.

"Tired of holding him, honeybunch?" Mama reached for him. Alyssa gladly gave him up and ran to get her doll.

Daisy scowled. *Whiny little* — on the other hand, maybe she'd get to hold him again. Alyssa waited till Mama's back was turned, then stuck her tongue out at Daisy.

Daisy had no time to bother with retaliation. She tugged at her mama's apron. "Mama, Mama, while you do the cookies, can I hold him again? Please, Mama?"

"Patience, girl. I just picked him up."

Eventually, the cookies were ready, and Mama had to attend to them. Daisy reached out to take the baby, just to remind Mama. She got to hold him until the Martels were ready to leave. As they said their goodbyes, she looked forlornly after the baby. Or rather, at the bundle of blankets, for he was well-wrapped against the January chill.

"If you need anything, just let us know," Mama was saying. "Daisy can drop by some days to help out if you like. She knows how to clean house and such."

Daisy could not believe her ears. "Oh, Mama, can I? Could I, Ma'am? Oh, could I, please? I'm a good worker."

"How very kind of you to offer," said Miz Martel, after a longish pause. "I'd love to have help sometimes, Daisy. You're most welcome."

The Aldens stood watching the old green pickup disappear around the bend.

"Oh, Mama," Daisy said. "When can I go see the baby — I mean, help..."

"Long as you get your chores and homework done, whenever Miz Martel says. Just mind your manners, Daisy. Try not to make a pest of yourself."

Sweet Child of Mine

A couple of weeks later, just as she was beginning to think it would never happen, Daisy got the word from the Martels. Saturday morning Daddy had to run into town for tractor parts, so he dropped her off at the Martels' gate.

A chill February wind was blowing fitfully from the north. She climbed over the gate, pulled her coat close around her, and started up the track under a leaden sky. The long driveway wound its way through a dense wood of scrub brush, winter-bare trees, and the occasional evergreen.

When at last the cabin came into view, she stared, enchanted. In the white winter setting, it had the look of something out of a fairy tale. Its roof was covered with snow, like royal icing on a gingerbread house. The window- and doorframes were carved so fine, with vines, leaves, flowers, and birds; almost as though they had been real once upon a time and now were frozen under the spell of a wicked witch.

At one side of the house was a garden, dead now, with the remains of sunflowers and cornstalks standing at one end, frost-blackened and drooping under the weight of the snow. Blue jays squabbled over the sunflower seeds, bright splashes of color in the otherwise monochromatic scene. The garden fence was a spiderweb of willow withes outlined in white.

Daisy smiled at the sight of a flock of sheep and goats munching hay in a pen next to the barn and chickens merrily scratching in the snow. A breeze stirred, and for a moment, she thought she heard the tinkling of fairy bells. Delighted, she glanced around; it was only chimes hanging from the eaves of the house and from the garden gateposts.

She recalled her mama remarking that the Martels were a bit strange and kept to themselves, mostly. They had arrived here way back in the seventies, to live off the land and, like many other hippies of that era, to drop out of society. Rumor had it that Mr. Martel had left law school and a cut-and-dried future in his father's firm; Miz Martel was a schoolteacher. They had met at a music festival and eloped, and then her daddy had disowned her. Or maybe it was the other way around. No one knew for sure.

At any rate, the Martels had moved into the old run-down farm over at Coon Hollow. The place was overgrown, but the orchard and grape arbor were still there. The young couple managed to hack a trail in from the main road (which was no great shakes itself in those days) to the house (or what was left of it). They camped in a tent under the trees, salvaged everything usable, burned the rest, and set to work building a cabin. It took them all summer to cut and peel the logs, but before winter set in, the walls were up, and the roof was on. They moved in and gradually finished the interior to their liking. During the following years, they restored the driveway, built fences, sheds and a barn, piped water to the house from a spring upslope, and eventually put in electricity.

They never invited anyone over but came out of the woods once in a blue moon to stock up on sugar, coffee, tea, and other staples. They coaxed the garden, orchard, and grape arbor to supply them with vegetables and fruit. There was plenty of wild game, and they soon acquired chickens, goats, and sheep.

Miz Martel carded, spun, and dyed their sheep's wool herself; during the winter, she knitted and crocheted. Mr. Martel built furniture and carved amazing things out of wood. Eventually, they joined the local farmers' market and set up a table every Saturday from spring until fall. Mr. Martel occasionally had to take a temporary job to make ends meet, like building a fence or shed for neighbors. Daisy remembered that was how her daddy had gotten to know him.

After word got out that Mr. Martel was a musician, he was talked into joining a local group, providing music for dances and other community social events. Soon he was much sought after for his country fiddle playing. Miz Martel seemed to enjoy dancing and visiting, but at the end of the night, they would retreat to their hideaway in the woods.

People whispered and gossiped, but the Martels didn't care about social amenities. They weren't unfriendly, but they let it be known that they preferred their solitude. More than one nosy neighbor learned the hard way not to impose. Daisy could understand that. People tended to meddle in their neighbors' business a lot.

She climbed the steps and knocked on the door. A curtain twitched at the nearest window, and hurried footsteps approached. The door opened, and Miz Martel greeted her with a smile.

"Won't you please come in, Daisy?" She gave a slight wave of the wooden spoon in her hand. Her long, dark hair was tied back with a red ribbon and hung to her waist, giving her a youthful look, never mind the gray streaks at her temples. "I'm just whipping up some muffins. Put your boots there on the rug and make yourself at home."

Daisy shyly murmured a greeting and entered. Miz Martel closed the door and swept across the kitchen to resume spooning batter into muffin tins. Daisy slipped off her boots, her eyes wide as she admired Miz Martel's long blue skirt brightly accented with huge orange flowers (half-hidden by an apron). She felt suddenly conscious of her own faded blue jeans and rather plain plaid shirt.

After the walk through the snow and icy breeze outside, she was grateful for the warmth radiating from the wood cookstove in the cozy kitchen. She glanced around; a collection of knickknacks on a corner shelf caught her eye: a kitten playing with a ball of yarn, a china tea set, and among the miniatures, a tall statue of a man in a green robe. It had been broken and repaired; hardly noticeable, but a line here and a small chip there gave it away. *Someone must love this statue a lot*, Daisy thought. In fact, the sweet face did invite affection. She would have liked one herself. Or maybe not; she could just hear her mama: *There'll be no graven images in my house!*

She glanced through the doorway into the living room. There, in a stone fireplace, a fire crackled. Near it stood a willow cradle. "Oh, can I?" she began.

"Yes, of course, you want to see the baby. He's asleep, but go ahead and look. I'll just put these in the oven."

Daisy made a beeline across the braided rug to peer into the cradle. All she could see at first was a colorful quilt of patches embroidered with fine stitching.

"Did you make this? Awesome!" She'd made quilts herself and attempted embroidery, but nothing so complex. Green velvet squares with silk-thread fences held gamboling lambs and kids. Red-winged blackbirds and blue jays sat in trees loaded with apples, pears, and peaches. Black satin crows picked up French-knot corn inside a fence, keeping an eye on the scarecrow standing among the stalks. Red chickens scratched at a tan patch. Blue silk flags, buttercups, pink satin roses, and daisies were stitched in clusters on patches of various geometric shapes. There were creatures straight out of fantasy: A fire-breathing green-sequined dragon that looked like a serpent with legs and wings rampaged across a long black satin patch. A phoenix was engulfed in orange flames on a large blue watered-silk triangle. The border was in shades of blue, with sun, moon, and stars stitched in metallic thread.

Then she saw the little face of the sleeping babe and forgot the amazing quilt.

Thomas realized he was as bad as Mamie about not being able to leave the baby alone for an instant. They took turns hovering over him, alert for any sign of a cough or sniffle, or even a cry that was a shade different. Though they had sworn off doctors long ago, much preferring herbal remedies and natural prevention, the unspoken threat of death haunted them, as well as the possibility that their baby had died because of some neglect on their part. They were determined not to repeat the mistake. They agreed to have a doctor treat the child, if necessary, even at the risk of revealing their secret.

To Thomas's amazement and relief, despite the baby's delicate appearance, he was healthy and strong; never was there a hint of cold or flu or any childhood disease. He didn't question this until later, when odd things began to add up, such as the child's apparent indifference to heat or cold that would adversely affect most people. He enjoyed the warmth of the fire in the hearth just like anyone else but never shivered with cold. And the first stubbed toe, cut finger, and scraped knee, proved that he healed at an amazing rate. Unnaturally so. What all this meant, Thomas couldn't guess.

Jude was a contented baby. While Mamie went about her household chores, he solemnly observed his surroundings with an awareness far surpassing that of other babies his age, it seemed to Thomas. And maybe those of another plane altogether, for at times he would turn toward a part of the room where there was no one (that they could see) and would bubble over with joy, his face lit up as he reached out his arms. And at times, his eyes actually glowed! As he grew older, he would laugh and chatter, as though carrying on a conversation with someone they could not see.

"He's talking to the angels again," Mamie would say.

Thomas often pondered the mystery of where he was really from and of how he had come to them. Whereas Mamie was content to believe that angels had brought him as a Christmas miracle, Thomas reserved judgment, though he had to admit that there was something about this he could not explain.

He had finally told Mamie about the more sinister side of the baby's arrival and of his lingering qualms. There was something not quite ordinary about the babe. Yet he felt that the child's beauty and sweet disposition must surely contraindicate demonic origins. Though Thomas doubted the reality of devils, he knew the horror stories, which had sown a mixed bag of seeds in his imagination.

He could see that Mamie too refused to see the child as evil, brushing off the fact that Satan, upon occasion, might very well appear as a child of light to parody the Christ Child. Thomas had at first caught himself eyeing the babe askance as it slept in Mamie's arms, fearing that glowing eyes would spring open in that tiny face to reveal a demon after all. He severely reproved himself for such pointless flights of imagination and managed to bury them deep.

For he soon grew to love the child as if it were his own. Even those "oddities" ceased to awe him and only caused him to become more protective. Thomas still did not understand what this meant, or what the boy was, but his eyes met Mamie's in tacit agreement. They must teach him to hide his oddities, for the world would not accept anything different, but would hound it to death.

At first, they kept him to themselves entirely, to forestall discovery of his strange gifts. As he grew, they taught him to conceal them.

Only Daisy was different. Thomas was amazed at the way she came to be part of the family almost by accident. At first, he and Mamie hardly knew how to say no to her mother's offer of help without seeming unneighborly and ungrateful. As it turned out, Mamie's health was not what it once was, and Thomas managed to persuade her to accept the girl's help, temporarily.

This arrangement would be of short duration, Thomas was sure. After a taste, Daisy would most likely decide not to come back. What ten-year-old would want to take care of a baby where she was stuck with no TV and must do chores and housework besides when she could be playing? It turned out that she was used to babysitting her little brother Beau; there were no surprises. And she actually liked it!

"I love that girl," Mamie said, after a time. "There is such a sensitive soul hidden beneath that plain exterior. And she's not one to carry tales, even to her own family. I love how she's drawn to grace and beauty, and all that constitutes what is known as culture. She's the kind of student that is a teacher's dream, with her hunger for learning."

"I say we give her free access to our collection of books," Thomas said.

"She's one in a million, humbly admitting her own ignorance, and happy to learn appreciation of the classics, opera, and poetry," Mamie told him, "And accepts suggestions for the correction of her speech without rancor; her grammar has improved tremendously. Without her noticing, even, I think, except, as she laughingly tells me, for her family's affectionate teasing."

"Did you notice how she was struck dumb the first time I played classical music on the violin?" Thomas chuckled. "Turns out she loves Beethoven, Bach, Mozart, Vivaldi—all of them. She said they seem to her like heaven's own music compared to the foot-stomping fiddle tunes she's used to. She begged me to teach her to play. What else could I do? She has no musical ear at all, but I couldn't say no to her. And I think she's actually making progress."

At Mamie's suggestion, Thomas put the violin in Jude's hands as well and gave him his first music lesson. The boy was only three at the time, but he'd always shown a love for music and already sang as sweetly as an oriole. Likely he'd also have a talent for playing instruments, Thomas reasoned. Even he was amazed at how quickly the boy learned.

It was clear that Daisy harbored no envy, even though little Jude soon surpassed her. Instead, she seemed as proud as though he had been her own child. By then, it was four years she'd been looking after him, and she'd never grown tired of it. In fact, she apparently enjoyed more than ever watching him learn new things.

Of course, Thomas had to admit, Jude was a unique child.

That winter, as they were enjoying an evening of music in front of a crackling fire, Thomas brought out a second violin. "You've heard of a Stradivarius. Listen to this."

All listened, intrigued, as Thomas played. The sweet, plaintive notes rose and fell, beautiful, poignant, bringing tears to their eyes by the time he had finished.

"It's like the angels must play in heaven!" Daisy exclaimed in delight.

Little Jude spoke up eagerly, "Let me play it, Daddy!"

Thomas ruffled his hair. "This is a very special violin, son. Look here, inside, where the light shines in. You can see the maker's initials: HH and a stag."

"Cool," said Daisy, craning her neck to see. "Where did you get it? And why play the other one when this one sounds so awesome?"

"That one's mine." Thomas chuckled. "This never was, really; I picked it up for four bits years ago at a New York City flea market. It was in a box of junk left over from an estate sale, in sad shape, with broken strings. I cleaned it up, bought new strings. When I tested it out, I couldn't believe it; I'd never played so well! And here I'd only bought it because I couldn't stand the thought of a musical instrument getting tossed out with the trash."

"But it's so pretty and sounds so fine," Daisy remarked. "Why would anyone throw it out or sell it at some flea market?"

"Actually, I did some research, and there's a story behind it," said Thomas. "This instrument is the handiwork of a German violin maker, Hubert Hummel, a contemporary of Stradivari, I believe. His few remaining violins are now valuable collector's items, identified by the symbol you see inside this one. It seems his family, all his heirs, were mysteriously wiped out, shortly after he himself died an old man. In fact, their entire village never recovered from the calamity, whatever it was. I couldn't find anything more about that, except that this violin later resurfaced. However, it was said to be cursed."

"Oh, dear," said Mamie, with a glance at the children.

Daisy shivered and cast a wary eye at the violin. "What happened?"

"No one knows for sure. The violin was packed up and sold with the rest of the ill-fated family's belongings. It seems to have traveled through Europe, leaving chaos in its wake. Or so the story goes. From one owner to the next, it went, passed along like a hot potato. No one had it for long; something always happened to it or its owner. Some said that its music was too sweet for this Earth, others that it was meant for a particular person, bringing catastrophe on anyone else. Bad luck did seem to strike all who possessed it."

"Daddy," Jude said anxiously. "You have it now."

"Thomas, should you be—" Mamie began.

Thomas smiled and held up his hand, bidding her wait and listen. "You know how stories get embellished in the telling. It's also said that the violin won't rest until it's in the hands of the person to which it rightfully belongs; that it'll seek him out and will know him. I know that sounds superstitious, but its history bears it out. A tragic tale. The violin has been stolen, or lost, time and again. Each time its owner met with an accident, died unexpectedly, or could no longer play. Nothing out of the ordinary, it might seem, but add them all up—and what with the rumors…"

"Oh, I see," Mamie sounded a trifle relieved.

"The violin finally reappeared around the turn of the century, when a wealthy German Jew acquired it and displayed it proudly, disdaining superstition. During World War II, his entire family was killed at Auschwitz. Their valuables were confiscated, and the violin fell into the hands of a high-ranking Nazi. After Germany's defeat, he was executed for war crimes. The violin went to his heir, who moved to America. By that time, no one would play the violin because of its bad reputation. When that owner met his doom, his heirs divvied up everything of value and gave the junk to a charity flea market.

"That's where I found the violin. Only later did I realize what a treasure I had. Though right from the start, I had an eerie feeling about it, almost as though it was alive, and calling to me, but I knew it wasn't meant for me; I was just saving it for someone else. So I always play my faithful old instrument; once in a while, I take this one out and play a few pieces to keep it in shape. I've always felt that I'd one day return it to its rightful owner."

He turned to Jude. "Okay, son. The way you play, I wonder if — go ahead and try it." With that, Thomas placed it in his hands.

A fire was crackling in the hearth; a faint aroma of woodsmoke permeated the room. Orange reflections danced across the floor, and shadows leaped about the walls. Mamie sat in her rocking chair, knitting socks. Daisy held one of the boy's well-worn Dr. Seuss books she had been reading to him.

Jude's face glowed with happiness as he lifted the violin to his chin. It was as yet too big for him, but even so, it seemed somehow to belong in those sensitive childish hands, as though it had indeed been made for him. He touched bow to strings; pure sweet notes rang out as he began to play. When the celestial sounds died away, a tear slid down Daisy's cheek. Mamie had stopped knitting, her cheeks glistening in the firelight, while Thomas surreptitiously dashed tears from his beard. To think that a child could play like that! But, of course, Jude had never been just an ordinary little boy.

Jude lifted his eyes and saw all the teary eyes focused on him. "What? I've been practicing."

At that, Thomas laughed, and the others joined in.

"The violin is yours, son," he said. "It was meant for you, no doubt about it."

"Mine?" breathed the boy, all thoughts of bad luck forgotten.

Thomas laughed a great booming laugh and swept the child into his arms. "Son, I don't know how or why, but if you aren't the rightful owner of this violin, nobody is."

The Accident

August 2005

Thomas squinted through the cracked windshield at the highway ahead, alert for the glow of eyes in the dark. Bright flecks danced in the high beams. Only insects, not deer (which also had a way of jumping out in front of you when you least expected it), but he eased up on the gas pedal, not wanting to hit one just because he was in a hurry to get home to Mamie with the good news.

She hadn't been too happy when he'd insisted on taking Jude and his violin to the music festival at the big Talequah rodeo. The boy was five already (six in just four more months) and had learned so much in the past couple of years, that he couldn't resist showing him off, just once. (Though he wasn't sure if a crowd that enjoyed dancing to the fiddle would appreciate the classical violin.)

Mamie had said if he wanted to enter the show with his buddies, fine. But to risk exposing Jude to the public eye was foolhardy, to her way of thinking. What if someone noticed that he wasn't really their child? Thomas reminded her that for five years, no one had come forward; it wasn't likely that they would now. She saw how much he wanted this, how proud he was of the boy and his gift for music, and reluctantly gave in.

Thomas smiled as in his mind's eye, he saw Mamie waving from the porch as they drove away. She had worried for nothing; the crowd and the judges all loved it, and they got safely away. How surprised she would be when they showed her the trophy! *Then all would be forgiven*, he hoped.

He glanced over at the child fast asleep in the passenger seat. Long lashes lay against the boy's pale cheeks; his hair was tousled. He'd relaxed his grip on the trophy, a golden violin, lying on his lap. Thomas's heart was full to bursting with pride. *My son.*

He rounded a curve, and a dark shape was right in front of them, full in the headlights.

"What the hell?!" He jammed on the brakes and swerved.

A deer? No. A man shape, but — it moved too fast, and that red glow of the eyes couldn't belong to a man. It was gone now, melted into the roadside shadow, but the old pickup was headed for the ditch. Thomas cranked the wheel hard. They hit loose gravel at the side of the road and veered into the edge of the pavement. The tire blew, and over they went. The pickup flipped and rolled, coming to a stop right side up in a patch of fireweed.

Sometime later, Thomas regained consciousness in the crumpled cab. How long he'd been out, he had no idea. Crickets chirped nearby; frogs croaked in the distance. The smell of gas was strong, the ticking of the engine loud in the night. *Got to get out.* He glanced over to check on Jude; the boy wasn't there. The window was broken, the seatbelt ripped off. That old worn one he'd meant to fix.

With a rush of panic, his first thought was, *My child!* Then, *Mamie'll kill me.*

"Jude! Boy, where are you?" he shouted. Pain seared through him, and a buzzing filled his ears. Through an effort of sheer will, he managed not to pass out again. Gradually his brain cleared. He considered opening the door, but when he began to lift his arm, the pain returned with a vengeance, radiating from his midsection. His body was held immobile in the crushed cab; he couldn't tell how. Even just breathing hurt abominably. "God." It was a prayer, not something he commonly did. To speak just one word was agony. *God, help me.*

A flash of headlights lit up the night as a car came around the curve. Without thinking, Thomas turned to look. Pain hit him, and he blacked out again.

The monk saw the taillights wink out as the vehicle ahead of him went around a curve. Then came a flash so brief he thought he'd imagined it until he rounded the curve himself and saw the glare of headlights shining at an odd angle from off the road. An accident. He pulled out his cell phone to call emergency services.

As he eased onto the shoulder, he spotted a pale form lying in the weeds beside the road. Quickly he braked and leaped out, emergency kit in hand. He hadn't taken more than two steps when he got a whiff of something rotten, so strong he nearly gagged, and felt a cold blackness, as of something evil. He glanced around just as a dark form melted into the night. Or maybe it was the play of shadow in the beam of his headlights; he couldn't be sure. The night often brought out the worst in the imagination. And yet it wouldn't be the first time he'd encountered something else. He reached into his emergency kit and took out a small bottle of holy water. He sprinkled it around even as he rushed over to the form in the weeds.

It was a boy, battered and covered in blood, and so still. He picked up the thin little wrist to check for a pulse. Nothing. He leaned close, and even in the dark, could see that the boy's face was ashen. The half-closed eyes held the glaze of death. As he laid his hand on the child's head to bless him, he felt the stickiness of blood and the grating of broken bone. A severe head wound. *Too late for this one.* He offered a prayer and sadly hurried toward the smashed vehicle.

A piercing shriek rent the night. He lurched, his heart pounding and his breath sharp and quick. *I'm getting too old for this.* He stopped for a half-second to listen. *A screech owl? No.* He shivered but hurried on. Priorities.

Even in the dark, he thought he saw movement within the crushed cab. Maybe the driver was trapped inside. As he drew near, he saw a man's graying head sunk on his chest and feared to find him dead, too. Then the man groaned. *Thank God someone's alive!* He peered through the broken window. The man lifted his head. Blood streamed down his cheeks and pooled in his thick gray beard as he turned dark eyes full of suffering toward the monk.

"My boy! Is he—?" He grimaced, and blood trickled from his mouth. The monk saw then that the steering wheel had broken and impaled him. He quickly shifted his gaze back to the drawn face.

Dead? Well, it was no use worrying him about that. The child was in God's hands now. Death was probably a mercy after the injuries he'd appeared to have sustained.

"He's fine," said the monk, fearing the man too was not long for this world. "Hold on, I've called for help. The ambulance is on its way." The man's eyes searched his face, and his lips moved, but no words came. He saw that the man had noted his clerical garb, and gently asked, "Are you Catholic?"

"No," the man managed. "But I—I think it's time. I don't know how to—"

"I'll help you." With trembling hands, the monk opened his kit and proceeded. A short time later, he concluded, "Thomas Joseph Martel, I baptize you in the Name of the Father, and of the Son, and of the Holy Spirit."

After Thomas was prepared for heaven, he gave a great sigh. The monk thought for a moment he had gone to meet his God, but then he heard breathing again, labored now. He anxiously glanced at his watch. What was taking the ambulance so long?

The man spoke, his eyes shining through unshed tears. "My boy…please take care of him. Tell Mamie I love her and…I'm sorry." He paused for a rasping breath, then went on, fainter now. "Father, forgive me for taking the child of another. But I did it for her. I did it for love."

The voice halted, followed by a faint sigh, and the monk saw that he was dead. He closed the man's eyes, wondering at those last words, and offered a prayer for him and his family. His boy. Well, he'll soon see for himself when they meet in heaven.

He became aware of the breeze stirring the treetops, of the sounds of frogs and crickets resuming their night music. As he walked back through the ragged weeds to check on the child, he heard sirens wailing in the distance. The pale and forlorn little body lay as he had left it.

But now there was a fresh, bright gleam of blood on the face.

The monk inhaled sharply. *Blood, flowing. Still alive? Impossible!* He hastened to the still form and bent down. Could that have been a faint sigh? Sure enough, the child seemed to be breathing, though every breath was shallow and slow. And there was a faint pulse. Horrified at his neglect, he rushed to get a blanket from his car and gently covered the boy.

The unnatural angles of the little legs and arms indicated broken bones. The child's face and body were covered in blood so that the extent of his injuries, and the original colors of his jeans and T-shirt, were not at once evident. The monk peered down at him, but the boy's face was obscured by shadow. He laid his hand on the cold forehead but was otherwise afraid to touch the boy for fear of causing him further suffering. If only the ambulance would hurry.

Suddenly they were there. The rescue vehicle arrived to extract the dead man from his pickup. The ambulance pulled up and stopped beside them.

"The boy is alive," the monk said. "I thought he was dead at first. Poor child."

The paramedics deftly splinted legs and arms and applied bandages, then eased the little form onto the stretcher and into the ambulance. "He'll be lucky to make it to the hospital," the nearer one observed to the monk in a low tone. "He's lost a lot of blood. Here, we'll get him hooked up to an IV."

"Yes, I thought he was dead at first," the monk repeated and turned a sorrowful gaze toward the boy. "But when I realized he was alive, I covered him with the blanket." Now he regretted not checking more closely. If the child died… and yet, he seemed better than he had before.

The medic nodded. "That may be what saved him."

No, I don't think so; it was the other way around. He followed the ambulance to the hospital and waited while the police filled out their report. The dead man's driver's license identified him as fifty-seven-year-old Thomas Joseph Martel. The monk waited while they searched for a telephone number (a signature was needed for the boy's treatment), but none was forthcoming.

"No phone number!" cried the incredulous nurse. "Impossible! Everyone has a phone in this day and age."

Not the Martels, apparently. Another nurse suggested phoning the Hanna storekeeper, Ned Farwell. He knew all the folks in the area and would have an idea of how to contact them.

While she was following that lead, the monk's gaze turned toward the gurney parked along the wall. The boy's slight form was so insubstantial there might have been nothing lying under the rumpled white blanket; only the spiky blood-soaked hair sticking out of a gauze bandage indicated his presence. The IV pole stood beside the gurney, its tube attached to a thin little arm on the other side.

The monk contemplated the forlorn figure and wished he could sign for him. He didn't realize he had spoken the thought aloud until the nurse kindly told him not to worry; the doctor would certainly examine the child, even without a signature.

He approached the gurney. The child seemed too still. Had he died, then, abandoned by all? *But, no.* As the monk drew nearer, he saw that the boy's eyes were no longer half open and glazed as before but were closed completely. As though he were only sleeping, not dead. The monk stretched out his hand. To his amazement, the pale, bloodstained forehead was warm, but not feverish. At his touch, the boy inhaled deeply, just as a healthy child might if his sleep was disturbed.

The boy was now breathing easily, almost as though he might awaken at any moment. Deep violet circles shadowed his eyes; otherwise, his face retained its deathly pallor, at least where it could be seen beneath the smears of blood and dirt. The monk wondered when someone would wash the pitiful little face.

Nurses scurried around, wheeling patients in and tucking them into beds in alcoves with curtains drawn. Beepers went, disembodied voices paged doctors, plaintive sounds echoed through the corridors. Doctors appeared at intervals to examine patients and scribble on charts. It seemed to the monk that everyone passed by the gurney as though the child on it was invisible. He tried to stop a nurse to remind her about the boy, but she tugged her sleeve from his fingers. Then she realized what he'd said and promised that someone would see to him soon and hurried away.

He wondered that no one seemed more concerned. Would the world just go on its merry way, heedless of a dying child? The boy had been dead, or dying, at the scene of the accident. He had not just imagined the severity of his condition; the paramedics had remarked on it. He glanced again at the boy. His condition seemed to be improving. *Praise God that he should witness a — no, it was too soon to —*

A tall gaunt man in green scrubs came out of nowhere, scanned a chart, and stopped beside the gurney. The monk stepped out of the way as the hawk-faced doctor scrutinized the boy. He thumbed back the child's eyelids and muttered something. A nurse rushed over and began gently peeling back the blankets to reveal the bandaged and splinted little boy in torn and bloodstained clothing.

"Get any X-rays of these bones yet?" The doctor asked, his eyes and fingers probing.

"No, sir, we're still waiting for the consent form," the nurse replied.

"Well." He observed the boy speculatively. "Is all this blood his? From the scalp laceration, I presume?" He indicated the bandage on the boy's head. Sensitive fingers sought irregularities. "No trauma to the skull, then?" The nurse stared for a moment, and the doctor turned to the monk. "You found the child?"

"Yes. Yes, I did. I, er, I thought he was dead at first. He didn't appear to be breathing or even have a pulse, and he was covered in blood."

"No crushed skull?" the doctor gestured impatiently. "According to the paramedic's report —" He turned to the nurse. "Are you sure this chart belongs to this patient?"

"Yes, of course, it does. Why? Is there a problem?"

"No, only —" He all but tossed the chart at her. "Get him cleaned up so I can at least see him. And I need those X-rays." With that, he went down the corridor and was gone.

The nurse sighed and glanced apologetically at the monk. "Please excuse him. It's so hectic around here. He's been on call too many nights and, well, he cares so much about them all." She turned her gaze to the boy. "He looks peaceful, doesn't he? Like he's only sleeping." A line of perplexity creased her brow as she glanced at the chart.

Anxiously the monk stepped forward, thinking at first that she meant peaceful as in dead. But no, the boy was only sleeping. The shadows around his eyes and in his cheeks had faded. It appeared as though the swelling around the broken bones had gone down; at any rate, the bandages were loosened. He wondered if he was imagining things, after all. Or witnessing a miracle? But he only said, "Thank God. It would be a real tragedy if Mrs. Martel lost her husband and child both at once."

The nurse frowned as she reread the chart. "Er, this is the boy who was in the accident?" She glanced up at the monk. "You were there?"

He nodded. "Yes, and this is the boy. Why, is—"

"Well. I'd better get him cleaned up before the doctor comes back." She seemed flustered for a moment as she covered the child with the blanket again. "Could you stay with him, please? We're so understaffed."

"I'm glad to help." The monk was intrigued now, not wanting to take his eyes off the boy. The nurse hurried away. Gently he tucked the blanket under the boy's chin and stood vigil, praying. He lost track of time, but after a while, the nurse returned with a bowl of warm water and a washcloth, apologizing for taking so long. She sponged off the boy's face and hands, blinking in surprise at the pale skin unmarked by cut or bruise.

"I don't understand," she said as she peeled away the torn and bloodstained shirt.

The monk leaned forward for a better view. The small chest rose and fell evenly. The skin gleamed white and unblemished as the nurse cleaned his chest and abdomen. "Then where did all the blood come from?" he murmured in wonder.

"There's got to be an explanation," the nurse said briskly. "Here, let's have a peek under this bandage." She unwound the gauze strip from the boy's head more slowly as she neared the blood-soaked pad directly on the wound. But it fell away easily without sticking. She drew in a quick breath and stared, speechless.

"What is it?" the monk said. When the nurse did not reply, he leaned in for a closer look.

She seemed disturbed as she smoothed back the boy's blood-spiked hair, parting it with fingers trying to be gentle and yet almost frantically searching. "There has to be a serious cut for that much blood. My God, where is it? Oh, sorry, Father."

"I'm sure we could use a prayer just now," he murmured. "Let me see. There was a cut. I saw it."

The nurse gasped in dismay, or perhaps wonder. "I don't understand. There's only this."

Where she had parted the hair, an easy task, since the dried blood had already fixed it in that position, there was nothing to show for damage except a thin reddish line.

"That's where it was, all right. Try washing there, gently, now." He watched in trepidation as she dipped the cloth in the basin and wrung it out again. She wiped the dried blood away, and the boy's hair began to shine its natural color. His skin gleamed pale and whole.

"Okay, really, what's this about?" she said.

The monk drew back as the nurse turned her eyes to him again. "I don't know what to say. That boy was battered almost beyond recognition. His skull was crushed. I saw it, felt it. There must be bruises or something."

"Yes, of course." The nurse's expression was doubtful, as though she was afraid to believe the obvious. "The medic's report claims that he — there must be some explanation," she said for the second time. "Unless someone's pulled a switcheroo here."

"No, I was here the whole time," the monk said.

The nurse surprised him when she spoke again. "I've, you know, seen a lot of things in this line of work — "

"Ah. Yes, I know what you mean."

Flustered, she turned back to the boy. "The doctor will be back shortly," she said without looking up. "Oh, if only the boy's mother would get here. We need those X-rays." She washed the blood from the child's hair and tucked the blanket around him before again leaving the monk alone to stand watch.

The monk was dozing in a chair by the child when the mother arrived around midnight. She was of average height, with a kindly, though unremarkable face, and dark hair graying at the temples, tied back and hanging nearly to her waist. She appeared to be fifty-something, like her husband — but both had dark eyes and complexion, nothing like this fair and delicate child. Was he adopted? Or were they the grandparents?

The woman hurried to the nurses' station, her eyes brimming with tears. At her side was a tall, rawboned man with blond hair hastily slicked back and pale blue eyes in a long face creased by laugh lines. Just now, his expression was somber.

At a few words from the nurse, all eyes turned in the direction of the monk. They began to come toward him, but the nurse called them back and placed a form and pen on the desk. She pointed to the X, and like an automaton, the woman signed. She seemed disoriented, but the tall man took her elbow, and together they hurried toward the gurney.

"I'm sorry for your loss," the monk said kindly. The woman's eyes met his for a brief moment, questioning. "I'm Father Paul Schultz; I was the first one at the accident."

The tall man shook his hand. "This is Mamie Martel, the boy's mother; I'm her neighbor, Zach Alden."

The woman had turned away and was regarding her son with sorrowful eyes. Tenderly she took the little face in her hands.

"He's asleep," said the monk, unable to think of anything more comforting at the moment, since the boy's condition had not yet been made clear.

The mother bent to kiss her child's brow, her eyes glinting with unshed tears. Her hands hovered over him as though she wanted to pick him up and hold him but feared causing him more hurt.

The nurse reappeared. "Yes, it's better not to move him until the doctor assesses the extent of his injuries."

The mother turned toward her with pleading eyes, her hand to her mouth, unable to speak. The nurse put a comforting hand on her arm, but she seemed frozen, isolated in her grief. The monk stood back, at a loss to help; she had avoided meeting his eyes after that first brief glance, and he had no wish to intrude.

"My husband," she said, turning to the monk at last. "You were with him at the end? Was he—"

"He was alive when I found him. He asked to be baptized and made his peace with God."

Mrs. Martel broke down and wept into her hands. The tall man patted her shoulder.

"We'll need you to identify the body, if you're up to it," said the nurse. "Come right this way, please."

"If you like, I'll come with you," said the monk.

She nodded, still weeping soundlessly. They followed the nurse down the corridor. The monk, at the tail end of the little procession, glanced back over his shoulder.

The emergency area was suddenly alive with nurses preparing to move the gurney. They unlocked the brakes and tucked the blanket around the small form, checked the IV, and the boy's vital signs. A lab technician swiftly drew several vials of blood from the thin little arm, slipped them onto a tray, and hurried away. The nurses pushed the gurney down another corridor toward the X-ray lab. Soon the nurse at the desk was alone at her station.

The monk turned and followed the others into a room where a body lay covered. The nurse drew the sheet back, revealing the waxen features of the dead man. Mrs. Martel managed to regain her composure and to acknowledge that this indeed was the body of her husband. Zach Alden's eyes were red as he again patted her shoulder.

"He looks so peaceful," Mrs. Martel said after a time. She seemed filled with unspoken thoughts and emotion as she stood gazing down into the still face.

"His concerns were for the boy," said the monk. "And of you. 'Tell

Mamie I love her, and I'm sorry,' he said just before he died." Other words came to him but were possibly bound by the seal of confession. Even if not, this wasn't the time for questions, he realized. Comfort was needed now. "He was a good man, Mrs. Martel, and is with God now, after his baptism."

"Please, may I have a few minutes alone with him?"

"Yes, of course," said the nurse, at once herding the two men out and closing the door. "When she's ready, just come down to the reception area; someone will direct you to the boy."

When the nurse had gone, the two men stood outside the door, a little ill at ease in one another's company. The monk attempted to start a conversation, but Zach gave only terse answers. It seemed not just a natural reserve – maybe distrust for strangers, or specifically, a Catholic monk. Mrs. Martel, too, seemed to share that distrust, though she had seemed comforted by the news of her husband's baptism. The monk resumed his silent prayer.

When at length they returned to the nurses' station, they were directed to a curtained alcove where the boy was tucked into a bed, sleeping. The splints and bandages had vanished, and he was wearing a hospital gown. The monk observed that he now appeared as though he had not been injured at all. The only evidence of the accident consisted of a few smears of blood the nurse's washcloth had missed and the spiky hair. The monk noticed that the boy's cheeks were wet with tears, though he still slept.

The mother hurried to his bedside and bent over her child with sorrowful eyes. "My poor boy. Mama's here now."

The monk was again struck by the contrast of physical appearance between the boy and his parents. What had the man said about taking the child of another?

The curtain stirred as the nurse poked her head in. "Oh, you've found him. The doctor will be here shortly."

Almost before she finished speaking, the tall doctor entered the alcove with an impatient twitch of the curtain. His hawk eyes swept the alcove, taking in the small group and coming to rest on the little patient. He glanced at the chart in his hand.

"Ah, yes, the little one," he said, as his keen eyes inspected the boy. "Curiouser and curiouser," he muttered. He folded back the blanket, and the child was revealed in all his perfection, like a little angel in his white gown. His entire body now appeared healthy and strong, as though it had never been injured. The limbs were straight and unmarked by scrape or bruise; the smudges were gone from beneath his eyes. His skin was pale but glowing with life. The monk recalled how ashen the skin had been and how battered the body when he found it. And now, not a bruise or scratch...?

"Yes, doctor," said the nurse in an even tone. "When I cleaned him up, this is what we found."

The doctor shook his head as he listened to the boy's chest and took his pulse (as though disbelieving of the chart in his hand), poked, prodded, and otherwise searched for the injuries reported by the paramedics.

"Impossible," the doctor said. "This cannot be. The paramedics set the bones, yet the X-rays show no sign of fracture. They record multiple contusions and lacerations; I see none." He paused to read what the nurse had written on the chart and checked the scalp. "Here, too, is a discrepancy. There's no mark on the scalp at all. Not a scratch. Certainly not a crushed skull and brain trauma. What's going on here? The boy is healthy as a horse. He's sleeping. Is this a farce? If so, I haven't time for it!" He glared around at those standing there but saw no sign of levity. He rubbed his hand across his face and groaned. "I need a vacation." As though coming to himself, he glanced at the perplexed faces apologetically. "Please excuse me. It's been quite a day."

"Doctor?" The boy's mother spoke diffidently. "If he's only sleeping, may I please take him home?"

The monk watched the exchange with interest. She seemed almost frightened of the doctor's scrutiny.

"Yes, of course," — the doctor glanced at the chart — "Mrs. Martel. There's nothing wrong with him, it seems, but —" he did not add, there ought to be. "The boy is fine. You're welcome to let him stay the rest of the night for observation. Sometimes these things —" He caught her darting, wary glance, and shrugged. "Yes, fine, take him home if you wish. Just let him sleep. Let him get all the rest he needs." He shook his head again.

"I don't understand," said the nurse quietly as she again tucked the blankets around the boy. "His clothing was bloody and torn, his bandages, the splints — they wouldn't have applied them had they not been necessary. I just don't see —"

The monk noticed that she glanced up in time to catch Mrs. Martel's meaningful glance at Zach Alden. "I'm sorry. If you want to take him home tonight, check out at the nurses' station. Right this way, please." She marched ahead of them. "I don't know for sure, but I've seen things, unexplainable things, in my line of work. Maybe God chose your child to reveal His mercy. His glory. I think it's quite possible that this is a miracle."

"Yes. Yes, of course," agreed the mother.

A little too eagerly, the monk thought. And where was the tone of wonder, of astonishment and awe?

When they returned to the alcove, the boy was awake. He gazed around sleepily, with a smile for his mother.

"Oh, my baby, you're awake!" she cried, tears in her eyes as she hugged him.

"Mama," he managed. "Was that scary monster just a bad dream then? But—where's Daddy? Mama? Mama!" (this last rather sharply). Then he seemed to wilt, like a flower, his eyes sad. "I dreamed that he…Mama, tell me it isn't so."

"Yes, darling?"

"The Lady in Blue came and took him by the hand." Tears welled up in his eyes. "She told me not to cry, 'cause he was going to Jesus. Daddy was shining like a star, like an angel. He glanced back and smiled, and then…then he was gone."

"Yes, my little one. He's probably looking down at us from Heaven now."

"But, Mama…" The boy dashed his tears away. "I didn't even say goodbye." He burst into sobs, and his mother held him close.

When the monk left to resume his journey, he knew he would not soon forget this night. It felt as though something significant had just happened, in some mysterious way changing the course of his life forever. *Odd, that.*

He sighed, suddenly exhausted. It had been a long night. Three days of retreat at the monastery would be more than welcome after all this.

Daisy

August 2006

Daisy and Jude established a routine of activities during the year that followed, to keep his mind off his daddy's death. Now that summer had rolled around again, berry picking was a favorite. Purple juice stained his mouth and hands, sweet little barefoot boy. She hid a smile as she straightened up and brushed back the sweat-dampened strands of hair that had escaped her kerchief, then picked up the bucketful of blueberries she'd gathered on their afternoon trek.

"Hurry, chinquapin. Your mama'll worry if you're not home when she gets back."

She shifted the pail of berries to her other hand and watched as the boy flipped a rock back into place and flitted up the hill toward her. It wasn't just his mama that worried. Daisy did too; ever since the accident, she'd had an unsettled feeling, as if a prevailing sense of doom hovered around them.

Nevertheless, she had to smile at how he could pass through brush and briars in bare feet without a scratch, so effortlessly. He was only six but could walk the legs off her any day. They would have been home already if he hadn't stopped to study every bird's nest, flower, leaf, spider, and beetle along the way, but seeing him take delight in things again was worth the dawdling.

As he ran toward her, he wasn't even breathing hard; it seemed he could climb a hill even in the broiling heat of summer without getting all red and sweaty. Even though his shoulders were bare (he wore bibbed overalls with no shirt), his pale skin never burned; nor did it tan, or even get one freckle. Heavens, her own arms were covered with the things! How she envied his flawless skin, unblemished except for that birthmark.

There was something so sweet about his face that she couldn't help staring sometimes, though Mama said it was rude to stare. The color of his eyes was such a wonderful blue, like sky or water or Mrs. Day's peacocks' feathers; not even glamorous Hollywood stars had such beautiful eyes. And his hair—how to describe it? When he was in the shade, it almost looked dark, though even then, it seemed to glow like flames, somehow. In the sunlight, it lit up around his head like golden fire. Perpetually ruffled even when there was no wind, it curled down the back of his neck and around his ears (ears so cute and pointed, like an elf's). Her mama declared that the child was forever in need of a trim. Well, the Martels had been hippies way back when and never did become fans of clippers. Daisy thought it a wonder the boy didn't have hair to his waist. Anyhow, she rather liked it longish. It was so pretty; she'd love to have hair like that, instead of her dishwater blond, which she felt was a dull, sad disgrace in comparison.

She felt his hand in hers and started. He was smiling up at her. *He has no idea the effect he has on people. He's only a little boy, after all.*

"My mama worries too much. My daddy said I'd be the man of the house one day and must take care of her when he's gone. That's now, but she thinks I'm too young. I'm not a baby!"

Impulsively, Daisy bent to hug him. "Oh, chinquapin. You're not a baby, course not. But you're only six. That's why I'm here." She grinned. "Else you might get lost, and a bear come along and eat you."

"I never get lost, Daisy. I know where home is. And a bear won't eat me. The Lady in Blue wouldn't let it."

"Aha. Remember that time you went for a walk in the woods by yourself, and it got dark before your daddy found you? You were scared then, I bet."

"Only a little, when I saw those yellow eyes glaring down at me from up in the tree. But the Lady took my hand and showed me where the purple flags grow. I was picking a bouquet for my mama when my daddy came and carried me home."

She sometimes wondered if he had imagined it, but his story never varied. "You're just lucky your daddy didn't take you out to the woodshed and tan your hide, worrying your mama like that," she said sternly. "I would have."

Of course, she wouldn't have, and he knew it. Not his Daisy. Still, a small frown creased his brow. "I didn't think of that. I was only two."

Her heart melted. "You're such a sweet kid," she murmured as she bent to kiss his brow.

Before she knew what he was about, he threw his arms around her neck. "I love you, Daisy Alden. You're so beautiful. When I grow up, I'm going to marry you."

"Pshaw, silly boy." She returned the hug, and though abashed, managed a no-nonsense expression. "I'm a good ten years older than you. You'll find someone your own age when it comes to marrying." She surreptitiously wiped a tear from her cheek; no one had ever called her beautiful before. "Come on; your mama will be back soon. Be sure to ask how her interview went."

They pressed on up the hill. At the edge of the oak grove, she paused in the shade to catch her breath, while the boy climbed to the highest point to survey the countryside.

"Hey, Daisy, I could see your house from here, except that hill is in the way." He shaded his eyes with a hand and scanned the other direction. "Look! What's that? There, through the trees."

She squinted into the brightness and finally saw a patch of reddish contrasting with the green. "Must be that monastery. I wonder if maybe they're building a tower." She shivered.

"It doesn't look very far away. I could—"

"Not far enough," she blurted out before she thought (he was only a child!). A sudden feeling of dread shook her. Her mama always said the place was cursed. All her life, she'd heard tales of criminal activity there during Prohibition, which stood to reason; according to mama, moonshine was the devil's drink. Daisy had no cause to disbelieve her. Of course, it was much later that the monks had moved in. She wondered which was worse—moonshiners or monks. But the moonshiners were long gone; the mystery surrounding the monks seemed, therefore, more sinister. There were tales of secret rituals involving blood sacrifice—or no, in all honesty, she had to admit that was merely idle speculation of some of the girls at school. But everyone knew monks were into all sorts of intrigue, just like in those movies. Not that you could believe everything that comes out of Hollywood, but Mama always said where there's smoke, there's fire, and—

"What does 'cursed' mean?"

Wide intelligent eyes pinned her down, made her think. *Did I say that out loud?* "Um, better just to stay away from there."

"That's what Mama said." He jumped down off the rock. "But I think it's calling to me."

"What did you say?"

He laughed merrily. "Not in words, Daisy, just a kind of speaking in my heart. But Mama said not to bother them; they're from Europe, she said, and might not take kindly to a wild American boy from out of the woods."

Daisy did not like the way he turned to gaze in that direction again. "You listen to your mama, chinquapin." She took his hand. "Come on; time to go home."

Jude trudged after Daisy, over the hill, down the winding trail, and across the flats to the creek, pondering the issues that threatened to change his life forever. If Mama got the teaching job, they could go to school together, she'd said. He felt a pang of unease. Up to now, his life had revolved around the cabin in the woods, except for the occasional excursion into town. He didn't know very many people.

He knew the Aldens, of course. And dear Daisy had been a part of his life practically since he was born, like a second mother to him. His mama didn't trust just anyone, but she said Daisy was sterling quality. She didn't have sticky fingers, she didn't gossip, and she wanted to learn. That especially impressed Mama, who had been a teacher long ago, before Jude was born.

Sometimes Beau came over with Daisy. He was a couple of years older than Jude, like a big brother. Tall for his age, Beau was, with pale blue eyes and sun-bleached hair just like Daisy's, and a slow infectious grin. Under Daisy's watchful eye, the boys fished for crawdads, collected bugs, tussled in the grass, and played in the sand pile. The Martels had no television to distract them from real play.

But Daddy was gone now. Everything had changed. Mama was going to work. She assured Jude it would be fine, now that he was six and about to start school. Of course, she had already taught him to read and write and basic math, so the discipline of lessons was familiar. It was the classroom situation with other students that would be a new experience. With a mix of anticipation and dread, he contemplated meeting new people. The few he already knew he could count on his fingers.

There was Whiskery Ned Farwell, who owned the Hanna General Store. He always gave Jude a candy stick, ruffled his hair, and called him a little man. Every time. That candy was a real treat; he didn't get sweets very often, just the homemade kind at Christmas and Easter, mainly. Mama said it wasn't healthy, but fruit and nuts were okay. He'd never been sick a day in his life, so it must be true.

Then there was Miz Emma, Ned's wife. She'd peer down at Jude like a hen eyeing a bug, with big blue eyes and glasses and red lipstick that was too bright. She sometimes asked him pointed personal questions that made him feel uncomfortable. Mama told him not to answer if he didn't want to, but to be respectful. Miz Emma always gave him an apple or an orange; aside from the questions, she was nice, too.

The Farwells had one daughter a bit older than Jude: Jasmine, a beautiful name like a princess would have. She wore a silver clip in her long dark hair and a flock of tiny butterfly combs that sparkled when she tossed her head. She had to be the most beautiful girl in the world. She didn't ever notice him at all. Mama said she was a little hussy.

Ira Finch at the gas station and car repair shop was a bony man with a snaggletooth grin who wore greasy coveralls and always looked as though he'd just crawled out from under a car, which he probably had. He'd wipe his hands on a grimy rag and search his pockets, eventually coming up with a stick of gum for a small boy. What a treat that was! Before the accident, Ira used to stand around talking to Daddy until his wife, Miz Lila Mae, would come out to stand in the doorway of their neat white house, her hands on her hips, and her eyes snapping beneath fierce black eyebrows. She'd stick two fingers in her mouth, and her shrill whistle would get Ira's attention in a hurry. With a sharp jerk of her chin, she'd signal him to get back to work. She probably figured he'd stand there chewing the fat all day and never get a lick of work done unless she cracked the whip, Daddy said once with a rueful little chuckle.

They had children, but Jude was overwhelmed by their number and boldness and only peered at them from behind his daddy's legs. Especially after he heard one outspoken girl say, "He don't look like no demon child to me, I don't care what Emma Jean says!" Why would someone say that? He'd tried to keep his oddities hidden, like Mama said. (Somehow, they must have slipped out.) Still, they were friendly kids, though Daddy never stayed long enough for him to overcome his shyness and get acquainted. Now, Mama assured him there would be plenty of time to get to know the boy Dace, who was about his own age, when he went to school.

Then there was Uncle Roy Oakley. He wasn't really his uncle; everyone just called him that. Daddy worked for him off and on, building houses and cabinets and such. Jude liked the logo on the side of his red van—Lionheart Construction—in interesting letters arched over a leaping lion.

Occasionally they stopped to visit Uncle Roy on the way home from town. Aunt Dolly would get Jude settled in a big armchair by the bookcase with cookies and milk, while Uncle Roy would bring out a Mason jar of white lightning and cards for a game of Five Hundred. After the game, Daddy would produce his trusty fiddle and strike up a tune. By that time, Uncle Roy was ready to cut a rug. He took turns dancing with Mama and Aunt Dolly. Jude, meanwhile, was lost in the world of *Ali Baba and the Forty Thieves*, Jack London's wild frozen north, or Robert Louis Stevenson's tales of the sea (a little deep for him, but there were pictures). Too soon, Daddy would rouse him from his wonderful fantasy world to play a tune or two.

Daddy was proud of Jude's gift for music and had him perform every chance he got; Mama preferred that they stay at home. Jude was happy enough with that, though applause from other people was gratifying. Daddy had said not to hide his light under a bushel, whatever that meant.

Beneath the cottonwoods and redbuds, sunlight dappled the water winding its way through the center of a rocky creek bed. After a sudden downpour, the narrow stream would become a rushing brown torrent, but for now, it was safe. Daisy kept her eye out to make sure Jude was following as she made her way down into the gully.

At the creek, he got distracted, peering down into the clear water. "See that fish, Daisy? Here, let me—" He grabbed hold of a rock the size of a tombstone.

"Whoa, there, kid! What did your daddy say about disturbing the natural course of waterways? Anyhow, your mama'll be home soon. Let's not dawdle." She marveled once again at the strength of those spindly arms, though she ought to be used to it by now.

They splashed through the water and up the far bank. The sinking sun was partly hidden by a stand of pines along one side of the jutting peak.

Jude pointed. "Once I climbed up there with my daddy. Cold air came out of a big crack in the rock, like an ice giant's breath. I thought a dead hand was going to reach up to tear my heart out."

"Jude!" she cried, shocked. "What a terrible thing to say! Where did that come from, anyhow? Just stop it, right now. Let's just go."

"Yeah. I don't like that place. There's something in there."

"My goodness, I hope not! Hey, there's the dogwood that bloomed when you were born. At least, that's what your Mama says." A curious thing, but better than ice giant's breath.

"Yeah, when the angels brought me from heaven."

Daisy smiled. "Course. Where else would someone sweet as you come from?"

A furrow creased his brow. "I can't remember angels—only the fire."

Fire? "You were too tiny back then to remember stuff, chinquapin. Maybe you dreamed it. Aw, would you look at that? A mama deer with two young'uns. Cute."

A doe and two half-grown fawns picked their way daintily along the trail, big ears twitching, great dark eyes watchful.

"The fawns don't have spots." Jude frowned as the deer vanished among the trees. "Shouldn't they have spots?"

"They outgrew them. They're big enough they don't need 'em anymore."

"You're grown-up, but you haven't lost yours."

"You're so sweet, I declare," Daisy said, laughing, and tousled his hair. "Let's get back."

She set a determined pace across a meadow yellow with buttercups. Jude ran to catch up, grabbing handfuls of the flowers. The sun was hot, and Daisy wished she had brought a bottle of water. She glanced a little enviously at the boy at her side, so energetic and oddly impervious to ordinary discomforts.

He began to hum softly. That lullaby again, the one he'd said the Lady in Blue had sung to him. Not his mama or angels. It was when he was falling down, out of the sky or a fire (or something like that), frightened and cold, crying for his mother. The Lady rocked him to sleep. When he woke, his daddy was carrying him home. The first time he'd told Daisy this, she put her arm around him and gently explained that dreams aren't real. He'd lifted glowing eyes to meet hers. Glowing! A startling thing—they seemed to pierce her very soul. Only with great difficulty had she torn her gaze from his.

"Daisy?" he'd then said, plaintively, "Are you okay?"

With eyes averted, she'd managed a strained, "Course, I'm okay." *What just happened?* she'd wondered but dared not meet his gaze. With a trembling hand, she'd brushed a strand of hair from his eyes. Those eyes, how had they—a trick of light and shadow, maybe? Finally, she'd managed to look into them again without losing herself, though her heart was still pounding. He'd seemed a bit anxious for her, but she'd managed to reassure him. Since then, she'd learned to be more careful.

They got to the creek that wound through the pasture and cooled their feet as they waded across the shallow little trickle. Goats and sheep lay in the shade by the barn. A flock of chickens sang and scratched in the dirt. The parking spot was still empty.

"Your mama's not back yet." Daisy wiped her brow.

"You go cool off and rest your weary bones, Daisy. Sit in the shade while I get you some lemonade."

He was so serious; she managed not to laugh. She went around behind the house. In the backyard, shaded by tall trees, was a large rectangular rock, perfect for a garden bench, though it resembled an antiquated tombstone more than anything else, she'd always thought. Moss streaked its weathered surface, even the smooth, somewhat polished front of it, on which was etched the image of an angel with a baby in his arms, surrounded by an intricate Celtic knot design. Daisy could almost imagine curlicue numbers and letters embedded among the fanciful vines, leaves, and flowers, but they somehow eluded her. The Martels had never talked about it, and she had never quite dared ask; she wasn't sure why. It was at the edge of the yard, by the flowerbed, where she'd often sat watching Jude and Beau as they played.

Now she sank down onto it gratefully and began sorting through the blueberries. She tossed out bugs, leaves, and twigs, shook the pail now and then until no more leaves came to the top. A sweet melody drifted down. Daisy set the pail on the grass and lifted up her eyes. Mr. Martel had pointed out an oriole's nest high in the tall tree nearest the house. If she was still enough, she might see the little songster himself.

She had learned so much from the Martels. The size of their library had overwhelmed her at first; she had never imagined so many books in one home. It was a treasure and a means of escape into other worlds. There, she made forays into learning and adventure. When the Martels had begun correcting her speech, she supposed that was only natural for a schoolteacher and was not offended. She hardly ever said ain't anymore and usually remembered the rule about double negatives.

She was ever grateful for another new and wonderful world they had introduced to her: that of classical music. On many an evening, she sat in front of the hearth listening to Mr. Martel's violin and little Jude's sweet singing. She and Miz Martel sang along when they could.

Under Miz Martel's wing, Daisy blossomed. No other teacher had taken such an interest in her. Where others saw only a plain face and mediocrity, Miz Martel recognized intelligence and integrity. After hearing her sister referred to as "the pretty one" time and again, Daisy thought it a fine thing to be valued for something other than looks, one thing she feared she sadly lacked.

Now, as she peered upward through the fluttering leaves, she saw a flash of orange; the source of that sweet melody. She liked to imagine that she was a princess in a fairy tale and that the oriole was a prince under a spell who sang just for her.

Someday my prince will come, she hummed softly, then sighed. *Get real, Daisy. Snow White, you are not.*

A clink of ice cubes snapped her out of her daydream. Jude stood before her, holding a tall, cold lemonade. Condensation fogged the glass.

"Thanks, Jude. You're a lifesaver. Hush, now. Listen," she said softly, pointing upward.

He smiled, tilting his head to look up at the oriole. "I bet I could play that tune on my violin," he whispered after a while. Tears sprang to his eyes; he blinked them away.

"Heck, yeah. Never mind the violin, you can sing that song sweet as that little ol' bird any day."

"I miss my daddy." He choked up.

She patted his arm. "Course, you do. But I bet he's up in Heaven smiling, watching over you every minute."

The boy stood still as stone, eyes fixed on the flash of orange among the green leaves, his fist clenched at his side. Sunlight glinted off the tear tracks on his cheeks. "Why did my daddy leave me?"

She set her glass beside the pail of berries and put her arm around him. Every muscle was tense, like the small, clenched fist. "He didn't mean to, chinquapin. He couldn't help it. Sometimes people have to do things they don't want to do. Your daddy'll always love you, forever and ever, and you'll see him again one day." She felt him trembling. "Go ahead and cry if you want. I'll hold you. I'll hold you."

"I'm not crying, Daisy. I got to be the man now to take care of my mama."

"Sometimes, even a man's got to cry, or he'll be like a stone. Stone breaks, chinquapin. You've seen how that tree bends in the wind? That's why it's not broken, but is still standing, fine and strong." She pulled him onto her lap. "Go ahead and cry. Your Daisy's here." She stroked his hair as he wept against her shoulder and felt tears of her own slide down her cheek.

Night of the Perseids

Foam rose in the bucket as two streams of milk alternated with a regular rhythm. Daisy leaned her head into the goat's warm flank, lulled by the sound of its munching of grain, her mind elsewhere.

"Daisy, Daisy! Mama's back!"

She jumped. "Hey, don't scare me like that," Daisy reproached the slender silhouette in the doorway.

Jude's hair was aglow in the sunlight. His long shadow stretched toward her across the straw on the barn floor. "Sorry, Daisy. Wait till Mama sees how many eggs I found!" With that, he ran off.

By the time Daisy finished milking, Miz Martel was walking up the path from her pickup to the house, all her attention on her child as he lugged the pail of eggs and chattered about his adventures of the day.

It struck Daisy that the boy had never grown to resemble his parents, like her mama'd said he would. He was still fair, his features fine, and though slender, gave promise of broad shoulders and height one day. His folks, on the other hand, were rather darker of complexion with brown hair (grayish now), and barely average height. She fancied their faces carved of wood with eyes of agate, his of marble with eyes of sapphire. She'd think he was adopted, except she knew he wasn't.

For a moment, Daisy imagined, as she sometimes did, that he was a fairy child exchanged in the cradle for the Martels' baby.

Then reality intervened, and she followed them into the house.

Miz Martel greeted her while Jude set the bucket of eggs on the counter.

"The interview went well," she remarked. "I'm pretty sure I have the job."

The boy brightened. "Are you going to be my teacher?"

"No, Mrs. Day will teach the little ones. She's very nice. Don't worry; I'll be just across the hall."

He sighed, a bit anxious, though also looking forward to this as a new adventure.

As they ate a supper of leftover ham and potato salad, Miz Martel filled them in on the details of her day. "Dace Finch will be in your grade, and he'll introduce you to his friend Cale Tremayne. You know, his daddy has the hounds."

"It'll be fun, you'll like it," said Daisy. "I miss that school. Just wait, I'm going to teach there someday."

"You'll make a wonderful teacher, Daisy," Miz Martel approved. "The children will love you. Now, remember what we planned for tonight?"

"To watch shooting stars!"

"And what are they called? What did we just read in the Star Book? Right, the Perseid meteor shower. We should be able to get a good view from the meadow on the hill."

"Yeah!" shouted Jude, grinning. "Daisy, we can make wishes!"

"Let's get these dishes out of the way," Daisy said, as she began running the water into the sink. "I'll wash; Jude, you dry."

"Are you staying overnight, Daisy?" Jude asked as he vigorously dried a plate. "Mama said we can make popcorn after the star show." He peered eagerly out of the kitchen window at the reddening western sky.

They went out into the warm night, carrying a blanket and flashlights. The sky was clear; the moon hadn't yet risen, so it was perfect for stargazing. Leaves whispered, and the fragrances of pine and newly mown hay came to them on a faint breeze.

They followed the circles of light down the path, through the barnyard. Slumbering animals stirred in the darkness as they passed by; soon, they had hopped across the creek and were on the trail up the slope. Up, up through the redbuds and the oak grove. Finally, they came to the meadow. They spread the blanket on the grass, sat down, and turned their faces skyward. The meteor shower was already in progress.

"It's so clear out," Miz Martel said. "So many stars!"

Daisy nudged Jude. "'Look at the stars! Look, look up at the skies!'" she quoted. "Remember Hopkins' poem, chinquapin?"

"'O look at all the fire-folk sitting in the air!'" Jude responded with the next line. "I like that one, Daisy!"

They grinned at each other, then lifted their eyes to the star-spangled sky and sat for a while in silent wonder. Soon the teacher came out in Miz Martel; she pointed out planets, individual stars, and constellations amid the storm of shooting stars. The boy was so full of questions that finally, even she was at a loss for answers.

"Someday, we'll know, Jude."

"Yeah. When we get to heaven." He was silent for a moment. "I bet Daddy knows all about them, now."

Even in the dark, Daisy saw Miz Martel's hand reach out to squeeze the boy's shoulder in silence. There was a glint of a tear on his cheek. Daisy stared hard at the sky.

Time passed quickly as meteors streaked the sky in abundance. The heat of the day fled; the breeze cooled. Daisy shivered and then was sorry she had because Miz Martel noticed. "It's getting a bit chilly. Maybe we should go in," she said, getting to her feet. Her silhouette was dark against the sky.

"No, Mama, not yet," Jude protested. "Look, there goes another one. Please, Mama? Just a little while longer?"

"Daisy's getting cold and, well, to be honest, I'm tired. It's been a long day."

"You go rest, then, Mama. Can't me and Daisy stay for a bit? She can wrap up in the blanket."

"That would be 'Daisy and I,' son," remonstrated Miz Martel, the teacher.

"Daisy and I?" Jude repeated obediently. "Daisy?"

Daisy ruffled his hair. "Sure, chinquapin, if your mama says. I should have brought my jacket, but the blanket'll do," she said to Miz Martel. "We'll be fine. I've got my flashlight right here."

"Well, don't be too long. I'll have the hot chocolate ready when you get back."

"And popcorn, too, Mama?" cried Jude.

"All right then." She kissed the top of his head. With a rustling of grass, she crossed the meadow and vanished into the shadows at the edge of the woods. The glimmer of her flashlight winked among the trees until it could be seen no more.

Daisy and Jude sat, watching the sky. Daisy had wrapped the blanket around them. They mostly sat in silence, though now and then exclaiming over a particularly dramatic display of cosmic fireworks. After a while, the moon began to show above the trees, stark and gleaming, the nimbus washing out the stars in its vicinity.

"Daisy," Jude said. "Do you know Dace Finch? Will he be my friend?"

"I don't see why not. He's a friendly kid. Always into mischief, but those twinkly eyes and that cute smile—it was impossible to get mad at him. His older sister, Birdie, is my age. We've been friends—"

She bit off her words at his sudden hiss of alarm.

"What's that smell, Daisy? Blech! It's almost like—"

"I just smell, um, hay and the piney-woods. Are you pulling my leg?" She laughed nervously. The night seemed suddenly dark and threatening.

His nails dug into her arm. No, he wasn't joking. "It's—what is it, Daisy?"

A chill went up her spine. She peered into the darkness so hard her eyes hurt but saw nothing but the grayish meadow and the black wall of woods beyond, even under the bright glow of the rising moon. "I don't know. I can't see —"

"Look, Daisy! Look, over there!"

She jumped. "Where?" *Gulp. Calm down, Daisy, you're the older one here.* But his fear was contagious; her heart pounded. "I don't see anything," she whispered.

"There! Look. There it is," he croaked, pointing toward a deep shadow that now she figured must be a patch of brush at the edge of the meadow where it began sloping upward to the hill above, though she could see nothing but black on black. "That thing over there. See it?" He clung to her, quivering like a leaf in the wind.

That frightened her nearly out of her wits. His mama often worried because he was so heedless of danger. Nothing much scared him, even when it ought to. The sight of him so terrified stood the hair up on the back of her neck. She felt around for the flashlight. Maybe if she turned it on...

"No! Don't move, Daisy!" he squeaked. "It'll see us!"

The blanket slid off her shoulders unheeded. Her shivering was not from the cold. "I can't see; it's too dark. What is it, Jude?" His ability to see in the dark like a cat was a marvel, but she'd grown used to it.

His face was stark white in the moonlight, his eyes wide. "It's coming," he whimpered. "No. No. It sees us. Its eyes are red; they're burning. Just like that one when Daddy — Daisy, it's coming for us!"

His terror was catching. She clutched his hand and scrambled to her feet. Something rolled against her foot. The flashlight. She snatched it up. What the heck, if it had already seen them, she meant to find out what it was. She flicked on the light.

Shadows moved, and her heart leaped into her throat. At first, she thought that was all it was, shadows. Then something flashed white as the beam passed over it. She moved it back to catch the thing again in the light. And wished she hadn't. There, a twisted triangular shape — *a face? No. Yes!* A nightmare face, eyes flaming red and glowing in the dark, just as the boy said.

The shadowy figure leaped forward with a strange gliding motion and was halfway across the meadow now, in a twinkling. *What is it? What is it?* No time to stand petrified.

"Run, Jude!" she screamed, pushing the boy ahead of her, thinking to distract it while — Jude was a fast runner — maybe he could make it home.

He clung to her arm as though he'd read her mind. "No, don't leave me, Daisy!" he shrieked. "Come on, let's run, let's hide!"

The thing was almost upon them. Now that it was closer, she got an idea of the look of it, like nothing she'd ever seen before. Not in real life, maybe in a movie. The white skull-like head had a patchy shock of ragged black hair and black eye sockets, from which the eyes flamed red. The mouth opened; fangs glinted in the moonlight.

Daisy and Jude ran for the trees. A snarl ripped through the night behind them, spurring them on. Grass caught at their feet; weeds snatched at their legs. They would never make it; the thing moved too fast. Daisy heard a rustling close behind them. Or was that the sound of their own footsteps? Every hair on her head stood on end. In an instant, the thing would have them.

Faster and faster, they ran. Toward the trees, hoping the thickets would slow it down. Unbelievably, they made it to the edge of the woods. Daisy dared not look back. Past the first oaks, she ran, holding the little boy's hand as they crashed through redbud, hickory, maple. Branches tore at her hair, slapped her face, caught at her clothing. On through the trees, down the trail. Daisy stepped in a depression, stumbled, caught herself, and ran on, gripping Jude's hand tighter. Horror of horrors, what if she lost him? His nails bit deep. He wasn't about to let her go either. She tripped over a fallen tree and scraped her knee. A sob caught in her throat as he dragged her to her feet, and they ran on, the bouncing flashlight all but useless.

Daisy was numb with terror. The back of her neck prickled; every hair rose as she imagined sharp claws reaching out. How could the thing not have caught them, the way it moved? So fast. It had to be right on their heels, but she couldn't hear it. She dared not glance back, or slow even the least bit. Not with a little boy depending on her.

A sharp yank brought her up short. Even then, Jude kept his grip on her arm. The flashlight flew out of her hand, and darkness closed in around them.

"Daisy, Daisy, don't stop now," Jude whimpered. "It's coming, Daisy. It's coming." He tugged at her arm, staring wide-eyed back up the trail.

"My shirt's caught!" she cried, frantically working to unhook it or tear it off, but it held fast. "Run, Jude! Run! Don't wait for me!"

"No, I won't leave you!" he shrieked. His eyes seemed to glow blue; they must have been reflecting the moonlight. No, impossible. The canopy of trees hid the moon.

"Jude! Listen to me!" she barked in a tone she had never before used with him. "Go tell your Mama! Now!" At his stricken expression, she spoke more softly. "She'll know what to do, Jude." With a sob, she choked out, "Go, now!" Anything to save him.

For an instant, it seemed as though he would do as she commanded, for he was an obedient child, but then he clung to her arm, his eyes pleading. "Daisy, I can't leave you." He threw his arms around her neck.

Then a voice dry as dead leaves crushed underfoot said, "Come to me, little one."

Daisy glanced up and stared, petrified. The faint illumination from the fallen flashlight picked up a misshapen form slinking toward them, the more terrifying because it was soundless. And because it had spoken in a voice not human.

What kind of a monster — this was a nightmare! She wrapped her arms around Jude and prayed. The thing reared up. Its skull-like head gleamed white in the meager light; its eyes glowed red. A long tongue whipped out betwixt sharp, pointed teeth. Skeletal white fingers with long claws sprang out of the blackness toward them. Daisy nearly fainted from terror; she felt Jude quaking in her arms as he turned wide eyes toward the apparition.

A blinding blue-white flash lit up the night. Daisy heard a loud snap and a strangled shriek. She blinked spots from her eyes and stared. The thing was writhing on the ground, its white face turned to the sky; it uttered a long, shuddering groan. Tendrils of smoke drifted up from between the white hands clawing at its chest. Daisy couldn't believe her eyes, but her throat burned with the stink of scorched flesh, hair, and fabric. Then the creature sprang up, and with a long, drawn-out wail, scrambled backward and vanished into the darkness.

In the dead blackness was a faint glow where the flashlight lay on the ground. Acrid gray smoke hung in the air above it, curling slowly upward. All sound had ceased, except for their panting. Daisy held the child in her arms, and they waited for a long time, it seemed, unable to believe that the thing was gone. Finally, Jude gave a little shake.

"Wha — what happened, Daisy? Daisy!"

"It's okay. It's okay now," she murmured, patting his back, full of wonder that they were alive. Still not certain that the thing wouldn't yet leap out of the shadows. "I think it's — I think it's gone." She hoped.

Jude clung to her with a grip of death, trembling. "What was it?" he whispered, his eyes wide. "What happened? What did you do?"

"I didn't," she murmured as she squeezed him tight for a moment. "It wasn't me." She couldn't stop shaking. Had that blue flash come from his eyes? No, impossible. Then what...? "We better go. Oh, my shirt's still caught. The flashlight's right over there."

He picked up the flashlight and handed it to her. "I see, Daisy. Here, just move a little this way. Okay. You're free." He hugged her tightly, then glanced quickly around. "Hurry. Let's go. What if it comes back?"

Calling in the Hounds

Their hearts beat fast, and they cast quick glances behind them as they hastened down the trail. Shadows seemed about to leap out at them at every moment as Daisy shone the light around. For her, the flashlight was essential, since the trees hid the moon. Jude didn't need it.

She'd often wondered why he wasn't like other children. Was he a demon child and his parents witches, as some said? No, Mama said those were rumors concocted by superstitious people who had nothing better to do than slander their neighbors. They ought to mind their own business, she declared. The Martels were nice folk; they just kept to themselves a lot, and some people just couldn't stand it.

Daisy was too shy to inquire about a subject like that; the Martels had never given her any reason to think they were in league with the devil—and she'd spent a lot of time with them. Though it did seem a little odd how Miz Martel continued to stick to her story about angels bringing the baby, even now that Daisy was fifteen and already knew the "facts of life." It would be impolite to contradict her, and anyhow, she decided, it was a much sweeter tale than the old one about the stork.

Soon they caught sight of the warm glow of light in the window. Daisy thought she had never seen so fine a sight. Even now, her spine prickled as though that thing was still creeping up on them. They dashed onto the back porch, tumbled through the door into the kitchen, and stood panting. *Safe at last!* Hard to believe, after all that had happened, but everything seemed right. The lamps were lit, the kettle was on the stove, and Miz Martel was setting a bowl of popcorn on the table. She glanced up with a smile.

Jude rushed over and buried his face in her apron. Her smile faded. "Is something wrong, my dear?"

Daisy rushed to explain, "I'm so sorry, Miz Martel. You know I wouldn't let anything happen to your little boy for the world. I tried to…if I'd known…"

Miz Martel gazed down into his little face, the huge, frightened eyes. "Are you hurt?"

The boy found his voice at last. "No, Mama, I'm okay. But Daisy skinned her knee. Maybe you should 'tend to it."

Miz Martel's brow furrowed as she directed a questioning glance at

Daisy. "Um, do you need a bandage? Let's have a look."

"It's only a scratch," said Daisy, her voice shaking now that it was all over, but she bared her raw and reddened knee.

Miz Martel cleaned the wound and put a bandage on it. "Tell me about it."

Daisy opened her mouth; the words seemed to stick in her throat.

Jude came to her rescue. "Something chased us, Mama. We ran and ran. Then Daisy's shirt got caught on the branch and—" His eyes grew large as he remembered.

Miz Martel frowned. "Something chased you?"

Jude gulped, and Daisy took over. "We couldn't tell what it was, but when I shone the flashlight on it—"

"It had a white skull-face and red eyes," Jude cut in. "Just like that time when—"

"It had fangs and long claws." Daisy shuddered.

"My goodness. Are you serious?" Miz Martel said, frowning. The teakettle began to whistle. "Here. Sit down. Let's have some popcorn and hot chocolate. Then you can tell me all about it." She retrieved the kettle, poured boiling water into mugs, stirred in the cocoa powder, and added a dollop of cream. She handed them out and sat down at the table. "Now, tell me what happened."

Daisy and Jude exchanged looks. Their frightening experience seemed unreal now, in the light and warmth and safety of the kitchen. Haltingly, they told their story.

"So, it wasn't a bear?" Miz Martel said when they concluded.

"Bears don't talk," Jude said. "It looked just like the one at the—the accident."

They stared.

"The accident?" his mama said. "What's this? You never told me about anything like that."

"I thought maybe I dreamed it. This time I was awake."

"Maybe it was a devil," Daisy said. "It was kind of like the ones in the movies. Its eyes glowed. Red. Jude wasn't dreaming, ma'am, or imagining it; I saw it, too."

Miz Martel sat silent, her frown deepening.

"I know it's hard to believe. I almost don't believe it myself, and I was there!"

Miz Martel got up and drew the curtains. "Okay. We'll say a few extra prayers tonight and check it out in the morning. Maybe we'll find tracks or some clue as to what this is about. Finish your cocoa and popcorn now, kids. It's way past bedtime."

The next morning after breakfast and chores, the three of them took a walk up the hill. Birds sang in the trees; the trail through the woods was dappled with sunlight. A faint breeze stirred the leaves. Daisy almost began to doubt what they had seen the night before, now, in the light of day. But it seemed Miz Martel did not discount their story; she examined the faint sign as they followed the trail all the way to the meadow. Only the forgotten blanket, a few bent grasses, and broken twigs indicated that they had been there. To Daisy and Miz Martel, at least.

Jude wrinkled his nose. "Phew. It still stinks here."

His mama nodded. It seemed to Daisy that Miz Martel knew something she wasn't saying. The way she stood staring up the hill from the meadow with a tight-lipped expression. A shadow seemed to pass behind her eyes.

"Well, all seems fine now." She turned a concerned look on Daisy and Jude. "But it's daytime. It won't hurt to be a little cautious after dark."

Daisy shivered. "Do you know what it was, then?"

"Let's not worry. It reminds me of something that happened, well, a long time ago. That's all." Her gaze rested on Jude for a moment, in a way that puzzled Daisy more than her words. "Though I can't see why, now, after all this time—"

"Maybe if I tell Daddy, he'll get Mr. Tremayne out here with his dogs and track it down," Daisy offered.

Miz Martel hesitated.

"Please, ma'am. You just never know. Daddy says Mr. Tremayne has the best hounds in the county. Wouldn't it be good to get rid of this thing once and for all, whatever it is? Before it hurts someone?"

"True," Miz Martel conceded, with a doubtful look. "I'm not sure we can, but I guess we ought to try."

Everything happened quickly after that. The Martels had a telephone now, ever since the accident. Daisy called her daddy and explained what had happened. He asked to talk to Miz Martel, and after she corroborated the story to his satisfaction, he agreed to call Jake Tremayne.

Early that afternoon, a cloud of dust rising above the trees announced the arrival of visitors. Daisy followed Jude and his mama out onto the porch as her daddy's old red pickup came into view. It bounced up the drive and stopped in front of the house. Daddy and Arlie had just gotten out when Mr. Tremayne cruised in. Three bluetick hounds rode in the back of his new gray Dodge, their salt-and-pepper muzzles lifted into the wind. One, and another, and then all three gave voice as the pickup came to a halt.

Daddy made introductions. Mr. Tremayne was a stocky, soft-spoken man. Daisy recalled that he and his wife ran a bed-and-breakfast over on Hanna Creek. He had a quiet way of taking charge that seemed to impress Miz Martel (she wasn't one to trust people much if she didn't know them well).

Mr. Tremayne opened the tailgate. The dogs needed no coaxing to jump out and surround their master. He snapped leashes to their collars and held on firmly as the dogs ran in circles sniffing the ground, eager to take to the trail. Their mottled black and white hides rippled sleek and shining as they strained against the tethers.

With words and gestures, Daddy explained what this was about and where they had to go. Mr. Tremayne nodded.

Daisy stood on the porch, watching while the two men and Arlie followed the dogs up the trail into the woods. Jude stood beside her, staring after her big brother with awe; Arlie was now eighteen and about to join the Army.

"Will they find it?" he wondered aloud in a small voice.

"Not if it only comes out after dark," his mama replied. "But maybe they'll find out what it is. Or where it went."

Daisy was silent. A thing like that might be hard to kill, whatever it was. But she was confident that her daddy could fix anything. And Mr. Tremayne's hounds seemed to know their business.

Miz Martel suggested that Daisy might help her prepare a lunch; the hunters would surely be hungry when they returned.

When the men returned with the dogs later, they were grateful for the offer of chicken sandwiches and iced tea. Mr. Tremayne tied the dogs to the rail, and at his request, Jude brought them water. They drank and flopped down in the shade of the porch, panting. The men went inside to sit at the kitchen table.

"Didn't find the critter, whatever it was," Daddy said to Miz Martel.

"The dogs found the trail," added Mr. Tremayne. "There's something out there, all right. Wasn't no bear or cougar, or we'd have it by now. No, ain't nothing like that."

"What do you think it is?" Miz Martel asked, a little diffidently, Daisy noticed.

"No idea. We ended up in that pile of rocks near the top of the hill; looks to be a deep crevice. I reckon there's a cave underneath, the way the dogs was sniffing around. But no way to get into it that I could see."

"That's where Daddy and me—" Jude halted as all eyes turned toward him.

"Tell them about it," Daisy encouraged him.

After he'd related the story, Mr. Tremayne gave Daddy a knowing look. "Maybe there's something to ol' Tom Rowe's tall tales, after all."

"What's that?" Miz Martel said.

"You recall him ranting about something prowling around his place at night, leaving animals laying around dead with all the blood drained out of them?"

"Oh, his stories about aliens? Yes, I remember."

"We thought it was his moonshine talking. But I ain't so sure of that no more."

Mr. Tremayne nodded. "In the past couple years, some other fellers have called me to bring my hounds out and follow a trail just like this. Seems nobody ever got a look at the thing, but calves, dogs, chickens and such, were found dead, just like ol' Tom said, with nary a drop of blood left in them. One feller said his cows and horses showed the same signs, though they survived. They had odd bite marks, mostly at the jugular. But it weren't no bear or cougar."

"Wasn't there a kid found dead like that over east of here?" Arlie put in as he munched on a sandwich.

"Hmm, you're right," Mr. Tremayne said. "Never thought of that being connected to these here animal killings."

"Could be," said Daddy with a proud glance at his eldest son.

"Anyhow," continued Mr. Tremayne, "There's something not natural about this. My hounds follow the trail and end up with nothing. Usually, they'll tree a critter; if it gets away, we know how. This thing's tracks just stop cold, like it vanishes into thin air."

"Or flies away?" said Miz Martel.

The men glanced at each other. "You might have something there," Mr. Tremayne said.

"And it only comes out at night," Arlie murmured.

"That's right," Mr. Tremayne said. "We went out during the night a few times; my dogs got a real hot trail, then—but it disappeared on them just the same."

"That crevice on the hill is too narrow for something that size to get into," Daddy added. "Normally."

"That's why I'm saying, it ain't natural," said Mr. Tremayne. "Heck, what kind of thing would it have to be, to do that?"

Daisy noticed that nobody said the word everyone had to be thinking. That would be crazy talk. There was no such thing as a vampire.

"Hey," Arlie said, "what if we cram a few sticks of dynamite in there? Boom! I'd like to see it survive that, whatever the heck it is."

"Now, son. I'm sure Miz Martel don't want us blowing up her hill."

"Anyhow, this area is riddled with caves," said Mr. Tremayne. "If the critter got into that crack, it's long gone by now; maybe clear to China, for all we know."

Arlie shrugged as he helped himself to another sandwich. "Just saying."

Goblin King

September 2006-Spring 2011

September came, warm and sunny during the day, but the nights were chilly, and the leaves had begun to turn bright red and yellow, flecks of color amongst the green. School started, and with it, big changes in little Jude's life.

He'd always known he was different, though maybe he hadn't realized just how different. His mama and daddy—and Daisy, too—had always taught him to conceal his oddities since other people might not understand. People tended to be afraid of what they didn't understand, his mama explained again when he was about to start school, so it was better not to excite their animosity. Whatever that meant—it sounded unpleasant, Jude decided. Mama was a teacher and sometimes used big words. Still, going to school promised to be an adventure; he'd never in his life strayed far from home—just occasional trips to the store and such. And of course, that fiddling contest.

He found out what his mama meant about being different after he started school and encountered bullies for the first time, and the importance of minding her warnings about not displaying his oddities. Like other boys, he sometimes wished that he could be, well—the king of the hill. He found out the hard way that tough may be cool, but freak is not. He should have known; even comic books could tell you that. Superman disguised himself as the nerd Clark Kent. And all those other superheroes kids admired—Batman, Spiderman, Hellboy and—all, all of them, proved that point with their disguises and such.

When Jude started school in the little unincorporated town of Hanna, the first month or so was fine—exciting, even. He had time to get settled into the routine, made friends, and learned team sports—things he hadn't had access to at home—and schoolwork was a breeze since he'd already learned to read and print.

Then it happened: he got his initiation into the real world. A rather rough one, it turned out. It seems every school has a bully to test out the new kid. In the school at Hanna, it was one Fenwick Cooper, though nobody called him that, except maybe the new teachers. Everyone else called him Stave. He'd managed to dodge the truant officer for the first month or so, but eventually got caught, and his daddy dragged him in by the scruff sometime in October.

Stave was a big hulk with a blond buzz cut and a gang of toadies to egg him on. J. C. Daws, Leroy Hayes, and Jasper Brown were the worst. J. C. and Leroy were skinny little blond yappy-dogs. Jasper was a tall black kid with a chip on his shoulder.

Luckily, Beau Alden (Daisy's younger brother) was there at the time, a couple of grades ahead. He was like a big brother to Jude and kept an eye on him, but of course, he couldn't be there all the time. And Jude wasn't about to be a rat.

Stave arrived, then, and the trouble started. Stave, J. C., Leroy, Jasper, and the others began their usual business of tormenting the little kids. Out in the schoolyard, mostly; initially, it was name-calling and mockery, but it didn't end there. Each time it grew worse. Jude and his friends managed to endure for quite a while, but eventually, the time came when Stave pushed things too far.

That fateful day, Jude and his new friends Dace Finch, Cale Tremayne, Violet Taylor, and Rosa Sharon McCoy were playing on the swings. Violet and Rosa Sharon were in the first grade too. Rosa Sharon was Cale's cousin, and Violet was her next-door neighbor (they'd always been friends), so they seemed to just naturally gravitate toward the three boys' group. Having them around turned out to be a lot of fun, Jude decided, even if they were girls. Violet had a good throwing arm for a girl, and Rosa Sharon's baseball card collection was something else!

When Stave and his gang started out with name-calling again, Jude and his group of friends did pretty well pretending they didn't exist until they started grabbing their swings and roughing them up. At first, they thought if they let the bullies have the swings, they'd leave them alone. They went off to a corner of the playground to play. That was when they found out the hard way that appeasement doesn't work with bullies; they just tend to see you as easy pickings. Stave was a few grades ahead and had been held back a couple of years besides, since he played hooky so often, so he was a lot bigger than most of the other kids in the school.

That day, Stave and his gang followed Jude and his friends across the yard, yapping and pushing them around until they had them cornered at the fence.

Jude, Dace, and Cale turned to face Stave and his gang, like heroes in those stories of King Arthur and his chivalrous Knights of the Round Table, and such, shielding the fair maidens from danger. (Though Violet was yelling some pretty unladylike things, as though she meant to take them on all by herself.) But when Rosa Sharon got hit with a dirt clod and started crying, that was it. Jude and his friends saw red; they turned and stood their ground, little fists raised.

Naturally, that didn't faze the bullies one bit. Stave was in the lead; his gang was right behind him. He swaggered straight toward Jude (Stave seemed to have it in for him, in particular). Jude was ready to defend himself, but he didn't really expect anyone to seriously want to hurt him. Well. Rude awakening. *Welcome to the real world, kid.*

Stave had a long reach, and before Jude could get a lick in, the bigger boy had him by the throat, pinned against the fence. He was easily a head taller than Jude and beefy. Jude was just a scrap of a kid. Spit flew in his face as Stave snarled words that no grade school kid had any right to know.

He was mad but scared too. He panicked.

A flash of blue light, like sheet lightning, came out of nowhere. Stave flew back and sat down on the ground, hard. He gawked at Jude, one hand clutching his smoking shirtfront. His gang stood stunned and staring for a half-second, then ran away screaming.

Jude didn't understand what he'd done, or even that he'd done anything, not even when Stave choked out, "Freak! What the hell are you?" as he scrambled to his feet and ran away, hard on the heels of his gang. When he reached the other side of the yard, he turned and shook his fist at Jude. "You're dead, you hear?" he bellowed. "You're dead!"

Jude just stood there bewildered, rubbing his bruised throat, trying to swallow.

"That was so cool!" Dace squeaked.

Cale crowed, "Wicked! Do it again, Jude! Make your eyes glow like that again."

The girls had seen the flash, but not its cause. Other children stared and whispered. Jude went beet red. He'd displayed one of his oddities for the world to see!

He was called to the principal's office, but no one seemed to understand quite what had happened, despite the witnesses. It must have sounded too crazy. Stave was three times Jude's size, but he was the one who'd got hurt. Jude wasn't about to say anything, even to his mama; she'd scold him for losing it. But Stave's daddy raised a ruckus. Apparently, he was the only one allowed to beat his kid.

School policy dictated zero tolerance for violence, the principal said. *No fighting on school property. Three strikes and you're out.* That was their first warning.

Mama—and Daisy, too—had always cautioned Jude that he must not hurt people, to keep calm and not to lose his temper, whatever the provocation. Even a six-year-old understands that, but even so, it was easier said than done.

If Daisy connected this incident to that night of the meteor shower, she didn't mention it where Jude could hear. And he didn't make the connection until years later.

Stave and his crowd knew enough to cool it when teachers or parents were within earshot, so things quieted down some after that. A number of minor incidents and a lot of verbal abuse but nothing memorable enough to attract attention.

Not until Jude turned eleven. Then things really went haywire. At that time, Jude began to experience an awkward stage, like most adolescents, a time of being all arms and legs. Unfortunately, his oddities seemed to intensify as well, often taking even him by surprise; he was never certain when or how strongly they would manifest next. It was a trying time.

Several incidents happened in rapid succession shortly after school resumed in January of 2011. Stave and his crowd must have made a New Year's resolution to outdo themselves, Jude thought. He tried to ignore their taunts and barbs, even when they pushed him around; he didn't dare display his oddities in that company—he knew he'd never hear the end of it. (Even now, he felt the repercussions of the first time he'd made that mistake.) Still, it wasn't easy. If he felt his temper rising, he avoided eye contact with them, thinking that this thing with his eyes was the most dangerous.

Maybe he really was a freak. Nobody else had eyes like that.

Still, he thought he'd make it through sixth grade. Spring was just around the corner. Though he was pretty edgy by then, what with his oddities coming and going without warning. When J. C. Daws dissed Rosa Sharon one day in the schoolyard, Jude didn't even think; he just hauled off and punched him in the eye. Surprised himself as much as he did J. C., but he couldn't be sorry he'd done it. A man's place was to protect women and children, right? And he'd done a normal thing—just used his fist.

Well, ol' J. C. had to be a rat about it. He ran crying to the teacher, and both boys ended up in the principal's office. Jude got a warning, his first that year (and he'd been doing so well!). Mama wouldn't be pleased. But J. C. had a real shiner.

Word got out that Stave and his gang planned to avenge J. C.'s honor. That didn't fool anyone; those hooligans didn't know the meaning of honor. They got their kicks from hurting people. Any excuse would do.

A short while later, they came after Jude and his friends again (the supervising teacher was nowhere to be seen). Their taunts pelted the little group like stones, but Violet had the safety on her hair-trigger temper, for once. And Jude cast his eyes down, afraid they'd start glowing again. Afraid he might hurt someone — or maybe afraid he'd enjoy hurting them. He did enjoy thinking about it sometimes. But Mama had told him time and again that that would make him just like them. It took a powerful effort sometimes, though. Daisy said never to hate but instead suggested that Jude ought to pity Stave. His father was a drunk and often beat him. Jude tried to remember that.

Besides, he couldn't forget the night he'd accidentally incinerated a fox in the henhouse. Killed it with just a look! He thought that was what had happened, anyhow. (It's not easy to believe something like that, even when you see it with your own eyes.)

He heard the hiss of a rock coming his way, right for his head. He'd have dodged it, but his friends were in the line of fire. So he caught the stone, flung it back with his usual unerring aim, and heard a yelp. Stave's forehead spouted blood. Jude ended up in the principal's office for his second warning. Stave got three stitches.

Then came the final straw. It happened one day when Mama stayed after school to mark some tests. To kill time, Jude went to browse Miz Lily's library. He was heading back toward the school with a load of borrowed books, his head in the clouds, when ol' Stave and his gang appeared out of nowhere. Before he could blink, they had him surrounded, mocking, jeering, pushing him from one to another till they had him backed against the eight-foot-high stone wall that ran along that particular stretch of sidewalk.

Jude clutched the bag of books to his chest. How would he explain to Miz Lily if anything happened to them? He felt the sudden swift heat of anger and at once dropped his gaze; still, they kept after him. A little desperately, he glanced up at the top of the stone wall and thought, *if only I was up there, I'd be out of their reach*. Then, he was up there, crouched on top of the wall. Below him was a sea of upturned faces, every single one of them white as a sheet. *How did I...* Jude was just as bewildered as any of them.

J. C. picked up a rock. "Get the freak!" he shouted as he wound up and let the rock fly. Jude dodged. J. C. cursed. Then, all of the gang picked up rocks and began winging them at Jude, cursing and swearing. He managed to dodge most of the missiles. The rest he caught and hurled back. The gang's song began to include yelps of pain, which then turned to shrieks of terror and frantic pointing, as though they saw some nightmare beast on top of the wall. Some of them started to run. Then, with a terrible clamor, the rest followed. Even Stave. Within seconds they had stampeded out of sight.

Jude realized then that his eyes were glowing. His heart sank. Was he a monster? Shakily he climbed down from the wall with the help of the ivy, tucked the books under his arm, and continued on to the school. He dared not tell anyone, not even Mama.

The next day at school was worse than he'd imagined it would be. Children stared wide-eyed from the playground as he strode up the sidewalk and the steps into the school; they eyed him fearfully from rooms and lockers as he passed down the hallway to his classroom. He heard whispers. Freak... demon child...

Those names were old news. It was the new one that hurt. Goblin King. He knew it came from the '80s movie Labyrinth (a cult classic now) with David Bowie as the Goblin King, who could do things that were humanly impossible: moving from one place to the next in an instant or defying gravity by walking up a sheer wall. However it happened in his own case, even Jude couldn't explain, but surely he was no goblin.

The name ran through the school like wildfire. People shied away, even some who were friendly before. Jude wanted to scream at them, *I'm a person, just like you!*

But was he? No, being thought a freak wasn't cool.

Mama found out, of course. She was furious; she took Jude out of school so fast, heads were spinning. She almost quit her teaching job; the board managed to talk her into finishing out the year. But not Jude; she resolved to homeschool him from then on.

Part III: Haunted

The Trip

Ashland, Oregon, 2012

He was already as tall as his mama by the time the next summer came; that first year of his homeschooling had passed quickly. He'd shot up like a bad weed that winter after he turned twelve and finished seventh grade with flying colors. That was when Mama decided they needed to get away for the summer.

So, they headed to her daddy's house in southern Oregon to take the old man up on his invitation to join him on a trip to Canada in his vintage World War II Army jeep. Jude was excited at the prospect of a trip and meeting his grandfather and his mama's brother Uncle Darren for the first time. His own relatives! Then they would head north to Canada, the land of adventure! To the Mile Zero City, Grandpa said, where he planned to join a convoy of veterans and army buffs to celebrate the seventieth anniversary of the building of "the Road," then travel north, all the way to Alaska.

There he met the girl who was part of his destiny. Of course, he didn't know that at the time. What struck him were her eyes — wonderfully black. Blacker than Dace's, even; like black currants. He'd never forget them. *Indian eyes*, Mama said. *Cool*, he thought, though to be honest, she didn't look Indian to him; why, she had freckles! And pale skin and brown hair with gold highlights. He'd always thought Indians had coal-black hair and copper skin, like Dace — whose daddy was half-Cherokee, he said. Jude shrugged; Mama was a teacher, and she ought to know.

But that came after.

When they first got to Grandpa's, Mama sprung a surprise on him — she had tickets to a real Shakespearean play! Ashland was only a skip and a jump from Grandpa's farm. The play turned out to be a memorable experience, but mainly because of an encounter with a mysterious lady.

He was amazed at the sight of the outdoor Elizabethan Theater, an exact replica of Shakespeare's own Globe Theater. (He'd seen pictures.) As he stared around, agog, he spotted a tall, aristocratic-looking gentleman in the crowd, wearing a long, elegant black cloak fastened at the throat with a gorgeous, jeweled clasp. Something like Dr. Jekyll, without the tall silk hat. Instead, his sleek black hair was combed back so that in the deepening shadow of twilight Jude almost thought for a moment that the man had horns. Then he moved, and the illusion was gone. He moved more like a cat than a man, with a graceful glide. *Odd,* Jude thought, but then he noticed a blond lady clinging to the man's arm. *Oh, she was so fine and fair.* Those blue angel eyes nearly took his breath away, and he stared in wonder. It felt as though there was some sort of bond between them. He would never forget those eyes.

As Jude stood staring, the gentleman turned slightly, so that he got a clear view of his face. A shock went through him. How startlingly white that face shone in the lamplight, and so perfect, like an angel's! His heart seemed to melt within him at the sight. And yet—there was something frightening about it. He felt suddenly terrified, terrified that the man would look at him—and yet, that he would despair if he did not.

Just then, the gentleman's eyes, so black in contrast to that white face, flashed strangely and stared straight into his. Why he should have noticed him in that crowd was a mystery. Or maybe he didn't, and Jude just thought he did; such was the power of those eyes. Jude's heart leaped into his throat; he was at once breathless with longing and dread. He wanted to run to him—so, so much. He gasped and shrank back behind his mama, clenching his fists with the effort to resist that headlong rush to destruction.

He felt his nails pierce his palms. Knew he'd drawn blood when those red lips parted with an audible hiss; and—and—the man had fangs! Or, maybe not... but in that instant, his eyes seemed to flare red! For just a moment, then the lady lifted her face to speak to him, and he turned to listen.

Just like that, Jude was released from that terrible hold those eyes had on him. He trembled in relief that he was still himself; that he was still alive. Dazed and thankful that she'd saved him from—from what? Of course, he'd only imagined it. Seriously, how could he hear him hiss over the noise of the crowd? And it was crazy to imagine that the man had fangs or that his eyes glowed red. This was real life, not one of those strange dreams he'd had all his life, with vampires and such.

Then again, didn't his own eyes glow? What could it mean? *Do I have fangs, too?* He resolved to check that out later. Terrified at the thought of what he might find—and yet, he had to know.

Who could they be? Jude took another look at the lady's face, at that sweet, beautiful profile, and trembled with the desire that she should glance at him, just once. The strangest feeling came over him that he knew her from long ago, from somewhere just beyond the reach of his memory. And that he should love her. Or had he only dreamed this? Often his dreams seemed so real.

He caught the scent of flowers—moonflowers, night-blooming jasmine and four-o'clocks—so familiar, though he knew not why. How could he? He didn't know what they were, even. The gentleman's hand touched her waist, and they moved on, while Jude gazed after her in heartfelt longing. But, him—there was something about him that made Jude's heart pound if he only just glanced at his face. And it took an effort to tear his gaze away. Was he Mr. Hyde, after all?

Then Mama took hold of his hand so she wouldn't lose him in the crowd and broke the spell. They found their seats and settled in for the show. Jude furtively scanned the crowd, but the gentleman and his lady had vanished. (They'd likely taken their own seats.)

The play was the most wonderful ever. Like magic. But it wasn't until afterward that the real drama happened. A dream? No, it wasn't. *I saw it; I know I did!*

As Jude and his mama were carried along by the surge of people exiting the theater grounds, he happened to glance up. There, across the way, he again caught sight of the tall, black-cloaked gentleman and his beautiful lady. Jude eyed them a little fearfully, but they didn't glance back, just moved with the flow of the crowd, on the alert and scanning the sky.

Weird. He felt a tingling of the senses again and wanted to run away, but couldn't move, just stood rooted to the spot, staring in breathless fascination. Though he was afraid that the man's piercing eyes would find him and invade his soul, he couldn't seem to help it; he didn't want to look away. There was just something about the man—almost as though he'd stepped through time from another era. Of course, that was impossible.

All this while, Jude was oblivious of the crowd swirling around him like a river around a boulder as he stood watching the couple swept along by a current toward another exit. The gentleman was a head above most of the crowd. His black eyes seemed to flash again. It was only a trick of the light, of course, as he passed under a lamp.

Or was it? His face seemed too white to be natural, and his lips too red, as though—was he made up to look like a vampire? But that made no sense. This was July, not Halloween. Hamlet was a Shakespearean tragedy with plenty of death and blood but nothing to do with vampires. Jude shook his head to clear it.

And then he got his heart's desire. She turned those sapphire eyes full on him. All the breath rushed from his lungs as he fell into blue depths, caught up in a kaleidoscope world of peacock feathers, flower gardens, sky, ocean. His heart took flight as though it had sprouted wings. This was paradise, and he'd known her from eternity. Within his soul, he'd always known her. He reached out to this—to her, his every dream come true. *Who are you that I should know you and feel that I belong to you?*

"Jude! Son, are you okay?" he heard Mama say as though from a great distance.

He fell out of seventh heaven and crashed to the ground. By that time, Mama had firmly but gently taken him by the arm, bringing him to his senses. No, he wasn't lying on the ground with his heart broken into a million pieces. He was standing amidst a fast-thinning throng, bewildered, as Mama tugged at his hand.

Still a bit befogged, he wondered, could she be the Lady in Blue? No, the Lady never left him feeling lost and alone. And this lady wasn't wearing blue. Her dress was silky black. She wore diamonds at her ears, an emerald on her finger, and was clutching a gentleman's arm. Who could she be? What was he? Jude felt a surge of disgust at his attraction to the gentleman with the power to annihilate his very soul twisting in his gut like a long-bladed knife, ugly and hateful. What had the man done to him?

"Mama, did you see..." he began, and would have pointed them out to her, but they'd disappeared into the crowd at the door. "Quick, Mama, I have to—" He dragged her with him as he forged through the press of people toward the exit.

"What, son? What's the matter?"

Once outside, he glanced around. Floodlights illuminated the parking lot under a star-sprinkled night sky. Where had they gone? Laughter and talking filled the night as clusters of people rapidly dispersed to their cars. Finally, he caught sight of them hastening across the lawn—not to the parking area, like everyone else.

"Over there, Mama," he whispered, pointing. "Look—oh!" He stared.

For as they'd paused in the shadow, the lady seemed to melt into the gentleman's arms. Jude caught sight of a flicker at his waist as he swept out his cloak to envelop them both. Then, between one instant and the next, they seemed to vanish into thin air. Jude rubbed his eyes, but they were gone.

"What, son? I don't see anyone," said Mama.

"But I was watching them, even before the play. And they saw me too." He stared hard into the night, but no one was there, where he'd just seen them standing. And vanish. "I just saw them a minute ago, walking right over there, and then they were gone."

"It's okay, darling," Mama said gently. "We'll go back to Grandpa's now."

Jude shivered. Had no one else seen them? Was he going crazy? No, he had seen them. Mama just wasn't looking at the right time. "Really, Mama, I saw them, a blond lady and a tall gentleman wearing a long black cape."

"Yes, son, I saw them too," said Mama with a small sob, though she quickly covered it with a tremulous smile. Jude felt her heart beating fast. What had she seen? "But then they went and sat far from us."

He sensed that she was grateful for that. She never did trust people much; he wasn't sure why. "What do you think—who are they?"

She patted his arm. "Never mind them. You're bound to see strange people now and then. But don't worry. I'm here. Your mama's always here to look after you." She forced a smile and led the way to where Uncle Darren waited in his Jeep Cherokee.

Later at Grandpa's, Jude checked out his teeth in the mirror. They were strong and straight and white, but not fangs. Or were they? How did they appear to other people? Not like that gentleman's, he hoped. Anyhow, what had that man to do with him?

A Vampire Tale

A cry echoed through the vampires' underground labyrinth, on and on, until finally it faded, and all was silent once more.

Bellatrix, notorious femme fatale even among vampires—which are by nature shameless and appear beautiful to those susceptible to their powers of mesmerization—clapped a hand over her mouth.

"Why would you scream like that? Right in the middle of my story," Little Lulu pouted. "Did you even hear what I said?"

"*¡Ay!*" Bellatrix cut her off. "You did not see, feel, that?"

Lulu gaped, clueless, as usual. "What are you talking about? I—"

"Listen, *comprende? ¡Ay de mi*! You notice nothing strange, just then?"

"Hey, I was talking. Uh, what?"

"It… it was like… " Bella glanced down at her hands, expecting to see them changed somehow, but no: her fingers were long and slender and white, nails exquisite as ever. Her long ebony hair hung straight and shimmering past her waist, over the graceful folds of her black silken cloak—nothing had changed. But something had.

"Like what?" Lulu prompted, curious now.

Bella flicked her a suspicious glance. How could Lulu not have felt that shifting? It wasn't an earthquake; no, nothing so physical. A movement of the cosmos? Or a tearing of the very fabric of space and time?

She frowned.

Whatever it was had been instantaneous. One moment, she was standing in this familiar narrow passage, half-listening to Little Lulu's incessant prattle while her mind was on more interesting things, like the coming of night and the thrill of the hunt. Then—like a bolt of lightning, she found herself swaying dizzily on the brink of a great yawning abyss where once the cave floor had been, terrified beyond all reason. That made no sense—a vampire had no fear of heights or abysses!

A ray of light had shot out from the black depths then, blinding her for a moment. When she could see again, the abyss had vanished, and all was as before. Except her.

In her mortal life, Bella had been a heartbreaker. Powerful men had sought her hand in marriage, for her beauty as well as her family connections. She took none of them seriously. As the only daughter of a wealthy Spanish nobleman who indulged her every whim, she had merely to raise a delicate eyebrow to be rid of a tiresome suitor. More than one had she thus cast into despair, giving him no more thought as she moved on to the next. She knew she would eventually end up with one whom her father chose, but that was far in the future.

So she'd thought. But the end of her good times had come upon her quite suddenly and unexpectedly — the end of the world, it had seemed to her at the time (as indeed it was, in a sense). It was in the year 1573, and she not yet eighteen when her father's health suddenly declined, and he at once took steps to assure her future. Already she was past the age when most girls were betrothed and must be married at once, he decided; for the first time, he was deaf to her protests. *¡Ay!* Marriage meant she would be under the control of another man — one perhaps not so indulgent as her dear papa.

Her life — ruined! All because of a certain young man her papa had chosen for her from a family he had long dealt with in the matter of fine wines. It seemed that their lineage was of the finest; noble, perhaps royal blood flowed through his veins, her papa said, a wonderful match. She pouted, picturing a pale, light-haired, ugly foreigner whisking her off to his ice castle in bleak northern climes, far from her beloved, lush, sun-drenched home. No more dreaming of a tall, dark and handsome caballero carrying her off into the sunset. No, no! She would not have it! She threw things about her room, even broke her favorite looking glass.

On the night of the fiesta, when she was to meet the prince (if he was a prince) for the first time, she had all but accepted her fate. But there was some delay, it seemed; his arrival was long overdue. Near tears, she'd run out into the gardens and gazed up at the stars, wishing he would disappear from the face of the Earth.

Her wish came true in a way she had not imagined — she also would disappear.

Old Tia Anna had trailed after her, complaining about the night air, mosquitoes and aching joints, but she shut out the sound and pressed her nose into a gardenia bloom. Its lovely fragrance transported her into a land of dreams. All sound faded into the background: Tia Anna's plaintive tones, the festive music from the veranda — all of it.

She stepped onto the lantern-lined path that led to the dense grove of jasmine and myrtle. Bright lights sparkled through the foliage, but from the happy crowd, she turned away.

The grass was velvet beneath her feet as she trod the light-splashed path between the lanterns to the fountain spilling crystal and pearls from six spouts of fine gold, among bulrushes and lilies. With a sigh, she gazed at her reflection. How fair her beauty shone, eclipsing that of all other maidens (as a poet so eloquently wrote). The stars shimmered like diamonds, reflected in the black water. Before her lay an enchanted world, cool and inviting. If she entered that magical door, could she escape her fate, and her betrothed, whom she scorned, sight unseen?

A fluttering in the bushes distracted her momentarily, as a sparrow landed and perched on a twig. *Listen!* it cried, *Go back.* His hand joined to yours shall bring light to the world. Else darkness will rule for fourteen generations.

She was suddenly frightened and shivered at what sounded like an omen. But this was a bird! A sparrow, she said to herself scornfully. What was it doing out here in the night? Tia Anna's frantic call came again; she hesitated, but only for a moment.

Then the decision was no longer hers to make. She'd thought she was alone, but as she was sighing behind her fan, a Dark Lord of the Night was watching, fire kindled in his proud heart. Like that ancient serpent, Charon invaded the lovely Eden of her father's garden. His sudden appearance caught her fancy, and she disdained the warning of the humble sparrow. A silly girl reaching for forbidden fruit, she was herself ripe for the plucking.

Charon beckoned. She lifted her eyes to his. A way out of that marriage she so dreaded! Never would she have to endure those old men, ever again. (How was she to know that this handsome dark-haired youth was older than all of them?)

There was nothing subtle about him. Of her life and innocence, he soon made an end. He bit her with scores of people nearby, just beyond the hibiscus hedge. She no longer heard Tia Anna calling her name as she searched for her in vain. None of that mattered anymore.

How well she remembered and would sigh if she could. Like a hero in one of her favorite romance novels, he had carried her off (after sunset, rather than into it). He took her to a cave in the hillside and turned her. Her family never knew what happened; she had just disappeared. But she cared nothing for that. Charon was her entire world, and she forgot them.

That was long ago and far away. This was the New World, three centuries later. In the summer of 1869, a total solar eclipse was once again in the offing; they must be ready for it. Tedious, but to Charon, this was about the fulfillment of his long-cherished dream. Obsession, perhaps.

Maps and charts lay piled around him in his study chamber. Many were rolled up and tucked away in their original cases; others lay open on the table with jars of ink or sand pots or polished stones weighing their corners down. On some nights, he pored over them for hours until the rising sun drove him to his sarcophagus and sleep. Bella knew that he studied many things, but the ancient prophecies were his main focus, comparing and connecting them to the signs of the times. This had been his preoccupation for centuries.

But once again, there was that familiar sense of urgency. When he once again commanded that they capture a virgin, Bella knew: this was about what he called his Black Sun ritual. They had gone through this many times before, but the innumerable failures did not discourage him. This time he would get it right. It was said that innocent blood spilled and tasted at the propitious moment would grant them immunity to the light of day. *¡Ay!* Never again to fear the rays of dawn! No more scuttling underground at the sun's rising!

Charon would rule the world, then. That was his ultimate goal.

Bella was out hunting each night at sundown until the light of dawn drove her underground. This was the master's dream, and she meant to be a part of it. Her own dream was to win back his favor; this she hoped to achieve by bringing him the prize.

But there was that ancient prophecy telling of a Consecrated One born of a line of kings, destined to destroy Charon on some future date, preventing him from carrying out his plan for world domination. The prophecy was of the kind carved in stone, unchangeable. A lesser being would have resigned himself in despair. Not Charon. A number of times over the centuries, he'd attempted to wipe the entire line from the face of the Earth in a sort of pre-emptive strike. Each time had ended in failure until three centuries ago when he'd finally succeeded, and it was said: the deed was done; the entire royal family massacred.

Well, everyone except the Prince, but he was no longer human and could not fulfill the prophecy.

Bella smiled. *Ay, there is no one to stop the master now!*

Charon was not so careless as to relax his vigilance, however. This sort of prophecy had a way of coming to pass despite all efforts to prevent it. If the Consecrated One should put in an appearance, after all, he must be captured at once, Charon said.

This would be no mean feat, he cautioned them. Bella was not impressed; she laughed at danger. Had she not heard and seen things to make one's hair stand on end, many times, over the centuries? Hah! She would soon have this one eating out of her hand, like any other man.

Charon's eyes, like shards of cold steel, cut through the frivolity. This was not just any man. According to ancient writings, the all-powerful Queen of Heaven favored this Consecrated One, because of his purity of heart.

Bella was not quite sure what that meant. She noted that other faces showed puzzlement too, but decided it was probably irrelevant. If the Consecrated One did indeed exist, she would catch him and destroy his innocence, if that was the problem. No mortal man could resist her charm. She had been around for a long time and had found that men were men the world over, in whatever era. The promise of peril only added to the thrill of the chase. And if she succeeded, she would be in Charon's good graces forevermore.

There was nothing to gain by being shy. Nyx and Styx and Pinkie and Lulu wouldn't hesitate. Bella didn't need a mirror to tell her that she was the most beautiful of them all. Her height and noble Spanish looks easily surpassed the others: Lulu was common and plain; Pinkie was a silly little blond with rosebud lips; Styx dainty and fragile-looking—that long, crinkled platinum hair her glory—but none too smart. As for Nyx... well, she was in a class all by herself. Bella cursed at the thought.

But for now, any virgin at all would do.

She recalled how she and Charon and all of them had gloried in the freedom of wide-open spaces and the comfort of solid earth beneath their feet after the long and arduous sea voyage from Europe on one of those blasted wooden sailing ships! How long had they endured the ominous swells of endless water, the creaking timbers, and the shrieking sails! Charon's entire coven of thirteen had made the perilous ocean crossing—and survived, though there had been moments of doubt.

It was an ordeal; on the one hand, the dread of daylight and, on the other, the incessantly moving water. Most of them hid below decks during the day, amongst the crates of Charon's possessions or clinging like bats in the dark corners of the hold. The constant lapping of water against the hull petrified them with terror, eventually lulling them into torpor. Only the proximity of the crate containing their homeland soil prevented them from going mad.

She'd tried not to think about how thin the groaning timbers were—the only barrier between them and mountains of water, the tossing waves that constantly heeled the ship over. Even now, she shivered at the thought. Never again.

Charon had had his stone sarcophagus; the rest of them had not so much as a plain wooden coffin and felt rather vulnerable. But the sailors were a superstitious lot and carefully avoided the deep darkness where the stowaways clustered during the day. No doubt the men felt, and feared, that eerie chill of their presence.

There was no lack of feeding during the voyage, a pleasure the master allowed as long as they were discreet. The night was theirs, and their prey had no escape. But they, too, were trapped; to avoid discovery, Charon forbade them to kill. A ship without men to sail it could not carry them safely to their destination. They dared not overstep their limits; even Charon was edgy surrounded by so much water.

After landing safely on solid ground once more, they'd wandered for a long time on the new continent, searching for a place to settle. They encountered many dangers but managed to survive them all and gained a few new members during this nomadic period. Eventually, they came to a cavern in the side of a cliff overlooking a river known as the Peace. There they settled in. Charon continued his study, searching for the means to rule first this new land, then the world.

It soon became evident that in the New World, and especially in the northern wilderness, mortals were not so numerous as in Europe. Charon took care not to destroy the food supply or reveal their presence. Thus they coexisted with the local inhabitants more or less in harmony for three centuries.

Until the summer of 1869. That was when their world fell apart.

Discovery at Clayhurst

Dawson Creek, BC. 2012

Jude and his mama rode with Grandpa in his little old Army jeep, which was slow, of course—it had been manufactured way back in 1942—which made it seem a long and somewhat tedious drive to the Mile Zero City—that is, Dawson Creek, British Columbia, in Canada. Well, it was about a thousand miles, he thought Grandpa'd said. Quite the adventure for a backwoods boy, nevertheless. Jude had visions of Jack London's frozen north and a land of great forests and rivers and voyageurs and so on.

A couple of Grandpa's army buddies had tagged along in their own vintage truck. They were all to gather at Mile Zero, where the convoy would start its trek north, up the Alaska Highway. Meanwhile, Jude got to explore the museum there—how he loved museums! Especially the wildlife exhibits, but in this case, it was another display that unexpectedly impacted his life—in a way he couldn't have imagined. It contained artifacts and a written account detailing the discovery of certain caves in the area.

He read the blurb under the map. It told of a local family out picnicking one Sunday afternoon on the flats of the Peace River's north bank, not far from the Clayhurst Bridge. Some of the boys were climbing the steep hillside, it said, when sixteen-year-old Nathaniel Moon slipped. He managed to catch hold of a sturdy bush in time to stop his downward slide into a hole hidden under brush and windfalls. The blurb continued:

"I think it's a cave!" Nathaniel shouted, "I'm going in!" With that, he slid down until his feet touched bottom. His teeth shone in a triumphant grin as he looked up from the dark hole. He had discovered a passage under the hill, narrow, but even at his height of six-foot-two, he could stand upright. Excited by the prospect of adventure, two of the other boys quickly joined him; the rest waited above ground. One ran back to the camp to get a rope in case the boys needed help climbing out.

Young Mr. Moon whipped out his trusty flashlight and led the way to explore. The tunnel appeared to have been well used at one time but long since abandoned. As they went along, more passages opened in the walls, branching off from the main one; these later proved to be part of a vast, sprawling maze. Despite their curiosity, the boys stuck to the main passage so as not to lose their way.

"Anyone got any bread crumbs?" Nathaniel joked, as they followed the passage

downward at a grade so gradual that they were hardly aware of their descent, except for the increasing chill. Stone walls and floor continued much the same until they came to a door. A real door, underground. It was ajar. With growing excitement, Nathaniel pushed it open, entered a small room, and shone the light around. The others followed and halted in amazement.

What first caught the eye were the wild geometric shapes daubed on the walls in garish primary colors — squares and triangles, spirals and concentric circles — as though some mad graffiti artist had been at work. Between these wild daubs of paint were delicate drawings of local flowers and wildlife, lovely and lifelike. And others, horridly vivid, of demons drinking blood and dancing in the torchlight. The boys shrank back, their skin prickling, their eyes wide.

They glanced around, a bit apprehensively. Just an ordinary room, it seemed. A bed stood against one wall, covered with a Hudson's Bay blanket so old it looked as if it might fall apart at a touch. On the opposite wall was a shelf holding some yellowed books, a pack of cards in a wooden box, a jeweled tortoiseshell comb, and a human skull. In the middle of the room were two chairs at a small wooden table. On the table was a chessboard with exquisite pieces carved of ebony and ivory set up in midgame and a leather-bound journal, inkpot, and pen. As though someone had just gotten up and walked away.

The print of the article swam before Jude's eyes as he imagined being there, seeing such things, and wondered what he would have done in Nathaniel's place. He turned to study the photographs of the drawings on the walls. They were a nightmare of contrast. Jude leaned down to get a closer view of the demons. Or were they vampires? They were similar to those in some of Cale's gory and frightening comic books.

At that moment, Jude was startled into the present time and place as a crowd of people pressed close. He tried to ignore the jostling; his attention focused on the fascinating display. If only he could visit the cave and see all this in real life, but Grandpa would probably say it was too far out of the way. He sighed and peered into the display case again at the collection of artifacts. The comb was labeled fifteenth-century Spanish. The journal was dated 1869. The human skull was carbon-dated 200 BC.

How did items so separated by time and place come together in a cave in northeastern British Columbia in what — *oh, 1869?* — he wondered. This was just the sort of mystery that intrigued him. How he wished he could get his hands on that journal and read it for himself! A printout did describe its contents, but that wasn't the same.

A group of boys nearby started roughhousing, but Jude hardly noticed, so absorbed was he in reading the fascinating account. The journal was said to have been written by a fourteen-year-old captive Indian girl. It sounded like she had quite the imagination, unless—was it true? Entries were written in a fine schoolgirl hand, the initials JMJ heading each page. She wrote of being carried off underground; of missing her family; of pain, and fear of "Sherone," a blood-drinking monster with long teeth and claws. (Jude shivered, reminded of his recurring nightmares in which he saw a terrifying creature of that description—even its name was similar—and he could see it only too clearly in his mind's eye.)

Her notes continued, "written," she said, "with a trembling hand." She referred to another as "the devil wearing an angel mask," whose look made her faint from fear, even as she longed to run to him. On a page smudged by tears was a prayer to God to send "Marie" to her rescue. But all was not so grim; during her captivity, a "kind lady" taught her games and brought her materials with which to paint and write.

Jude glanced back at the blurb, which explained that the cave had been hidden underground in 1869, but after a hundred years of exposure to the elements and harsh northern winters, erosion and frost heaves had done their work, causing the collapse that finally opened it to discovery.

"Sweet, eh?" The black-eyed girl's voice broke into Jude's deep speculation. He nodded. (How those eyes intrigued him since he'd first noticed them outside in the sunlit parking lot!) Then she added, "My brother Nat was the one who found it. I'm Phaedra."

"Cool," was Jude's awed response as he peered into the case again. He'd often read about people finding dinosaur bones or lost cities. It was quite a thrill meeting someone whose brother had made such a discovery.

He absently touched the glass top of the display case. About that time, one of the boys shoved another, and he crashed into Jude, causing him to stumble against the case. His fingertips touched the journal—or no, the glass was in the way (*wasn't it?*)—at the same time his elbow brushed the girl's arm. There was a blinding flash, and everything went white. A purple afterimage of the case and its contents shimmered before his eyes.

He blinked as the face of an Indian girl came into view, reflected darkly in the glass. *No, that wasn't glass. Was it water? How…* He gazed down into the pool. No, there was no water, just a vast abyss. That Indian girl was just kind of there. The image wavered, then steadied.

As he stood swaying on the brink, she reached out a slender hand, her dark eyes pleading. "Help us. The beast rises. Find the diamond and drink the cup of bitterness to the dregs. Only you can save us, Jude Martel." Then she faded and was gone.

He stared. He had no idea what she meant, but he'd never forget her words or that expression on her face. He felt dizzy suddenly.

Then he fell. Down, down he went, into the bottomless emptiness, into thick darkness, his senses reeling. He couldn't see, or hear, or feel. There was no up or down. He thought he was falling but was no longer certain. He tried to yell, but couldn't.

He'd just been in the museum! What had happened? Was this an "episode" (as Mama referred to the visions he sometimes had when he played his violin)? But how? He wasn't playing his violin. Where—? Or maybe he was asleep, and this, a nightmare.

Wake up, wake up. Why couldn't he awaken? He was terrified. *Jesus, help me*, he prayed.

Then he heard a voice. It wasn't Jesus. It was a rasping voice, like the rustling of dried leaves that somehow formed words. What words? No...no... It was coming from everywhere and nowhere. Everything was black. Deep, dark, and the sound of a drum, pounding, pounding through his head. More noise filled the air, of screaming and snarling and cursing, and always, always, that infernal drumbeat. Then he saw them—white faces, glowing red eyes, fangs. Claws reaching out toward him.

Jude felt as if hell had been ripped open and he was in the nightmare scene—yet it seemed like he was seeing it through the eyes of another person. How...? Or, was this a dream? *No...no!*

He yelled, but in the midst of that cacophony, no one seemed to hear. Still falling, he reached out in desperation for something to hold onto, anything... anything...

The Prince

Clayhurst Crossing, BC. Spring 1869

A small band of Indians arrived to set up their fishing camp on the river flats, right at the vampires' doorstep—just as they had every year, like clockwork. When Bella and the other vampires emerged at sunset, there it was, like a banquet laid out before them. But Charon kept a short rein on his crew, for many dangers existed, even in the northern wilderness.

The time of the solar eclipse was fast approaching. Would they find the virgin required for his ritual sacrifice in this camp of perhaps a hundred mortals busy about their task of surviving in this harsh land? A fair question, Bella decided. She had long ago given up on the belief that innocence even existed and deemed this endeavor a waste of time. But the master had spoken.

They had always been particularly cautious nearest their lair. Even mere mortals posed a danger if they happened upon a vampire while it slept. These mortals were as tough as saddle leather and would have no mercy, especially since the priests had come and all but eradicated the vampires' link to these peoples.

Shamans traditionally communed with the spirit world; the promise of power was ever tantalizing. They saw in these creatures of darkness a means to attain it, not batting an eye even when Charon demanded a virgin in exchange. He knew they'd keep these meetings secret rather than risk either death by furious vampires, or the wrath of the populace and exile (which in this land of harsh climate and savage peoples amounted to the same thing). The Indians feared those consorting with demons even before the arrival of the missionaries. They had no tolerance for them afterward.

Nor did Charon underestimate priests and their potential for disaster. One would visit the fishing camp several times a summer on his regular rounds. It did no harm to be cautious.

After the breakup of ice on the river, when the spring melting covered the flats, the riverbank lay empty of humans yet awhile as the water receded. Only when the long pools and inlets had shrunk to reveal banks of muddy sand and round river rocks did the Indians move in. After nightfall, the vampires awoke to the sight of campfires blooming like bright flowers along the shore. Dark, sturdy men prepared to fish and hunt. Women put up racks for smoking fish and meat. They would stay through summer and autumn to harvest chokecherries and berries, if all went as usual.

They did not know that this summer, the sun would be blackened. Charon knew, and meant to see the fulfillment of his dream. With quill in hand, he pored over maps, star charts, and centuries of calculations. During those days, Bella noted that the Prince was the only one taken into confidence; he even dared point out a flaw here or remark on an equation there.

Bella had often seen the two of them with their heads together, working out a problem or arguing a point. Sometimes she lingered just to catch a glimpse of them, of him, the unattainable Prince. She was accustomed to getting what she wanted, and her failure to do so in this case was infuriating. She didn't hang around long — that wouldn't be wise. The Prince was now the master's favorite; he had been for ages. And the Prince had eyes for no one but Charon, except maybe Nyx. Bella cursed. How she hated Nyx!

The Prince was cold. Even Styx could not light his fire, and she, his own creation! She'd probably thought that when he gave her the gift of immortality, she would own him forever. Likely he got tired of her clinging, Bella thought vindictively. Vampires are solitary creatures, after all. The Prince cared for nothing but power — and blood, of course. Was that why the master showed him preference, seeing in him a reflection of himself? Bella slouched with the weight of futility. Maybe there was more to this than even she could guess.

She'd never forget the night Nyx brought him home, in defiance of Charon's express command to kill them all. And the master, instead of annihilating him on the spot, as they'd all expected, had turned him into a god.

At the time, Bella was Charon's favorite, his new pet, just snatched from her father's garden. Charon had been tracking the Holy Grail when he got as far as Old Barcelona and lost the trail. There he'd found her and thus consoled himself while waiting for Nyx to complete her mission.

Nyx had been sent to find a ring given to an ancient king as a sign of favor, supposedly by his god. A legend had grown up around it. He who rightfully possessed the Ring would rule the world, it was said. Charon maintained that at one point, he had rightfully acquired it. And in some way, this Ring was apparently essential to his Black Sun ritual for achieving world domination.

Bella remembered well the night a messenger announced that Nyx had targeted the wrong family; there would be a slight delay while she sorted things out. Charon's eyes flared fire as he looked down at the unlucky bearer of bad news quaking before him. Even Bella thought he'd fry the messenger where he stood, but he only growled, *"Tell Nyx I want that blasted Ring now!"* The messenger bolted, no doubt relieved to have escaped unscathed.

As it transpired (Bella eventually learned), Nyx had turned one member of that royal family, instead of quietly slaughtering the lot of them, as directed—and she'd wiped out a whole village! Not only had she defied orders, but she'd also drawn undue attention to the existence of vampires. Even Bella knew that put them all in danger; it was probably part of the reason they had to flee Europe.

The night Nyx returned with the Ring, the party in the Great Hall was in full swing, a gathering of vampires with a number of mortal guests. Some of these were minions. Others were invited in for feasting and drinking and dancing, then served as the entrée for their hosts, perhaps to die, or to survive, to attend future orgies.

Charon was on his throne as usual, with Bella on his knee, when Nyx arrived. The crowd parted for her, then continued on with the music and dancing and feeding. Bella had heard of Nyx, but was not prepared for the reality. Nyx was more beautiful and powerful than she'd imagined. She burned with jealousy and felt her heart sink as she began to appreciate where Nyx stood in the hierarchy of the Vampire Brotherhood.

Nyx flashed her a look of daggers as she approached the master.

An object lying in the palm of Nyx's hand got Charon's attention at once. Bella lifted her eyes to follow his gaze and was transfixed by the sight of a large ruby that flashed in the torchlight. So *this* was the fabled Ring of which Charon was so enamored!

Then Nyx turned and beckoned. A figure behind her stepped into view. Nyx placed the Ring in his hand and urged him forward. Charon stiffened, his gaze at once piercing and deadly.

Bella stared. He was even more gorgeous than the Ring! (No wonder Nyx couldn't resist turning him!)

"Look at the beauty I've brought home," Nyx said, with false lightness. Bella saw that Charon knew at once who (and what) this creature was; his face darkened. Storm clouds were gathering. "For you," Nyx quickly added.

Even Bella could see Nyx was scrambling for a peace offering. So maybe even she feared the master's wrath.

Bella felt the stone-hard tension of Charon's body, the fierce grip of his claws at her waist. She went still as death. If he meant to bite someone's head off, she did not want it to be hers. Jealousy stung her for a moment that someone else should get Charon's attention. (Up till then, she'd had him all to herself!) But when she took a second look, with narrowed eyes, at this forbidden prize of Nyx's, she was stunned anew. Intrigued, she watched him stride forward. He was nearly as tall as Charon, and oh, so lovely and strong. *That face! Those eyes!* What she wouldn't give to—

Thankfully, Charon was distracted. Only when she caught Nyx glaring did Bella close her gaping mouth. She lifted her chin in defiance but dared not meet her eyes.

He stood before the throne, gazing up at the master with wonder, but also a kind of unconscious arrogance. Bella admired his spirit. Or maybe it was just ignorance, and he was not aware of his peril.

Nyx's eyes were on him, filled with a strange mix of hope and pride and indulgent satisfaction. But her long, slender fingers clutched at the edges of her cloak in anxiety. Only a fool would not have quailed. Charon's eyes were hard as steel gimlets, boring holes through the unwanted intruder.

The dark eyes met Charon's with unflinching boldness.

Too proud, too proud. Bella felt a thrill of excitement. Would he last the night?

She met his eyes briefly (was that a flicker of interest?) and was shocked at herself for the traitorous thought. Since she'd been turned, she'd had eyes for no one but Charon, but now she was intrigued. Then the power of the master's gaze caught and captivated him—from that day to this!

What I would not give to have him look at me like that again. But it seemed he had forgotten she existed.

Charon's tongue snaked out; the newcomer leaned slightly toward him. (Or maybe he was drawn.) He dropped to one knee and inclined his head, then lifted his gaze to the master's face. "My lord, I give you this Ring, and with it my fealty, now and forever, to do with as you will."

Bella nearly swooned. That voice! Had he beckoned just then, she would have flown to him at once. She watched, entranced, as he reached out his hand to Charon; the Ring glittered on his palm.

Charon took the Ring, his eyes glowing with a fire exceeding that with which he'd looked upon her for the first time. "Ah, the Heart of Orion returns to me," he murmured, turning it over in his hands.

Heart of Orion? *¡Ay de mi!* But wasn't that the Ring he'd spoken of? The one that he'd vowed would soon be his? With the ruby named for the red star in the constellation Orion—for which he'd affectionately named her? Bellatrix, the Hunter's heart—*my heart*, he'd said, holding her close.

This precious Ring, it is my namesake. She turned adoring eyes upon Charon. But he was staring at the Ring. It flared in the palm of his hand, reflecting the fire of his eyes.

"I have won, Praetorius!" he hissed, "I have won at last!"

Slowly the master lifted his gaze to the tall figure still on one knee before him. Those eyes, dark as night, dropped respectfully.

"My lord," he said, lifting his eyes once more, as though unaffected by Charon's unpleasant expression. "I come to do your will. Command me."

Charon's eyes narrowed. He leaned back, his claws tapping the carven armrest. After a long moment of tension, he reached out his hand and beckoned. To Bella's dismay, he seemed pleased now. What impact would the master's interest in this new pet have on her place in his affections?

"Rise. Come to me," the master said.

He rose and stood at the master's feet. Charon leaned forward, his eyes hungry.

Bella saw that Nyx awaited in dread the fate of her forbidden prize.

"I'll take him." Charon extended his hand. "Drink."

Bella stared, fascinated, as always when Charon exercised his power. A flash of uncertainty crossed the new one's face, and then he reached out to take Charon's proffered hand. The master nodded, and those perfect white teeth sank into the smooth pale flesh. Blood poured out, black and cold and thick, into his mouth and down his chin. The new vampire's eyes blazed like windblown coals. Bella clung to the master's throne in an ecstasy of excitement.

Would he kill? No. No. This one was too beautiful to have it all end here and now. He was taking too much, too much. Bella remembered how even just a taste had sent her sky-high for hours, whole nights, sometimes. Charon suddenly sank his teeth into that perfect throat—so enticing! She trembled with anticipation. Would the master share?

"Hands off!" Nyx hissed, grabbing her arm. "He's mine!"

"Let go!" Furious, Bella tried to pull away. Flashes of silver suddenly danced before her eyes. Then her vision cleared, and she realized. *She slapped me! She dares, while I sit next to Charon?*

"Keep a civil tongue in your head when you speak to me!" Nyx snarled. "And if you ever touch him, I'll—"

Bella's first impulse was to snap back, but there was something about Nyx that checked her. *Well,* she thought, hotly, *Two can play at this game.* (Brave words, as long as she kept them to herself.)

Nyx seemed to forget her at once as she turned with an anxious frown to see the outcome of the little drama enacted before the throne. Other vampires paused in their activities to surreptitiously observe. Their mortal guests were not so circumspect, maybe unaware of the danger, and watched openly with expressions varying from curious fascination to dawning horror.

At that moment, the new vampire tore himself from the master's wrist, his mouth glistening black and his eyes blazing with fierce unholy fire. In a flash, Charon pinned him to the floor and crouched over him, a deep growl rumbling in his throat. He was lord and master here. This proud young upstart must know his place.

Bella narrowed her eyes; it seemed even Nyx was worried—very nearly biting her nails. With good reason. If there were a shred of rebellion there, Charon would taste it, and that would be the end. Well, this one would probably not last the night. She'd just resigned herself to the momentary pleasure of watching Charon tear him apart, when she took another look and saw that he lay trembling and subdued at last. The master rose gracefully and, in one fluid motion, was on his throne once more.

It seemed he had forgotten Bella, but she dared not presume. Any movement in his vicinity could be an invitation to dinner. *His.*

Even Nyx was cautious. When at last, he gave a slow nod, she ran to the motionless form and took the still face in her hands. The eyelids fluttered and sprang open. She drew back as the black eyes flashed fire. In one fluid motion, he whipped to his feet and bowed gracefully to the master. His flashing gaze boldly met Charon's once more. "My lord. I exist only to serve you. Command me."

Charon's laughter boomed out and resounded through the Great Hall. "A child after my own heart. I see that fire in your eyes! Come to me another night, and I will show you how to use it." Then his own eyes glowed. "Ah, sweet victory! I take the heir of my royal enemy and make him my own. From this day forward, he shall be my crown prince."

Thereafter, he was known as the Prince.

Child of the Sun

Dawson Creek, BC. August 2012

Jude reached out, but both hands clutched at nothing but emptiness, and he thought he was lost forever. For a minute, an eternity. He knew he was in the museum, and yet it seemed he was not. Had he broken through to some other world by touching that journal and bumping into that girl? What was this? Who was she?

He couldn't breathe. It was so dark. Darkness surrounded him. Or was it water? He tilted his head back and lifted his eyes up, up, up. Faraway, he saw a pinpoint of light. Sky, maybe, like he was at the bottom of a well ten miles deep. A frightening thing.

Mama! he cried. Then, *God, help me!* over and over, a heartfelt prayer screamed silently to the heavens.

In that instant, he flew upward. With a splash of brilliant droplets, he broke through into the light, high above the surface, like a breaching whale, and gasped for air as though he'd been drowning. Far below him was a black abyss. He shivered at the sight of it and lifted his face to the warmth and light of the sun. Free at last, after that eon of hell.

He came to himself in the museum.

"Oh! You gave me a shock," said the girl with the freckles and the black eyes, laughing a little as she rubbed her elbow. She was so reassuringly real, standing beside him, solid and human, after —

Oh, okay. It wasn't sunshine, but soft artificial light in a room teeming with — *Oh! People! Thank God. Not —* He turned his head slowly toward the sound of the girl's voice. *Where am I? Who is she?* He took a deep, rasping breath, as though he really had just come up out of the water. Had he blacked out there for a minute? He felt so cold. His knees went weak, suddenly, and he caught himself against the case.

"Stupid, what're you, stoned, eh?" a boy in the scuffling pack near him sneered.

Jude closed his eyes for a moment. When he opened them, his fists were pressed against the display case to keep his balance. He tried to appear as though nothing was wrong.

"Are you okay?" said the girl, with a concerned expression.

He was about to say, *sure, I'm okay,* when a kid nearby laughed raucously.

"Look, the Yank is crying," he jeered.

Jude lifted a hand to his cheek. It was wet with tears. He didn't remember crying. He tried to think, but his brain felt numb.

The girl's eyes snapped. She made a threatening move, and the boy flinched.

His buddy cackled. "Watch out, man, or she'll gimp your other leg for you."

Then Jude recalled her kicking the boy in the shin earlier, in the parking lot—when he got lippy, maybe (he couldn't quite remember).

The boy scowled and edged away as fast as he could in the press of the crowd. Even his buddy subsided in a hurry when the girl turned her glare his way.

"What is the meaning of this?" said an authoritative voice.

Jude turned to see a woman in a museum security uniform. Vaguely he wondered why she was talking to him; he wasn't the one shoving people. She gripped his arm. "Young man, you are not allowed to touch the artifacts."

He followed the direction of her gaze. In his hand was the journal. He stared; he couldn't recall how it got there. Wasn't it just…? He dropped it into the display case, right where it had been in the first place, hoping to amend matters. His first visit to Canada and in trouble already. The slogan he'd heard somewhere came to him: the Mounties always get their man. There was no running away. *Uh-oh. I'm in for it now.*

Her eyes wavered as they met his. She seemed a bit dazzled for a moment or two, then blinked and managed to set her mouth in a grim line once more. Her face went white, and her expression altered to a mix of fear and revulsion—that all-too-familiar look people got when they saw his eyes start to glow. He quickly dropped his gaze.

"What, er, how—?" she spluttered.

He quickly apologized, hoping to avert disaster, though with no idea what he'd done. She was looking at him strangely, her hand on his arm. "I, um, I put it back. I didn't know…" he added, visions of being put in jail large in his imagination. He hadn't meant to—what had he done? There was Mama, trying to get to him through the crowd.

"Excuse me," she called, trying to be heard above the din. "Excuse me. That's my son. Please let me through."

"I saw you put it back in the case," the woman muttered, distracted and frowning.

"Yes, I did, ma'am," Jude said politely, in an attempt to mollify her, at least until Mama got her attention. Mama was good at handling tense situations, being a teacher.

"How? That's what I'm wondering. How did you do it?" she said accusingly, giving him a little shake.

He eyed her warily. He was no longer touching the artifact. Surely his fingerprints hadn't done irreparable damage. Still, it seemed safer to give her some kind of an answer.

"Er, I, um, dropped it?"

"I'm warning you, don't give me any lip!" she blustered. "There's a lid on that case, and it's locked! You have some explaining to do, young man!"

Her anger bewildered him for a moment; it wasn't like he'd stolen state secrets! Or—maybe she was just scared. He could understand that—sometimes he scared himself! "Well, I, er—" he began and stopped. Now there was a glass top on the case, and the journal was beneath it. "But there wasn't a lid…" His voice trailed off. He shivered at the faint shadow of a memory of the image of a great black abyss, of dark shapes, screams, and the fluttering of wings. *No.*

"Excuse me," Mama interrupted breathlessly as she finally reached them. "Will you please let go of my son's arm? He's not going to run away."

The woman fixed Mama with a piercing stare. "So, you're this boy's mother?"

Mama met her gaze with a hard glare of her own. "Yes, I am. Now, if you'll kindly take your hand off him and tell me what's going on?"

"Mama," Jude said in a low tone. "There really wasn't a lid on it…before."

"There has always been a lid on that case," said the woman firmly, but released his arm. "Your son was handling the artifacts. That is not permitted—no matter how cute he is!" She turned red and appeared confused, as though she hadn't meant to say that.

Mama ignored the woman's silliness and gave Jude a level look. "Did you touch the artifact, son?"

Jude dropped his gaze. "Yes, but I didn't—it, um, maybe jumped into my hand?" How could he explain when he couldn't remember what had happened in that instant, that eternity of—what? He cautiously eyed the case, thinking there should be a warning sign saying, *Abandon all hope, ye who enter here.* At that, something unpleasant flickered at the edges of his consciousness. He couldn't recall, didn't want to, and felt a little dizzy. *No, don't think about it.*

"Since he hasn't really hurt anything," Mama was saying, her eyes narrowed, "please accept his apology, and we'll just go, if that's okay."

When she spoke in that tone, people just naturally backtracked.

"Yes, of course. Everything seems to be in order now." The woman's eyes darted to Jude again. "Er, you seem a little pale, young man. Are you okay? Should I call an ambulance?"

Jude very nearly put up his hands to fend off her barrage of well-meaning questions but managed to resist.

Mama hastily intervened. "No, thank you, he'll be fine. Please don't concern yourself. I'll handle it."

The woman pursed her lips and flicked a glance toward the case. Her eyes went wide with shock; her face paled.

Jude flicked a glance at the case, and his mouth fell open. The journal lay open to a page near the end. On it was written a single entry: *She tells me it is Aug 7, the day I have been waiting for. I go to him now for the last time. Then home. She promised.* On the page opposite was a drawing of a girl in a long white gown, her dark eyes sad. He recognized her as the girl who'd pleaded to him for help.

Taste of innocent blood. Taste.

Bile rose in his throat. With an effort, he choked it back. Unpleasant images flickered at the edge of his conscious thought; he felt he was about to be sucked into that scene in the journal. *No, not again!* He forced the images back, to save himself. From what? *Blood...taste... No, no!*

"No need to trouble yourself, ma'am," Mama was saying to the security officer as she gently took Jude's arm. She tried not to appear unduly hasty as she guided him to the exit. "I knew we shouldn't have come," she muttered. "We should have stayed home."

It was all Jude could do to make it out the door before he threw up. Outside in the bright sunshine, Mama sat him down on a wrought-iron bench in a patch of lawn. The heat of the sun felt good after the cold, dark—*No! Not that.* He didn't want to go there, wherever, whatever, it was. He closed his eyes, willing the nausea to pass. Mama fanned him with her kerchief. He couldn't explain, and she didn't press him.

"So, there you are!" Grandpa growled, suddenly beside them. "I was searching everywhere for you. I got hungry. Figured we should have some lunch."

"Yes, Dad, in a minute." She fanned Jude faster. "Are you okay, son?"

Jude opened his eyes. It took an effort, as though he had to drag them open. He'd have replied to his mama's question, but couldn't manage words yet. He felt so cold. The dizziness was fast receding, though.

"What the hell's wrong with him?" Grandpa said gruffly.

"Oh, Daddy, we were in the museum, and he had one of his—"

"What the hell are you doing to him? Women! You pet him and coddle him—and now look at him. He's turning into a sickly boy, a sissy. Hell's bells, woman, he needs a dad to raise him to be a man. Get up! On your feet, soldier! Hubba hubba! Are you going to be a pansy all your life?"

Jude nearly wilted under his tirade. He was only a child, never mind that he was as tall as his grandpa. It got him thinking, though, what it meant to be a man.

"Dad, stop it!" cried Mama, nearly in tears. "You don't understand." She smoothed Jude's hair.

He pulled his head away. No wonder Grandpa said she petted him!

The old man snorted in disgust. "What did you see in there to make you sick, boy? Was there some blood on the grizzly's claws?"

Blood. So much blood. He cut off her head, and blood poured out on the ground. He picked the severed head up by the hair and lifted it high for all to see. Blood ran down his arm, dripping, dripping. He turned his face to the sky to scream defiance and victory. *All that blood.*

Jude turned and threw up on the grass.

When he'd finished, Grandpa was gone. Mama tried to help him, but he brushed her off, though he accepted the kerchief to wipe his mouth. No, he'd be tough, like Grandpa. The old man had fought in a war and survived. He was a hero. In that moment, Jude resolved to make Grandpa proud of him one day.

"Are you okay, dear?" Mama asked but didn't touch him again after the rebuff.

Jude mumbled something unintelligible as he scrubbed at his mouth, trying to rid himself of the bitter aftertaste. Finally, he stood up, determined to ignore the dizziness. He'd be a man, whatever the cost.

"I'm okay now, Mama," he managed, finally. "Let's see if Grandpa still wants lunch." The thought of food nearly made him heave, but he didn't want Grandpa thinking he was a pansy. "Later we could go look at the art gallery and…and maybe see that video in the museum about 'the Road.' Think Grandpa's picture's in it somewhere?"

Prowling the Peace

Clayhurst Crossing, BC. Spring 1869

Bella perched on a rocky ledge, observing the Indians gathered around their flickering fires and mulled over how the Prince had established himself at Charon's side since that night so many centuries ago. None compared to him in beauty or might. No one dared to challenge his position.

She watched the Indians poking at flames and chattering among themselves. August seventh was fast approaching—the day on which the sun would go into hiding, the master had calculated. Bella knew that Charon would chant the words of power and perform a particular ritual dictated by ancient lore. He—and all of them—would drink of the innocent blood and be transformed. Never again to fear the light of day! The entire world would be their playground. She smiled at the thought.

Time was running out. All were out searching for the requisite virgin— or trying to appear as though they were. In other words, everything was proceeding as usual. Until Charon announced that he sensed the Huntress nearby.

Panic! Bella shivered at the mention of that name, as did nearly every other vampire. The Huntress could be anywhere, blending in among ordinary mortals. She was made to hunt and slay. Most vampires wisely tried to avoid her, though tales were told of certain bold creatures that dared much.

The Prince was one of these. He had in past centuries faced a Huntress, or two, or three. He had survived the encounters; they had not. Apparently, it was the drinking of their potent blood that had so enhanced his power and beauty. Though the Brotherhood admired and envied his feats of valor, most were not so inclined; the danger was real, death the most likely outcome.

Bella slipped from her perch as she sensed shadows drifting down around her to warily approach the campsite. Dogs got to their feet at the edges of the firelight, hackles rising as they faced the pale cliffs. Low rumbles issued from their throats.

Close around the campfire, mortals' faces gleamed bronze in the dancing light of the flames as they spoke in low tones over cups of tea and bowls of moose stew. Several men sat near the wagons, cleaning their rifles. Two women repairing a net slapped at mosquitoes until someone tossed a few green sticks onto the fire. Smoke billowed up, dissipating the clouds of pests, so that the humans were able to get on with their chores.

They were as yet unaware that a larger and more deadly type of bloodsucker watched from the darkness.

Just past the line of wagons, horses tethered in a grassy hollow stamped their feet and whickered nervously. This alerted the humans, who glanced around, dark eyes sweeping the shadows. They were not able to sense the vampires' approach, but their animals could. The dogs' growls did not go unheeded. One man rose to investigate the restlessness of the horses. Human eyes could only see what might have been shadows from the smoke of their fires, no more.

After a cursory inspection of the campsite, the vampires drifted away, leaving the mortals to their unease. No need to frighten them away before seeing if they had what the master desired. Not to mention that Huntress none of them cared to meet. Other nightly entertainment would have to suffice for the present. Game was plentiful, but with humans so near…

Bella floated on the night breezes, her cloak trailing and her long black hair riffling in her wake. Stars glittered like beads of crystal scattered across the deep purple velvet of the sky. She reached out with all her senses and flowed through the night, no more than a blur of black to even the most observant of mortals.

The soft whispering of leaves spoke to her in a myriad of voices, voices lovelier by far than that of the demanding and voracious river. How she feared that sound! *Why would Charon set up headquarters so near it?* she'd often wondered. With an effort, she managed to relegate the hated voice of the river to a faint background static.

Muffled footfalls and the occasional cracking of a twig or dead branch traced the progress through the bush of prowling night hunters or other beasts seeking water under cover of darkness. Most men would stay close to their fires.

As Bella drifted away from the fishing camp, listening, she caught the rush of swooping wings and the shrill squeak of a hapless mouse. A squirrel family chittered as it settled down for the night within the bole of a hollow tree. From a hidden trail came the sound of a prowling lynx's soft, padding feet. And *¡ay!* there, human footfalls crunching down the path to the river. Hunger bestirred itself within her. One man alone; she'd attend to him shortly.

Other scents wafted to her on the breeze. A moose drank from the river, unaware of the man's approach. Upslope, a fox carried a rabbit in its jaws. The fresh blood piqued her interest, but not enough to rouse her from the luxury of her wake-dreaming above the treetops. Not for a rabbit. Beneath the layers of warm and living smells were those of damp clay and sand of the shore and old leaves carpeting the forest floor. Pungent fragrances of spruce and pine stirred in the breath of wind.

A human shriek of terror pierced the night and was suddenly cut off. Bella's ears pricked up, all her senses homing in on the disturbance. A familiar scent, overwhelming and irresistible, brought her to a halt. Then she was there, above it. She stared down at the thrashing beneath the trees. The confusion of figures blended into deep green foliage and purple shadow. She growled in irritation. Someone else had found the prey she'd neglected to claim. She dropped from the sky, the scent sharpened; warm, live, human blood. Hunger exploded within her.

The willows quivered, disturbed by the action on the ground. Then she saw: two vampires crouched over a man. Down on his back, he flailed about, his hard leather boot-heels digging grooves in the ground. An empty water bucket lay nearby.

Suddenly she felt tears inside. *Daddy! Don't leave me!*

Who — where had that come from? Furiously she crushed the sensation and forced herself to turn to the matter at hand in the forest below. And caught the scent, so tantalizing. *Be cautious.* Who would be tormenting their victim? Not the more powerful vampires; they'd have had him mesmerized into bliss in a heartbeat. *¡Ay!* someone she could bully into giving her a share.

In the blink of an eye, she descended. The faces turned to her as one, blood running down their chins, hot, fierce red eyes glaring. Bella laughed aloud, exultant at the prospective feast. It was only Blue Boy and Pinkie. They always hunted as a pair and did not welcome interference. Victims of one of Charon's sweet experiments (as he termed it), they were twins in their mortal life and, oddly, still clung to each other after they were turned. It was not natural for vampires to be so close. They were meant to be loners.

Bella's tongue flicked out. Pinkie and Blue Boy, in their excitement, forgot themselves and growled a warning; she ignored them as she savored the scent.

Neither had forgiven her for turning Blue Boy's head for a short while. She couldn't see why they harbored a grudge against her for that. He was a pretty boy, and she was irresistibly beautiful. She'd soon lost interest; he was much too shallow for her taste, she told herself. And they were sister and brother after all. Her biggest disappointment was that the Prince did not get jealous or even take any notice of her short flirtation with the twin.

Entranced by the blood streaming from the mortal's mangled throat, Bella dismissed the twins entirely. They went back to their feeding without further protest. No doubt, they were as ravenous as she and were not about to let their prey bleed out on the ground while they fought over him.

They could have the jugular. Bella had her own style. She captured his gaze with her own; his expression of terror dissolved into rapture at once. Oblivious of Pinkie and Blue Boy at his throat, he fixed adoring eyes on Bella with a faint ecstatic smile. She leaned in to kiss him. Felt, tasted his euphoria as she sank her teeth into the hot flow of life, of blood. She wanted to drown in it.

Nothing could ever match this feeling.

Unless it was the blood of the One. But—she was already higher than a hunting hawk's flight, from this ordinary mortal. That one must be unimaginable bliss!

Still, this was better than just drifting high in the night sky, dreaming. Pinkie and Blue Boy and fantasies of the Prince and the Consecrated One faded along with the world around her. All that mattered was this one sweet mortal. The blood, and the heartbeat strong and fast, made her feel so alive! *Almost.*

As blood poured down her gullet, she felt, saw, lived the rush of memories: of a childhood of happiness and sadness and anger and pleasure and growing up. All those wonderful human things through all the years of his life, until this, his last day on earth, when he'd pitched camp, hobbled his horse and set off with a pail down the path to the river for water, where the dark agents of death dropped down on him. His last conscious thought was of his wife and children, with a sense of regret and loss; and anxiety for the state of his soul as he was struck with the realization of his peril and the possibility of dying. But by then, it was too late.

Bella took him from the terror and pain, took him to the stars with her, a trip of fantastic, exhilarating speed such as she was certain he had never known. She climbed to the heights with him, felt his rapture, and... *oh, what could be better than this?*

Then he died.

She tore herself away, and they left him lying under the scrub willows, his mouth and throat and red-and-blue-plaid flannel shirt torn and stained with blood. His face was ashen, his black unseeing eyes open to the sky. As

Bella stood regarding the dead man, a stab of remorse struck her at this useless destruction of life.

What the hell?

She shook off the terrible, unnatural feeling and threw herself at Blue Boy to lick the blood off his chin. The wave of bliss returned with a vengeance, and she gave a squeal of exuberance. Blue Boy laughed, and then they had to drag Pinkie away, she was so greedy, trying to go back for more when the man was already dead. But Bella was too high and happy to make her usual scornful comment. Blue Boy and Pinkie were too drunk to care, and everything was funny and beautiful. Bella kissed Blue Boy, and he laughed again, and Pinkie did not even get mad. They cavorted through the bush down to the sandy shore of the river and back to the small clearing where the man had set up camp, perhaps to find another mortal thereupon which they could continue their feast.

But the man had been traveling alone. Never mind the horse. Time to move on. Pinkie suggested they go back to the fishing camp and find another victim. What a greedy little thing she was! Still, it was a tempting thought. It was difficult to stop once started. Especially with only one mortal among the three of them, whetting their appetites for more. Not to mention the thrill of killing.

Still, one of them had to have some sense, Bella decided.

She reminded Pinkie with exaggerated seriousness that Charon would not thank them for frightening the people away or killing virgins, if there were any. He wanted them for himself, she added. At that, they burst into peals of laughter. She grew serious once more and made Pinkie and Blue Boy promise not to tell that she had said that, even if it was true. The master may not see the humor in it. But he also wouldn't want them to be so careless as to get themselves killed. High as they were, the possibility was not all that remote. Especially with the Huntress about.

By the time they returned, the people at the fishing camp were mostly asleep, from the look of it. A few men were still outside, banking the fires and checking on the animals. One old woman was pouring a last cup of tea to take into her tent.

Bella told Pinkie and Blue Boy they were only going to observe but would not touch anyone, and they said, yes, of course, and giggled foolishly. It was so much fun. They crept near so silently that even the dogs and horses did not seem aware of them. They watched the humans from just outside the firelight, with their bloodstained mouths open to catch the scent on the night breezes.

A man checking the horses' tethers had finished and, with one last pat on a horse's neck, began walking back toward the row of wagons. Bella could smell the dark wool of his jacket, the tobacco in his pocket, traces of gun oil on his hands. Too soon, he would be back at the relative safety of the camp. Somehow she had lost track of Blue Boy and Pinkie.

She only realized that she had moved toward the man when she saw him right in front of her, reaching into the wagon, under a canvas tarp. Too late, she wondered how that had happened. The sharp smell of the canvas she immediately dismissed. She leaned toward him, tasting the air in eager anticipation, savoring the human scent, so tantalizing, the smoke, and—

He turned and seemed startled to see her there. She smiled and looked deep into his black eyes. Fear flashed in them, and he lurched back against the wagon. *Oh, yes, the fangs. And the—ay.* Self-consciously she wiped her mouth with the back of her hand. His eyes darted to her gleaming nails. He seemed to realize what she was, then, and opened his mouth to shout a warning or to scream with fear; she did not wait to find out which. She was upon him in an instant, her trademark kiss stopping any sound he had thought to make.

Then she was lying on the ground, wondering what had happened. No time to think. A flash of steel in the man's hand arced downward, but she was already across the clearing and in the deep shadow of a willow thicket.

In a state of shocked disbelief at his quick defensive reaction (how was it that she had not mesmerized him?), she observed from her hiding place that his eyes darted around in search of her. He panted from fear, a naked blade in his hand. The horses stirred restlessly, snorting and rolling their eyes toward her hiding place.

She couldn't think what had happened. How could he have resisted her? She had learned from the best, much as she hated to give Nyx credit for anything. She had the gift, Nyx had once said.

Her shock melted away, but her craving was still as sharp as the man's blade. Dare she make another attempt? Surely, he wouldn't expect... she watched in mounting anticipation as he sheathed his knife once more. As soon as he turned his back...

In the next instant, she would have been upon him, and there would have been no reaching for that knife ever again. But before she could make a move, he turned toward her refuge (almost as though he could see her, but he could not, surely!), and made the Sign of the Cross.

Her shriek rent the night as a great sheet of pain slammed her into the thicket. In that instant, her powers of self-preservation took her, without conscious effort on her part, to relative safety some distance away. *Puny mortal! How dare he!*

She stared, trembling, agog with disappointment and disbelief. Who would have thought that an ignorant backwoodsman would think to do such a thing? It seemed that the Enemy had made inroads everywhere. Just as the vampires had come halfway around the world to this new land, so had He.

Bella's indignation rose at having been so easily and thoroughly foiled. What she might have done, she'd never know. For a blow to the side of her face knocked her to the ground. She leaped to her feet, snarling, and saw — Nyx had slapped her! She fell to cowering at once but managed not to reach up to touch her stinging cheek.

"Fool!" Nyx hissed, eyes aglow with fury. "Can't you remember the master's command for one minute?"

Bella quaked and hated herself for it. "I will not do it again," she choked out.

Shadows drifted past, and Bella stiffened, hoping they hadn't noticed. She had her pride, just as when she was mortal. In her estimation, most of the vampires were mere peons putting on airs, whereas she... only she was of the true nobility, her superiority inborn. Except for the Prince. Some said he came of royal blood.

Bella sincerely hoped he hadn't seen her impulse that could have meant the ruin of them all. His attention she longed for with all the strength of her being, but humble she was not. And yet, what would she not give to have him speak to her, just once? For whatever reason. But he was nowhere in sight.

Nyx had turned away, dismissing her as of no importance. How she hated that! How she hated her! Bella lifted her head and stood tall once more, with as much dignity as she could muster. No one ventured any comment as she drifted back toward the cave to nurse her battered ego.

She heard a shout, then, from the midst of the camp, as the man raised the alarm. Other men sprang up, with guns or clubs in hand, on the alert at once. A few women peeked fearfully from the tents, shushing their awakened children in low tones.

The vampires scattered.

Betrayal

Hanna, Oklahoma. August 2012

Lily, the librarian, paused in the midst of dusting the bookshelves to glance out the front window. The sight of the unkempt grass of the front yard reminded her of how she missed her little handyman, though not just because the lawn needed mowing. Jude and his mama had been regulars at her little library ever since he was a little tyke. After they'd chosen a stack of books to borrow, she'd invite them for tea and cake or cookies to make sure they stayed to visit. She loved her tea, but it wasn't the same with no one to share it. They'd enjoyed many lively discussions about books over the years.

That boy loved to read, a good sign of intelligence, curiosity, and eagerness to learn, like her nephew Lee. As a child, Lee, too, had been a bookworm, eventually going on to the university. He'd majored in archaeology but also excelled in a wide variety of related fields. Now he had his doctorate degree. Jude could do as well, Lily decided, if his mama didn't hold him back. This Canada trip would be a good experience for him.

At the sound of an approaching car, she glanced out toward the road. Speak of the devil. It was Lee in his black BMW. She tossed the feather duster aside, patted her frizzy white hair into place, and hurried out to the kitchen to put on the teakettle.

How long it seemed since he and his friend Roger had last stopped by while on their summer vacation some years back, on their way to explore some caves. A lovely visit, but the last of those regular, frequent ones. Since then, she had seldom seen him, and his visits were brief. Young people nowadays, always running, like hamsters on a wheel.

He was coming up the walk, a slight figure in a white golf shirt and tan slacks. She hastened to open the door, and there he stood on the welcome mat, the sun glinting off his slick platinum hair, his hand raised to knock.

"My dear boy, it's so good to see you again," she cried, with outstretched arms. She gave him a hug and was so pleased to see him that she hardly noticed his lack of enthusiasm as he returned the hug. "The teakettle's on." Just then, a piercing whistle came from the kitchen. "Have a chair, Lee, dear, while I get that."

She brought the teapot and a plate of coffeecake to the table where Lee sat absently appraising her library.

"I'm on my way to Dallas for a genetics conference," he replied to her initial volley of questions, with a conspicuous lack of emotion. "Thought I'd stop in for a visit since it's on my way. Life is so hectic; I'm always on the go. Usually I fly but decided to drive this time. Don't often get to see this great country of ours anymore."

Odd, how his manner didn't jibe with his words. She asked him about himself as she served cake and poured tea. His dry report ended rather abruptly (the itinerary of a busy professional, she supposed). She filled the ensuing silence with chatter, at intervals offering more tea and cake. Lee seemed bored or maybe distracted.

He barely managed to repress a sigh after she once again lamented the fact that her little handyman was on vacation, and finally, he broke in with, "If you like, I'll mow the lawn for you. At your age, Auntie, you shouldn't be pushing that mower around in this heat."

"Why, thank you, my dear boy. That would be so kind." She was glad to finally catch a glimpse of the old Lee. "I can't seem to get good help nowadays, other than Jude, that is. He rakes leaves, too, and weeded the flowerbed last year when my back gave out. He's a wonderful boy."

For a minute, she thought that Lee was rolling his eyes. But no, that was impossible; he'd never been rude, even as a child. Fun-loving, yes. Apparently, he'd outgrown that. He seemed to take life so seriously now.

Still, he nodded and smiled in all the right places (though in an oddly unemotional way), so she was encouraged to pursue her favorite subject. That is, Jude Martel, who'd read every book in her library several times over and, well, she just couldn't say enough about him. Eventually, she paused for breath, and Lee went outside to mow the lawn.

When he'd finished, Lily invited him to supper. He almost refused; he was anxious to be on his way. But he was famished, he admitted. The mouth-watering aromas emanating from her kitchen apparently decided him. He stayed.

"You should hear him sing," Lily resumed over supper. "Like an angel, and he plays the violin so beautifully—you think you've died and gone to heaven. More scalloped potatoes, Lee? There's another slice of ham; here, have some. I can't eat that much anymore. You look like you could use some more meat on your bones, dear." She passed the serving dishes to him, and he finished them off. No mean feat for one so thin.

"And the poor child. I just don't understand why the other children treat him so badly," she continued. "He's the nicest, most delightful—well, children can be cruel, I know. Maybe they're jealous since he can run so fast and—"

"So, if he's so fast," Lee interjected as he folded his napkin and refolded it, "couldn't he outrun them? I mean, if they're picking on him."

"Oh." Lily was startled. It was the first comment Lee had made for some time. "Er, you know, it's kind of, well, they'd corner him or bully him, then they were the ones running away. Things happened; nobody quite knew what, or how. It all started in first grade; he knocked down that big bully Fenwick Cooper without even touching him, so they claim. Something about his eyes glowing; silly, I know, but that's what they said. They started calling him freak then and never let up. This whole business went on for years, I believe, without anyone in charge ever really taking notice. Finally, last winter, his mama started homeschooling him. About time too, I say."

"Yes?" Lee urged, his eyes like nails, piercing. "What happened?"

Lily set down her fork and dabbed at her lips with a napkin. "It seems Fenwick, et al, cornered the poor child just down the road there. He ended up on top of the stone wall, out of their reach, though they couldn't agree on how; it happened so fast. Some said he ran up the wall like a lizard; others said he flew. Nonsense, of course. How could anyone do that? Maybe they'd got into some weed. I don't know. They began calling him Goblin King, the cruelest cut of all. You've seen the movie *Labyrinth*?"

"I've heard of it," Lee sighed, then something seemed to dawn; his eyes took on a certain gleam. "So, Auntie, what then?"

"Sure he has these, well, odd things about him. But he's such a sweet child. Why is it that—"

"Odd things?" Lee leaned forward, his pale eyes avid. "It was true, then?"

"No. Well, maybe." Lily paused for a moment while Lee sat tensely waiting. "Actually, I sometimes noticed that he was here one moment, there the next. Almost as if he'd moved faster than the human eye can see. Impossible, of course. I can't explain it. It wasn't consciously done but only happened if he was frightened or anxious. I think his mama instructed him; she was always concerned about people asking questions."

"For example?" said Lee, his eyes burning.

Lily hesitated. She didn't like that look in his eyes. "Oh dear, I'm such an old gossip. I shouldn't have said anything. It's not something they discuss with just anyone. They talk to me sometimes; at first, because I was concerned about Jude reading in a dark corner. It came out that he was able to, well, see in the dark."

"See in the dark, like a cat?"

"Um, yes, I suppose."

"How old did you say he is?"

"Er—" she was disarmed by the unexpected question and answered before she thought. "He's twelve now."

"Twelve." Lee muttered some quick calculations under his breath. "When's his birthday?"

"Right around Christmas. December twenty-second, I believe. Why do you ask?" Though perplexed by Lee's sudden interest, she couldn't help being pleased that he'd finally become truly involved in the conversation.

Suddenly, she found herself revealing more than she should have, maybe, like the boy's physical description (and the fact that he looked nothing like his parents), where he lived, that his daddy had died when he was five, and other irrelevant information, like his friends' names and what they did for fun.

Then Lee abruptly left.

Lily began to have second thoughts. She'd so enjoyed Lee's visit; she'd been lulled into thinking it was just like old times. But it wasn't, she realized. For the first time, she allowed herself to consider how Lee had changed—between one visit and the next, it was. He and Roger had stopped by that summer. Ever since then, Lee was no longer Lee, but a cold stranger, as though an alien had taken on his form or inhabited his body, like in some of those science fiction stories. But this was real life!

Still, he'd changed, and not for the better. He was no longer the smiling, innocently curious boy she once knew, but a cold and calculating man. Of his work, he'd say no more than that it was classified. At first, she thought he was joking, but no; he seemed to have no sense of humor (or any emotion at all that she could see). *Odd, that.*

Why had she told him about the child? She felt uneasy, now that she had time to think. She frowned, trying to remember what had triggered his sudden interest. He'd seemed bored for most of the visit (no more than one would expect, of course, of a busy young man listening to his old aunt's prattling over tea).

She had only meant to recall the fun they'd had, desperate to bring back the old Lee. Now she felt a frightening knot in her stomach over the way his pale eyes had suddenly become almost hungry when she'd mentioned the boy. The thought of that expression turned her cold. How was it she hadn't been more wary, more discreet?

She breathed a sigh of relief as she watched his taillights disappear around the curve in the road.

Vindicated

Clayhurst Crossing, BC. Spring 1869

Back at the cave, Bella scowled. Nyx was so indulgent with her own children, yet chastised her as though she were a rebellious child! It couldn't be that Nyx was jealous; Charon had always been hers, so it was said. Or, was this about the Prince?

She heard a quiet laugh behind her. She whipped around. "Oh. It's you."

It was the Sandman, with his mischievous half-smile. "Ah, Nyx again?"

"Go ahead and laugh; she likes you. She has ever hated me."

"The feeling is mutual; I've no doubt."

"True." She cursed, her eyes flashing sparks. "You heard her. Any excuse to cut me down."

The Rocket came up just then. "Ha! You think you're the only one she slaps around? Get over it. You're just spoiled."

Bella rounded on him. "Call me spoiled, you little piece of —"

Nose to nose, the fire in their dark eyes clashed. Slender as a blade, the Rocket was, and elegant. He might have been beautiful, Bella had decided, but for that perpetually sulky look. And that temper! Sparks were bound to fly whenever they met.

"Easy there." The Sandman stepped between them.

"You heard what she called me!" squeaked the Rocket in an offended tone.

"Listen," the Sandman said. Their curiosity roused, they forgot their tiff and turned to him with questioning looks. "Nyx actually did you a favor, Bella. The Huntress is right here in the camp."

"*¡Ay de mi!*" Bella shivered. "And I was there, so close!"

"You gave us away!" The Rocket squawked. "Now, we can't even go out at night."

Bella turned to lash out, but the Sandman stopped her with a gentle hand on her arm. "No, Nyx said that because of Bella, we discovered it before any of us were taken."

"I'll never get an apology from her," Bella scowled. "Not in a thousand years."

The Rocket shifted his feet, mumbling an apology of his own; he looked relieved when Bella's gaze softened. "At least you and Pinkie and Blue Boy caught a live one tonight," he added in a placating tone. "No one else did."

"Luck," she said generously. Her fond recollection was unpleasantly disrupted by the thought of that fleeting sense of compassion that had unaccountably assailed her.

"The Huntress," the Sandman mused, oblivious. "The master did warn us. But Nyx has an ace up her sleeve—or the knave, rather. A shaman! We just have to avoid the Huntress for the next couple of months, that's all. Or kill her."

"Two months!" the Rocket groaned. "Or kill her... sure, you just run right out there and bite her, hero."

The Sandman shook his head, still smiling. "Not me. Maybe the Prince will. He's our 'Jack the Giant-Killer,' ain't he?"

"Huntress-Killer, yeah," the Rocket said. "Hey, Bella! Would you brave the Huntress?"

"Not a chance." Then she thought of the Prince. *He* would. "Or, I'd maybe help, if someone—"

"Ah, you mean the Prince?" the Sandman cut in with an infuriating grin.

The Rocket smirked.

She glared daggers at them. Was she so transparent that even these peons...?

"Is there a problem?" said a new voice, softly menacing.

Bella's frown faded. Rojo. He was so fine; he always had her back. She'd turned him soon after their arrival in the New World. Thin-faced and wiry, with flame-red hair, he was instantly labeled Red Fox. It suited him well enough, but he took it amiss and transformed into a whirling fury. Bella loved that fiery temper so like her own, and his gorgeous long red hair. He did accept her affectionate name for him, *Pellirojo*. The others had difficulty wrapping their tongues around it and shortened it to Rojo. He accepted that.

"We were discussing the Huntress," the Sandman explained. "Have you heard what's in the works?"

"No. Just that the top dogs are on it."

The Rocket frowned. "I've never seen a Huntress, ever, and don't want to. They can leave me out of it."

"Me, I think I'll have a look around," Rojo said.

"Don't be a fool." Bella ruffled his hair. "I would not have you lost to me."

Rojo took her hand from his hair and held it against his cheek. His devotion was as ardent as the fire of his fury. As one of Charon's cast-off pets, Bella was starved for that sort of attention. She knew Rojo disdained the sidelong glances and sneers aimed at these public displays of affection and was prepared to defend them both with ferocity at the least provocation. Of course, she was capable of taking care of herself, but still, it was rather a fine thing.

A soft but authoritative voice interrupted them. "Children."

All heads whipped around as Nyx materialized, her star-studded cloak shimmering, her boots eerily quiet on the stone, those slinky, loose-fitting trousers she wore giving no hint of a whisper. She looked down her fine narrow nose at them.

Children? How Bella hated that. She was not a child; certainly not Nyx's! But she'd learned not to express such feelings in Nyx's hearing.

"The master will see you now. All of you." The firm tone did not invite comment or question.

They followed in silent apprehension through the labyrinth, down, down, deep underground, to the Great Hall. There sat the master, tapping his nails on the ornate arm of his throne. Members of the Brotherhood poured through the entrances. No one escaped his hard-eyed scrutiny. It made one shiver, that look. The members of the elite were arrayed on each side of the throne, facing the crowd. Next to Charon stood the Prince (no less imperious than his master) with Styx at his feet. Bella hated the way she gazed up at him with naked desire—so vulgar and low-class.

Nyx took her place, shadowed by her newest boy, Sweet William. Bella eyed him appreciatively; he was quite handsome. Tall and lanky with dark hair—the Latin look to which she was so partial. One day, if Nyx turned her back long enough… Her chances were good, she figured. Nyx was never so particular with her other boys as with the Prince. *And I have tasted them all.* Bella allowed herself a faint smile of satisfaction.

The Genie was in the forefront; old as the hills he was, from long before Bella's time. Craggy-faced and a little scary-looking, not someone with whom you got too familiar. His loyalty to the master was second to none. The same with Reed, the tall, thin colorless one, his crony the feisty Arab, Sirocco, and their following; all Charon's from time immemorial.

With Bella, the Sandman and the Rocket gazed with undisguised calculating ambition at the position of privilege they all so ardently coveted. Bella felt a pang of loss; she had once had a place there. It was a demotion she shared with a long line of pets from before and after her through the centuries, each in their turn cast off to the sidelines. Lulu, Pinkie, and Blue Boy, to name a few. All had joined the ranks of the dispossessed, the trash.

No, there was no point in being bitter. They had their own society; they who had that one thing in common, if nothing else. Not exactly friends, but companions, to a degree acceptable in a vampire. It was not as if Charon had forgotten them. He still claimed them as his own and demanded fealty, but he had lost interest at about the same rate as they lost their humanity. Or at least that was how Bella figured it. Only by displaying something uncommon or intriguing about oneself could one continue to hold his interest. Like the Prince had — even though Charon had not turned him himself. His was a special case, for reasons unknown to Bella, and anyone she had ventured to question about it.

With dreadful longing, Bella wished she could be the one to find him a new pet, or better yet, his next sacrificial victim; then, she would once more be worthy of his notice. But now there was the Huntress to avoid. Another complication.

The shaman! Why did I not think of that? With my beauty and charm, I could persuade him to…if I can only get my hands on him before Nyx does.

Charon's deep voice interrupted her plotting. She cursed her momentary distraction. But Rojo and the others were listening; she'd catch it later. Now the master warned that this was no time for frivolity (with a sharp look in her direction, it seemed to her).

A solar eclipse lasted but a short while, and if innocent blood was not tasted at precisely the right moment, and the ritual completed, it would fail this time too. Back to the drawing board for Charon. Long, hard study of sky charts to predict another solar eclipse, to calculate the precise location of its totality. The master would not be pleased if they had to move again. And they would all suffer.

Charon emphasized the need for strategy. There was no point in recklessly descending upon the camp, only to be dispatched by the Huntress. Or to risk revealing their lair, so near the camp of the Enemy. Even the master was vulnerable as he slept through the day.

How he did chafe at his bonds! Though master of all, he was held underground by a curse most vile, Bella had heard. Long before her time, an ancient enemy had spun an invisible web of magic to bind him. As Lord of Darkness, light was the bane of his existence. Not only that of the sun, now. He had once been able to venture out on the darkest of nights (such as that moonless night, Bella recalled, when he'd found her) but the web continued to tighten over time until even starlight burned him. Now he was bound to his underground realm as though by adamantine chains.

He vowed that he would break the power of that curse. He would walk the Earth again — not only at night but during the day as well. The prophecies spoke of a Key.

He meant to find it.

Home Again

Hanna, Oklahoma. August 2012

Jude couldn't wait to share the excitement of the trip to Canada with Daisy. When Mama finally allowed him to visit the Aldens, he ran all the way. As he sped down the long driveway, he could hear the singing of the chickens and the incessant bawling of a cow in the corral behind the barn. The old clapboard house soon appeared through the trees, a welcome sight—seemed like he'd been gone a year. A scruffy brown dog came running out, barking, but the bark soon turned to yips of recognition. Jude scratched the dog's ears. It wriggled happily, then ran ahead of him up the steps onto the porch.

At Jude's knock, Daisy's mama appeared at the screen door, wiping her hands on her apron. Her face lit up as she saw him, but she frowned at the dog. "Go on, Skeeter! Shoo! Leave the kid alone, will you? Howdy, Jude. That dog's such a pest, but he sure does like you. It's good to see you again. How was your trip?"

"A lot of fun, Miz Alden. Is Daisy around?"

"Daisy's away at summer school."

At that, his face fell, and she quickly went on. "But she'll be back next week, honeybunch. She wants that job teaching here this fall, and it's the only way she could qualify." She opened the screen door a bit, then quickly closed it. "Darn flies. If you want, you're welcome to come on in and tell me all about your trip. Or, Beau's out in the barn; maybe go out there. He'd love to see you."

Jude managed a smile. Miz Alden sure liked to talk. Of course, he wanted to see Beau too. Skeeter ran down the steps and streaked toward the barn, as though he knew exactly where Jude was going.

He followed the dog through the open barn door. Beau glanced up from pitching hay into the row of mangers, where cows tossed their heads and munched. A lone cow still bawled across the back fence, beyond the calves cavorting in the corral outside. Dust motes floated in the narrow rays of sunlight shooting through the cracks between the weathered boards of the barn wall. A stray beam caught Beau's lank, sun-bleached hair, setting it aglow, white-gold against his sunburnt, freckled skin.

"Hey, Jude," said Beau with his slow grin, his pale blue eyes twinkling.

"Back in one piece? No bears or wolves done mauled you? I see you still got your nose and ears."

"Wha—?"

"No frostbite, I take it?" grinned Beau by way of explanation as he tossed another forkful of hay into the manger.

Frostbite. *Cold. Cold, so cold.* Jude shivered as the gurgling rush of the voracious river blasted his senses. Curses shredded the air; his soul shriveled within. *Mama, don't let them!* Unwanted memories rose up to clamor at the gates of his consciousness. *No, stay back!* Something bit deep and dragged him down. *I didn't want… I didn't!* The hot flood slammed into him, pulsating through every vein, every capillary in his body, sending him sky high. To the stars. *Ecstasy. What's this? No, no, not that. Cold, so cold. No, must not. Go. There.* He shuddered with the effort to stay above the surface, repressing the memory of—no, it couldn't be a memory. Just imagination… or was it a dream? He realized suddenly that Beau was giving him a rather quizzical look.

"Er, I mean, no, it wasn't cold at all. Nice! Yeah, it was real nice. Hot. They have summer up north too. Honest. The lakes are great for fishing, but they've got a million bugs that eat you alive. And flowers. Mama liked the gardens. Yeah, we were surprised too. It's all kind of different than here. Trees like toothpicks and—"

Beau lifted an eyebrow, and Jude realized he was babbling. He shut his mouth and his eyes, just for a second. And shivered again.

"How about we go hunt squirrels after I'm done here?" said Beau easily into the ensuing silence. "Got some nuisances over in the granary. Ain't had time to take care of them, what with helping Daddy in the fields since Arlie done joined the army last spring. The dang little critters are getting out of hand."

Jude sat on a bale, grateful that Beau had covered for him again. He inhaled the scent of fresh hay, of cows, and the dust of old straw, familiar smells of home. Better than—*no, can't go there.* The cows tossed their heads and rolled great liquid eyes at him. It was good to be back. "Squirrels, yeah. That'll be fun. Hey, Beau, you shoulda seen that museum. All kinds of animals and birds. Eagles, a wolverine, grizzly, moose—"

"Cool." Beau finished tossing the hay and stabbed the fork into a nearby pile. He brushed bits of hay and chaff off his shoulders and shook them from his hair. "Done, for now. We'll let the cows out later. Squirrels, here we come!"

Jude followed Beau out of the barn and waited as he latched the door. "You coming crawdad fishing tomorrow? I'm inviting everyone for a feast.

Be nice if you could come. Seems like we were gone for a year. Had fun, though, fishing with Grandpa and his buddies. We saw a wolf on 'the Road,' near the Yukon border."

"Yukon! Hey, I remember that from school. The gold rush. Cool! Sorry, li'l bro, can't go tomorrow. Wish I could, but Daddy wants me to plow that far twenty acres. And the fence needs fixing." Beau gave an exaggerated sigh. "There's always something. But I'll take a rain check on that."

"One day soon, maybe?" said Jude, disappointed.

"Sure. I'll make time somehow. Wait right here while I run on up to the house and get my twenty-two."

"Instead of the slingshot?"

"Yeah. This is war. Slingshot's just for fun."

"Reckon Goliath would disagree," grinned Jude. "Squirrels might too."

"We'll go with the twenty-two this time."

"I should have brought mine," Jude said regretfully.

"It don't matter. We'll trade off." Beau loped away to the house.

Jude glanced up as the breeze stirred the tall pines just past the chicken house. Squirrels chattered, running up and down the branches. He had to smile when he saw Beau's tall, lanky figure coming from the house, a rifle in each hand.

Beau grinned. "I walked in, and there was Arlie's twenty-two setting there looking pretty. He won't mind."

"Good going!" Jude hefted it. Beau tossed him a clip.

"Lucky we got them squirrels to take care of," said Beau. "Mama was just about to give me some more chores. Never mind that I got company. But she done give in when I mentioned squirrels. She hates the dang things. Seems like the work never gets done, anyhow. I'm looking forward to going to school this fall. Yeah, I know. Never thought that would happen." He chuckled and heaved a long sigh. "I don't know what Daddy's going to do without me to help."

"School! Dang! I'll never get to see you."

"Yup. The hazards of high school. I don't like riding the bus for miles, but that's life, I reckon. You homeschooling again this year?"

"Yeah. Forever, I reckon. I miss my friends."

"There's still weekends. Too bad about Stave and his gang throwing a monkey wrench into the works. You should have told me. I'd have straightened them out."

"I'm no rat fink. But Mama heard, and that was it for me. I could have worked it out myself. Grandpa says I got to stand on my own feet and be a man. You're the only big brother I got, but I can't expect you to bail me out forever."

Beau slapped Jude on the back. "I reckon you'll do fine standing up for yourself, li'l bro. Dang, I got to quit calling you little. You're pretty near as tall as me."

They laughed and ambled down the path past the chicken house to the granary. Squirrels chattered and scampered up the roof and into the nearby trees, where they scattered, only to dart out from branches high overhead, scolding.

"Yeah, whatever. Take that." Beau raised his twenty-two and fired. A squirrel dropped to the ground, twitching.

Jude nudged it with his toe. "Right through the eye."

"I dare you to beat that."

Jude raised Arlie's twenty-two and fired off two shots in quick succession. Two squirrels flopped to the ground. He grinned. "Two through the eye."

"We ain't done yet. Wait'll I get two with one shot."

"This I got to see."

"Come on, let's go. There's a lot more where these come from. You should see the mess they made in the grain."

The competition was on. It was child's play. Not only because of the squirrels' impudence, but because both boys had a good eye and a natural aptitude for marksmanship. Or rather, Beau's was natural. Jude's was more than just natural, like his eyesight, and other things. Not something they talked about, though, just a fact of life.

Once the obvious varmints were out of the way, the boys investigated the scrabbling noises coming from inside the granary. Beau climbed into the shed and flushed the remaining squirrels out, while Jude picked them off with quick shots as fast as they appeared. He lined them up. Skeeter happily guarded the row of little carcasses.

"Oops. Which ones are yours?" Jude said. "I think I mixed them up."

"What?" called Beau from inside the granary.

"Never mind. You selling the hides?"

"Yeah," came Beau's reply. "Less'n you want 'em."

"You heard that well enough," Jude murmured. He raised his voice. "We can split them fifty-fifty. I'll skin mine with my new knife."

Beau appeared. "New knife?"

Jude handed him the knife.

With shining eyes, Beau tested it out by cutting a loose thread on his overalls. He grinned. "Pretty sharp."

"Grandpa gave it to me," Jude said, proud.

"Cool, you finally meeting your Grandpa. Come on, let's finish this." Soon they had the squirrels' nests cleaned out. Beau nailed slats across the holes in the granary. "Well, this'll have to do."

Jude eyed the carcasses with a mischievous grin. "Too bad we lost count. I'm pretty sure I got the most."

"Hah! Think so, huh?" Beau laughed. "It don't matter. Like you said, we each get half." Beau gave one last blow with the hammer. "Done!" He brushed the grain dust off his clothing. "Shoulda stayed in the woods, little varmints, and you'd be alive today."

Jude turned toward the pines, wrinkling his nose as a breeze wafted toward them. "Phew! What's that awful stink?"

"Squirrel nests? Oh, you mean you can still smell that? Well, I reckon you can. Come on."

Jude shivered as the stench hit him again. His breath caught; his skin prickled. *Evil. No, Beau, don't make me—* But Beau had already started down the well-worn trail into the thick stand of pines. With a deep trembling breath, Jude followed. Of course, Beau wouldn't make him go if he knew. But Jude wasn't sure himself why he was afraid. No, he wouldn't be chicken.

Dead needles and twigs rustled beneath their feet. Jude glanced upward warily as a breeze stirred the branches with a soft soughing sound and spiraled downward toward them. The scent slammed into him, cut off his breath like a blow to the throat. *No, no—*

Music is blasting, a syncopated rock beat, and a wailing like lost souls. Jude looks around in a panic. Where…? There are no tall pines, only a vast cavern, rank with the smell of death. A majestic figure sits on an ornate throne. High above, half-obscured by the acrid smoke of pitch-burning torches, is a macabre crown of human heads stuck on spikes.

Jude stares, fascinated. *Is this a dream? People are dancing. No, not people. Or, yes, people, too.* Their thrumming heartbeats stir something inside him, a thrill of hunger. *Blood. Warm. Sweet. No, no, what's happening to me?*

He feels himself drawn to the throne, and what sits on it, against his will. First, he sees black boots, half concealed by the hem of a long cape, then is compelled to look up, up. Terror fills him; he tries to look away. *Can't. Cold. So cold.*

On the beast's lap sits a fair maiden, its white hand at her waist holding her captive. Her pleading eyes meet Jude's; tears slide down her cheeks. It's up to him to save her. His heart shrivels within him. *I'm no hero. What good can I do?* The white hand moves, then, drawing sharp claws across her throat. Blood streams down to stain her white dress. And Jude lifts his gaze to look into the face of the beast—a white face, the mouth red with blood. Dead black eyes fix on his, pull him in. *Blood, so fascinating, so—*

The sudden presence of the Lady in Blue is a reproach; he sees clearly what he's doing and is ashamed. *O my God, I'm heartily sorry for—* With all the strength of his will, he resists those terrible eyes. Then they flare, and a shaft of white-hot fire shoots out to pierce his heart. With a cry, he falls into an abyss.

"Right here. See this?" Beau said, as though nothing was out of the ordinary, standing there in his old overalls and straw in his hair, smelling of the barn.

Jude glanced around, a little disoriented. Oh, okay. This was the familiar piney-wood at Aldens' farm. He managed to breathe again. His chest hurt; he couldn't think why. Never mind. Be a man, Grandpa'd said. He willed the pain to pass. Whatever it was.

"Hey, you okay, Jude?"

"Course. What're you talking about?"

"Er, nothing, I reckon." Beau sounded dubious. "I was just saying, you got to see this here."

Jude leaned down to see what Beau was pointing at; it took an effort to concentrate, to ignore that smell of death, the chill on the back of his neck, and the prickling of his skin as his hair stood on end. He saw claw marks on the tree; and on the ground, though these were almost obliterated by dog tracks.

"Looks like Mr. Tremayne's hounds treed something," ventured Jude. "Was it the phantom again?"

"Yeah, only this time—wait, you ain't gonna believe this."

"So surprise me."

"It was that time me and Daddy done your chores, and we was about to head back home when we seen it."

"Not the phantom?"

"Yeah. Or anyhow, kind of a blur of black and white, like a ghost. It come out of nowhere, stared at us, screeched, and vanished. Right spooky, them glowing red eyes. Just like ol' Tom said, and nobody believed him. We seen it, Daddy and me both. Just like what you and Daisy said you seen that time. Well, we drove home, but the whole way we felt something watching us. Ol' Skeeter was barking his head off, up at the sky! If he barks, there's a reason. Well, we got into the house right quick. I woulda brung Skeeter in, too, he was so scared, but Daddy said he's an outside dog, and that was that. Poor old Skeeter."

"I see Skeeter's still kicking. What happened next?"

"We hear this terrible screech out behind the barn. And the cows a-carrying on like there's no tomorrow. Well, you know Daddy. Anything touches his critters and, well—he done lit out behind the barn. Whatever it was sure skedaddled, but it was carrying off a calf like it was light as a feather. And it was a hefty one, too!" Beau shook his head. "You shoulda seen Daddy's face. He couldn't believe it!"

"I can," whispered Jude, grabbing hold of a tree for support.

"It weren't dragging it, nor running, Daddy said, it was a-flying! It done flew right over the fence and into the woods, not very high and kind of crooked-like. Like it was into ol' Tom's still. You shoulda heard Daddy cursing and swearing—no, I reckon it's better you didn't. Anyhow, he lost track of the thing in the dark of the woods and come running back to the house, yelling at Mama to call Tremayne to get his hounds out here, pronto. The phantom done stole Li'l Betsy's calf. Poor Li'l Betsy was hollering up a storm at losing her young'un. I could hear her from clean inside the house. I sure didn't want to go outside. No sirree."

"That's her I hear by the fence, bawling?"

"Yup. Well, Tremayne come right out and set the hounds on the trail. It took a sight of sniffing around, 'cause of the thing flying. But once in the woods, it dragged a little low. I reckon it wanted to hide and eat the calf."

"Or suck its blood?" said Jude, before he thought—and flushed red, needlessly ashamed, as though he were the guilty one. "I've, uh, heard the stories."

Beau gave him a compassionate glance and went on. "The hounds was baying. They had it treed. What with the calf bawling and that thing a-snarling and a-hissing to beat the band, it was a terrible commotion. We run into the woods. I stuck pretty close to Daddy, I can tell you. Well. Look at the claw marks on this here tree. The dogs was like to rip it down. I never seen the like."

"The thing didn't fly away? You said it flew, right?"

"Daddy and Mr. Tremayne was shining flashlights around, and pretty soon we spotted it perched in the tree, sucking the calf's blood. Them glowing red eyes—man, what a nightmare! The calf was squalling, but it was out of reach; we couldn't do nothing. Look way up."

Jude wanted to throw up, not look up. But the scent was merely residue from the week-old incident. And it was daylight. The thing wouldn't be jumping down out of the tree at them. He lifted his gaze. On the limb was a tuft of reddish-brown hair.

"'Way up there? Tell me you killed the dang thing!"

"When Tremayne started blasting, the phantom screeched and threw the calf down, then vanished into thin air, like. I couldn't tell if it got hit."

"It—it got away…?" Jude was breathless with terror. *Come to me, little one.* "What does it want? Me?"

"Shucks, li'l bro, don't even say that. Just hungry, I reckon," Beau said, without conviction.

"It followed you from our place. Our place, you said."

"That don't mean nothing. Anyhow, it didn't take none of your critters. Daddy made sure. One day it'll get too cocky. The whole county's got their eye out for it. We won't let it get you. Hey, you don't look so good. I bet Mama's done baked chocolate chip cookies. Let's go check. We'll skin the squirrels after."

"Sure, sounds good. Squirrels won't be going anywhere," said Jude with a quick, half-fearful glance back at the tree as he hastened after Beau.

Jude's four friends from school came by the next day in response to his invitation to the crawdad feast. They sat out on the back lawn under the afternoon sun, cracking shells and dipping crawdad tails into dishes of Mama's homemade melted garlic butter. Violet and Rosa Sharon chattered as though to make up for lost time. Their excuse was that they'd hardly seen Jude since his mama had taken him out of school, and then he was away half the summer; they had a lot to catch up on. When they paused for breath, he gave them the Mile Zero Post pins he'd brought back as souvenirs.

"This is so cool!" Violet's dark curls bobbed as she took off her red baseball cap and proudly attached the pin. "All the way from British Columbia. Gee, thanks, Jude."

Rosa Sharon brushed some strands of red-gold hair out of her eyes and surreptitiously dashed away a tear. "I can't believe you thought of us when you were having so much fun. This'll go right in with my baseball card collection." (The ultimate honor, coming from Rosa Sharon.)

They all listened with rapt attention as he regaled them with tales of his travels. The girls admired the new clothes Grandpa had bought him, with a rush of compliments and protestations of envy. Dace and Cale exclaimed over the Swiss army knife. The boys allowed Jude his time in the sun before recounting their own adventures of hunting and fishing and exploring the woods. It sounded like so much fun that Jude almost wished he'd stayed home or could have been in both places at once.

Both places at once. No!

He got queasy at the thought. It brought what had happened in the museum too close to consciousness for comfort. He didn't want to remember that. Dared not. He forced himself into the present. He missed his friends; he saw so little of them, it seemed, since he wasn't in school anymore, but — *no, not two places at once.*

The afternoon went by quickly. Too soon, Miz Taylor arrived to pick up Violet and Rosa Sharon to drive them home. The boys were allowed to stay longer, but before darkness fell, Mr. Tremayne came for them. The phantom had left its mark. Residents of the county had become wary of letting their children play outside after the sun had set.

The Huntress

Clayhurst Crossing, BC. Spring 1869

Bella preferred to hunt alone or with Rojo, but this time Little Lulu tagged along. Her black ringlets bounced, and every one of her annoyingly cute dimples was showing as she jiggled in excitement when Bella pointed out a mortal approaching from the edge of the firelight illuminating the Indians' camp. A rare sight since the humans had learned of their presence. Now, even before the sun went down, they herded their children to safety, and even many of the adults retired to their tents. And now the very boundaries of the camp seemed to repel the vampires in some mysterious way.

Nyx deemed it likely that someone had sprinkled holy water around the perimeter since they couldn't cross that invisible barrier. That was perhaps just as well, with the Huntress about. They hadn't yet seen her, but nights passed in dread that some of them would be missing when dawn came.

Lulu squeaked in excitement. Bella waved her to silence and tasted the air; this one was male, so not the Huntress. But others could pose a danger too, as she'd recently learned. She signaled Lulu to stay and glided toward the intended victim. The scents of woodsmoke, leather, wool, fish, and of the mortal himself, drew her. The craving gripped her, sudden and powerful, like a thunderbolt. She caught herself. *No. Stop. Remember to ask —*

She drew nearer to that heart-pounding, so enticing. He pressed forward, his eyes searching. Shadows shifted. Breezes rustled through tall cottonwoods and scrub willow. Bella hesitated. Was he bait set out by the Huntress to trap an unwary vampire? A wave of heat struck her, the heartbeat thrummed through her, and then she was on him. She took his face in her hands. There was that irresistible pulse, flickering with every beat of his heart. She shook herself. *Oh, yes, yes, the question.*

She gazed into his eyes; he was instantly enraptured. *But wait, I must not lose my one golden chance.* Reluctantly she drew back. "A virgin. Bring me one, and I will spare your life."

He heaved a deep sigh, adoring eyes on her face. "So pretty…"

Impulsively she bent to kiss him; he melted in her arms. Her teeth sank in, and blood flowed. Priorities! The question. But there was no stopping now…

She felt a tugging at her cloak.

"Bella, Bella, stop! Remember to ask— oh, let me have some, please, Bella." Little Lulu was alternating between trying to pull Bella off and pressing close to lick the blood from her face. "You said—oh, let me have some?"

With an effort, Bella tore herself away. The man lay panting on the ground, his mouth torn and bleeding. He reached out pathetically. What had she meant to say? Lulu bent toward him.

Bella hissed, "Not yet!" and Lulu shrank back. She peered into the man's pleading eyes; her hand slid to his throat. That racing pulse… so entrancing. "Watch the path!" Bella snarled and tried to get hold of herself as Lulu slunk a little way away. There were more important things than to satisfy Lulu's greed! She drew the man to his feet and held him close for a moment, then resolutely pushed him away. He clutched at her cloak. She yanked it from his fingers. "Go now." It would not do to kill him, however much he wanted it. "Meet me here tomorrow night."

"Here, tomorrow night," he repeated mechanically.

"With—?" she prompted.

"The girl, as you said." He frowned. "No, not you…?"

So he was out here to meet Nyx. She glanced around in apprehension. Nyx would not thank her for interfering, but—who cared what Nyx thought?

"Yes?" she growled. "Spit it out!"

He lifted his eyes to meet hers. They were calculating, greedy. "And you will give me the power to command those of the spirit world?" His tobacco-stained teeth showed in a snarl. "I must rid us of the priest!"

Her eyes blazed; he at once fell all over himself, groveling.

"I—I'll bring her—" he croaked, fawning. "Tomorrow night!"

"And you will have your reward." With an anxious glance around, she nudged him on his way.

Lulu's mouth drooped at the corners as his footfalls retreated toward the camp. "You didn't even let me taste," she whined.

"Quiet!" snarled Bella. "Do you think I wanted to let him go? Just think of our reward when we bring in the prize."

Lulu subsided, pouting. "But I was hungry, and—"

Bella gestured impatiently, and Lulu's mouth snapped shut with an audible clack of teeth. The underlings knew not to push her too far.

However, her rages were like flash fires, and when she spoke next, it was in a softened tone. "Cheer up. The night is young."

They drifted into the night. Bella did not really expect to find any humans out wandering around, now that they'd been warned, but as she and Lulu half-heartedly cast about for scent, they heard the sound of giggling over the ever-present roar of the river. Enticed by the sound, they drifted downward over the dunes toward the shore.

There, in a hollow out of sight of the camp, a boy and girl were entangled, delighting in their escape from the watchful eyes of their elders. Bella and Lulu glanced at each other. Naughty; so almost too easy. Not to kill — that would be taunting the Huntress. But these two would want to keep their tryst secret. Perfect prey.

Bella plucked the boy off the sand in mid-tickle and drew him to herself, ignoring Lulu's miffed, "But I wanted him!" Tough. She wished Rojo were there instead. He liked girls, or anything — the younger, the better. She smiled at the fond memory of how, not long after she'd turned him, he'd come upon a group of children playing outside at night. He'd darted in among them like a fox among chickens and tore their tender throats out. The children's piercing, terrified cries brought the wrath of the townsfolk upon their heads, of course, and they were obliged to flee in a hurry. But that was long ago; he had learned much about discretion since then.

The boy's black velvet eyes showed a moment of startlement as they met hers, then filled with rapturous surrender. Lovely. *Only a taste, though*; that was all they dared if they wished to avoid discovery. Bella was quite taken with this tall, handsome boy, but they'd been warned. Perhaps later she could turn him.

They left the two on the riverbank, bewildered, but otherwise unharmed. At least not so anyone would notice.

Rojo was eager to accompany Bella the next night after she told him what they'd found on the shore. But first, the shaman. Lulu squealed in anticipation; she meant to get her share this time. Bella quaked at the thought of Nyx finding out.

As they approached the place of rendezvous, they paused to listen. All seemed as usual at the Indian camp: the crackling of fires, the occasional bark of a dog, the whickering and nervous stamping of horses, the muffled cry of a child inside a tent, the low murmuring of adults over tea. Night fell and deepened; a breeze gusted through the trees, rustling the leaves. The smells of smoke and fish and humans wafted toward them.

Concealed within the shadows, they waited. No sign of Nyx, or any of the others. Darkness settled in, and with it, both man and beast. Frogs resumed their nightly chorus. Where was that blasted shaman? Bella nervously glanced around. What if Nyx came looking? Nyx always knew when she lied. That didn't stop her, but she'd learned to duck whenever Nyx raised her hand.

There, a footfall! Bella cursed her daydreaming. A man was approaching from the camp. She peered through the branches and tasted the air. The shaman! At once relieved and anxious, she signaled Rojo and Little Lulu, then drifted down to the path. The man started in sudden fear as she emerged from the shadows. With him was a slender girl with long, shining black hair. The man tried to speak, but his voice failed him. Was it Bella he feared, or—? Her gaze swept their surroundings. *No, no Nyx.*

She broke the tense silence. "You have one?"

"Yeah," he croaked, pushing the girl toward her.

The girl's eyes opened wide, and she shrank against him. "Uncle, what is that?"

Bella looked intently into those wide dark eyes, but the girl somehow resisted her powers of mesmerization. Baffled, she turned to the shaman. Felt a sudden wave of disgust. What sort of man would do this? *No, wait, what was—why would she care?*

"You are certain?" she growled to cover her confusion.

He grunted an affirmative, then looked into her eyes and instantly fell under her spell.

"Who is this, Uncle? Uncle?" The girl tugged at his arm, her fingers tangled in the fringes of his jacket sleeve. When he made no reply, she lifted her eyes to his face. "Uncle? You said Auntie was waiting for us out here. Where is she? I only see this, this—" On her face was an expression of confused horror.

He roughly took her hand from his sleeve. "Go with her, Josie. Now. She'll take you to Auntie."

"What's wrong, Uncle? Why do you sound so—" She clung to him in terror as Bella took her arm.

"I'll take you to your auntie, Josie," said Bella softly. "Come with me." She leaned toward the girl.

With a cry, Josie tore loose and ran down the trail.

"Catch her!" Bella snarled. Rojo was after her like a streak. "You!" she barked at the shaman, "Stay!" She turned to Lulu. "Watch him."

The girl didn't get far in the dark; she tripped and fell headlong into a thicket, and Rojo was on her. But she was putting up a fight, if the thrashing of the bushes was any indication. The piercing shriek Bella heard next came from Rojo. The girl leaped up and ran like a deer, a knife in her hand, its bare blade gleaming in the moonlight. Rojo sprang up, snarling, but Bella had already gone after the girl herself. She wasn't about to lose her prize now; she dared not let her reach the ring of firelight.

Josie stumbled through the darkness, panting; Bella flowed smoothly just above the ground. It was no contest. "Come here, you." Bella dropped down on the girl and snatched her up. The knife flew from Josie's hand. She fought like a wildcat, but Bella only laughed and tucked her under her arm. Charon would love this one! She started back to where Lulu waited with the shaman, while Josie kicked and strained to free herself. "Don't make me hand you back to Rojo," Bella said in an ominous tone. Josie paused, her eyes darting toward Rojo, who was swearing revenge as he held his side. "Did she hurt you with her one long tooth?" Bella taunted.

He gave her a black look.

As they neared the shaman, something seemed wrong. Bella paused, every sense alert. There he was, lying on the ground with Lulu at his throat. Bella was instantly furious. The greedy little—she knows we may need him yet! *I let her out of my sight for one minute and* —

There was a flash in the moonlight, and Lulu was writhing on the ground, shrieking, clutching at the wooden stake that pierced her through. Bella stared in horror as a young woman with flowing black hair stepped over the supine shaman and reached down to grip Lulu's dark curls. With one graceful move and a swiftness Bella had thought impossible for a mortal, she cut off Lulu's head with her long-bladed knife.

This had to be the Huntress!

She straightened up and turned to face the vampires. Her blue cotton dress swirled around her, revealing moccasins laced to the knee. Fringes swayed as her leather jacket swung open. Across her chest was a bandolier studded with stakes, knives on the belt at her waist. A bow and arrows were slung across her back.

"Fly, Rojo!" shrieked Bella. And he was gone.

Josie cried, "Help me, Marie!" as Bella turned to flee with the girl.

The young woman's black eyes were cold and steady. The bow appeared in her hands like magic, arrow nocked and released in one fluid motion. A feathered shaft quivered in the trunk of a tall cottonwood. *Too close!* Bella fled, still clutching the girl. She didn't mean to lose her prize after all that.

With long, swift strides, the Huntress came after her, another arrow nocked and ready. Bella dodged behind trees, hither and thither. *¡Ay!* Where to go? She dared not lead the Huntress to the cave. Frantically she threw herself into the willow thickets, trying to lose her in the dark and the tangle. Branches snagged her cloak and yet seemed not to slow the Huntress at all.

Bella rounded a copse.

There was the Huntress waiting with an arrow aimed at her heart.

She held the girl close.

The Huntress paused, then loosed the arrow. Bella turned to flee and felt a tingling between her shoulder blades where the shaft was sure to strike. From the corner of her eye, she saw something red and black flash between them and heard a thunk and a shriek. Rojo had taken the arrow meant for her!

Bella was torn for a moment, but the Huntress didn't stop to cut off his head or even slow down. She leaped over him and came straight for Bella. She raised her bow in mid-stride and loosed a third arrow. Bella threw herself down and felt the shaft tug at her hair as it passed over her head.

Then she was up and fleeing again—no longer flowing, but scrambling, desperate. Lulu was gone, Rojo down. The Huntress was swift and relentless, ever gaining, yet Bella dared not let go of her captive. Her key to Charon's favor—if only she could survive.

She'd lost all sense of direction in her headlong flight. Suddenly before her jutted a sheer cliff, rearing up to a steep hillside covered by scrubby brush and cactus. She came to an abrupt halt and glanced back.

The Huntress had paused, waiting for her to choose her direction. In her hand was the bow, nocked and ready.

Is this how it ends? With one last hope, Bella turned, snarling, holding the girl in front of her. Surely the Huntress would not harm an innocent. This woman was not like other mortals. She was frightening; coldly unafraid and implacable, deadly calm, her jaw set in grim determination, her black eyes like polished stone. She lifted the bow, her aim steady and true. Bella gripped Josie's hair in one hand, the nails of her other hand pricking the girl's throat.

That gave the Huntress pause. A vampire's sharp claws could slit a throat even in the throes of death. Yet her glittering gaze never wavered. Vampire and Huntress stared at each other across the clearing. Bella could hear nothing but the whisper of leaves stirring in the breeze. Even the night birds were silent.

The Huntress tucked away her bow, reached inside her jacket, and drew out a stake. Bella couldn't take her eyes off that instrument of her destruction. Her snarl was one of sheer desperation.

The Huntress started across the clearing, eyes fixed on her target. Her long, graceful strides ate up the space between them. Bella panicked and flung herself up the cliff, still clutching Josie by the hair, but in the process lost her death-grip on the girl's throat. The Huntress broke into a run and threw herself up after Bella. With her free hand, she snagged Bella's cloak and flung her to the ground. Bella lay a bit stunned for a moment, wondering what had happened, her fingers still tangled in Josie's hair.

Then the Huntress was astride her, her upraised arm descending toward Bella's heart. Bella hissed in panic, pulled Josie to her, between her heart and that deadly stake. The girl was no good to her dead but better that than—

She hadn't reckoned on the Huntress's quick reflexes. The stake stopped a fraction of an inch short of piercing the girl where she lay.

And right before Bella's eyes was the Huntress's throat, vulnerable as she leaned down. A chance! She lunged upward. But before she could so much as graze the skin, a gleam of silver swung toward her from the top of that blue dress. A blast of pain slammed her back against the ground. For a moment, everything went black, and it was as though a gong sent wave after wave of unbearable sound echoing through her head, shattering her brain.

She heard her own shrieks as though from far away. When her senses began to clear, she realized that she was lying helpless on the ground. The crucifix swayed above her. She felt numb and could do nothing but watch in horror as the Huntress deftly untangled Josie's hair from her limp fingers. Bella knew that next, the stake would be in her heart, and there was nothing she could do about it.

Then, utter pandemonium. There was no warning. The Huntress just tumbled over her head, her long, black hair fanning out and a startled expression on that impassive face at last. Vampires were everywhere, flitting among the trees, shrieking and snarling, hissing, and growling. And Bella was free. The terrible crucifix had gone with the Huntress. She didn't stop to think, just grabbed Josie and was across the clearing and into the bushes.

"Flee, Bella!" the Prince barked. "We've got this."

"Go, go!" (*Nyx?*)

Bella stared in astonishment. But there was no time to waste. The Huntress was already on her feet, the stake in one hand and a long, gleaming blade in the other, ducking and slashing as vampires came at her one after another, and then in a rush. Vampires fell screaming and writhing before that darting stake and razor-edged knife. Some disintegrated into dust. The Huntress's glittering eyes missed nothing; her hands seemed to blur, they moved so fast.

Bella began to fear that an army of vampires was not enough. The Huntress was like a whirlwind, leaving destruction in her wake, while she herself remained untouched. Rojo! Bella felt a pang at the thought of his demise, but there was no time for that now.

Eerie how, despite that fierce attacking army, the Huntress was yet in command of the situation, almost as though she had a bubble of protection around her, some sort of invisible shield.

It seemed unlikely that they'd overwhelm her by sheer force of numbers. *How does one kill a Huntress?* Bella wondered.

But the Huntress had turned her face toward her once more. Like magic, the bow reappeared in her hand, with arrow nocked. Bella fled the scene; she could hear the chaos but dared not glance back.

Josie opened her mouth to scream; Bella clapped her hand over it. The girl's cheeks were wet with tears now, as her hope of rescue faded along with the sounds of battle. She drooped, all resistance gone. Bella pressed her close and savored the precious warmth and racing heartbeat.

The entrance to the cave was a long, narrow crack running diagonally up the face of the cliff, mostly concealed by wild rose bushes. Bella flowed through the opening, carrying her tender burden, while Josie clutched at her cloak, trembling and afraid in this strange, dark place.

They followed the winding passage of the labyrinth, down and down. *Safe at last*! The Huntress wouldn't follow them here. Even she wouldn't dare meet the master on his own turf.

Blood Brothers

Dace and Cale were allowed to visit Jude quite often during the rest of the summer, even though everyone knew that the area haunted by the phantom centered on Coon Hollow. In broad daylight, it seemed safe enough. The three boys, therefore, resumed their favorite pastimes: climbing the hills, fishing and hunting, swimming in the creek, and playing war in the woods, just as they had every other summer since they'd started school.

Now and then, Dace and Cale referred back to details from Jude's trip. Out of the mishmash of ideas gleaned from that and Cale's dad's hunting magazines came elaborate plans for the three of them to go on moose and grizzly hunting trips to Canada one day. They crammed every minute together full of real or imagined adventure, now that Jude was back. Summer needn't be a total loss just because he'd been away for a few weeks.

One sunny day they climbed the hill, scaling some rocks as they followed a deer trail up through the scrub brush to the top. When at last they reached a small meadow near the summit, they threw themselves down on the grass to catch their breath. Jude took the new knife out of his pocket and let the sunlight play across its shiny red-and-silver surface. A useful tool, but especially treasured because Grandpa had given it to him.

"Wish I had one of those," said Dace. "Looks sharp. Can I see it?"

"Sure," said Jude, tossing it to him. "I tried it out already, on the trip; whittled sticks for toasting marshmallows and cleaned fish and such."

"Course, it's sharp," said Cale. "It's new. Mine's kind of dull. I got to get Daddy to sharpen it proper for me one of these days."

Dace opened up the longest blade and tested it with his thumb. "Ow, it's sharp, all right." He stuck his thumb in his mouth.

Jude drew a sharp breath and shivered. He glanced up, but the sun was shining bright and strong; no cloud had covered it, nothing to account for the sudden chill.

"I wish we'd gone with you, or you'd stayed here," Cale rambled on. "We're like the three musketeers. All for one and one for all. It ain't the same without all three of us."

"That's what I was thinking," agreed Jude.

"Like blood brothers," said Dace. "Hey, cool! Let's be blood brothers!"

"That means we got to mingle our blood, like in stories?" Cale said dubiously.

Jude sat up slowly, suddenly apprehensive, for some inexplicable reason. "Reckon we ought to?"

"Sure," Dace said. "We can use your new knife."

"Rad," said Cale. "Then nothing can separate us, ever. I always wished I had brothers. If I had my pick, it'd be you two. Let's go for it now, while the girls ain't here."

"Course. No girls allowed," said Dace. "As for brothers, I got more than enough, but they're already my blood." He tossed the knife to Cale. "Here, dude, my thumb's already bleeding. Your turn."

"How'd they do this again?" said Cale, blanching. "Er, Jude, it's your knife. You want to go next?"

Jude shrugged, trying to act natural. "You got the knife. I'll go after."

"Chicken, Cale?" laughed Dace, a little wildly.

"I ain't chicken," scoffed Cale. "Here goes nothing." He cut his finger. Blood welled up, and he held out the knife. "Your turn."

Jude inhaled sharply and stared at the ruby red droplet glistening against the pale skin. Something stirred inside him.

"Jude, the knife!"

Jude started. "Oh, yeah," he said, a little discomfited, not quite sure what had happened there for a moment. He took the knife and pressed the blade's edge against his finger. A faint line of blood appeared and dripped. "Okay, now what?" He felt unaccountably breathless, couldn't think straight, for some reason.

"We mingle our blood and say 'blood brothers forever,' and swear to stand by each other till death," Dace said.

As though in slow motion, Jude reached out his bleeding finger to those of his friends. They touched, and their blood mingled. With a snap and a crackle, the boys' laughter faded into the background, and Jude quivered as a jolt went through him. He stared at the blot of crimson on his finger.

Or a jewel that caught the light. Ruby red flame shot out and danced across the walls. *No, wait; that was a dream. It's not the Ring; it's blood.* Its scent seemed to catch in his throat, and his heart leaped. A pounding filled his head, like wild drums beating—*oh, how he longed to taste*—the very sight of that red droplet blasted him with a rush of ecstasy so sweet, so ferocious he thought his heart would burst. He wanted it to never end. Wanted to live forever, wanted to die. *Forever… forever…*

"Jude, say it! Say 'blood brothers forever'!" Cale and Dace's shouts finally penetrated the sweet red-gold haze that enveloped him. "Jude! What are you doing? Why are your eyes glowing? Jude?"

Glowing? He cast them down at once and shuddered with the effort of coming back to reality. "Blood brothers forever," he managed, slowly, with great difficulty. Forever... forever... The words kept echoing through his mind. His heart was pounding. He dared not face his friends. *What had he done? What had he been about to do?*

Then they were laughing and clapping him on the back, oblivious of danger. "We done it!" Dace laughed, and Cale shouted, "We're blood brothers, forever and ever. Wicked, man! Nobody can separate us now, ever. Right, Jude?"

"Yeah." Jude slowly lifted his gaze to meet theirs. *Unless I kill us all. Wicked is maybe right. What the heck's wrong with me? I nearly — what was I doing? Blood?* He shuddered at the image that loomed like a monster from his subconscious and quickly repressed it. "Let's, er, let's go up top, okay?" Without waiting for a reply, he turned abruptly and started toward the peak.

From where Jude stood balancing on the highest point, he could see for miles around. His friends puffed and grumbled and finally caught up.

"Man, would you look at that?" Dace panted, as he reached the top and squinted into the distance. "I never noticed that house there before, the one with the little windmill. Or that red one over there, with the tall blue flowers. Cool!" He pointed.

"You're right," said Cale. "Where'd that come from? And that horse barn with the pasture full of Tennessee Walkers just to the left of it. See that — where that sign above the gateposts says 'Calloway's Double-H Ranch'?"

Jude gave them a quizzical glance. "What're you talking about? They've always been there." *But only I could see them at this distance*, he realized. Had something sharpened their eyesight all of a sudden? Made it like... his? That ruby red drop came to mind, for some reason. A frightening thought. He shot a glance at his friends, but they seemed oblivious, agog as they were at this unexpected phenomenon. Well, he certainly wasn't about to say anything. *Anyhow, maybe it wasn't... that.*

Jude spread out his arms and closed his eyes, reveling in the sunshine hot on his face and the wonderful wide spaces and the warm breezes that ruffled his hair and plastered his shirt against his body. It helped him forget whatever it was, whatever had happened to him at the museum. He shivered at the memory of the cold feeling in the pit of his stomach; or was it his heart, dead? *No. No.* Where had that come from?

For some reason best left unexplored for now, he dreaded the loss of light and warmth and space (as if such a thing were possible). He'd never been afraid of the dark before, nor had cold ever caused him discomfort. Until the visit to the museum. Ever since then, he'd felt that he'd never be warm enough again, that there'd never be enough sunshine. Or space. Walls seemed to close in on him sometimes, making him mad to escape. To fly — *no, not that*! In the effort to shove the thought from his mind, he swayed on his precarious perch.

"Jude! What are you doing? You can't fly, you know," Dace said, only half-joking. "You okay?" His tone was touched with concern.

Jude started and opened his eyes. "Uh, yeah, sure." He let his eyes rove the countryside. *What am I? Well, whatever. Be tough. Be a man.* Grandpa! Grandpa would know the answers, if anyone did. Grandpa always came up with little sayings and words of wisdom out of the blue, even when you were unable to articulate a question. He looked forward to visiting Grandpa again soon.

Josie's Lament

Clayhurst Crossing, BC. Spring 1869

Bella narrowed her eyes in suspicion. Why would Nyx create a diversion so that I can bring in the prize? So she may gain the glory? She ground her teeth. *No – not this time!*

The girl seemed to weigh nothing at all as she carried her deep into the labyrinth. All was black as pitch down here, but that was no inconvenience to Bella, who could see in the dark, as all vampires could. For Josie, it was a different story; she clutched at Bella's cloak, terrified. Until they rounded a curve of the passage and a flickering light appeared up ahead; only then did she ease up on the death-grip. It was from an open door that tongues of light danced out across the floor of the passage onto the opposite wall.

Bella carried Josie through the doorway into the small chamber especially prepared for her, where a fire snapped and crackled in the hearth—the source of the light. On the walls were daubed garish primary colors in geometric shapes and concentric circles, as though by some mad painter. Against one of the walls stood a narrow bed with a bright new woolen Hudson's Bay blanket folded at its foot, and a bookcase against the opposite wall. In the center of the room was a small table with two chairs.

Most mortal guests did not enjoy the privilege of an individual room but were merely lavishly wined and dined, then invited to the Great Hall to serve as entrées for their ravenous hosts. A few were turned; others died. Those who survived were invariably eager to return. No, Josie was not one of them; she was a special case, Bella knew, requiring particular care.

Bella gently placed the girl on the bed. Josie clung to her arm and lifted frightened eyes to meet hers. "I want to go home."

"In good time, *chica*," Bella soothed.

"My name's Josie," the girl corrected her bravely, even as tears traced lines in the smudges of dirt on her face.

Bella smoothed the hair back from her brow and her little round ears. So cute. Not like pointed vampire ears. And that pulse... She shook the thought away. The girl must be tidied up, her face washed and *¡ay!* her hair was a rat's nest after the flight through the bush! Her clothing was somewhat the worse for wear too.

"Sleep now. Sleep," Bella crooned softly. She dared not chance the girl wandering off while she went to find a dress and wash water. Terror and excitement had taken its toll. Josie fell under the spell of the vampire voice. Her eyes closed.

When Bella returned, Josie was still asleep. She washed the girl's face and combed her long hair with her own jeweled tortoiseshell comb. She removed the thick gray sweater and torn calico frock and dressed the girl in an elegant white gown (Charon preferred that virgins wear white).

Josie didn't stir but lay still and beautiful as a princess waiting for Prince Charming to wake her with a kiss. How pleased the master would be! But it was cool underground, even in summer, and mortals tended to suffer from cold, Bella knew. The white dress was silky, not warm at all. She covered the girl with the blanket, closed the door to shut out the draft, and stirred up the fire; warmth spread through the room.

Bella gazed at the sleeping form, fascinated by the rise and fall of the coverlet with each breath. A good sign. It was important that the captive feel safe and happy. Charon liked them willing. Maybe their innocence protected them somehow? But why would anyone want to resist the master? In any case, he always got what he wanted.

She pulled up a chair and sat beside the bed. Josie would need reassurance when she awoke. *¡Ay de mi!* Her own uncle betrayed her! Bella wondered uneasily if Little Lulu had killed him. Nyx would not be pleased. But as long as Charon was, that was what mattered, she assured herself.

She sensed a vampire's approach, heard the whisper of a cloak. Instantly alert, she sprang to the door and looked out. Rojo! He'd survived!

His progress was slow and labored. When he caught sight of her, he moaned, "Help me. This arrow in my back, it hurts, oh, it hurts."

She glanced back as Josie stirred in her sleep. "Shh. Don't wake her."

He cast his eyes down, his brow creasing in reproach at her lack of sympathy. (Rojo was so melodramatic!) After several pathetic moments of trying without success to reach the horrid feathered shaft protruding from the middle of his back, he finally lifted tragic eyes to her face. "Please." Softly, wary of Bella's temper.

Well. He'd taken the arrow for her, after all. She went to him and, with deft fingers, took hold of the fletched end. It had missed his heart and lodged against a rib. "Fine. Just don't yell; the girl is asleep. And no biting; I am not in the mood."

His claws tightened on her arms as she shifted the arrow and thrust the sharpened flat triangle of silver out between two ribs. A whimper escaped him as the shaft followed, shining with black blood. He ground his teeth and fell to his knees.

"Here is your trophy," she said briskly. "You should be proud. Shot by the Huntress and still able to tell the tale." He closed his eyes and turned away but took the arrow. "I saw," she said in a softer tone. "That arrow was for me. Sleep, now, and heal."

He stood gingerly and regarded the deadly shaft in his hand. "Damn! That hurt! I swear, next time, I'll put this arrow into her!"

Bella gave him a thumbs-up as he crept away down the corridor. When she re-entered the chamber, the girl was awake, her eyes wide with fear. The quickened heartbeat drew Bella; she shook herself. "Are you warm enough, *niña*?"

"When can I go home?" Josie countered.

"Later," Bella lied, "After you are presented to Charon."

"Charon? What is that?"

"The master." No comment. "You are hungry? There is food." Josie shook her head. Bella went on cheerily, "I combed your hair and brought you a lovely new dress."

Josie's eyes were like those of a frightened deer. She tugged at the blanket, trying to cover her bare shoulders. When Bella moved to tuck it around her, she cringed.

"I won't hurt you," Bella said, but the girl's eyes remained fixed on her, big and scared. Bella sat beside her on the bed and smoothed her hair. The girl sat very still. "When I first meet Charon, ay, he is so handsome and charming—to know him is to love him, I promise." Bella noticed that the girl was not reassured. "But then you may go home."

"Why are you still here, then?"

The question caught Bella by surprise. "I, er, I wanted to stay." (Better not to mention that Charon never let you go.)

"I'd like to go home now," the girl said in a rush. "I want my mom and dad. I—I don't want to meet him."

Bella kept her voice soft. "After. I promise."

Why do you lie to her?

What the hell? Who said that? ¡Ay de mi! What is the matter with me? Bella dashed a hand across her eyes to clear her mind of the disturbing thoughts; those waves of unaccountable emotion couldn't possibly be her own.

Josie's eyes filled with tears. "I—I'm afraid."

Bella composed herself with an effort. "Shhh. Dry the tears. Charon will not be pleased with the weeping."

Josie sat up and scrubbed her cheeks. As she did so, the blanket fell from her shoulders. Mortified, she clutched it in front of her. "Where's my sweater? And my own dress? I hate this one."

Bella allowed her some space for her little rebellion. "The sweater is dirty and your dress is torn. You must wear this one."

"I don't want this dress. It's too bare." Josie's implacable expression was disconcertingly like that of the Huntress.

As if that will matter where you are going, you little —! Bella gritted her teeth, but caught herself and forced a smile. "It's dark. No one will see." Did she know everyone here could see in the dark?

Josie got off the bed. She wasn't very tall; the dress covered her feet. So sweet and innocent. How would her blood taste?

"Stop staring at me like that!" Now there was fire in those eyes.

"Y-you look so like an angel," stammered Bella, unsure if she had flicked out her tongue. "The dress, it is very pretty on you."

"I hate it, and—and I hate those ugly scribbles on the walls! And—and I don't want to see Charon. Ever!" Josie sulked for a moment. Then, "What is this place? Where am I?"

Bella smiled. "You are nearer to home than you think, but farther than you can imagine."

The girl frowned. "Riddles. Father says the devil speaks in riddles to deceive."

Priest! Bella thought furiously, then forced a laugh. "¡*Caramba!* Charon will not be able to resist those big dark eyes of yours."

At that moment, Bella sensed the approach of more vampires. She went to the door. The crew was back; those that had survived. She watched the ragged procession flow past. Harried, haunted, they slunk toward the throne room where Charon awaited. Even the Prince was haggard and drawn, his eyes filled with pain. That conjured up horrid images in Bella's mind about what must have happened out there. That the mighty Prince should be wounded! With a shiver, she reflected upon how the weapons of the Huntress caused vampires so much hurt, beyond the natural. They were composed of materials like silver and ashwood that warded against evil, it was said, and worst of all, were blessed by a priest.

Nyx remained as the others disappeared from sight. "Let's see what we've got. It better be worth it."

Bella's anger flared. Nyx always managed to cut her down with a word or a look. With a silent snarl at Nyx's back, she followed her into the chamber.

Josie stood at the hearth. She glanced up as they entered. Bella stared, transfixed. A vision, radiant in white, with hair black as night, star-bright eyes and golden skin; if only she could remain so, always. But a mortal was too fragile to survive the ritual.

Oh, why do I feel such sorrow, such pain? How can I bring this doom upon a girl so innocent and alive, as I once was? Bella tore her gaze from Josie, horrified. How could she think such a thing? What had the girl done to her? Then she realized; the thought, the feeling, had come from within. But no — it couldn't possibly be her own. *I like what I am. I wouldn't change if I could.* She shook herself, a little frightened, hoping Nyx hadn't noticed.

But Nyx's eyes were on the girl. She couldn't fail to be impressed, surely. After her initial inspection, she smiled at Josie. " I have sent for refreshment." She indicated a chair, and Josie sat down at once, staring at her with huge dark eyes.

Of course, Nyx had mesmerized the girl without a thought. Her expertise far exceeded Bella's considerable talents in that line. That ever pricked at her pride. She snarled behind Nyx's back. Nyx proceeded to do with ease what Bella had been stumbling over. She sat at the table with Josie and soon had her confiding in her, telling of her hopes and dreams. Her tears dried; she seemed to have forgotten her predicament.

Bella could see Nyx taking all credit. Though furious, she dared not show it, but subsided ungraciously to sit on the bed and nurse her injured dignity. Better that than to entirely surrender the field to Nyx. She'd watch and await her chance. Cautiously. Nyx would tolerate no rebellion — even the thought of it — as Bella had long ago learned.

Tiny Tina appeared in the doorway, holding a crystal goblet in trembling hands. Nyx signaled. "Bring it here, wench."

Tina rushed in and set the glass on the table. Water slopped out as she did so. She fluttered despairingly.

Nyx froze her with a look. "Get out! Bella, clean up this mess."

Tina fled. With a strained smile, Bella leaped to her task. Nyx turned back to the girl. Josie eyed the glass apprehensively. She was assuredly more used to tin cups than crystal goblets.

"You must be thirsty," Nyx suggested, smiling. "Have some fresh spring water while you await your dinner."

Obediently the girl drank it to the last drop, then regarded the cup with an expression of distaste. "There's sand in it!"

"These underground springs," Nyx said, with a dismissive wave of her hand. Bella went weak with relief at Nyx's look of satisfaction. The girl had passed the test, unfazed by the emerald powder stirred into her drink. Innocent, then. Nyx lost no time in verifying her fears. "It is well for you, Bellatrix, that she is suitable."

It was all Bella could do not to throw herself at her in a frenzy of rage. She showed her teeth in a silent snarl. Fortunately, Nyx had turned back to Josie.

Nyx drew the girl's gaze to meet hers. "Sleep now." Josie put her head down and fell asleep. Nyx went to the door and was gone.

When Nyx returned sometime later, Bella was glad she had stayed where she was. Had she moved, Nyx would suspect her of touching the girl. Not that she hadn't thought of it. A mortal in such close proximity was hard to resist. Nyx glided over to the table. Bella scowled behind her back; she felt it was her prerogative to present the girl to the master, but she dared not defy Nyx.

Josie raised her head, groggy and bewildered, as Nyx gently touched her shoulder.

"Come," said Nyx softly. Charon will see you now."

Stark terror flashed across the girl's face. "No! I don't want to." She clung to her chair. "Marie! Help me, Marie!"

Bella's every sense came alert. *Marie. Ah, yes, the Huntress.*

"Come, my dear." Nyx took her arm.

Josie jerked away. "Jesus, help me, Jesus, help me, Jesus, help me!"

Bella cringed. Nyx's lips were drawing back in a snarl. Her eyes began to blaze, and her hands formed claws as though she would rip the girl to shreds in a minute. Strange what that Name could do. *No!* It would not do to ruin the plan now.

With a terrible effort, Bella leaned close to murmur into Josie's ear, "You will be fine. I'm with you." Each thrum-thrum of the girl's heart sent a thrill through her until she was nearly undone. She concentrated. "Do not be afraid," she managed. "I am here."

Josie stopped saying the words, and Bella nearly collapsed in relief. The girl's eyes filled with tears as she clung to Bella. Nyx scowled but saw how things had to be. Bella managed not to gloat openly. She dried the girl's tears and took her hand; Nyx followed.

The sound of drumbeats and a wailing, as of lost souls, grew louder as they entered the Great Hall. Josie stopped, perhaps chilled by what must have seemed a vision of hell. A writhing, milling crowd leaped and swayed to an awful yowling and a frenzied beat.

As though upon a signal, all sound abruptly ceased. Vampire eyes instantly fixed on the girl, glowing like fireflies in the dark. Teeth gleamed; tongues whipped out to taste the air. Mortal guests paused to stare. Bella urged the girl forward; Josie gripped her hand tightly and bravely walked through the parted crowd. At last, they reached the foot of the tall throne at the far end of the vast Hall, where the elite lounged around, as was their custom.

Charon gazed down upon them with heavy-lidded eyes, his long white hands stroking the ornately carved arms of the chair, his lips curved slightly into an anticipatory smile. How often had Bella dreamed of this! Surely, he would take notice of her, as well.

She bowed. "Master. I present to you this maiden." His glance flicked to her, just for a second, before settling on Josie.

She should have swooned with rapture. Instead, she felt suddenly cold inside, filled with a nameless dread, as if some terrible force within was about to rend and tear with the claws of a panicked creature desperate to escape. No one else seemed to notice; all eyes were on Josie. Bella swayed, a little dizzy, and swallowed hard. *Now was not the time to...*

Charon beckoned to Josie. "Come to me, little one."

Josie stood as though rooted to the spot, her eyes wide. Like a rabbit hypnotized by a snake, she couldn't tear her gaze away. Charon's eyes glimmered. Bella remembered how it was, and... well, she'd settle for crumbs. She urged the girl forward.

His eyes glowed, and Bella was consumed with envy as she recalled how at one time, she had been the one to set him on fire like this. He picked Josie up and sat her on his lap; his tongue flicked out to taste. She tried to push him away and turned to Bella with reproachful, terrified eyes.

Bella was baffled by her reluctance. Suddenly a wild impulse seized her; it was all she could do not to throw herself between the poor child and the monster on the throne, to save her from her fate. She shuddered in an effort to rid herself of this madness before anyone saw; she quickly glanced around. *¡Ay de mi!* But no one else seemed to notice. She turned once more to Charon and his prey.

With exquisite claws, he drew Josie's hair away from her neck. And she was resisting! Oh, the injustice of it! (Bella would gladly have exchanged places with her.) Of course, resistance was futile. Josie whimpered as he bit. That brought back memories of those long-ago nights when —

She felt a hand on her arm and spun around. *Nyx*?!

Utter confusion, and then the realization that she — how long had she stood there gazing up at him in naked longing? Mortified, she glanced around. But no one else was paying attention to her. The band was playing again — violins and accordions, as well as the ancient instruments Charon had brought over from the Old Country — and all were caught up in that hypnotic drumbeat, dancing and feeding... and whatever took their fancy.

"I must wake Rojo," she said inanely. "He'll miss the party."

"Let him rest," Nyx said. "We'll need everyone in prime condition. With the Huntress on the prowl, Charon's big event will seem a long time coming."

For the first time, Bella clearly saw the looming danger. Two months! And the Huntress would stop at nothing to rescue the girl.

Kidnapped

Jude pushed the droning lawnmower across Miz Lily's yard. His mama had dropped him off to mow Miz Lily's grass and trim the hedges while she ran some errands. He was to meet her at Whiskery Ned's general store after he finished. He worked through the hot afternoon, so taken up in daydreaming that he was oblivious to either the sweet fragrances of new-mown grass and full-blown roses or the occasional harsh whiff of exhaust.

Daisy was coming home this weekend!

People came and went, mostly mothers bringing their children to borrow books from the library, which Miz Lily operated out of her home. A few ladies dropped by for tea (Miz Lily loved company and always had the teakettle on). Some of them waved at Jude, and he nodded back, conversation being impossible over the noise. This was a small rural community where everyone knew everyone else.

So, he was a bit surprised when a sleek black Lincoln Town Car with tinted windows and a lot of chrome cruised up and stopped. It flashed in the sunlight as the doors opened, and three men emerged. Jude couldn't help staring. It was like they'd stepped straight out of a movie!

The driver had dark curly hair and a swarthy complexion; he wore his light sport shirt and slacks with flair. As he reached up to adjust his sunglasses, a diamond in his onyx signet ring flashed; bulging biceps strained at his sleeves. His jaw and physique were those of a Marvel Comics superhero. With a casual look around, he strutted up the walk. A smaller man in a narrow-brimmed hat and a gray summer jacket got out of the passenger side. He resembled a weasel, or maybe a hitman from an old gangster movie. Furtively he glanced around, then slunk after the driver. A third man clambered from the back seat. His loud Hawaiian shirt was stretched almost to bursting across his heavy chest and shoulders. Sunlight glinted off his shaved head and a lone silver earring as he briefly scanned the area; then, with an ape-like stride, he followed the others.

None of them gave Jude a second glance as he made his noisy rounds of the lawn. He wondered absently what had brought them to this little out-of-the-way library. They didn't seem the bookish type or the kind that would drop by for tea with Miz Lily.

The sun was a great bronze disc hanging halfway to the horizon by the time Jude locked up the garden shed and knocked on Miz Lily's back door to let her know he was finished with the work. After a long wait, he was about to knock again when quick footsteps approached from within. The door opened, and Miz Lily peered out at him with bright, birdlike eyes and a forced smile.

"Oh, there you are, dear boy. Finished already?" She sounded a little out of breath, as though she'd run all the way to the door. "Thank you so much." She pressed some bills into his hand. "Your mama will be expecting you at Ned's store right smart now." With that, she closed the door firmly in his face before he could say a word.

He started down the road, puzzling, casting a glance back over his shoulder a time or two. Miz Lily hadn't even invited him in for a cold drink after working the whole afternoon in the hot sun! He'd been looking forward to a glass of her homemade iced tea. His mouth was dry, his throat parched. How unlike her to rush him off without even a drink of water!

He stopped and turned. The black car still sat at the curb in front of the library, now partly shaded by the trees across the road. Could Miz Lily's odd behavior have something to do with those strangers? They had appeared rather sinister, and no one else was around. The book-borrowers had come and gone.

He considered going back to see if Miz Lily was okay. What if the men were crooks, holding her hostage? He shook his head. No, he was letting his imagination run wild again; his teachers had often complained about that. Anyhow, this wasn't your classic getaway car, in movies, at least. Too flashy. And Mama expected him to meet her at the store. Miz Lily would scold him if he went back, for worrying his mama. And Mama would worry if he was late. What could a twelve-year-old kid do, anyhow? He'd tell Mama; she'd think of something.

He hurried on, turning his mind to more pleasant thoughts. Like Daisy. Only a few more days and she'd be home! He'd tell her about his trip. About fun stuff, like the Hamlet play, the wildlife they saw, the hot springs they swam in, and moose along the road. And about the other things—some of them, anyhow.

Not that thing that had happened in the museum. *No, never.*

Anyhow, he couldn't recall what it was, exactly (didn't want to, really). But ever since then, it seemed his recurring episodes and dreams were no longer the entertaining, childish fairy tales they'd once been. They'd darkened and become bleak and forbidding. More often now, he saw that girl; that fair damsel carried off by—not a dragon, maybe, but some fell beast. He never could quite see what it was. But her face was etched in his mind; so real, he'd know her if he saw her. He was sure of it.

It was up to him to save her from—*what*? Could it be that vampire he'd seen in his dream of that castle in the land of Grimm? Charon. He shivered at the thought. Sometimes he got the feeling it would spring right out of his nightmare and into the real world. What that had to with the Indian maid pleading to him from the abyss, he had no idea, but it was connected somehow, he knew. And why did he get the feeling that the fate of the world lay in his hands? Impossible—that could never happen! Maybe it was just his imagination again. But his dreams often seemed so real.

The purring of a motor jarred him from his reverie. He glanced around just as a black car rounded the curve. He stepped off the asphalt onto the gravel shoulder to give the vehicle plenty of room. It didn't pass but instead slowed and came to a halt beside him. It was the Lincoln Town Car he'd seen at Miz Lily's.

Ah, so they weren't holding Miz Lily hostage after all. Still, when the driver's window hummed open, and the sleek, angular face turned toward him, Jude stepped back warily. The diamond flashed from the hand at the wheel. Sunglasses hid the man's eyes; his smile was false.

"Excuse me, sonny," he said in a hearty tone. "Mrs. Longstreet says you can show us the way to the monastery."

"You know Miz Lily?" said Jude, relieved. *So that's why they're here*, he thought innocently, laughing inwardly at how far his wild imagination had gone astray.

"Lee suggested we stop by his Aunt Lily's for directions," the man explained. "She pointed you out and said if we could catch you, you'd show us the way."

Jude remembered Miz Lily mentioning a nephew Lee. And this wouldn't be the first time he'd had to direct someone to the monastery. City people tended to get lost easy in these parts. Well. Luckily, he hadn't run back to Miz Lily like Chicken Little crying that the sky was falling.

But why had Miz Lily hurried him off like that? She never passed up the chance to chat over tea, iced or otherwise. Even if he was a kid. He leaned down a bit and saw the weasel-like man staring at him from the front passenger seat with bleak, gray eyes too close together; his lips were thin, almost sneering. At that moment, the back door opened, and the bald man stepped out, smiling broadly. The smile seemed like it was pasted on.

"Just scoot on in the back with Joey there," said the driver.

The big bald man nodded vigorously, still smiling.

Jude belatedly remembered Mama warning him not to ride with strangers. "My mama's waiting—" he began, hesitantly. Then again, if Miz Lily'd told them…

Joey gave a great flourish and a bow, indicating the back seat. "Won't take long," he rumbled. "Aunt Lily says it's not far, and you look like a smart kid."

"Yeah, just up the highway a bit, then turn right at—" Jude sighed. *Smart, yeah;* didn't look as though he could say the same for them. But if they were friends of Miz Lily's nephew… "Oh, all right. But Mama'll have your hides if I'm late."

They laughed heartily, as though he'd told a joke.

"You just hop right in here, kid," Joey said.

Jude climbed in, misgivings allayed by awe at the soft leather seats and luxurious red interior. What must it be like to be rolling in dough? Even Whiskery Ned's old Caddy wasn't this ritzy. And it was so cool compared to the summer heat outside; that must be air-conditioning. Mama would love that. Someday he'd buy her a car like this, of her very own. No more old clunker of a pickup truck for his mama, hot in summer and cold in winter, that broke down at the most inconvenient times, so she had to poke her head under the hood and tinker with it to get it going again. She wasn't a mechanic like Grandpa. Jude vowed that from now on, he'd pay more attention to what Dace's daddy tried to teach them about cars. One day he'd take that chore off his mama's hands.

So enraptured was he that he was unaware of the self-satisfied smirks on the men's faces. Joey closed his door and climbed in on the other side. The motor purred, and the locks clicked shut. The car rode smoothly, even over bumps in the highway. Jude basked in the luxury, imagining himself as some high-class dude. Too bad Mama wasn't here. It was almost like flying.

Hey, wait a minute. Jude straightened up to peer over the driver's shoulder. The speedometer gauge had leaped up alarmingly fast. "Better slow down," he advised. "You'll need to take a right at that turnoff up ahead there."

"Got it," said the driver, but he didn't slow down.

The turn was coming up fast. Jude pointed. "There it is. It's real sharp."

"I hear you, man," the driver said as he sailed past.

"Hey, you missed it," said Jude, a little exasperated. "I told you. Now you got to go back. There's a pullout just ahead, past that curve," he added helpfully.

"You just settle down, boy, and buckle up. We're in for a lo-o-o-ong ride."

"Here you go," said the big bald man, indicating the seat belt.

Jude stared at the man in disbelief, trying to sort things out. His gaze slid to the two men in front; they stared straight ahead.

"But the monastery. It's… didn't you say…?"

The weasel glanced around and laughed unpleasantly. "Just don't give us no lip, kid, and we'll get along fine. Joey, buckle him up. Move it, Paco," he said to the driver.

Joey reached for the seatbelt. Alarmed, Jude tried the door handle; it didn't budge.

"Joey, deal with him," said Paco in a tone of warning.

Jude stared around wildly, his heart racing.

"Just calm down, kid, and let me—" began Joey, pushing him back so he could draw the seatbelt across.

Jude's heart leaped into his throat. He wasn't used to being manhandled, and this was a stranger, to boot. The beefy hand pressed against his chest. He pushed the brawny arm aside, surprising the big man as much as he did himself. The seatbelt flipped back to its starting point. Joey's expression was suddenly grim; he leaned over and pressed Jude against the seat with a forearm like Popeye's, nearly crushing him with his weight as he attempted to buckle him in. Jude tried to wriggle out of the man's grip, without success.

He kicked out wildly, fighting panic, remembering what Grandpa had told him: animals panic; people use their brains to reason out what to do.

"Damn it, Paco, slow down till I get this wildcat buckled up," Joey grumbled. "Stay put, kid, damn you."

Paco swore a blue streak and stomped on the gas pedal. "We're on a schedule here, Joey. We wasted enough time back there with Granny and her tea."

Jude took advantage of Joey's distraction to dive for the door and yank at the handle again. It had to open! Nothing happened; it stayed locked.

A hand gripped his hair, dragging him back. He whipped around to flail at Joey. Surprised, the man eased up on his grip momentarily, and Jude flipped over to make another dive at the door. He scrabbled at the lock; it wouldn't open. Joey grunted as Jude's foot caught him in the stomach and growled as his head got slammed against the other door.

"What the hell's wrong with you, knucklehead?" snarled the weasel. "Can't you deal with one measly kid?"

"He ain't a kid; he's a cyclone." Joey cursed and lunged for Jude again.

"Damn it, Dobbs, tell him to stop the car and help me out here."

Suddenly the man had him in a bear hug. In renewed panic, Jude jabbed his elbows one-two into Joey's ribs and got a surprised grunt, but the big arms tightened around him. *No, Grandpa said not to panic.*

He panicked.

A blue light flickered along the doors; all their hair stood on end. With a sharp snap and a boom, a hole appeared in the roof of the car, blackened around the edges. The smell of phosphorous lingered in the air.

"What the—?" Paco cursed and slammed on the brakes.

Dobbs glanced up at the smoking ceiling and croaked out a streak of profanity. Joey stared, and Jude felt his grip loosen. Paco and Dobbs turned toward him. Their expressions left him in no doubt of their intent.

With a panic-stricken glance at the double threat from the front, Jude kicked out. His foot connected with the side window. The glass honeycombed and then disintegrated. Jude slipped like a fish from Joey's arms, flipped over, and was out the window headfirst.

He hit the ground with a thud, the gravel sharp against his shoulder, and the breath nearly knocked out of him. Oblivious to the shower of broken glass pattering around him, he tucked his head in, rolled, and was up and running before the men overcame their shock. He heard shouts behind him. Car doors slammed; boots crunched across the gravel. Fear spurred him on.

He sailed over the ditch, up the bank, and into the woods. The trees were a blur as he flowed between them, dodging branches and gliding over windfalls. Dry leaves rustled faintly at his passing, hardly disturbed by the lightness of his feet. His long strides rapidly put distance between him and his pursuers, who weren't so lucky, judging by the curses and cries of pain gradually diminishing behind him. *City dudes.*

When finally he paused to reconnoiter, he saw that he'd come out on the highway further on. Faintly he heard frustrated shouts and curses and crashing about in the woods, but the voices had to be some distance from the car. They wouldn't be driving just yet. He exhaled slowly. Sarah's Draperies was just down the road. There he'd be safe. Miz Sarah would let him phone Ned's store, and Mama would know what to do.

A quick glance around assured him that the coast was clear. He sprang out onto the road and ran for all he was worth toward Miz Sarah's.

Chimes signaled his entry into the dim, cool drapery shop. A fluttering and twittering of birds greeted him from a tall wicker cage standing just inside the glass door. He couldn't resist poking his finger in and wiggling it. The small yellow birds only twitched, turned bright eyes toward him, and twittered some more. He heard a rustling in the back room. Must be Miz Sarah.

He glanced outside. His pursuers hadn't got this far yet, but the thought that they soon would urged him on. He made his way through a forest of swatches and bolts of drapery fabric, racks of rods and other hardware accessories, past the counter and into a cluttered back room. There, another tall wicker cage housed several budgies in varying colors. They tilted their heads and eyed him curiously as he peered in at them.

"Hi, little guys," he greeted them.

"Hi, guy. Hi, guy," one of the birds answered. The others squawked in unison.

He couldn't help laughing; they were so funny.

"Oh, it's you, Jude," said a soft voice behind him. "Is your mama in here somewhere?"

Jude turned to see the trim elderly woman. "Hi, Miz Sarah. No, she's not. Er, can I use your phone? I need to call her. She's at Whisk—er, I mean, she's at the store getting groceries." He started to tremble, now that he had time to think.

"Of course." She indicated the telephone behind the counter. "Is something wrong?" she added with a little frown of concern.

Jude ran to the window. No black car in sight yet. "Those men—"

"What men?" Miz Sarah hastened to the window and peered out. The parking lot was empty except for her little station wagon, and not a car to be seen on the highway; cows in the field across the road lay about chewing their cuds. "I don't see any men."

"They tried to steal me, but I got away. I didn't know what to do, so I—I ran here." Jude rushed back to the telephone and punched in a number. "Mama? Er, Mr.—uh, Farwell, is my mama there? I mean, is Miz Martel there, please?" There was a long pause; Jude kept glancing toward the window. Finally, he turned his attention back to the phone. "Mama, come quick and get me. Some men are trying to—"

"Jude, honey, quick!" shrilled Miz Sarah. "Give me the phone, please! Get into that closet over there and close the door. Right now!"

As Jude ran for the closet, he glimpsed a shadow falling across the door at the front of the store. The closet door shut behind him just as the chime sounded, and the yellow birds twittered. Miz Sarah was saying into the phone in a low tone, "Mamie, your child's here, come quick! Some men are— I'm calling the sheriff right now!"

A bit later, Jude heard the click of the receiver, and Miz Sarah calling out in a voice loud enough to carry over the racket her birds were making,

"Good afternoon, gentlemen. May I be of assistance this fine day?"

Without a pause came the smooth reply. "Hello, ma'am. You wouldn't have seen a boy come by here just now?" *That was Paco.*

"A boy!" Miz Sarah laughed. "This isn't the kind of store where you'd likely find a boy. Oh, you're serious! Why, have you lost one?"

"Yeah. My nephew," grunted Joey. "You can't miss him; a pretty child. My sister'll kill me if I've lost him."

To Jude, crouching in the clutter of the closet, the voices were a little muffled, but he recognized them and shuddered.

"Oh, dear. That sounds a bit extreme." She tittered with fake laughter like the sounds of her little yellow birds. "You lost him, did you?"

"Well, you see," said Paco. "We had to make a pit stop up the road, when—"

Dobbs rasped out. "Little brat run off chasing a squirrel. Maybe couldn't find his way back to the car. We thought he mighta come in here."

"I'm sorry, I can't help you. But if you leave me your number—?" As she picked up a pen and paper, she noted their hesitation and went on without missing a beat. "Or you could wait here in case he shows up. I've just made a fresh pot of tea."

About that time, Jude heard the familiar rumble of Mama's old pickup. A horn sounded from the parking lot out front, and at once, there was a chorus of super-polite, but hurried regrets at being unable to stay, and the sound of the chimes. Jude opened the door a crack to peek out. The men were gone.

Mama came through the front door, and Jude ran into her arms. "So, what's this all about, son?"

"They're gone, Mama. Soon as you showed up, they high-tailed it out of here. You must have looked pretty scary."

"Actually, the sheriff was right behind me. A flashy black car peeled out of here, and he took off after them. They must have been up to no good— whoever they are. What's this all about?"

"I told the sheriff some suspicious-acting men were in my store," said Miz Sarah. She chuckled. "I even offered them tea, but they were in a mighty big hurry to get out of here. Must be crooks, with that nose for the Law. The sheriff was pretty quick; maybe just down the road when I called. Don't worry; I didn't mention you."

"Who could they be?" Mama said with an anxious frown. "What were they doing here, and—"

"Mamie, I hate to say this," Miz Sarah said. "But, I think those men just tried to kidnap your son."

"Whatever for? We're not rich or famous," said Mama, then went white and added faintly, "Oh, dear." Miz Sarah gave her a quizzical look, but Mama only said, "Thank you, Sarah. That was quick thinking on your part. Really, I've no idea who they are, or why—" Mama seemed to choke up.

"Let's go home, Mama," said Jude, all of a sudden, realizing that a sheriff meant questions. He didn't feel up to explaining things like flashing blue lights and stuff. He'd endured all that sort of thing in the principal's office often enough to guess how it would turn out. People already thought he was a freak. He'd had enough of that.

"Yes, son, I think we ought to," agreed Mama. She turned to Miz Sarah. "Please don't say anything to anyone about this."

"Of course not, Mamie. But if you need help or anything—"

"I just want my child home safe, without getting the law involved. You know what a hassle that can be."

"Are you sure?" said Miz Sarah. "It'd be good to put a public menace like that behind bars."

"With what evidence?" Mama got defensive. "After they traumatize my innocent child with the third degree, they'll say for lack of evidence they can do nothing. No, thanks, Sarah. I prefer we remain off the radar screens of both law enforcement and lawbreakers."

"Of course, Mamie," Miz Sarah agreed meekly. "You're absolutely right. Would you like to stay for a cup of tea?"

"We'd love to," Mama said, "but I left my groceries on the counter at Ned's. I think I'd better rescue them."

Jude waved at Miz Sarah as they drove away.

Shaman's Revenge

When Bella carried Josie from the Great Hall later that night, she was only asleep, not dead. Charon was saving her for the big event. He'd only tasted; other mortals would satisfy his hunger this night.

The fire was crackling; food and drink were on the table. Josie stirred but did not wake as Bella placed her on the bed and tucked the blanket around her. She appeared to sleep more easily now that she was no longer in that disturbing presence. It was Bella who was in a state of excitement. Charon had noticed her! Not as he once had, of course, but... she'd settle for crumbs.

But what had happened back there? Those appalling emotions were not her own! Couldn't be—she was a vampire! Was she picking up on some mortal's feelings?

Bella bustled about, straightening books on the shelves, setting out a deck of cards, a chess game. She could teach Josie to play; chess was the master's favorite. Maybe then she...

Despite her activity, Bella felt herself drawn to the girl and soon was standing by the bed, staring at her. How vulnerable she seemed, lying there asleep. Bella felt the heat of her breath from where she stood; she let herself be taken by the rhythm of her heartbeat. Surely that was allowed. She was not touching her, after all.

Then she was touching her. Her nails slid along the soft cheek to smooth strands of hair away from her brow and her neck. She stopped, her eyes drawn to the flicker of a pulse at her throat. She leaned down slowly and felt the hunger leap within her, strong and wild. No! She sprang back. That was a sure path to destruction.

She flung herself out the door, locked it, and stood trembling at the close call. She hurried to the Great Hall, desperate to sink her teeth into a mortal. Only then would she be able to resist.

Bella returned sometime later, aglow, and feeling warm and alive, almost. She'd been quite piggish enough to put even Pinkie to shame. But she dared not take chances. When she got to the door, she fumbled at her belt for the key, and remembered to dab at her mouth and chin with a handkerchief, wiping away any bloodstains.

But what's this? A low murmur from inside the room brought her up short. Josie, talking? Bella strained to hear. Dire possibilities flashed through her mind. Charon would not be pleased if anything untoward befell his new treasure. If Josie was not alone — Bella was the one with the key, and it would be her head on the block if…

On the verge of panic, she opened the door. The atmosphere felt heavy, oppressive. Struck by some unnamed terror, she turned to flee. *No, stop.* She forced down the panic and glanced around. There was no one except Josie, kneeling by the bed. Praying — *no, not that!* Bella closed the door behind her and locked it. Terrified of being trapped in the Presence of this — this —

"Josie," she managed. "Don't do that."

Josie jumped, startled. She got to her feet and stared. "Are you — Who — ?" she began uncertainly.

"You know me. Bella."

"Bella? But you, you seem so —"

And she realized. After feeding, she must appear less gaunt, with maybe a bit of color. "Yes. Just do not — you know."

"What? Oh, pray, you mean?" At Bella's short nod, Josie gave her a strange lost look. "Why not?"

"I cannot — just don't, please." How she hated to beg!

"But, but I —" The girl's lips trembled.

"Don't cry. I will not leave you; just think of me as your mother," Bella babbled, so relieved was she at the lightening of the atmosphere as soon as Josie was distracted from her prayers.

The girl's chin went up. "I don't need you to be my mother. I'm fourteen. And I already have a mother. She taught me to pray when I'm afraid. You maybe wouldn't hurt so much if you prayed."

Bella was indignant (she wasn't hurt!), then touched. The girl seemed genuinely concerned. "Believe me, it will not cure what ails me." Startled by her own words, she stammered a bit in confusion. Josie was staring, perplexed, so she smiled a little.

Maybe it was the smile, but Josie seemed to relax. She sat on the edge of the bed and frowned. "I woke up and was afraid, so I knelt to pray. Was it only a dream? But there's blood here on my dress, see? And, oh, my neck hurts." She reached up beneath the long hair, gingerly rubbed the back of her neck, and winced. Her dark eyes turned to Bella, trusting, for some reason.

"Yes, I see." Bella went to reach for something on the top shelf. "Here, we'll try this." She opened a small jar of yellow ointment.

Josie pulled her hair aside and bowed her head as Bella applied the remedy. "Oh. It feels better already."

"Of course. Letha mixes herbs from her garden and the forest to make medicines."

"My grandmother is like that," said the girl. With a sigh, she added, "Can I leave now? You said after—"

"Just as soon as Charon gives the word," Bella said. Josie opened her mouth to protest, but Bella cut in briskly. "Look. All the food you can eat." With a sweeping gesture, she indicated the laden table and the entire room. "And things to do. See, there are books, games, paints, brushes." She smiled as she gestured to the wild wall art. "You could create something better than that. And here are paper and pens; you may even write a journal if you like." Josie was growing more distressed, so Bella rushed on. "I know it's cold. We have made a fire and put a pretty blanket on your bed."

Josie burst into tears. "But I want to go home."

Nonplussed, Bella put an arm around her tentatively and stroked her hair. "I'm here. Cry all you want. I understand." She was pleased to find that she could hold this mortal body close without feeling the temptation to bite. Well, only a little. She murmured comforting words, and gradually the girl quieted. "That strange feeling you have," Bella said softly, "is a sign of Charon's favor. What a wonderful privilege it is to be so chosen."

Josie frowned. "I can't remember," she said, almost apologetically. "But no, it's something bad. And I'm... afraid."

"There's no need." Bella patted her. "Trust me. The rapture you'll experience is beyond imagining, if only you—" Josie's doubtful frown cut into her fantasies. "What I mean is," she amended, "Well—just do as he bids, and you will see."

"I don't know... No! Whatever he did, it was evil!" Josie furiously dashed tears from her eyes.

Bewildered by such vehemence, Bella fumbled in her pockets for a kerchief. Truly, she didn't understand the girl. "*Ay, mi querida*. No one can resist him. Why should you be different?"

Josie lifted dark eyes to meet Bella's; they were forlorn and sad. "But it's a sin! I need to see Father, to go to confession."

This caught Bella by surprise; she gnashed her teeth. Fortunately, Josie had cast her own eyes down, so she didn't notice. Bella managed to speak calmly. "Really, there is no need."

"But there is," the girl said slowly. "I feel this evil, like a great shadow eagle, coming over me."

"What if I teach you to play chess?" Bella offered. "Charon will perhaps be pleased if you challenge him to a game."

She felt the girl's great sorrowful eyes upon her as she set up the game. But Josie caught on quickly and seemed to forget her sorrows for a time. While they played, they talked. Bella was pleased to discover that Josie had started writing a journal and had made wonderfully lifelike sketches on paper. On the following days, the girl took up the paints and brushes and began to fill every available wall space.

Bella was the one who fetched the girl for Charon on the nights the summons came. It was she who consoled Josie afterward when the girl awoke wailing from nightmares. Words seemed to bring no comfort; Josie only wept the more. Bella could only shake her head.

She had begun to find herself actually enjoying the girl's company. They settled into a routine. Bella was amazed at Josie's painting. She would have liked to read the journal too, but it repelled her as though warded somehow.

Charon did eventually play a game of chess with Josie, but that was not his real interest. Each session with the master seemed to bring her to the edge of despair, but if Bella left her to herself for a time, she would find the girl more at peace upon her return. In her eyes would be less resignation and more fire of resistance, no doubt due to her reliance on prayer, Bella guessed, unhappily.

Then Charon decided to share his Josie-girl with the Prince. From then on, her eyes were haunted anew. Bella groaned with longing; to Josie, he was a nightmare. Charon could mesmerize at a glance, but the Prince—! A mortal had only to glimpse his face or hear his voice to be instantly enraptured. Josie had no words for it, but Bella knew. Not even vampires were unaffected by his charm.

Bella watched the Prince receive the summons to the throne. He spoke but one word, and a tear spilled from Josie's eye in an agony of self-reproach as she reached out to him. He took up one of her hands as though to kiss it, turned it over, and sank his teeth into her wrist; his eyes glowed like wind-blown embers, while Charon observed with heavy-lidded eyes. Bella tingled with the expectation of what he would do next; she'd settle for second-hand thrills.

"Hey, cool it, Bella. Nyx is watching." The voice at her elbow made her jump.

"Don't sneak up on me, Rojo!" she snapped.

Rojo laughed. "I've been standing here like forever, while you —"

"Watch your tongue, or I'll rip it out!" she snarled.

Rojo jerked back, his mouth clacking shut. With a swirl of her cape, Bella turned from his pleading gaze and stormed to the far end of the Great Hall. One glimpse of her glowering face cleared the way through the crowd on the dance floor. But at the door, she stopped short. She dared not be hungry later when attending to the captive. Resolutely she turned and scanned the crowd for a victim.

That night in the chamber, Bella was enthralled as Josie confided her woes, though she managed an appearance of sympathy. *No one could resist the Prince's charm*, she assured her. Still, Josie accused herself. Bella could not countenance it.

When her tears had dried, Josie resolved that next time would be different. But that was a vain hope. It was always the same.

And the Prince smiled coldly through it all.

It turned out that Lulu hadn't killed the shaman. He came back one dark night to exact payment. Bella was waiting for him. It would be her pleasure to send him to that other world of which he was so enamored.

She should have suspected something when he demanded his reward without groveling. But how was she to know of the power of the shaman? Mortals posed little threat to vampires under ordinary circumstances. Except for the Huntress and the holy ones of God, which the shamans were not — and that was about all she knew of shamans. She had no idea that this one's link to the spirit world was an evil deeper than her own.

When she set upon him, he didn't resist. She thought nothing of it since one bite commonly creates in the victim a desire for more. Until she tasted bitterness. She sprang back, hissing and spitting. A terrible weakness came over her, and she fell to the ground.

The shaman fixed her with cold, reptilian eyes. "You try to kill me, vampire? Now I take your head. Vampire skull is good medicine." He drew out a bone-handled obsidian knife.

She stared at the shiny black blade in the rough brown hand. What was this thing that appeared to be a man but had blood to poison a vampire? He'd seemed normal when she bit him before. Numbness crept over her, a tingling sleepiness in every limb. She watched in helpless horror as he put the blade to her throat.

Suddenly the knife flew out of his hand. Bella couldn't move but lay staring up through the leafy canopy to the stars above. Soon a curtain of blackness began to obscure her vision.

"Why do you turn on us, shaman?" she heard Nyx say, as though from very far away. "I promised you the reward."

"Then where is it?" he said coldly. "She tried to…"

All sound faded, and Bella could no longer hear the shaman's voice or Nyx's. Not the leaves whispering in the breeze, or the shaman's heartbeat or breath. Panic. Was she dead now, rather than undead? *No, I am here. Where was here?* She couldn't feel or see or hear, as though trapped inside a dark, soundproof box. *Help me – ?*

At last, a sensation. She had no idea how much time had passed, if any. Something was stinging her lips. *Burning. At least it was feeling, but oh, how it hurt!* She wanted to scream, but couldn't move. The burning spread to her tongue, her mouth, and down her throat. Fire raged into her stomach, surged through every vein and artery, to the very tips of her fingers and toes. A nightmare parody of its antitheses, the ecstasy of drinking mortal blood. She opened her mouth to scream but managed only a pathetic whimper.

A voice spoke in her ear. "It's going to be all right, Bella." She groaned, then heard Nyx say, "You'll be fine. The shaman's blood is now poison, but I've given you a dose of mine to counter it."

The pain soon subsided. Bella sprang to her feet, trembling and furious. "Where is that God-forsaken shaman?"

"An apt description," Nyx remarked. "But never more can we drink his blood. He has become less human than we are. I was obliged to send him to Letha for his reward. She'll see to him."

Bella let loose with a string of curses. She gave Nyx a shrewd glance. "You saved me. He would have cut off my head."

"True. Or you might otherwise have been trapped there forever. Now come. We have much to do."

Bella shuddered. Trapped, forever? Whatever Nyx's motive, she could not but be grateful.

The Phantom

Hanna, Oklahoma. September 2012

Mama made a point of sticking close to home after that kidnapping scare. Jude was glad. He could always find things to do and enjoyed taking care of the sheep and goats and playing with the barn cats. Dealing with people often turned out to be a perilous undertaking, in his experience. When his friends were busy elsewhere, he roamed the woods and hills alone. One day he sat on the peak, as he often did, thinking about the meaning of life (particularly his own, which seemed to him somewhat different than that of anyone else he knew) and other things of importance.

Sunlight bathed the slopes angling down to the creeks on each side of the ridge. Behind Jude, the mountaintops rose from a summer haze. Before him, a mirror-blue lake glittered through distant trees. The woods lay between, and meadows of swaying grass, rippling waves of green dotted with yellow and purple wildflowers. Down in the hollow was home. And over there, a patch of red tile roof showed above the trees — the belltower of the new basilica. From here, he could also see part of the stone bridge. He felt an attraction to the monastery, always had. Yet it made him uneasy too; he wasn't sure why.

In his wanderings of the woods, he had on occasion found himself at the edge of the abbey grounds, not quite certain how he'd gotten there. Sometimes he'd watch cars drive up to disgorge passengers at the basilica steps, and he'd long to enter those big doors himself. But Mama had said... And anyhow, he felt an insurmountable barrier between him and them, something that he didn't understand.

So, he would remain hidden among the trees, observing as the monks tended gardens, vineyard, and farm, and when they filed into church as the bells pealed loudly, echoing from the wall of surrounding trees and hillsides. Why did he find this mysterious lifestyle so intriguing? He had no answer.

One day he'd advanced well beyond the shelter of the trees without realizing; a monk took notice, called out, and started toward him. Startled, he'd fled. He'd heard that some of their neighbors didn't cotton to trespassers and were pretty handy with the shotgun. (Maybe they hadn't meant the monks, but there was no use in taking chances.)

Exploring the countryside had always been a favorite past-time, whether by himself or with Dace and Cale. At one time, they'd been overly curious, to his mind, about the crack in the side of the hill. But no longer. They'd soon learned that he'd have nothing to do with it and thereafter resigned themselves to adventures elsewhere.

The truth of the matter was that one time Jude had (against his inclination) stood watching while Beau poked in the crack with a stick. He'd felt a stirring beneath them, and a noxious vapor wafted out. He'd staggered back, choking. Beau stared in astonishment, having perceived no such thing, but seeing Jude's distress, led the way down the mountain. And that was that. Jude had made sure to avoid the place ever since.

Now he knew: the inhabitant of the crevasse was known locally as the phantom. He recognized the smell, the sense of it, now, same as on that night of the Perseids. So it hid beneath the haunted hill during the day and emerged after sunset to roam the countryside, raiding farmyards, just as people said. That must be why he'd sometimes sensed a presence when he was outside after dark. He hadn't realized what it was until the night of the Perseids when he'd seen it. Ever since, though, he made sure never to wander far from the house in the evening. Somehow he knew that he was safe inside.

Only one time did his vigilance slip, which resulted in the only close encounter since the Perseid incident, and confirmed his fears. He'd been distracted that afternoon, mulling over that incident when he'd climbed the wall to escape Stave and his gang—not so much disturbed by the bullies' reaction to the situation, as that of his own body. What did it mean when he could move so fast that the human eye was unable to detect it? Or that he could climb a sheer wall like a fly? Or whatever had happened (he was still not sure).

He had to be alone to think, to try to work it out in his head. Was he going crazy? He'd walked uphill and down that afternoon, thinking; evening came before he noticed. Usually, he kept better track of the sun, but he must have been off in la-la land; when he started awake in the real world, the sun was riding the hills. He scanned the area, trying to get his bearings. Okay, there was the steeple of the basilica above the trees, red in the last rays of sunset. Beyond was the hill sheltering Coon Hollow and home.

How had he wandered so far, unknowing? Careless of him. Mama was sure to be worried; it was already starting to get dark. In a bit of a panic, he set out down the road.

His long legs ate up the distance, but the sun soon dropped behind the hills, and twilight fell. Darkness didn't hinder his vision, but the thought of the phantom turned his will to water. *Grandpa had said not to be a pansy*, he reminded himself. There was no cause for panic, at least not until he felt the telltale prickling of his hair standing on end or caught wind of that foul smell. Anyhow, it was not like the phantom came out every night. Or did it? That thought hurried him along faster.

Mama would have a light burning in the window. A comforting thought; he tried to hold onto it, but questions interfered. What did the phantom want with him? For it *did* want him. Beau was only trying to set his mind at ease by dismissing the notion. Didn't he say it stared at him and his daddy and then fled? It didn't want *them*. And Jude had never forgotten that night of the Perseids, when it had spoken to him. *Come to me, little one.* He was struck with terror even now, just thinking about it.

He ran a little faster, out of the woods and down an incline. The gravel road just ahead ran past the monastery property. Only a few miles to go. But as he climbed out of the ditch and onto the road, he felt his hair stand on end. *No, not now!* Not when he was so close to home and yet so far.

But what if he was running right toward it? He froze, his heart in his throat. It was close; he could feel it. He tried to listen, but all he could hear was the pounding of his heart and his panting. *Can't stay here. Must. Go. On.* He stood listening, trying to calm his breathing. He scanned the area; nothing seemed out of place. No unaccountable shadow. No sound at all. Just that prickling and his hackles rising. No foul odor, yet. He exhaled slowly, took a step, and another. Down the road. He quickened his pace. *Don't panic.* Soon he'd see the glow of lamplight in the cabin window. *Home…*

He found his stride and sped down the road. The way was smooth and clear. He realized he was moving faster than was natural and slowed a bit. But there was no one around to see. And he was in kind of a hurry. Mama had long ago forbidden him to run his fastest. It didn't look natural, and people might wonder, she said. About what, she didn't say. Only that most folks tended to panic when something was out of the ordinary, so it was unwise to reveal things like that. She didn't say what exactly might happen; she didn't need to. His imagination filled in the blanks, with men in white coats hauling him away to an underground experimental station or some such place, like in games and movies. So, he mostly minded what his mama said.

Then he smelled it. That foul stench of death, of rotting blood, smoke, and sulfur, faint on the warm night air, but unmistakable. He halted, shivering. His heart beat triple time. He glanced around, trying to pinpoint exactly where he was. Too far. Too far from home. He wanted to crouch down on the spot, quivering like a hunted rabbit. That was no good. The phantom could probably sense his presence, hear his heart pounding and his frightened panting, and it could see in the dark. Better to keep walking. No use in standing here like a brainless rabbit, waiting for death. He took a deep breath and continued on down the road, though a little more slowly than before.

Then the stench slammed into him, caught in his throat. His hair stood on end, for real this time. With an involuntary sob of fright, he broke into a run. Down the road he raced, his feet barely touching the ground as he fled faster than the mortal eye could see. But he didn't care anymore.

Just as he was thinking, *almost home*, he felt a blow to the back of his neck that flattened him face down on the road. Gravel bit into his cheek and forehead. Something weighed him down, heavy on his back. The stench was overpowering.

He gasped for breath and spat grit from his mouth.

The thing on his back shifted its weight; it felt light and yet pressed him to the ground. Claws gripped his shoulders; a face leaned down to touch his. Cold, silken skin. He felt the mouth open, fangs against his cheek, almost a caress as they slid to his throat.

With a howl, he whipped out of its grasp and flung himself away, not knowing or caring in which direction he fled. Off the road, into the ditch, up the other side, through the woods. He crashed through the underbrush, heedless of thorns and branches. Heard the phantom shriek its fury behind him. Ahead was a fenced pasture, an orchard, the smell of a barnyard.

A house — must be a house — would he find safety there? He couldn't think where he was, whose place this was; sheer terror sped him on. The sound of flapping wings filled his head. The thing was gaining on him. He imagined claws reaching out, piercing his back. Cold crawled up his spine.

A fence. He took it in a single bound. Soared over it, but the thing had to be right at his heels. He could feel it. A sob caught in his throat as he saw distant lighted buildings. *Too far.* He couldn't outrun the phantom; it was too fast. He saw the familiar outbuildings, a stone bridge, a tall spire. The basilica! *This was the abbey!*

If only he could make it. Even monks wouldn't turn him away. Not if they saw what pursued him. Something caught at his foot, a vine, a root, a tangle of long grass, and he fell headlong. With a terrified whimper, he glanced back to see the phantom rocketing through the woods like a heat-seeking missile, its eyes like red glowing coals in the darkness.

Its mouth opened to rend the night with a terrible shriek.

Jude leaped to his feet and ran toward the lamplit windows, so near and yet so far. His feet felt like lead. No hope. The phantom would have him in about one second.

Halfway across the pasture, he heard a terrific snarling and hissing behind him, though it seemed it had not gained on him.

He dared to turn and stared, astonished.

The phantom was still in the woods beyond the fence, ripping branches off trees and clawing up the ground in a fit of rage. Its shrieking set his teeth on edge; its eyes burned like the embers of hell's own fire.

But it wasn't touching the fence, wasn't crossing it. Almost as though something held it back, as though the property line was an invisible barrier that it couldn't breach. Had the monks warded their boundary? It hadn't prevented him from entering. He felt suddenly uneasy, like being caught between the devil and the deep blue sea. He glanced back at the phantom again.

Its rasping voice carried across the meadow. "You are mine! They stop me here, but what is meant to be, will be. Your fate is written in the stars since time began." And then it was gone.

Jude blinked and stared. *What was that all about?* Or, had he only imagined it? Was it only the branches rasping in the breeze? No, he'd seen, felt, smelled it. *Heard it.*

He turned his feet toward the monks' driveway. Though he knew that darkness concealed him from the eyes of mere mortals, he couldn't help an apprehensive glance toward the lighted windows as he gained the driveway and ran for the road. But no monk was in sight, nor did any watchdog raise the alarm. Anyhow, the phantom was gone now. He could sense that the night was clear and clean of its presence.

Soon he saw his mama's light in the window. At the sight of her worried face, he resolved to be less self-absorbed and more considerate of her wishes from now on. Of course, she demanded an explanation. He was still trembling from the scare and couldn't hide anything from her. She suggested that the phantom was something evil and that the holiness of the monks had somehow repelled it.

"If they're holy, why don't you like them, Mama?" he dared to say, voicing the unspoken question that had bothered him for so long.

She went quiet suddenly and blinked several times, her eyes reddening. Then she spoke softly. "I—I don't dislike them, son. It's just that—er, sometimes when you're not living according to... well, Daddy and I were never married in the Church, and I always felt I would be judged a sinner by those who did live the way they ought. Just felt guilty, I think, and didn't know what to do about it, so… oh, why am I telling you this? You're just a child. And it's late—"

"Thank you for telling me that. I'm twelve years old, Mama, not a baby. So we can be friends with them? They are our neighbors, too, aren't they?

She pressed him close. "Yes, of course. You're right. I should have thought of that myself a long time ago."

In his bed that night, he shivered at the thought of the phantom on his back, cold, heavy, the pricking of its claws on his shoulders, and those teeth! *It was going to bite me! What is that thing? What does it want with me?*

The Long Walk

Clayhurst Crossing, BC. August 7, 1869

Finally, the day arrived of the solar eclipse, the virgin sacrifice and the ceremony to accomplish Charon's dream. This time the ritual would not fail. This time they would be freed.

Everything was falling into place. The celestial event was at hand; the vampires resided within the predicted umbra, and the victim was still pure and unsullied. Charon was as tense as a drawn bow. After centuries of study and planning, of innumerable failures and disappointments, he saw the fulfillment of his dream almost within his grasp. The curse lifted; he need not fear even sunlight.

He would attain his ultimate goal of world domination—and defeat his ancient foe at last.

All vampires had an internal clock to tell them when it was time for waking or sleeping. Thus, even when deep underground, Bella knew that the sun was high when she was awakened and summoned to the sacrificial chamber. They'd all looked forward to this day with great expectation, yet with some dread, as well. Even though she knew they were hidden from the faintest light of day, she couldn't help being a bit afraid of what would happen. Maybe nothing, as all those times before. Still, she wanted to be there, as they all did, to share in the good fortune the master had promised.

Bella prepared Josie for her special moment, combing her hair with her own precious tortoiseshell comb until it shone. The girl was solemn, dark eyes sad, but she stood unresisting as Bella arranged her long black hair to hide the unsightly bite marks on the back of her neck. Even the ointment could not obliterate them when more were added every few nights.

"Do I have to do this?"

"Yes, of course. This is your big day." Bella wiped a tear from the girl's cheek. "Chin up. Like a queen. You go to meet your lord."

"No, he is not, Bella. I told you. Only Je—"

Bella's smile froze as she stopped the words with a shake of her head and fingers against the girl's lips. "Hush. Do not say that Name. It is forbidden here." Josie's eyes grew sorrowful, but she said no more. "You will be home soon, I promise." Inexplicably, Bella was overwhelmed by compassion. "My dear, how I will miss you," she murmured, impulsively embracing Josie.

And was shocked at herself. These feelings of affection couldn't be her own; a vampire doesn't become attached to its prey. She quickly released the girl and stepped back. At once, a feeling more in keeping with her vampire nature kicked in, and she eyed Josie hungrily. The girl will soon be gone forever. *If only I could taste her blood, just once.* Before she realized, she had leaned close and was nearly undone. With a sob, she tore herself away.

"I'll miss you too," Josie said, putting her arms around Bella. "Don't cry."

It was all Bella could do not to laugh. *She's comforting me!* But when she thought about it, the joke was on her, after all. She'd grown quite fond of the girl in a way that she did not understand.

Not that she regretted that the girl was destined to die rather than go back home as she thought. Seldom had Bella encountered anyone interested in the things that constituted culture. She'd quite enjoyed the games and the discussions, even if they were often strained and their differences irresolvable.

She glanced at Josie and shivered at the thought of how close she'd come to tasting, to disaster. Charon would sense any such transgression at once; she knew that.

"I will be fine," she managed in a tone she hoped sounded suitably grateful for the unwarranted concern. "One more time, okay? We make it good."

With renewed resolve in those solemn eyes, Josie took a deep breath. "I'm ready now."

Bella took her by the hand to lead her through the thick darkness of the underground. Distant chanting echoed through the labyrinth, gradually growing louder, until at last a faint glow lit up the passage ahead. They were soon in a chamber of substantial size.

Vampires lined the walls; their eyes lit up at the sight of the girl, but they didn't interrupt their chanting. Charon stood in the center, beside a large ornate altar, magnificent in his sweeping black cloak, his eyes ablaze. Flame from the Ring on his finger flashed across the white faces with unaccountable brilliance. Bella felt a pang of loss as she recalled that Charon had once compared its beauty to her own.

Now his eyes glowed with a ruby-red light as he gazed upon the girl. She shivered at that predatory look and clung to Bella's hand. Bella murmured something encouraging about home, so when Charon beckoned, Josie took a deep breath and went to him.

All of the elite had gathered around the altar. Nyx's eyes lit upon the girl with greedy anticipation. The Prince stood beside her, coldly imperious. Others were there, but to Bella, they were of no account in this long-awaited moment. Charon took Josie's hands in his and drew her close to obscure her blinding white dress with the black of his cloak. Bella stood admiring the sheer poetry of it, the elegant symbolism! Just so would Light be devoured by Darkness!

A stir of restless movement rippled through the chamber. Every vampire was suddenly nearer; all eyes fixed on the girl, drawn to her without conscious thought.

Charon placed her on the altar. Josie whimpered like one having a bad dream as the Prince stretched out her trembling arms so that she lay in the position of her crucified Lord. Charon's lip curled at the mockery. Bella had often heard him challenge God to save this innocent or that one. Then he'd destroy the victim and laugh, while the rest of them capered with glee.

She was suddenly filled with horror, terrible tears welling up inside. Horrified, she quickly glanced at Charon (had he noticed?) but he was intent on his ritual. The incomprehensible feeling faded.

Charon's black cloak swirled around him as he spoke the words of the ritual. He nodded, and the Prince took hold of Josie's chin in graceful, tapered fingers and turned her head to expose her throat. The chanting grew faster and wilder. All were whipped into a frenzy. First, a victim sacrifice, then the world!

Bella leaned forward eagerly. The Prince touched the girl's throat, and a crimson line appeared. The chanting ceased; vampires surged forward with a collective hiss, set afire by the scent of blood. Only their fear of the master restrained them from swarming the victim.

Charon first marked symbols in blood on the four corners of the altar, then he tasted. Lightning flashed from his eyes. He nodded, and the Prince leaned down and drew the girl's gaze to meet his. She gave a long sigh; a faint smile of rapture curved her lips, and she lifted her chin of her own accord.

A gem-encrusted, brazen goblet appeared in Charon's hand, flashing with color. Beautiful, but not so fascinating as the blood that streamed into it. Steam rose in the chill air as Charon raised the cup to the sky and roared out a chant. The crowd shouted out a response. Bella peered up at the ceiling with the rest of them, expecting the cave to open magically to the black sun.

Nothing happened. Later, maybe?

Charon drank, then set down the cup. He beckoned to Bella and the Prince, then lifted up the girl's hands and held one out to each of them. "Taste, Bellatrix. Prince, my chosen one, taste."

Each acknowledged the honor with a small bow and took a wrist. They bit and were connected. It was rapture! For a moment, an eternity. Then a shadow fluttered at the periphery of Bella's vision as Charon joined the feast. His power shot through their veins like a bolt of lightning. Bella felt she might have been blasted from existence had not the Prince's defenses sustained her.

Josie's living heart was beating for them all.

Bella felt so alive—*oh, if only this could go on forever*! She knew that was impossible—a mortal could not long survive the shock. But surely it was pure bliss even for one so doomed! The signal came then. Bella and the Prince reluctantly withdrew, leaving the prospective bride to the master alone. It was time to complete the ritual.

That didn't happen.

For at that moment, there seemed to be some confusion at the door. Before Bella could think, a blue flash like sheet lightning slammed her to the stone floor. A terrible sound like a gong shattered her brain into a million pieces. She heard her own shrieks echoing through the tunnels of her mind.

When she came to herself, she tasted blood, smelled it so near, so tantalizing, that she opened her eyes. She was lying next to a lovely crimson pool… Couldn't think where… how… why… couldn't think at all. She raised her head, but *ay, the pain*! She fell back, groaning. The smell of blood revived her eternal hunger; her tongue flicked out— and she was shocked into awareness.

All about her was utter chaos—a mad scene of struggling figures writhing and fluttering, shrieks and roars of pain and rage, terror and frustration. In dull incomprehension, she watched vampires scatter, vanishing through cracks in ceiling, walls, and floor. Then everyone was gone, except for those lying dead.

And she herself.

With that realization, her survival instinct kicked in. She lurched to her feet and scrambled into the nearest crack in the wall. There she clung, trying to recover from the shock. What had happened? Her head still hurt, but the nausea was fading. She saw the pool of crimson on the floor near the altar and knew. That sweet innocent blood she'd ingested, and its power, wasted! But to re-enter the chamber now would be to invite destruction.

Charon and the Prince were nowhere to be seen. After some laborious thought, she vaguely recalled them dematerializing in an instant. Why couldn't she do that, instead of being paralyzed by... whatever it was?

Then she saw her. The Huntress.

Of course, only she could cause such devastation. She was now clearly visible from Bella's hiding place in the shadows, with her crucifix on a leather cord about her neck. A daunting array of weapons seemed to spring into her hands as needed. The priest was with her, and a small ragtag band of mortals armed with all sorts of makeshift vampire-killing weapons. How had they found them in these depths, to surprise them in the midst of their ritual?

With increasing desperation, Bella watched while the Huntress went about dispatching any vampires that remained. The priest directed some of the men to wrap Josie gently in a blanket. He himself carried something covered by a silken cloth of gold, something from which she was compelled to turn away her eyes or be blinded by its light. It was even more powerful than the Huntress's silver crucifix.

At the sight of it, she felt a momentary leap of delight within her. But such a feeling could not be her own—she was a vampire! At that thought, she felt a terrible, inexplicable sense of desolation.

The priest proceeded to say some Latin prayers and sprinkle holy water all around, while the other men kept watch with wary black eyes. The Huntress went about her business of making certain no vampires would rise again, while some of the men spirited Charon's Josie-girl away.

Bella crept further into the narrow opening until she came out into a passage on the other side of the wall. She flitted from shadow to shadow to avoid the lantern lights of the enemy, who now emerged from the chamber to search the labyrinth. The Huntress and her crew had been so sudden and swift, so efficient and the devastation so complete; had anyone else survived? Bella finally reached the throne room and was relieved to see that the master was there, bleakly counting heads, a pitiful remnant.

Nyx was there with a goodly number of her own children under her wing; among them were the Rocket, Sweet William, and the Sandman. And the Prince, with Styx at his heels. The Genie, Reed, and Sirocco trooped in, ashen and bedraggled. It had been a close call indeed. Too many were yet missing.

Bella's eyes darted about, searching the crowd, but that flaming red hair was nowhere to be seen. Her dread grew. A movement at an archway caught her eye; her head spun around in joyous expectancy.

It was only Blue Boy and Pinkie, hurrying in to be duly noted by the master. Still no Rojo. *He could be late, like others who were straggling in,* Bella told herself, but felt a cold lump of dread inside her. His harebrained ideas often got him into trouble before he thought. Surely he wouldn't face the enemy on his own. *If he was such a fool, he deserved what he got,* she told herself. What was that pang she felt (*not sorrow, surely*!) at the thought of losing him?

"Where's Rojo, Bella?" Pinkie said, her voice shaky.

"How should I know?" she snarled.

Pinkie jumped back, her eyes wide.

Bella calmed herself; it wasn't Pinkie's fault. She retracted her claws and added more softly, "I only just got here myself."

Blue Boy put his arm around Pinkie defensively. "We almost didn't get away. I haven't seen Rojo since—"

"He was beside us when the Huntress came in, but everyone just scattered," offered Pinkie.

"I swear I'll take a strip off his hide when he does show up," Bella growled.

Several long minutes later, she heard a shout from the doorway. "Bella, Bella!" She turned and saw flame-red hair fluttering wildly as Rojo flew toward her, his face smeared with blood. He threw himself at her feet. "Oh, Bella, you're here!"

She held him to her and stroked that beautiful long hair. "Of course, I am." She nearly choked up. "What took you so long?"

"I thought she killed you," he moaned. "You were lying there so still. Just lying there, in all that blood, and—"

"Do you think I die so easy?" she derided him, though she quaked at the memory.

"I thought I'd lost you forever. Then she came for me and I, well, before I even knew, I'd slipped through that space under the altar and was hidden from her sight." He sank to his knees. "I'm sorry, Bella. I should never have run away and left you, but I couldn't help myself. She—I was mad with terror." His voice sank to a whisper. "When all was quiet, I crept out, but you were gone! She'd done away with everyone! I heard the screams, and I thought—"

"I understand. Get up. There will be a reckoning. I swear it."

He stood slowly, uncertainly. "I—oh, Bella, if anything happened to you,

I—"

"Be still, *niño*." Bella frowned. "What is that blood on your face?" She bent to taste it.

"I just couldn't leave it lying there."

"What? You took my—" She knew the instant she tasted it that he'd drunk from the pool on the floor.

"I couldn't help it," he whined, clearly expecting to be slapped down. "It was going to waste. How could I resist? It tasted of you." His eyes blinked madly as he sank down to kiss the hem of her cloak. "I thought you were gone, and though I suffered terribly after the Huntress and her minions fouled that chamber with their holy water, it seemed a way of having part of you."

Silly romantic fool. As she reached down to lift him up, he squeezed his eyes shut, waiting for the blow to fall. *Flattery—I love it.* "My Rojo. Again you brave the Huntress for my sake."

"I'll give it back," he gabbled in terror.

Bella snickered at his reaction. "Let us see what Charon wishes of us. And then I will take you at your word."

Puppy Love

Hanna, Oklahoma. 2012-2013

Finally, Daisy came home, and the Aldens invited Mama and Jude over for a Sunday afternoon barbecue. Mama made potato salad and peach pie; Jude took his violin. As they drove into the Aldens' yard, the screen door flew open, and Daisy rushed out to greet them. She looked so dolled-up with a stylish haircut and light green skirt and blouse that Jude almost didn't recognize her. He took a second look — it *was* Daisy!

As soon as the pickup came to a stop, he jumped out and ran into her arms. "Daisy! I haven't seen you in a coon's age!" He had to lean down as she threw her arms around him.

She hugged him, then stepped back. "Gosh, chinquapin! You've grown so tall this summer. Is it really you?"

He laughed. "And here I was wondering why you're so short, Daisy, but I didn't think I ought to mention it."

Beau had come out grinning behind Daisy. "Yeah, li'l bro, gotta watch what you say to these modern women."

Jude gave Daisy an appraising look. "I have to say, you been gone too long. I hardly know it's you. You look like a city girl, or maybe one of those Hollywood stars."

"Star, my eye! Don't tease me," laughed Daisy. "I'm a teacher now. I have to dress appropriately."

It was so good to hear her voice. How he'd missed her.

"Holy! Big words," teased Beau. "Who are you, and what have you done with my sister?"

"You just never mind, sweet pea," she said, cuffing him playfully. "Here, Miz Martel, let me help you with that."

Jude glanced around. His mama was climbing out of the pickup, juggling the bowl of potato salad and two pies. "It's okay, Daisy. I'll get it." He easily hefted the load of food. "Go grab my violin. That is, if you'd care for a tune, after."

Daisy ran to the pickup, scooped up the violin, and hugged it close. "You're not getting away without serenading us. I'm holding your baby hostage, chinquapin, until you do. I so missed hearing you play and sing while I was in Tulsa."

"No more than I missed you, Daisy. I'll play tunes for you forever, and sing, too. Anything you want, just so you'll stay."

"Why, thanks so much. I got homesick like you wouldn't believe." She walked beside him to the house, carrying the violin. "That city life isn't for me; I'll always be a country girl at heart. I'm so excited that I finally got the job teaching here like I always dreamed. It was worth all the trouble."

"I'm glad your dream came true. But my heart nearly broke when I got home to find you gone again. I wanted to tell you about Grandpa and our trip up north. It was fun, er, mostly." He glanced around, discomfited for a moment. "Gosh, I'm starved. Something sure smells good."

"Yeah, Daddy's got the steaks on the barbecue, and potatoes." She led the way to the backyard. "See there, Mama's already got the veggie platters out, and fresh-baked cookies. Let's put your mama's potato salad right here, and, oh, my—how I've missed her peach pie. I'm so glad to be back! For good, I hope."

"Howdy, neighbors!" Zach greeted them, red-faced as he lifted the lid of the barbecue. He glanced at Beau. "Johnny-boy, run get a dish for these potatoes, will you? I think they're about done." As Beau dashed into the house, Zach turned to Jude. "Got your plate ready?" He stabbed a sizzling steak with his long-handled fork.

"Sure do," said Jude, inhaling the mouth-watering aroma.

Zach slapped a steak onto his plate and a scoop of potatoes. "Here's your steak, too, Mamie. Just how you like it. And Daisy…"

Liz rushed out to greet Mama and Jude and to direct everyone to the spread of food on the table, making sure no one missed out on anything.

Jude grinned at Alyssa, who was lounging in a lawn chair in the shade, sipping a cold drink and listening to music on her iPod. She gave him a distracted wave.

After they dished up the rest of their food, Daisy led the way across the yard to a picnic table under a pecan tree.

"'Johnny-boy'?" Jude said in a low voice, with a quizzical smile.

"Yeah, daddy's taken to calling him by his little pet name ever since Arlie left home," Daisy laughed, shooting a quick glance toward Zach, "and I went to Tulsa to teacher's college, and—well, Alyssa's about to fly the coop too. I suppose it's his way of hanging on to his baby boy." She noted Jude's quirked eyebrow and added, "Beau's full name's John Beauregard Alden—you didn't know? Okay, I guess that's understandable; we mostly just called him Beau. Now, tell me all about your trip."

Jude dug into his food and his narrative. About Grandpa, Uncle Darren, their dogs, Hamlet, and had just begun on the trip, when he paused. "Oh, yeah, I nearly forgot. I brought you a Mile Zero Post pin." He drew it from his pocket and gave it to her.

"Thanks, chinquapin." She glanced up with tears in her eyes. "I'd give you a big hug and a kiss, but the table's between us."

"Later, okay?" he laughed, blushing. "Was nothing, anyhow. I wanted to get you something classy but didn't have the money, and —"

"I'm just teasing. I'll treasure it always. Now, tell me all about your grand adventure."

Between bites, Jude went on with the story of his summer traveling. He tried to make it all happy and carefree, but he should have known Daisy would see through all that.

"That's so fine." She lowered her voice. "But there's something you're not telling me." He hesitated, and she pressed on, "So, what is it? Come on; you can tell your Daisy."

"Well, a couple of things, aside from the usual," he admitted, with an anxious sigh. "When we went to see Hamlet, a gentleman and his lady vanished into thin air right before my eyes. Sure seemed like they did, anyhow. Maybe I'm losing it, but — no, Mama seemed a little freaked too. Something to do with them."

"Well, of course, if they disappeared like that."

"She didn't even see that. So, I don't know; she won't say."

"And you? What's your take?"

"They were beautiful, like angels almost, but he gave me the shivers. There was something not quite right about him. It's hard to explain."

A little frown of concern creased Daisy's brow. "You didn't know them?"

"No," he said slowly. "They seemed familiar, somehow, but —"

"That's not the whole story, is it?"

He shot her a glance, then shrugged, uncomfortable. "I just don't know how to explain. There was something worse. A lot worse. At the museum in the Mile Zero City, I saw —" he shuddered. "No, I can't recall. I just can't. Like one of those episodes, but — Daisy, I wasn't even playing my violin! It was so bad! If I try to remember, my heart pounds so hard I can't breathe! It was like a nightmare come to life."

"Oh! Like the phantom? And all that other. Maybe there's a connection."

The phantom! He felt a chill. "Gosh, no wonder they call me a freak." He cast his eyes down in shame. "Other people can't do stuff like that. Was it real, the fox getting blasted into ash? I saw it, but…"

"Just be careful," Daisy said softly. "And try to keep calm."

"I know. But it's hard sometimes. I can feel it coming on, the glowing thing, and still— But why's the phantom after me?" He lifted his gaze to meet hers. "You know, Daisy, used to be when I sensed the phantom, it'd just fade away. It didn't do anything, just scared me. This time was different." He told her about the phantom's attack and the surprising sanctuary. "I don't get why it couldn't cross the boundary."

"Maybe 'cause it's evil, and they're good, like your Mama says?" She reached out to pat his arm. "I think I'll get some pie. Want some?"

He nodded. But what about those weird flashbacks? And—blood brothers. What had happened there? No, he couldn't tell anyone—not even Daisy—about that. Not yet.

"Here you go. Peach pie with ice cream." Daisy scooted a plate across the table to him.

"Thanks, Daisy. But you could have brought us a whole pie to share," he teased, in an attempt to lighten the mood.

She laughed. "Your mama said we had to leave some for the others." She took a bite. "Mmm. This is heaven. So. What do you think the phantom really is, now that you've seen it up close? A ghost?" she chattered in an attempt to put him at ease.

He shook his head as he took another forkful of dessert and went with it. "No, it was solid. You've seen it; it's no ghost. It felt cold as death, though, and I felt cold where it touched me." At the thought of it, the coldness started to engulf him in its grip.

"Are you okay? Hey, chinquapin?" The warmth of Daisy's voice brought him up out of the dark, into the sun-drenched backyard. He found himself sitting on a bench in the shade of the Aldens' pecan tree.

"Yeah, sure." He shivered, wondering what had just happened. He quickly took another bit of pie onto his fork, but his hand shook so that he lost it halfway to his mouth. Mortified, he fished the pie off his lap and ate it; it seemed tasteless as cardboard now.

"It's okay. You can tell your Daisy," she said softly. "Wouldn't it be fun if I could teach your grade? That is, if your mama let you go to school again."

"That'd be great. I miss my friends and playing baseball and such." He felt tears spring to his eyes and quickly looked away, trying to pull himself together.

"But your mama knows best, of course," Daisy chattered on, as though nothing were amiss. "I'll see you often now that I'm back home. You can tell me anything, no matter how crazy. You're my chinquapin, and I'll love you forever." She reached out and squeezed his hand.

He felt comforted and grateful. He opened his mouth to tell all when there came a rustling of footsteps in the grass.

"Is this seat taken?" said Beau with a grin.

"Of course, sweet pea. We're saving it for you. What took you so long?"

Beau sat down and started in on his heaping plate of food. "Do you want that in twenty-five words or less?" he said between mouthfuls.

"Just because I'm a teacher doesn't mean I expect a ten-page essay," smiled Daisy. "We'll settle for the short version."

"Your daddy made you sing for your supper, did he?" Jude managed to laugh, now that the cold had receded.

"Hey," protested Beau. "It ain't funny. Daddy makes me do everything."

"I've never heard that line before," said Daisy dryly. "Ho-hum. Used to be Alyssa. And probably me, at one time."

"Hah! What's he going to do when I'm in school?"

"All the work, as usual," Daisy teased.

Beau set to and soon finished his steak. "I better get some of that pie before it's gone," he said with his irrepressible grin back in place. "Nobody makes peach pie like your mama, Jude." He hurried away.

"Did you tell Beau?" Daisy said, her brow furrowed.

Jude was bewildered for a moment (*oh, yeah, the phantom*). "Er, no, not much, anyhow. He won't push it if he sees I don't want to talk."

"It's okay, just asking."

The scare of the phantom was so real and immediate that Jude felt he would never be free of it. Never again, it seemed, would he tread the familiar sun-dappled woods of his childhood in freedom and happiness; it had become a dark and frightening forest, teeming with monsters—one, anyhow. Now he couldn't roam the hillsides even in daytime without glancing over his shoulder at every little noise; night brought with it terrors of glowing eyes and that cold presence. Until a devastating event unexpectedly brought about an easing of the situation.

One day Uncle Darren called to inform Mama that Grandpa had died suddenly of a heart attack. Uncle Darren had come home from work and found the old man lying in the yard with his dog standing guard over him.

Jude was in shock. *Grandpa, dead?* How could this be, when he'd just begun to get to know him?

Zach promised Mama that he and Beau would keep an eye on the place and feed the animals while they went to the funeral. Mama couldn't afford plane tickets, so she and Jude caught the Greyhound this time. Even for that, she had to rob her scant savings account.

Uncle Darren met them at the Ashland bus depot and drove them out to the old home place. The house seemed empty without Grandpa. His old dog Scorpion stuck his nose in Jude's hand, welcoming him warmly, though the soulful amber eyes seemed to say he knew his master was gone for good. *What would happen to the dog now*? Jude wondered. Uncle Darren assured him that this was the dog's home as long as it lived.

The funeral went without incident, attended by a goodly number of neighbors and a few relatives. Mama wept, but Jude stood dry-eyed as the clods fell on the coffin, thinking about how, if he took a trip to Oregon after this, nothing would be the same. It seemed so unfair. Just as he'd begun to get a sense of belonging, Grandpa was taken away forever. His hero, gone. No more crotchety old man giving him blunt advice whether or not he asked for it.

He hadn't wished to attend the viewing of the open casket, but Mama made him go. It turned out that just as he was thinking it didn't really look like Grandpa there in the coffin, dressed in the suit he'd always wore to church, he got the feeling that Grandpa had just dozed off and at any moment would awaken and wink at him. Just like he remembered him. He would have cried then, but there were no tears, it seemed — not when he wanted them, only when he didn't, like at the museum.

He'd never forget Grandpa admonishing him to be a man. That he would be, he vowed. If only Grandpa were here to help. How he missed him. First, his daddy, now his grandpa. Why did life have to be so full of heartache? Where was God in all this?

That evening they made their farewells to all the neighbors who'd showed up for the get-together afterward, bringing dishes of food, paying their respects, and reminiscing. There were relatives that Jude had never met, distant cousins. Uncle Darren and Mama were Grandpa's only children; Jude, his only grandchild.

Jude didn't know many of the people, and he didn't feel much like eating, so he went outside to sit on the back step. Red streaked the evening sky, and a dust devil whirled away across the valley toward the haze of distant hills. A fitful breeze lifted Jude's hair and stirred the long brown grass against the woven wire fence beside the old gray barn. He caught a glimpse of olive drab there, in the lean-to. The army jeep. Memories sprang to mind of the trip north. He felt a rush of nostalgia and unutterable loneliness. Grandpa, come back.

He heard the soft padding of footsteps. Scorpion. The old dog gazed up at him sadly and rested its head on his knee. Plainly Scorpion missed

Grandpa too. Jude scratched the dog's ears, thinking how nothing would ever be the same again for either of them.

A shadow fell over them as a tall, gaunt cowboy with a gray handlebar mustache and a ten-gallon hat came out on the porch. He sat down beside Jude.

"Howdy, son," said the rough-hewn old man. He set the hat beside him on the step and balanced a plate of food on his knee. "Thought I'd come out and keep you company. Getting a mite stuffy in there. Me, I can't take the indoors for too long. Or them crowds." He paused to eat a few bites of food. "Taking it right hard, I see. I'm Jim Dalton. I live down the road a piece. Yup. There wasn't nobody quite like your Grandpa. Couldn't find a better friend than he was, nowhere." When Jude didn't respond, he went on. "I see you met Scorpion. You got a dog at home?"

"No," Jude mumbled. He wanted to be civil, but his heart was heavy. The old man meant well, but that wouldn't bring Grandpa back. Still, he was brought up to be polite, and he could hardly treat one of Grandpa's friends with disrespect. He made an effort, and soon old Jim had drawn out of him more than he'd intended to reveal. Where he lived and what he enjoyed doing, and what Grandpa'd taught him about how to train a dog, and how much he liked Grandpa's dog, Scorpion, and Uncle Darren's dog, Basher, and wished he had one of his own.

"Tell you what," said Jim, with a twitch of his long mustache. "I have a batch of pups just weaned and ready to go to new homes. One, I reckon you'd like. Looks just like old Scorpion. Black. White tip on his tail."

Jude's spirits soared for a moment, then sank. "Uh, how much? I only got what's in my piggy bank, and Mama'll say we can't afford it 'cause she spent all that money on bus tickets, and —"

The old man chuckled. "No, I don't want a red cent. I've got homes lined up for all the other pups, but this one. He's the runt of the litter. I just want him to go to a good home. He needs a boy just as much as you need a dog. With your mama's permission, of course."

Early the next morning, when Uncle Darren drove them to the depot so that they could catch the bus home, Mama had her one old suitcase, while Jude gripped his own in one hand and a somewhat worn carrying case in the other. Old Jim had said not to worry; he could return it next time he came to visit.

He peered through the mesh at the black puppy curled up inside. "Hi, little pup."

Its eyes shone like shoe buttons, and its tail thumped in response as it poked its wet nose at the mesh and the pink tongue flicked out. It whined.

Jude smiled and whispered, "Good boy, Li'l Scorpion. We're going home. You'll see. We're going to get along just fine."

And so he had his dog and a remembrance of Grandpa. At home, he wandered the woods with just the pup for company, trying to walk off his grief. Mama stood by helplessly, knowing that nothing anyone could say would mitigate it. Only time. She'd balked about the dog at first, but now she could see that it was a godsend. Li'l Scorpion followed Jude everywhere and soon had his eye on him just as old Scorpion had eyed Grandpa, eager to obey his young master's every command. He was a brave watchdog right from the start, and with him at his heels, Jude no longer felt the need to shy away from every dark shadow of the forest.

Sometime later, the will was read, and Mama received her share of the inheritance. To her surprise, it was enough for a living for her and Jude, and then some. Uncle Darren got the old home place. He sent Jude Grandpa's fedora and said he remembered how Jude had admired it and that Grandpa would want him to have it.

Jude treasured the hat and wore it often. It made him feel close to Grandpa.

After he turned thirteen, Jude occasionally worked for Lionheart Construction, doing custom cabinetmaking and other fine woodwork in the finishing process of building houses. Uncle Roy said with that knack he had for coaxing beauty and grace from pieces of wood, he must take after his daddy.

He still did odd jobs for Miz Lily now and then. She always offered him iced tea afterward, and he never mentioned the time when she hadn't, though it was foremost in his mind at such times.

Mama had advised him not to tell anyone about the attempted kidnapping, for fear of the "professional snoops," as she referred to lawmen, government agents of all kinds, welfare workers, and anyone else who might come around asking questions that she deemed none of their business. Jude waited in vain for Miz Lily to bring up the subject, so he could maybe find out who those men were. She never said a word about it but continued on as though nothing had happened, favoring him as she always had.

He had grown to a height of six feet and was rangy, though his broad shoulders promised to fill in with muscle one day. He got a job working for Ned at the Hanna General store, stocking shelves, delivering groceries, and cleaning up. It was his dream come true, ever since he'd developed a crush on Jasmine.

Even as a child, he'd felt a certain fascination, but now she was ever on his mind. He lived to catch glimpses of her passing by the door or coming into the store to grab a treat. A whiff of her delicate, flowery fragrance was heaven. If, upon occasion, she cast a condescending glance upon him, his heart beat high. The few offhand remarks she sent his way he treasured as pearls and rubies dropping from her lips. If she hardly noticed him, that was understandable; she was a few years older than he was, and he feared that to her, he must seem just a dumb kid.

Some days he had to stay late to finish his tasks. Ned had given up on hiring more help for the simple reason that he couldn't find kids who were willing to work. They generally were lazy and unreliable, he declared (and that was strong language for the easy-going storekeeper).

At first, Ned had been hesitant about hiring a thirteen-year-old but was too kindhearted to refuse to give work to a widow's only son. Miz Lily put in a good word, and time proved her right. Ned was pleasantly surprised when Jude never failed to arrive on time, and he always completed his work.

One evening when Jude stayed until after dark to finish stocking the shelves, he was surprised to hear the crunch of gravel as a car stopped out front. He glanced out the window. A shiny dark blue car had pulled up outside, one of those '50s Chrysler models with the big fins. In fair shape, too. Ned had already placed the "closed" sign in the window and was counting the till. In answer to Jude's unspoken question, Ned commented off-handedly that it was just a boy coming to pick Jasmine up for a movie.

Jasmine had a boyfriend? Jude's heart sank to his shoes at the thought.

With a feeling of dread, Jude pictured the driver as a suave gambler. Or, more realistically, some pimply-faced teenager whose rich daddy bought him that classic car so he could impress girls. Jude lamented the fact that he had no daddy to buy him a car. He sighed at the injustice of it. To a rich man's son, Jasmine was no doubt just one more pearl on a string; to him, she was the most beautiful girl in the world. He could picture himself throwing his coat on the ground for her to walk across a puddle without wetting her feet, like Sir Francis Drake was said to have done for Queen Elizabeth.

His heart beat fast at the thought that he might catch a glimpse of her as she left the house.

Then he felt the telltale prickling of his senses and lost his breath. Something evil was near. Not the phantom! No, how could it be? Jude glanced over at Ned, but he seemed unaware. Should he warn him? He opened his mouth to speak, but what would he say? Before he could articulate his concerns, Ned went into the backroom to put the money in the safe.

Uneasily, Jude turned back to the shelves. There was the sound of quick footsteps and a murmur of voices. Then the door burst open, and he smelled the familiar fragrance. His heart leaped as Jasmine rushed in, her beauty filling his world, the sweet cherry-red lips, lightly rouged cheeks, shining dark eyes, and beautiful long hair.

But to his horror, the smell of death followed close at her heels, blasting him with that sense of the proximity of evil. He shook. *The phantom? No, it wasn't, after all.* Still. Could this really be her boyfriend?

"Hey, Jude," said Jasmine, without even glancing in his direction. He sensed mockery in her tone and made no reply. Nor was one expected. "Just grabbing some Coke, Dad," she called out as she opened the cooler. She turned to her date. "Or would you prefer root beer?"

Jude stared openly, but the man didn't acknowledge his existence. No, he wasn't the phantom, but there was something sinister about him; he was tall and gaunt with longish tangled hair, but that wasn't it. He appeared at first glance to be young, yet oddly ageless, and too handsome to be real. And there was something wrong with the way Jasmine seemed to melt when the guy spoke or looked into her eyes.

He fixed an angry glare on the man and wanted to kill him. That scared him. Where had such murderous thoughts come from? He took another furtive glance. How pale the man was. *He looks dead*! Jude's breath caught in his throat. That sense of evil reminded him of the phantom, all right, except this guy appeared more human. So what was he?

"It's all the same to me, sugar," the boyfriend softly murmured into Jasmine's ear (though to Jude, with his keen hearing, it was audible even from clear across the room).

He scowled and was surprised to see the gaunt face turn toward him as though he had spoken his thoughts aloud. The man put a hand on Jasmine's waist in a proprietary way and directed an unpleasant smile at Jude. His eyes were flat black and cold, like a shark's. Ghastly, in that white face. Jude shivered. Where had he seen eyes like that? And that smell — vampire? Despite all his dreams and weird experiences with the phantom and the museum, the idea just seemed too fantastic, like something from a nightmare coming into real life. Other people didn't believe in… *No, no.*

The man nuzzled Jasmine's neck.

She giggled. "Ooh! You're so cold."

"You'll warm me up, baby," he said with a low laugh.

Jude's hackles rose. "You. Leave her alone."

The man turned his head slowly to fix those oddly flat eyes on him. Jude managed a steady stare of his own, which seemed to disconcert the man, who shifted his gaze uneasily. His lip curled, and he snarled faintly; Jasmine was oblivious, intent on digging the pop out of the cooler.

"Little boy," the man sneered. To Jasmine, he said, "Who's your knight in shining armor?"

"Who? Oh, him! That's just the kid who works in the store," she said with a dismissive little wave of her hand.

Jude flushed. But, of course, she wasn't herself. The man—this thing— had hypnotized her somehow, he was pretty sure. He held the man's cold gaze and tried to think of what to do. Jasmine must not leave with him.

Jude's fear for her safety blended with his anger in the sort of desperation that had proved explosive upon occasion. This time he had no inclination to suppress the telltale heat that rose behind his eyes.

But this man was sharper than Stave Cooper. His gaze wavered uncertainly as Jude took a step toward him. Before he'd taken another step, stark fear flashed across the man's face. Jude knew then that his own eyes were glowing. For once, he was glad of it, whatever the consequences.

The man sprang back from Jasmine, and with one frantic glance at Jude, went for the door. He vanished down the hallway, a strangled scream trailing after him. Jude stared in surprise. That strange gliding gait, so fast that he seemed to blur as he fled—where had he seen that before?

Outside, a motor revved. With a spattering of gravel against the curb, the car peeled off. The rumbling of the motor quickly faded into the night. Jude tried to think what exactly had happened. There was something he should remember but couldn't, didn't want to.

A sharp slap across the face jarred him to his senses. He saw stars and the flash of Jasmine's eyes.

"You little creep!"

He touched his stinging cheek. "Sorry, Jasmine. He—"

She slapped his other cheek, harder, nearly spinning his head around. "What did you do to him? What—" Her voice sank to a whisper. "What the hell's wrong with your eyes?"

Self-consciously he dropped his gaze to hide the glow. His cheeks burned from the slaps. But that was nothing, as long as she didn't call him a freak.

"Here, what's going on?" said Ned gruffly, appearing in the doorway from the back room.

Jasmine burst into tears. "Oh, Daddy! He—he—" she wailed and ran from the store. The door slammed.

Ned glanced quizzically at Jude. "Yes, and —?"

Jude slowly raised his eyes, "I'm sorry, Mr. Farwell, I only meant to help." He paused. Ned seemed to be waiting for him to continue. "Um, that man was up to no good, Mr. Farwell. Anyhow," he added defensively, "I, er, I didn't do anything."

"I see." He didn't, of course, but nothing much ruffled Ned. "You go home now, son. I'll call you when I need you again."

Jude hung his head. Was this another way of saying he was fired? Mama wouldn't be pleased. How often had she warned him to control his temper? Still, he couldn't be sorry. That man (or whatever it was) meant harm to Jasmine. He lifted his head and fixed Ned with a level gaze. "Mr. Farwell, that man is evil. Even if you're firing me, I'm glad he's gone."

Ned sighed. "I'm not firing you, son. Just keep a low profile until, well, you know, until things blow over. When that girl's in a temper —" He paused and shook his head. "You have to understand something about women —" he began, then seemed to think better of it and continued on another tack, "She'll have her mother in on it and, well, just give it time." He patted Jude's shoulder. "I'll deal with it. You're a good boy, Jude. Have a good night, now."

Jude avoided the store after that until Ned called him back in to work. It pained him that Jasmine had her nose in the air whenever he caught a glimpse of her, now not even acknowledging his existence at all, even to mock him. His heart was sore, though his face burned at the memory of her slaps. He sighed.

One day Mama told him to quit mooning around and forget the little hussy. Anyhow, she added, he was too young for that kind of nonsense.

He'd never told her. How did she know?

China Boy

Clayhurst Crossing, BC. August 1869

It was still full daylight; Bella and the others could do nothing but wait and watch in helpless dread as the Huntress and the priest proceeded through the labyrinth, methodically laying waste to their home. She couldn't see them but could hear screams and the murmuring of voices echoing through the passages. Prayers, she knew, by that sense of dread she felt. The two of them were a lethal combination; she annihilated any vampire they happened upon, while he pronounced the prayers of exorcism and sprinkled holy water on walls and floors and ceilings to cleanse them of evil.

Bella and the other survivors scattered at their approach, hiding in dark corners and anywhere else they could find refuge. Some of the newer vampires didn't realize until too late that the Huntress had no mercy for their kind; or rather, she believed mercy meant releasing them from their unnatural state by staking or beheading.

When night fell, the Huntress and her escort withdrew. Even they would not tempt fate that far, apparently. In any case, the Huntress would know that vampires didn't easily let go of their prey, once claimed. No doubt she would herself watch over the girl Josie, to prevent her from falling back into their hands.

Though she couldn't get them all in that spiderweb of a maze, the means she and the priest used effectively spoiled it as a home for them. In the space of one day only, Bella lamented, ruined!

She could see that Charon was furious — his ritual had failed once again, he'd lost his Josie-girl, and they must pack up and move at once; heading south, he said. He couldn't travel openly above ground even at night, like an ordinary vampire, but had to be transported within his great stone sarcophagus.

Bella was surprised at how quickly minions arrived with mule-drawn wagons. She oversaw clearing out the lair. Minions could load the master's books, maps, weapons collections, and such; it required vampires' preternatural strength to manage his heavy throne and coffin. Eventually, the wagons were packed and ready.

After all that time in one place, the move wasn't easy, but they'd wandered before, and they could do so again. Still, a long, arduous trek lay ahead. Arrangements to get the master's wagon underground before each sunrise demanded the most meticulous planning, scouting ahead to assess the terrain and the movements of the human population. The minions could cautiously continue south with the other wagons.

Then the Prince, with a cold light in his eyes, announced that he would remain long enough to retrieve the master's Josie-girl and kill the Huntress. Bella's heart leaped. Most of the others were not so eager to volunteer until the Prince promised all who survived a taste of her blood. That caused them to reconsider. There was much power to be gained from the Huntress's blood.

Nyx was torn. She wanted to go with the Prince but didn't want to leave Charon. The Prince assured her that neither did he mean to abandon his master; the going would be slow, so it was well that they'd have a head start. He swore he would not be long taking the Huntress's head and the girl, so Nyx opted to stay, after all. She herself chose trusted mortal minions and an elite vampire guard to accompany Charon's wagon. As far as Bella knew, Nyx had always taken care of him; he was her creation, it was said.

Just after sunset, the Prince and his crew watched the ponderous wagon train set out. They sat tight for the next few nights. Bella knew that they were waiting for the priest to depart; he had a large mission territory to cover, and the Prince had calculated that he'd soon be on his way. The Huntress was challenge enough; with a priest, she'd be impossible to take. Each night they awoke anxious lest the Huntress had slipped away too, as they slept. Then one night, the priest was gone, and the Huntress was still there.

The Prince set his plan in motion at once. He ordered his little band to haunt the area just enough to entice the Huntress into the open, but not to warrant calling the priest back to perform another exorcism (they wanted no more of that!). They resumed a downscaled marauding, to stir the Huntress to action.

Bella took Rojo with her to the shore each night, though it didn't seem likely that she'd find her boy, since their cover was blown. But their persistence paid off; they again found the guilty pair giggling in the tall grass. Alas, there was no time for play. Rojo sprang from the shadows and soon left the girl dying on the shore, abandoned like a broken doll. He stood guard while Bella finished with the boy. Turning him in the open was a perilous undertaking. When she was certain that he was hers forever, she carried him to the cave. She dared not leave him for the Huntress to stake the instant he died.

The vampires were using a secondary entrance downriver from the camp; the sprinkling of holy water had ruined the main one. Only this cramped and less hospitable section of the network of caves remained untouched by the priest's minions.

With Bella's able assistance, the boy died that day; the next night, she helped him rise, a perfect monster. Alas, his honey-brown skin she so loved quickly faded to the color of ash, but she knew that in time it would transform to a vampire sort of beauty. His hair was like polished ebony, his eyes black as night. He was a head taller than Rojo. Bella preferred the Latin look, and he was — well, close enough, if with rather an Oriental cast to his features. So she called him China Boy. Nyx kept threatening to do away with him until the Prince stepped in and put an end to the harassment.

It turned out that Bella's deeds once again furthered their plans. The girl had been found lying on the dunes.

As expected, the Huntress came out alone after sundown, on the warpath. Clearly, a small army of vampires no more daunted her than facing them one-on-one. Stars sprinkled the black sky above. The Prince had loosely arrayed his forces facing the grassy, open area where he deemed she would appear. They hid in the shadows. Aside from the breeze stirring their cloaks, they made no movement but waited, still as only vampires can be.

Rojo was at Bella's right hand, China Boy on her left. He needed careful watching, for he as yet knew nothing of his powers or his peril. He hadn't even had a chance to feed. Bella dared not leave him, fearing that Nyx would do away with him. She meant for him to benefit from the promised taste of the Huntress's blood.

The Huntress was a silent stalker, but their keen hearing picked up her soft-soled steps on the leafy carpet as she came down the path. Of vampires, there was no outward sign, but she sensed their presence soon enough. She stepped over the invisible line onto their chosen ground, and the battle was begun.

The river Peace knew no peace that night.

On the vampires' side were fear and fury and desperation. The Huntress remained cool, methodically picking them off one by one. Nyx was right about China Boy, Bella had to admit; he was more hindrance than help. Still, she clung to her resolve. They'd survive. Or not. But to give him up, to give Nyx the satisfaction? Never.

The clearing was soon a scene of utter chaos. Vampires sprang, scuttled, and flew around, toward, or away from the focus of their malevolence. A shrieking, snarling demonic din filled the night. No doubt, all mortals within hearing shivered in their tents. Only one dared brave the darkness for the sake of all. She stood at the center of the maelstrom, cool, and as yet unscathed.

Her hands blurred, so fast did they move — almost as fast as those of her foe. Nothing could escape her dark flashing eyes, it seemed, or her deadly weapons. Bella couldn't help admiring the Huntress as she went about her work as calmly as a woman cleaning house and with equal efficiency. Already vampires lay scattered about the clearing in still heaps of black or writhing and screaming in the throes of everlasting death. Some had disintegrated into dust.

A daunting prospect: their crew had been small, to begin with. Most of those remaining melted into the shadows and wondered, would any survive the night? The Prince remained coldly confident; Bella could see. He would not give up on his purpose. The Huntress would die, whatever the cost. He meant to have her blood.

Though terrified, they dared not defy him. When he signaled them to converge once more on the Huntress, Bella commanded China Boy to stay and joined the others. The unflagging attacks were part of the Prince's strategy to wear down this foe, she could see. An arduous task, and exceedingly dangerous; this was no ordinary mortal. But all he sought was a split second of inattention.

After that mad charge, Bella pulled up, trembling, and rejoined China Boy. It had been a close call. Rojo shrieked vengeance and streaked across the clearing, bent on destruction. He was such a hothead, too impulsive. China Boy was eager to join the fray, but he was too new. With great difficulty, she managed to restrain him.

The Prince roared a command, and at once, others flew into the attack. Bella caught sight of her little red fox trying to sneak up on the Huntress. Impossible. There was a giant cottonwood at her back. And it seemed that she knew what he was about. The stake in her hand changed like magic to a long-bladed knife.

Bella saw him slip a hand inside his cloak. The Huntress whirled and slashed. ¡Ay! She was going to behead him! Bella called out in her best imitation of Josie-girl, "Marie! Help me, Marie!"

The Huntress's glance flicked toward her for an instant. Rojo took the fleeting momentary opening, not to flee, as Bella expected, but to attack.

The long, flashing blade descended. Bella saw the sheen of blood on

Rojo's cloak as he tumbled to the ground at the Huntress's feet. He started to rise but fell back. The Huntress glanced down.

No-oo-ooo! With one hand fiercely clutching China Boy's plaid flannel sleeve, Bella could only stare in horror as the Huntress turned to get a clear swing at him, certain that was it for Rojo. But just then, Nyx and the Sandman flew in. They drew the Huntress's attention for a split second. Her long blades missed them by a hair's breadth, then they were away.

Bella screamed, "Flee, Rojo!"

He didn't even glance in her direction. Something flickered near his hand. The arrow! Ay, he meant to put the arrow through the Huntress! Fool. The Huntress was deflecting another attack by the Prince and Styx. Styx dodged death by a hair; the Prince danced out of reach of that long knife. Up went Rojo's good arm, aiming the deadly shaft toward her back, just above the kidney.

Good boy, Rojo, through the gut! That will put her down. And then she'll get a taste of the Prince's brand of mercy.

As Rojo thrust the arrow upward, the Huntress shifted her stance to slash at the Prince once more. The arrow missed its intended mark and instead plunged into her thigh. She cried out, her deadly calm disturbed at last. With a grimace of pain, she turned to dispatch her assailant, but he was no longer there. She whirled to face new attacks and inadvertently put her weight on her wounded leg. Her knife flew out of her hand as she stumbled and went down.

In the blink of an eye, the Prince stepped on her long hair to pin her to the ground. He snatched up her knife, and with one swift slash, cut the leather cord that hung around her neck. The little crucifix cut a silver arc through the night and vanished. The vampires scattered, hissing. But the Huntress was disarmed, and they converged at once, drawn by the smell of blood.

Now it was her blood, shed for the first time that night. And the last, Bella gloated, proud that Rojo had been the cause.

The Prince gazed down on the Huntress lying at his feet. "Where is our Josie-girl? Give her to me now."

She lifted her eyes to the Prince's face (unaffected by his charm, unlike ordinary mortals). "She is not yours. You will not have her."

The Prince sneered. "Then we will kill you, and after that, we will take your kin one by one until we find her."

"Even if you take me and all my kin, you will not find her here."

The Prince stared down at her, coldly, then his eyes flashed in sudden fury; with a snarl, he caught her up. She punched him in the jaw but may as well have hit a rock, for all the good it did. He drew her into his embrace. (How Bella envied her that!)

The Huntress's hand went behind her back and reappeared, gripping another knife. Bella was stunned by her swiftness—she was still quite capable of taking off a vampire's head! But the Prince's hand closed over hers like a steel trap; the knife dropped to the ground. Nyx kicked it away and gave the arrow a nudge with her boot. The Huntress cried out, her face twisted with pain. How Bella gloated at her disgrace and their Prince's conquest!

The Huntress strained to free herself, but he pressed his cheek against hers. "Away, filthy beast!" she cried. "Jesus, help me!"

The vampires shrank back, hissing at that forbidden Name. Even the Prince flinched, but he swiftly recovered, bent his head to her throat, and bit deep. She gasped, then her lips moved in prayer. Bella's lip curled. As if such mumbo-jumbo would stop the Prince!

Rub-a-dub-dub

Hanna, Oklahoma. April 2014

Exuberant whoops rose with the steam from the hot tub out under the trees. The three boys' only reaction was to shrug and grin as they put away ladders, paint, and brushes. It had taken them all afternoon to paint the garden shed. Cale closed the door of the garage, and they trudged across the yard toward the house. The chilly breath of spring hissed through the tall pines, sighing around the corners of the big log house and three cabins that comprised Tremaynes' Hanna Creek Bed and Breakfast. The sun was fast sinking in the west, gilding Cale's daddy's new black four-wheel-drive Ford pickup and his mama's blue Toyota sedan. The guests' silver Chrysler 300 outclassed them both.

"Nice wheels," Dace smirked. "What do we have here? Mob bosses?"

"Holy cow. Look at them dash lights. Leather seats too." Cale peered through a tinted window. "That's one sweet ride."

Jude shivered. Leather seats. The reference to mob bosses. But it wasn't a black Lincoln Town Car. He'd never forget that one.

The racket coming from the Jacuzzi had silenced the nightly chorus of frogs and crickets.

"City slickers," said Cale with a curl of his lip and a sardonic glance toward the deck across the yard.

"Look at it, just a-steaming," said Dace. "Hey, wouldn't it be funny if a bear come along and says, 'Somebody's mama's cooking dumplings. Let's eat!'" He laughed uproariously at his own joke.

"They sound a little pickled," Jude said. "I thought your mama didn't allow rowdies, Cale."

"She don't. They seemed okay, I reckon. Took the far cabin and kept to theirselves, mostly. They been here a few days already, but it don't look like they're hunting or fishing." He shrugged. "Maybe got bored; looks like they're into the booze."

"Ain't here for the scenery, neither, I reckon," Dace said, without much interest. "Hey Cale, you going to show us that new game of yours?"

"The new Fable?" said Jude eagerly. "C'mon, Cale. I hear it's a real sweet one."

Cale brightened. "Yeah, man, you gotta see these graphics."

As they mounted the steps to the porch amid avid discussion of the new game, the door opened. There stood Cale's mama with an armload of folded towels.

"Oh, thank the Lord, you're just in time," she burst out, flushed and sweating, her strawberry blond hair escaping its tie. "Boys, could you please run this stuff out to our guests in the hot tub? Not the cabin, the tub. Okay? I promised I'd have everything ready before they were finished soaking. What a day!"

The boys groaned but relented when she gave them a stern look. She loaded Cale up with a stack of towels. "Just one minute, Dace, Jude. I'll get the clothes. Can't have them running around in the buff." She gave them each an armful of freshly laundered clothing. "There, that's done. Thank you, boys."

As they turned away and headed down the long boardwalk toward the hot tub deck, they heard her muttering something under her breath about being thankful the royal pains would be leaving tomorrow.

Raucous laughter and a babble of male voices sounded loud and out-of-place in the serene woodsy setting. A cloud of steam obscured the view, but not enough to hide the fact that four men sat in the water, hair slick and faces red. Empty liquor bottles littered the deck.

Cale led the way to the wooden bench and deposited the towels there. Dace and Jude followed with the stacks of clean clothing.

"Hey, we got company," laughed a swarthy man with curly black hair and an enviable set of gleaming muscles.

All heads spun their way. Dace and Jude ducked shyly as the attention of these city folk zeroed in on them.

"Hello there," said Cale politely, more accustomed to out-of-town guests. "Your towels and clothing, sirs, fresh out of the dryer."

"Shucks," said another man, his shaved head and flabby tattooed shoulders shining above the surface of the water. "For a second there, I thought they was chicks."

"At the price we paid for this dump, you'd think they'd supply them free of charge," said the first.

"Never mind chicks. I'll take one of these. They're pretty enough," a third said loudly, as he bobbed in the water. Wet, rust-colored strands of hair were plastered to his head. To Jude, his fat face resembled nothing so much as a lump of dough after Mama'd punched it a few times. And the eyes—they were like blue-green cat's-eye marbles someone poked into the dough. Now they seemed to pierce him through. "Come here, my fine young lad," the man leered with an oily laugh.

Something about the expression and tone made Jude's hair stand on end.

"Shut up, knuckleheads," rasped the fourth, a weasel of a man with a big nose. "Remember why we're here. Pass me that bottle, will you?"

Jude felt thankful for his intervention. Until those bleak eyes turned toward him. He shivered at the look; suddenly, he couldn't wait to get out of there.

"No, I'm serious!" the doughy one bellowed. "I'll make it worth your while, kid."

"Er..." Cale began, but even he was at a loss for words, for once. The other two shifted their feet uncomfortably, wanting to politely escape but not knowing quite how.

The weasel took a long pull from the bottle while the swarthy one eyed the boys with a mocking grin. The shaved-head's stare merely made them uneasy, but when the redhead ran glittering eyes over them, it chilled their blood.

"Okay, kid. The towels," rasped the weasel. "Now go on, get out of here. Scram! I ain't got no tip for you."

That was all the encouragement the boys needed. They scuttled away as fast as they could while still retaining a shred of dignity, pursued by crude jokes and loud guffaws. They paused at the steps of the house.

"Dang!" said Cale. "If Ma heard that, she'd lay the boots to them!"

At the same time, Dace said, "My mama'd skin that old perve alive!"

"Think we should sic our mamas on them?" said Jude, managing a grin. "They could take them easy. There are only four of them, and they're city dudes, to boot."

"Yeah!" Dace agreed, laughing. "Ain't no sucker alive can stand up to my mama! Not even four of them against one of her!"

"Or how about the dogs?" shouted Cale. "My daddy's hounds'd eat 'em alive!"

"Cool!" whooped Dace. "Nobody'd ever find 'em again."

"Yeah. Too good for them, I reckon," Jude put in. "Calling this a dump." But that wasn't what made him shiver as though the long finger of evil had reached out and touched his spine.

The door opened, silencing them at once. All three pairs of eyes turned toward Cale's mother in the doorway.

"What's all the noise out here?"

"Nothing," they replied in unison.

She gave them a look.

"I, er, was just telling Dace and Jude about Fable," Cale hastily explained. "They was coming in to see."

She raised one eyebrow to let him know he hadn't fooled her. "Only for a few minutes. Jude, honey, you know your mama wants you home before dark."

She stood aside, and they followed Cale inside and down the stairs to his basement game room. The demonstration stretched out to fifteen minutes and then a half-hour. Cale's mother poked her head in the door and reminded them that it wasn't getting any earlier. Reluctantly, Jude got up to leave. His friends accompanied him outside for the final farewells.

The noises at the hot tub seemed to have died down. Cale grinned and shrugged. "Think they're dead?"

"No such luck, I reckon," said Jude, suppressing a shiver. "Well, I better go."

"See you tomorrow at the crack of dawn," said Dace.

Jude gave them the thumbs-up and started down the driveway, already daydreaming of the crawdad fishing expedition they had planned for the next morning.

"Meet you down at the creek bright and early," Cale called from the shadow of the tall pines by the garage where he and Dace stood watching.

Jude turned to wave.

"Six o'clock sharp," added Dace, who was waiting for his daddy to pick him up a little later when he came out to deliver machine parts to Mr. Tremayne.

Jude could have caught a ride with them, but Dace's daddy would likely be late and was sure to stand around talking for a while, besides. Mama'd start worrying if he wasn't home before dark. He squinted at the sky — well, he'd just about make it. He didn't mind walking; it wasn't far — only a few miles. And he'd seen no sign of the phantom since that time when he was twelve. He was a kid, then. Now he was fourteen, nearly a man. And the scare had lost its edge over time.

Anyhow, that tingling of his senses would warn him. He felt pretty confident in his growing strength and speed; the phantom wouldn't find it so easy to take him down, now. Maybe it was scared of him, he exulted, then common sense intervened, and he reminded himself that now he had a dog guarding the place, so maybe that was what kept it at bay. Li'l Scorpion was very protective. And he wasn't home yet.

The sky shone red in the west; long dark shadows were rapidly creeping across the landscape. Not that it mattered with his catlike night vision, but Mama'd start to worry once the sun set. He lengthened his stride; his long legs ate up the miles quickly. The nippy April air made small clouds of breath when he hit the low spots. He passed the school, Miz Lily's, Miz Sarah's, Whiskery Ned's, and soon left Hanna behind. While he was lost in thought, his feet seemed to find the way of their own accord.

Mama'd save scraps of leftover cooked chicken for them to use for bait. Hooks and lines were ready to go. He anticipated a big catch the next morning and smiled as he recalled the girls' excitement when he'd invited them over for the afternoon crawdad feast. Violet and Rosa Sharon loved that.

Gravel crunched behind him, and headlights topped the rise, pulling him out of his daydreams. Then he heard the purr of a motor and saw where he was — on the gravel road already, just a mile or so from the gate. Trees verdant with new growth crowded the lane ahead. A few stars twinkled in the darkening sky.

He moved to the shoulder to give the car room to pass on the narrow lane. The flash of headlights glinted off the trunks of trees and ran glowing lines along the barbed wire fence as it drew nearer. He expected it to drive on by, but it slowed beside him. He could tell by the sound that it wasn't any of his neighbors. Surprising – not many strangers had occasion to use this little back road.

It crunched to a full stop, and he glanced over. A silver car, too elegant for this neck of the woods. *Wait a minute.* Wasn't that the Chrysler 300 from Tremaynes'? Couldn't be. When he'd last seen the guests, they were soaking in the hot tub, wasted.

As the driver's window hummed open, he caught a whiff of alcohol. *Okay, maybe these were the same men.*

The muscular, sun-tanned arm at the wheel gave him a feeling of déjà vu. As did that signet ring on the broad hand that raised the sunglasses to eye him appraisingly. Sunglasses, in the dark? That struck him as familiar. And not from the hot tub.

Paco! Of course, that other time. These were the same ones that had stopped and asked him for directions. He was only a kid then. How had he not recognized that sleek dark face in the hot tub, the jutting jaw?

Jude's heart lurched within his chest.

Different car, but the same men. There was Dobbs in the passenger seat, bleak eyes fixed on him. Those eyes, how had he not recognized them — the weasel in the tub who'd told them to scram! The Tremaynes' city slicker guests. No wonder he'd sensed something familiar about them. *Not this again!*

He was vaguely aware of others sitting in the back seat but couldn't see them clearly through the tinted windows. His heart pounded. *No. They wouldn't catch him this time!* He knew what they were about. How could they think he was that dumb? He was at once poised to run, when the driver's short laugh stopped him in his tracks.

"Not so fast, sonny. Have a look."

The back window hummed open, and a sweet fragrance wafted out. *Jasmine? She was sitting in the middle, on the lap of a smiling man. No, not a man. Horror of horrors, there was that smell of death again!* And the long white fingers, with claws, long and shining. He shivered at the horror of it, without quite knowing why. Took in the others at a glance. Joey was wearing a white tank top, exposing a tattoo on each shoulder. Yes, he was the slick wet thug in the Jacuzzi with the coarse laugh and the stare. On the opposite side of the back seat was a stocky man wearing a scowl, a rumpled gray suit, and a flat gray cap. He hadn't been with them last time, but the mashed face, the piggy little eyes—this was the doughy man with the red hair he'd seen in the hot tub. The one with the twisted glitter in his eyes.

Jude's stomach lurched with revulsion. What did they want? And why was Jasmine with them? Her cheeks were streaked with tears and mascara as she turned pleading eyes toward him.

"I'm sorry," she said faintly. "I—I didn't know. Please. Help me."

His breath came faster as he tried to think what to do. He couldn't leave Jasmine to their mercy. At the sound of the driver's door opening, his every muscle tensed. He stood trembling.

"Easy, easy," said Paco softly, as though calming a shying horse. He and Dobbs slowly got out of the car.

Jude backed away. The back doors opened; the other two men got out.

"You get the picture. Come quietly, and nobody gets hurt," the weasel said, sauntering around the front of the car. A bulge under his light jacket looked ominously like a holstered pistol. And there were four of them—plus that thing, holding Jasmine.

Jude's eyes darted around frantically as the men slowly converged on him, making noises meant to be soothing. "Easy, boy, easy," said Paco. "Come here now."

Jude wanted to run, but Jasmine was in danger! No time to think. He darted between Joey and the redhead and leaned into the car. His unnaturally swift move shocked the men into immobility for a moment. He took hold of Jasmine's arm. Her captor held tight until he glanced into Jude's face.

Jude felt the heat behind his eyes and knew they were glowing when the sneering smile faded. The man began to babble incoherently, then flung

Jasmine at Jude and was out the open door on the other side. He scrambled across the road, into the ditch, and up the far bank, wailing. With a weird flapping sound, he vanished into the night. His piercing shrieks echoed through the woods, higher and higher, fading in the distance.

Jude stared in bewilderment until Jasmine's whimper brought him to himself, and he saw her terrified gaze on him. Didn't she know he'd never hurt her? Her eyes, like great violet pools, met his. They seemed to draw him in somehow (or was it the other way around?). He saw trust there and acquiescence. It gave him a strange and heady rush, a feeling that she'd do anything he asked.

A rustle of movement reminded him of their predicament. He caught her up in his arms. She clung to him as he drew her out of the car and stood her on her feet. For a moment, he held her close. His heart skipped a beat; he very nearly forgot his peril. He pressed his cheek to her hair, breathed in the sweet scent, and was amazed at how soft she felt. How often had he dreamed of this moment? If only this feeling could last forever.

Loud swearing broke the spell. The shocked and temporarily immobilized men came alive at last. At the crunch of footsteps on gravel, Jude gently disentangled himself from Jasmine's death grip. He turned her toward the open road. "Run, Jasmine! Go!"

She clung to him, staring up into his face with wide, frightened eyes. "But it's dark, and—"

A flicker of movement behind him told him she had only a matter of seconds. He pried her hands loose. "Run to Tom's, Jasmine. Hurry! Call for help."

Her gaze flicked suddenly from his to a point somewhere behind him. With a whimper of terror, she spun on her heel and ran down the road. There were shouts and curses from the men behind him as the sound of her footsteps blessedly diminished.

"Joey! Get the girl! Don't let her get away!"

Jude's heart raced as he turned to face the enemy. No wonder she was terrified. Four men advanced toward him, their eyes glittering with menace. He wanted to run, too, but no, he couldn't let them get Jasmine.

At Dobbs' shout, the man turned to chase Jasmine. He was big but fast, like a mean bull. Jude threw himself at him, fists flying.

The big man was solid but grunted with the impact, then brushed him off with a brawny arm as though he was no more than a pesky fly.

"Get the kid, Paco, McCabe!" Dobbs shouted.

Jude paid them no mind but darted at the big man again to give Jasmine time to escape. He rained blows on him, hitting the man wherever he could. It seemed as though his punches had no effect, but he kept at it.

Finally, the man stopped in his tracks and, with a roar, threw a swing at him.

Jude felt the wind of the flying fist ruffle his hair as he ducked and gave the big man a kidney shot. The man grunted.

Paco and McCabe rushed at Jude, gleeful as they thought to have trapped him between them.

"Okay, here we go," said Paco, grinning.

"Come here, my pretty," McCabe leered.

With a sinuous movement, Jude slipped away from the grasping hands, leaving the men in a tangle. Furious, they surged after him. He leaped aside, but they pinned him against the car. He fought with a strength and quickness that seemed to surprise them.

Jude smacked Paco's jaw.

"You little piece of—" Paco snarled, his ham-like fist coming straight for Jude's face.

Jude dodged the fist as easily as he had the rocks of Stave Cooper's gang.

Dobbs broke into a mirthless laugh at Paco's roar of pain as the fist slammed into the car, denting it. Paco shook his hand but didn't relax his death-grip on the front of Jude's shirt and threw him down. Jude's flailing fist caught Joey in the eye. The bald man swore and flung himself at Jude just as McCabe took one of Jude's flying feet in the groin. He squealed.

Jude saw him falling and tried to roll away, but the redhead fell on top of him, and the breath went out of him in a great rush.

"Don't... let him... get... away..." The big bald man's panting breath was hot and rank in Jude's face as he pinned Jude's shoulders.

McCabe moaned and clutched his middle as he lay heavily across Jude.

Jude labored for breath; Paco pinned his legs to the ground. Desperation. A short, fierce struggle ensued, during which Jude managed to slip a hand free to latch onto Joey's throat. He squeezed, hard, and felt the pinning of his shoulders ease as the man fought to dislodge the chokehold.

Dobbs stopped laughing and turned the air blue with curses. Jude saw a boot coming at him, and then he was whirling through the stars and blackness.

Awareness slowly returned; pain rolled over him. He gasped under the weight crushing him to the ground. Tried to think what had happened. Finally, he realized that the weight was Joey sitting on his chest. Joey was clawing at his own throat and still fighting for breath. A sharp pain shot up Jude's arm, but he managed not to cry out and noted vaguely that the weasel's boot was grinding his hand into the gravel.

"I almost thought youse was the three stooges," Dobbs was saying as he got a firm grip on Jude's hair. "Quit your whining, McCabe. Let's get this over with."

McCabe stopped moaning and began searching his coat pockets. Gravel bit into Jude's back. His jaw ached, and a sharp pain stabbed his arm again as Dobbs shifted his weight. Jude heard the clink of something metallic and slid his eyes over to see. A thin line gleamed in the moonlight. *A needle! No! Panic seized him. No, don't panic.* But the heat built up behind his eyes again. There was a loud snap, and blue light flashed like sheet lightning. A branch hanging over the road exploded in a shower of sparks. *Mama, help! What's happening?*

With a superhuman effort, he heaved his entire body, and the three muscular men went flying in as many directions. He sprang to his feet, dislodged Dobbs' grip on his hair, and sent him flying. He winced as pain streaked the length of his forearm. The men snarled and grunted, falling over each other, but soon scrambled to their feet and came after him again.

"Grab him, Joey," Dobbs shouted. "Don't let him get away."

Jude whirled to dodge, first Joey's clutching hands, and then McCabe's. He paused, panting, and for an instant, the car was encased in a shimmering blue light. *Nooo! What is it?* Everyone's hair lifted from the static in the air.

"What the hell?" squawked Joey, scanning the cloudless sky in bewilderment.

Jude felt lost and alone, wondering as much as they what was happening.

The men exchanged glances and then turned to stare at Jude uneasily.

"Snap to it," Dobbs snarled. "What are you scared of? He's only a dumb farm kid!" And he dived at him.

Jude slipped through the clutching hands, then paused irresolutely and panting as he cradled his injured wrist. Pain shot up his arm each time he moved; he had to grit his teeth to keep from crying out. He swept his surroundings with a frantic gaze, seeking escape. The air crackled as balls of fire burst into existence among the branches, then fell in globs and showers of sparks to wink out before they hit the ground.

McCabe whimpered. "What the hell is it, Dobbs? Nobody said nothing about this!"

Jude stared as a streak of blue light flickered just above the road, sizzling, then zapped away into the woods. Something burst into flame, throwing sparks, and then was gone. He closed his eyes. *What's wrong with me? Wherever I look, wherever I look —*

"Some kind of voodoo," croaked Paco. "I ain't having nothing to do with that."

"Lee'll have our hides if we let the kid get away again," shouted Dobbs, cursing. "Don't you chicken out on me now!"

Jude opened his eyes again, warily, afraid of what they'd do next. But those men. He needed to see.

Joey glared. "I'm going to kill that kid!"

As one, they rushed at him. Paco was the unlucky one charging straight on. A blue flame knocked him to the ground; he lay on his back, unmoving, his shirt front smoking. Jude stood frozen with horror at the realization that he may have killed a man. He thought of the fox. Was it his eyes? Could eyes really do that? For a moment, the men stood like statues. Dobbs swore. "What's with you girls? Get the freak!"

Paco groaned and stirred, and Jude breathed again. The man was alive! He was so relieved that being called a freak didn't carry its usual sting. The others swarmed toward him again. He twisted away, out of reach, still favoring his injured wrist. He felt the heat rising again, and a fence post across the road burst into flame. Never mind, at least Jasmine was gone, out of harm's way. Now all he had to do was run.

A sharp little pain touched his thigh, no more than a pinch, a mere annoyance. Nothing much. He brushed at it without thinking and began to run. There was a faint clink on the gravel as something fell away.

At the first step, his legs turned to water, and he was down on the ground. He tried to get up but only managed to get to his knees. His body didn't want to obey; his brain felt numb. What had happened?

"Quick! Grab him," snarled the weasel. "Where's that rope?"

"What the hell did he do to Paco?" said McCabe, bending over the supine form of his comrade. "Are you okay, man?"

Paco groaned, and with McCabe's assistance, sat up groggily.

"No wonder the vampire ran away," Joey muttered. "It musta knew something we didn't."

"McCabe!" shouted Dobbs. "Get over here!"

Head hanging, Jude felt them dragging his arms behind his back. Pain shot up his injured arm as they forced his wrists together and tied them tight. He clenched his jaw to keep from crying out. There was no strength in his muscles to resist; he vaguely wondered what was wrong but couldn't think. The weasel grabbed his hair and pulled his head back to peer into his face.

"Look out, man," said Joey nervously. "It's his eyes. See what he done to the trees and —"

"He don't look no different than any other kid," Dobbs speculated, amidst a stream of obscenities, "except maybe prettier." He laughed a mirthless laugh.

"He ain't any other kid, man," Joey croaked. "He damn near tore my throat out. Hey, McCabe, how come he ain't put under yet? I thought you—"

McCabe turned, looking up as he helped Paco to his feet. "What the—? He ain't out? Impossible! I dosed him but good!"

Paco touched his chest gingerly and whimpered, "His eyes. Watch out for his eyes." He lurched and fell against the car, panting. "What the hell kind of freak are we dealing with?"

They all turned to stare at their prisoner. Jude could feel the eyes, smell the fear, hear the heartbeats racing. His eyelids felt so heavy he almost couldn't keep them open, but somehow he knew he must not give in. What would Mama do if he didn't come home? He hated to think of her worrying, looking out the window and down the driveway for a sight of him. Quieting the dog's whining as it sensed her unease. The lamp would be lit and supper on the table, waiting. At the thought of food, his stomach felt queasy. He grimaced in an effort to keep from emptying it in front of his foes.

"I say we blindfold him," said McCabe uneasily. "I don't want those eyes on me. He should have been out by now. Twice over, at his weight. I give him a double dose, like Lee said."

"A double dose?" said Joey slowly, with a suspicious glance at Jude. "Why would you give him so much?"

"Lee never says no more than he has to. You know that," McCabe growled.

"He did warn us to remember the last time," said Dobbs. "Said the kid's stronger than he looks, and—" He fixed his bleak gaze on Jude. "What the hell are you, boy?"

The others unconsciously moved back a few steps, but Jude didn't answer. He didn't know the answer. Besides, he was afraid that if he opened his mouth, he'd throw up. If only he could concentrate, if only he could gather his thoughts, but they seemed to slip from his mind to scatter in every direction.

"I don't know as I want to be in the same car with him," wheezed Paco. "Unless you knock him out first."

"Let me hit him," rasped Joey, brandishing a fist. "I'd like to hit him, just once."

"The hell with all this babble, girls," Dobbs said. "Just toss him in the trunk, and let's get out of here. "He ain't going to do nothing. Give him another dose if you're scared, McCabe."

McCabe swore. "Yeah, and we'll be in Dutch for sure if it kills him."

"Fine," Dobbs snarled. "Joey, you drive. Paco and McCabe, you sit in the back with the kid. Have that needle ready in case he livens up. We don't want no fiasco like last time. Quit your whining, Paco, and move it!"

Paco ensconced himself in the back seat, with a lot of moaning and his hand to his chest. Goaded by Dobbs, Joey and McCabe laid their hands tentatively on Jude and lifted him to his feet. He couldn't seem to do anything about it, couldn't even stand by himself. Reassured of his helplessness, they got a bit braver and dragged him toward the open car door. Jude feebly tried to resist, the thought piercing the fog of his mind that once they had him in the car, all hope would be gone, but a black tide kept trying to pull him under. He managed to keep his head above it. All that cursing and swearing must mean something, though he hardly knew what he was doing.

"The hell with this noise!" rasped Dobbs. "Shoot him up again, McCabe. That oughta tame him." McCabe hesitated a bit too long. "Do it now!" Dobbs snarled.

The others paused in their efforts to stare uncertainly as McCabe fumbled in his pockets. "This is all I got," he grumbled. "What if we need it later?"

Dobbs swore. McCabe eyed him dubiously but drew the syringe from its plastic case and advanced on Jude. Even through the numbness of his brain, Jude recognized the threat. He was leaning against the car, beside the open door. He braced his feet, thinking to run, but Joey choked him back, a muscular forearm at his throat.

He saw that metallic glint again, and his heart raced. As the needle neared him, he shied back in panic, straining against his captor.

"Hold him still," growled McCabe. "Damn, Lee better give me my quality time with him, after all this!"

Joey's beefy forearm tightened as Jude strained to break the hold and to evade the needle stalking him. Pain streaked through his arm, and again, he felt the heat gathering behind his eyes. All sense of control scattered and was lost. Static crackled. Tongues of blue flame rippled through the trees; the acrid smell of smoke and panicked cries filled the air.

A glare of yellow light suddenly blinded him. The restraining hands vanished, and his world tilted. Something slammed him in the side of the head. When the stars and planets stopped spinning, he opened his eyes. Feet were rushing past at an odd angle. It came to him that he was lying on the ground. He vaguely heard shouts and sounds of a scuffle. Had they forgotten him? *Run.* He panted with the effort but could not seem to move. The black tide washed over him.

He emerged from the fog and heard running footsteps, the slamming of car doors, the revving of a motor. Gravel pelted him as the car peeled off. The rumble of its motor receded and vanished. The glaring yellow light was still there. Footsteps approached, and his heart fell. What would Mama do when he never came home? Gravel crunched beside him. Jude opened heavy-lidded eyes and saw shiny black shoes and a long black skirt. Trying to see made him dizzy; he closed his eyes. A hand gripped his shoulder.

He jumped, his breath coming short and fast. No, the blue light, the flame—no good to panic.

"Oh, thank the good God you're still alive," rumbled a male voice. *Skirt?* Jude thought, and then a little frantically, or cape (remembering the beast on the throne in his nightmare)? *No, no, that wasn't real. Or was it?*

The kindly voice interrupted his anxious rambling thoughts. "I've sent the thugs packing. This knot is pretty tight. If you'll just hang in there, I'll cut these ropes off." His rescuer began humming a tune as he sawed at the bonds. Jude groaned involuntarily as pain shot up his arm. "Oh! Sorry, I didn't—wait a minute! Looks like you might have a broken wrist. I didn't realize. Here. I'll be careful. I've got a first aid kit in the car. Oh. You want to get up? Let me help."

Strong hands lifted Jude to his feet and steadied him as he stood trembling, favoring his injured wrist and trying to get his bearings. He opened his eyes cautiously, on guard against the return of dizziness or the blue flame.

"Thanks," he mumbled. "I—I gotta get home." His mouth, his head, seemed full of cotton.

For the first time, he got a look at the stocky older man, not quite his height. He took in the bluff, good-humored face with heavy jowls, a wide, generous mouth, twinkling eyes of an odd greenish color, and sandy-red hair in rather a wild disarray.

Those eyes. Where have I seen them before?

He suddenly noticed that the man was wearing the long black robe and cowl of the monks at the monastery. Sharply he drew away from those helping hands. The man didn't try to restrain him. Jude's first step was more of a lurch. He staggered, breathing heavily, and caught himself against the small blue car parked there. Something was wrong, but he couldn't think what. He had to get away. Mama would worry if he didn't get home soon. What if she came searching and those men were still on the prowl? Anyhow, the monk made him uneasy. What was he doing here?

"You don't look so good," said the monk with a concerned expression. "Let me drive you to the hospital."

Jude came to himself with a start, wondering why he was leaning against the car with his head hanging. Suddenly the monk was closer, as though he'd moved to catch him if he fell. Jude forced himself to stand upright. Finally, he realized what the monk had said.

"No. No hospital. I'm okay." He frowned, trying to puzzle out what that white box the monk held in his hand could be.

"Okay, no hospital. But you're in no shape to walk. I'll drive you home, then." The monk put a gentle hand on his shoulder. "Let me take care of that arm first." He set the white box on the hood of the car and opened the lid.

Jude realized then that it was a first aid kit. "No need," he said (or thought he did), but the monk went ahead and began to put a splint and bandage on his arm. He had no energy to resist and stood half-dazed until the smell of coffee and the sound of the monk's voice jerked him into awareness. He must have zoned out again.

"I was just saying, maybe this coffee will help. You look as though you need it. I'll drive you home if you point the way. Come now. I don't mean you any harm."

Never ride with strangers. "Who are you?" It was hard to get the words out. After a long time, it seemed, he noticed a steaming mug in his hand and wondered vaguely how it got there.

"Sorry, I should have introduced myself. I'm Father Paul Schultz," the man said in a cheerful tone. He reached out to shake hands, then stopped; Jude held the coffee in one hand, and the other was bandaged. "And you are—?"

Something made Jude want to trust him, though he couldn't think what it was. In fact, he couldn't think straight about much of anything. He took a sip of the hot coffee as he tried to reorient himself. "Jude Martel," he slurred, finally.

The monk seemed to understand him well enough, for he repeated it with a curiously speculative look. "Martel?" he murmured softly. "Ah."

Suddenly he was rushing around. He opened the front door on the passenger side, picked up a heap of books and papers, and transferred them to the back seat next to a gym bag. "Here we go," he said finally, cheery and red-faced. "Come on, son. I'll drive you home." While Jude tried to comprehend, he added, "I can't leave you here. Those hoodlums probably won't be back, but I wouldn't chance it. And you're in no shape to walk."

Jude couldn't deny it. He allowed the monk to assist him into the car, where he sat breathing hard, fighting dizziness. It wouldn't do to throw up now.

"You okay?" said the monk as he handed back the coffee cup (Jude couldn't remember him having taken it). The monk closed the door and went around to get into the driver's seat. The car purred as he eased onto the road. "I think what you need now is to get home and sleep it off. How you can still function after the dose they gave you, I can't imagine. I found the syringe," he added, shaking his head.

"Just down the road here a ways." Jude panted from the effort of trying to get the right words out. "A white gate, um… our driveway." (The monk nodded; he must have understood.) As they rumbled along the gravel road, taking it easy where there were potholes, the trees sliding past made him dizzy, and he had to close his eyes. He zoned out again… smelled flowers.　And sprang into consciousness. *Jasmine! How could he have forgotten?* He clutched at the monk's sleeve. "I have to find her. Jasmine! I can't—"

The monk glanced over at him sharply. "Jasmine? You were with someone?"

"No, they were going to—I don't know. I told her to run. You didn't see her down the road?" Laboriously, he lifted his gaze to search the monk's face.

"No, I didn't see anyone."

Jude sat back, worried now as he imagined what might have happened to her, each scenario worse than the last. What if she was wandering in the woods, lost and frightened in the dark, or lying in the ditch with a sprained ankle, or retaken by the hoodlums, or that vampire? At that, he felt a bit of panic. "I told her to run to Tom Rowe's." It took an effort to speak, to think. Fat lot of good he was, trying to be the hero and save her. "Stop the car. I have to find her." He began fumbling for the door handle.

"Hold on, now," the monk said. "You stay right where you are. I'll call this Tom Rowe. Do you have his number?" A cell phone appeared in his hand, glowing blue.

"Number?" Jude concentrated. After a few false starts, he finally retrieved it from his memory. He managed to enunciate the digits without slurring too much, he guessed, since the monk seemed to understand. While he placed the call, Jude sipped from the cup; his shaking hands nearly spilled the coffee. If anything happened to Jasmine, he'd never forgive himself. She'd done something foolish, true, but had depended on him for rescue. She wasn't used to running around in the woods; didn't have his night vision. Had he sent her to her death?

"Rest easy," the monk said after a short conversation on the phone. "She's fine, aside from a bit of hysteria. Tom Rowe drove her home. Ned Farwell was just gathering a posse to come and rescue you. They're glad to hear that you're safe and on your way home."

Jude sighed with relief. Jasmine was safe; for now, that was the important thing. Except Mama would be worried. He was probably later now than if he'd caught a ride with the Finches; it seemed he'd left Tremaynes' a lifetime ago. He took another sip of coffee. Must not doze off; must be awake so Mama would know he was okay.

Jude glanced at the monk. The lights of the dash highlighted a somewhat lumpy face, a kind face. Had he really whipped four thugs by himself? An old guy like that? A monk? Suspicion entered his mind. "How did you happen to come along just then?" He tried to keep his voice steady.

The monk's swamp-water green eyes flicked to Jude's face and back to the road, almost as though he'd forgotten the presence of his passenger until he spoke. "I was on retreat at the abbey. Have a meeting with the bishop at lunch tomorrow. Lucky for you, I decided to get an early start and head back to Tulsa tonight."

Jude's heart skipped a beat. The thugs had mentioned the monastery when they asked directions, or no, that was the other time. But was there a connection? "Were those men at the abbey?" he said warily.

"No, they weren't." Then monk seemed to catch the note of suspicion in Jude's tone. "No. I've never seen them before."

"But you whipped them by yourself? All four of them? No. You couldn't have. Just one old guy? Where is your army?" Jude halted, abashed at how that came out.

The monk gave a great booming laugh. "My army? I only have the invisible kind, son, and I may be old, but the element of surprise somewhat evens it out." He sobered. "You weren't doing so bad yourself, for a youngster. I can see you're quick and strong—but some training would do you no harm. No, I'm serious—I'd really like to see what you can do. Sorry I arrived so late in the game—a few minutes more, and it might not have ended so well for you."

He gave Jude a quick glance, and unfazed by Jude's lack of response, went on. "I haven't seen you at my classes. Or maybe you haven't heard. I teach martial arts at your school gym here two nights a week. Part of an outreach program to keep kids out of mischief. All kinds of kids—you'd fit right in. And you'd be surprised at the difference a bit of training makes. Control, self-discipline, and practice—it'll do wonders for your confidence and skill. Come and join us. Mondays and Wednesdays, seven sharp. I'd like to see you there."

The cheerful tone faded to a faint buzz as Jude zoned out again, until the familiar sound of Li'l Scorpion's bark brought him out of his fog. It seemed they were slowly bouncing up the driveway. He felt something in his hand—oh, okay, the thermos cup. He lifted it to his lips, but the little that was left was cold. The aroma revived him a bit. Li'l Scorpion's bark had changed, the deeper tones trailing off into yips and a whine that meant he recognized his master.

Mama must have noticed, because a bright beam leaped out from the door as it opened. Her silhouette cast a long shadow toward them. The car came to a halt. Jude was trying to think what to do next when his door opened, and the monk was there beside him. Mama was on the porch peering into the night, trying to shush the dog and call Jude's name at the same time.

He felt a gentle hand on his shoulder. "You're home, now, son," said his rescuer kindly. With strong arms, the monk lifted him out of the car and to his wayward feet.

At once, Li'l Scorpion's exuberant greeting overwhelmed them. The cold nose poked at him as the dog wagged itself between them and out again to circle around, whining. Still trying to gather his scattered wits, Jude leaned on the solid shoulder and let the monk guide him to the house.

A background orchestra of crickets and frogs gradually resumed after the momentary interruption. Evergreens whispered, and deciduous trees rattled in the night breezes.

Mama ran down the step toward them when she saw that it was really Jude come home. "What happened to you, son?"

There was no hiding anything from her. He meant to answer, but nothing intelligible came out.

"He should be okay once he sleeps it off," the monk said, "but if you like, I can drive him to the hospital. He didn't want me to, but it's your call."

"No! No hospital," she burst out, and then took a deep breath. "I mean, thank you very much, but we'll be fine. Oh. We've met before, right? You're—"

"Father Paul Schultz. Of course. The name Martel did ring a bell. The car accident, yes, a few years ago."

"Nine, actually. And you found him—them—that time, too. How, er, what happened?"

"Tonight? Well, I chanced upon your son in the midst of a little altercation just down the road."

Jude was only too glad to let the monk explain. His mind was still fuzzy, and he didn't think the words would come out right. He let the monk and his mama help him up the steps and into the house, where they eased him onto the couch. He sank into the soft cushions, his eyes heavy-lidded. He sensed rather than saw his mama's concern.

"I'm fine, Mama," he mumbled, trying not to favor his injured arm too much.

"Yes, darling, you just rest," she said, smoothing his hair. "Sleep now. You can tell me all about it tomorrow."

Only then did he relax. *All was right in the world.* Mama was listening to the monk's tale. The murmur of voices faded in and out. He thought he heard the monk say that even a sparrow does not fall without the Heavenly Father knowing. He couldn't think what that had to do with anything but was so tired that he drifted off to sleep before he could hear more.

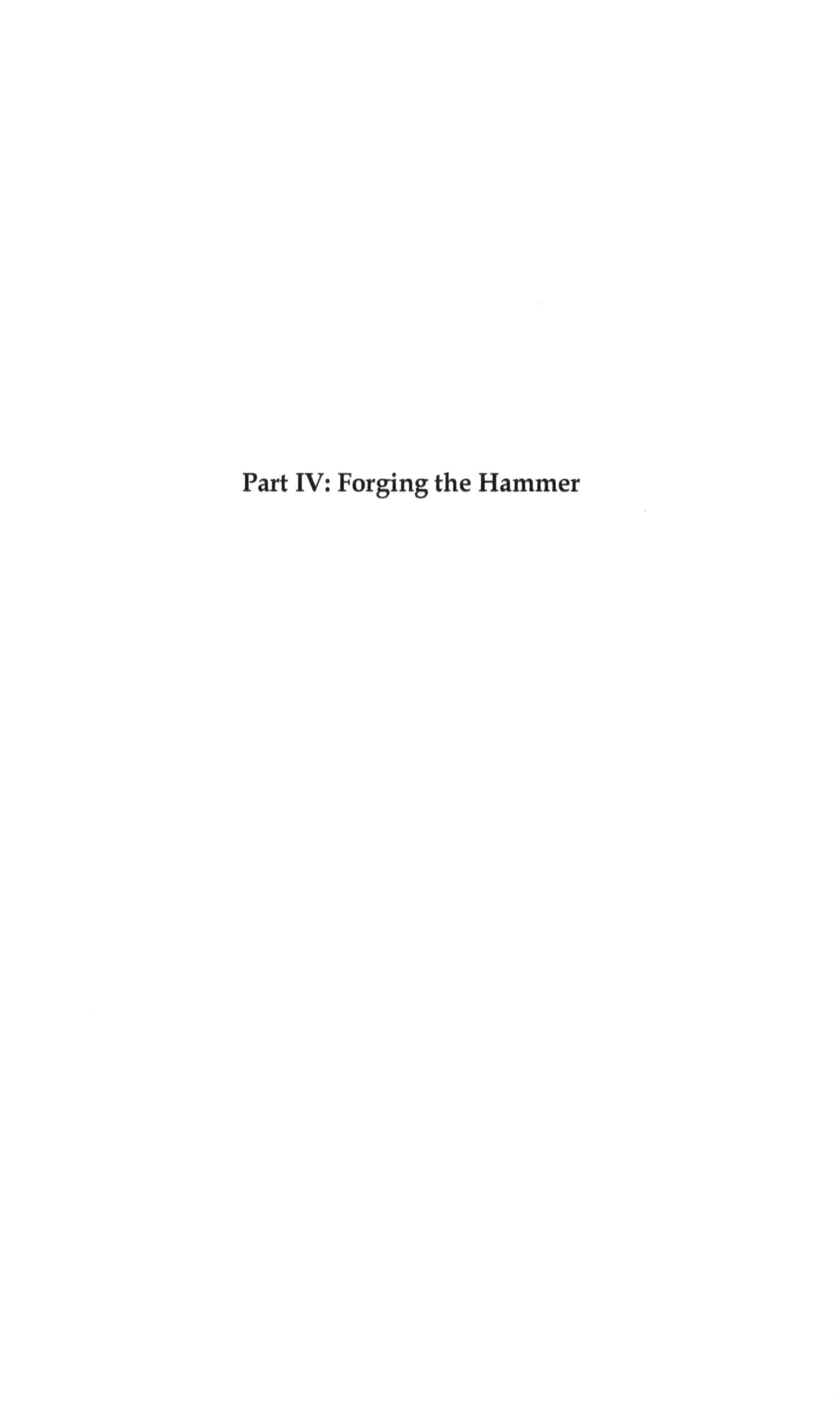

Part IV: Forging the Hammer

Guardian of the Ring

Father Paul Schultz had not thought of the Ring in decades, not since he was eighteen and leaving home for college. His father, like Tobias, had taken him aside to impart some words of wisdom before his son embarked on this venture into the wide world. The young Paul had listened with proper deference, but in his anticipation of adventure, his mind wandered. He should have paid attention. He was the first in fourteen generations born with the distinctive olive-drab eyes that marked those of his family destined to be a Guardian. Though it was not until much later that this duty was thrust upon him, and in a way quite differently than he had ever imagined.

"The Ring, and what our illustrious ancestor has written concerning it— are you listening?"

Startled from his reverie by his father's sudden roar, Paul stammered something inane, but that raised eyebrow gave him his cue. "Of course, the Ring. The one in our family's charge since… which my illustrious ancestor, er—"

His father sighed. "Listen. You have the green eyes. Very likely, you may one day be called upon to serve."

"Yes, sir," Paul said in a tone suitably grave, though other things, of more immediate interest, occupied his mind.

His father rather gruffly intoned the familiar creed. "His journal specifically states that one of our House must guard the Ring always. Not only from those who covet its power and would use it for evil, but also for those to whom it rightfully belongs. Only they may safely possess it; only we may hold it in trust for them. Woe betide all mankind if it falls into the wrong hands, for then the world will be darkened, and fiends from hell shall reign."

Father Paul had heard the story since he was knee-high to a grasshopper. Of how a High King (or was it God?) had long ago bestowed the Ring upon a certain king known far and wide for his uprightness and wondrous valor. A ring of gold, set with one large ruby and three small sapphires. Upon this solemn occasion, their own ancestor, loyal vassal of the favored king, had signed an oath in blood, binding those of his House in perpetuity as Guardians of the Ring. They were given the honor of preserving the gift for those of that lineage, wherever — or whenever — they might be. Political intrigues and wars had long since swallowed up said Royal House. Yet it stood to reason that there were individuals out there, somewhere, with that royal blood coursing through their veins, and one day the Guardian may be obliged, for the sake of the world, to find them and serve — to the death, if necessary.

The story itself had been written down long after the fact and passed on from one generation to the next, preserved in an ancient, faded, leather-bound journal — one of the family's most treasured possessions. Never mind that it was almost illegible. To read it was hardly necessary; memories were long and storytellers rife in the family of Guardians. The journal was merely the visible, palpable proof, impressing upon each new generation the sweet burden never to be forgotten. All accepted it as their birthright.

Father Paul had never seen the Ring. Nor had his father or grandfather. That was irrelevant. They could recognize the Ring if they saw it, just as they would know those of the royal blood, as though it were ingrained in their DNA. In a way it was, due to that oath. They could no more deny their dedication to this end, their devotion to it as to a sacred duty, than break any other religious vow. It was a matter of honor, of destiny, of a promise of the highest order, though, throughout history, their involvement variously waxed and waned along with the fortunes of men and nations.

According to family tradition, the Ring had disappeared back in the sixteenth century. (Was there mention of vampires here — no, that couldn't be right, could it?) The Protestant Rebellion was in full swing, the Ring all but forgotten, as the family was caught up in the affairs of the time. However, their destiny was bound to that ancient oath and never altogether lost. It only lay dormant, ready to awaken when its time came.

Father Paul had long since put it on the back burner with all other medieval considerations. For years, he had hardly thought of the Ring at all; he told himself it had perhaps found its way back into the hands of those to whom it rightfully belonged.

Alas, he had recently come to believe otherwise.

In this modern era, man was so caught up in the busyness and noise of industry and technology that he had become deaf to important things — notably, the Voice of God. Father Paul knew that in some way, He would make Himself heard, but at this late date, it seemed unlikely that the call would come in his lifetime (never mind the green eyes).

So when he opened the newspaper one fine day in the early twenty-first century, he was shocked out of his complacency. On the Science and Technology page was a photograph of a display of ancient artifacts — and there, among them, was the Ring! According to the caption, two young college students, Roger Lewis and Lee Davis, had discovered the artifacts while exploring caves. Though authentic, they were apparently of debatable importance, according to a spokesman for the scientific community.

Father Paul knew nothing of that, but he recognized the Ring. There was no doubt in his mind what this meant. Priest or no, he dared not shirk his family responsibility.

He had indeed found adventure upon leaving home those many years ago. He'd gone on from college to the seminary — which pleased his parents, who had prayed that God would choose one of their sons for His own — and in due time was ordained. His family was renowned throughout the ages for its soldiers and priests. He chose to be both when he subsequently joined the Marines as chaplain. He survived the war in Vietnam and, in due time, came back to resume his place in civilian society.

Nothing was the same. Even he was not. He had been to hell and back. But his experience had taught him much of both the good and the evil in man, and he was the wiser for it. He was also a lot older than those few years would indicate. Sadly, the veterans were not welcomed home as heroes but reviled as imperialists and worse, even by some of their own people. He told himself that even Jesus was betrayed by one of His own and counted himself lucky; he had faith. Some had nothing that they could see. He made the transition relatively smoothly and tried to help others. The fact that they were marked as psychotic killers did nothing to ease their re-entry into society.

As the years went by, young people wandered, lost and questioning. Many turned to Eastern and New Age cults, to ultimately end in despair. Others turned to drugs and crime, with the same result. The loss of such potential, and souls, was a travesty. Father Paul did what he could.

Martial arts became the fashion. At first, like many others who sought a way to stem society's headlong rush toward chaos, Father Paul was saddened by this one more example of man seeing violence as a solution to his problems, but he soon realized that this new trend was potentially a defense against violence. With proper instruction, youth could become protectors of the weak and the champions of good: modern knights.

Though no longer a spring chicken, Father Paul had his Marine training, and he'd kept fit; the reflexes were still there. Ah, here was a way to give a generation of lost youth direction in their search for the meaning of life. Fired by a newfound enthusiasm, he managed to gain permission from his superiors. "To get the kids off the streets" was his argument that tipped the balance. He would teach them self-discipline, generate self-respect, and instill a sense of purpose in their lives. He juggled his busy schedule to fit in martial arts classes. He loved the challenge. The results were satisfying, with youngsters on the road to perdition quite turning their lives around due to his efforts — and God's intervention, of course.

Then he saw that newspaper article and was instantly in turmoil. Would he have to change the course of his life now, at this late date, when he had such a good thing going? Abandon his troubled teens to go on some medieval quest to return the Ring to its rightful owner? A difficult thing, making changes when one was past sixty. If only one of these two young men was of the family to whom the Ring rightfully belonged, there would be no reason to get involved. Of course, that would have been too easy.

Father Paul tossed the paper aside and forgot it until a couple of weeks later when he was giving his quarters a thorough cleaning. There was the paper, under a chair, the photo face up. He put it in the pile destined for the trash and went on sweeping; tried to ignore it, but his conscience would not be still. With a sigh of resignation, he retrieved the article and took down the information. His father (*may he rest in peace*) would have said he was still trying to run from responsibility.

One day soon after, he happened to be in Chicago. He inquired at the office of the university and was told that Davis was off-campus for the weekend, but young Lewis could be found in the lab at almost any time. He had absolutely no social life. Father Paul was soon knocking on the door of the lab. By then, he was resigned to attending to this family business. He'd get it over with and then get on with his life. Unlike Roger Lewis, Father Paul had a life, a very busy one, and did not relish the thought of interrupting it. Granted, there had always been that possibility of being called forth at a moment's notice; the fact that nothing had happened in five-hundred years meant nothing.

And in whose possession had the Ring been all that time? The denizens of hell, it would seem, considering the sad state of the world. That would make young Mr. Lewis quite the hero for retrieving it. But if he was not of the royal blood, he was only an unwitting pawn in this deeply serious chess game of circumstance. Father Paul could not stand by and do nothing while an innocent bystander was set to take the consequences.

Even so, he sighed deeply. The door finally opened, and a rather rumpled young man peered out at him through thick glasses and croaked a greeting.

"Roger Lewis?" Father Paul said.

The young man took in the monk's habit at a glance and gulped. "Sorry, Father, er, uh —" He collected himself. "I get so involved in my work, I —"

"No need to apologize. I came unannounced, after all." Father Paul hastily introduced himself and made a brief mention of his purpose. "If you're too busy right now, I can arrange to see you another time." He wanted to say that time was of no importance, but no, he could not let his father down or the generations of family that came before. He would get no rest until he had attended to this matter.

Roger Lewis hesitated, then abruptly invited him in. "Now is as good a time as any, Father. Have a seat." He rushed around, clearing papers and various items from a couple of dilapidated chrome-and-plastic kitchen chairs that stood near a small table. "My apologies for the mess." He scooped up an unwashed coffee mug and an empty McDonald's bag from the table, put the one in the sink, and tossed the other in the garbage. He gave the table a cursory wipe with a damp dishcloth. "I wasn't expecting visitors. Just a minute, I'll get us some coffee."

He plugged in an electric kettle and spooned instant coffee into two clean mugs. Father Paul cringed (being a real coffee man, himself). When Roger set a giant jar of Coffee-Mate on the table, he fervently thanked God he drank his coffee black.

He was tempted to classify Roger as the proverbial absent-minded professor. He hadn't the aspect of a prince, or — what would royalty look like? All would be revealed in good time, he was sure; his first priority was the Ring. He took a chair and tried not to gaze in horror at the sorry excuse for coffee as he laid the news clipping on the table.

"I saw this article and would like to know more about your discovery, Mr. Lewis. If you don't mind, that is."

The young student glanced at the clipping only momentarily before lifting his eyes to Father Paul's face rather apprehensively. "What would you like to know?"

"Well, for starters, how and where you found these artifacts. And, if I may, to see them."

The little line of worry between Roger's brows faded. "I appreciate your interest in my work, Father. I spend so much time in the lab, the days run together. I was afraid I'd forgotten Sunday Mass again. It wouldn't be the first time, I'm afraid. My pastor gives me a call now and then to remind me. I try not to neglect my spiritual life after, er, what happened. Sorry, that probably isn't... "

Father Paul decided that this babbling was perhaps a form of self-defense after the professional drubbing he'd received when his wild tale broke the news. That could account for his nervousness in the presence of an authority figure. But over coffee, which Father Paul managed to choke down rather smoothly, Roger relaxed and told his story.

Had it not been for Father Paul's own equally fantastic story, he may have dismissed it outright, as others had.

Roger told of how he and his friend Lee had explored many an underground cave over the years while on vacation, collecting fossils and taking photographs. In the summer of 2010, they'd made the discovery of a lifetime because they'd taken a wrong road. They ended up in a cave that wasn't on their map. Amidst a network of passages was a chamber so vast that even these many months later, Roger described it with a sense of awe. Like a cathedral, he said—in size, that is, for there was nothing of holiness in it; the sense of evil was almost palpable.

Even though they had the best of flashlights, the darkness seemed oddly thick and black and oppressive. Roger noticed figures drawn on the walls—perhaps letters, he realized, upon closer inspection. He had studied various scripts and languages of ancient times, but this was unfamiliar. Filled with excitement, he whipped out his camera and began to take pictures.

Then Lee pointed out to him that there were torches fastened high on the walls, only recently extinguished. With a chill of apprehension and a quick glance around, they decided to move on. They chose at random one of the passages branching off from the huge cavern and followed it. Roger had never before been afraid, but there was something about this place. Lee pressed on, as though driven; Roger reluctantly followed. And they found something they'd never dreamed of. Here he paused in his narrative and lifted his gaze to meet that of the monk.

A vampire, tucked away in a corner, asleep.

A vampire! Father Paul almost laughed but saw that Roger was serious. *Ah. No wonder he'd gotten himself into hot water with the scientific crowd.*

The young man said matter-of-factly that it wasn't quite what they had expected (but he didn't backtrack!). This demanded a serious readjustment of Father Paul's ability to suspend disbelief—even coming from a family rife with tales of vampires. But that was way back when people were superstitious and actually believed in such things!

The two young scientists were no doubt disbelieving of their senses as well. But when the vampire's eyes sprang open and glowed red as live coals, they nearly died of terror on the spot. Roger froze, Lee ran. Not back toward the surface and the safety of sunshine, but onward. When Roger heard a terrible shriek from the direction Lee had gone, he managed to come to his senses. He backed away from that terrifying apparition, turned, and ran down the passage, after his friend. Around the corner, he found Lee standing, petrified. Yet another vampire seemed to be holding him in thrall with its hypnotic gaze. Roger yelled. Lee didn't respond. With eyes averted from that deadly gaze, Roger grabbed his friend's arm and dragged him away, back up the passage.

They ran, back the way they had come, as near as he could figure. Crushing darkness was all around them, but they rushed on, following the scant beam of the flashlight, the sound of their panting nearly drowning out a distant wailing and flapping of wings. Vampires? Roger found himself praying, something he hadn't done in years.

All at once, he'd measured his length on the floor. Had something hit him? Or maybe he'd tripped—he couldn't be sure. At any rate, he'd lost his grip on both Lee and the flashlight. All was pitch black; the light had gone out. There was no sound from Lee. Roger groped about in the dark; no luck. In desperation, he promised God never to miss Sunday Mass again if he got out alive. Then he felt the flashlight under his hand and breathed again. He flicked it on and shone it around. There was no sign of Lee.

And he was in a strange place. He felt a bit of panic but then realized that he was in a small room cluttered with all sorts of things hung on walls or lined up on shelves: ancient charts, maps, weapons, books, and human skulls. A pile of papyrus scrolls sat on a table in the center of the room; one lay open as though someone had recently been studying it. What a find! As Roger eagerly shone his light around, a flash of red caught in the beam. A ruby ring!

He heard a rustling sound then. Lee? No, that was no human sound. In sudden panic, he snatched up the ring and the scroll, crammed them into his backpack, and fled.

From behind him came the echoing sounds of flapping and squeaking, like bats. Were they bats or vampires? *Dear God, what had they awakened?* Distant screams and growls were growing louder, nearer. Something was following, tracking him in the dark!

He prayed as he hadn't prayed in years. And ran on.

Like in a nightmare, the way seemed never-ending, but at last, he saw a spot of light ahead—the cave entrance! He threw himself out, into the sunlight, and not a moment too soon. Flame shot out of the cave after him; a horrific scream made the very air shiver. A nauseating cloud rolled over him, the stench of smoke and sulfur and death.

Beside himself with terror, he'd scrambled down the hillside, heedless of thorns piercing his clothing and tearing at his flesh. Better that than claws and teeth!

He didn't stop running until he reached the campsite, got the jeep packed up, ready to go, and — *oh, no! Lee*. He couldn't just abandon him! He eyed the pile of rocks on the hill and paced, chain-smoking as he waited for his friend to appear. Time seemed to crawl. Still, he waited.

After the sun had passed its zenith, he'd kept glancing at his watch, his nerves frazzled. He had to be long gone by sunset. *But — Lee!* He despaired of ever seeing his friend again. He knew in his heart that if something emerged from that cave after the sun went down, it would not be Lee, and he did not mean to be there. It was time. He had to leave now, with or without him.

He'd stubbed out his last cigarette and started the jeep. He glanced up the hill one last time. There was Lee, sauntering down the trail, his hair neatly in place, and his clothing hardly rumpled, just as though he'd been out for a Sunday stroll in the park at the university. Not like he'd been running for his life.

Roger still couldn't explain it, but Lee had not been the same since. He seemed cold, preoccupied.

"So. Is he a — ?" Father Paul dared not say the word.

Roger shook his head. "No, he isn't a vampire."

If that were even possible, Father Paul thought. He was only just getting used to the idea that vampires actually might exist, after all.

Roger and Lee had continued to work on projects together, but Lee seemed driven to accomplish some mysterious work of his own, besides. Something he called the Ponce de Leon Project.

"As in Ponce de Leon and his search for the Fountain of Youth?"

"Apparently. Only he claims to be ahead of the game on this one. The explorer of old didn't have modern resources or technology, whereas he knows what the Fountain of Youth is and will soon have it in hand. Then he added, with a cold laugh quite unlike himself, 'This is a secret that will rock the world, my friend. We'll be rich as Croesus.'"

Roger shrugged. "I don't understand. We've always been friends — played, worked, and studied together. I've never known him to be preoccupied with wealth or power. Knowledge, yes. Something happened to him in that cave. But what?" Roger shook his head. "It's as though he's caught a weird strain of gold fever."

Roger brought out his artifacts for Father Paul's inspection. It was the Ring, all right. His fingers itched to make away with it, whatever the cost.

He didn't quite dare tell even Roger his own harebrained story. *Truth is often stranger than fiction*, he realized.

Father Paul soon ascertained that Roger was not even remotely related to either the family of the Guardian or the Royal one. Thus his possession of the Ring was a danger to his life and his soul, but only Father Paul knew that, and he had to keep it to himself for the present. Roger wasn't ready to accept the truth yet.

But, vampires? That was hard to swallow, notwithstanding mention of them in his own family history. Like most people, Father Paul had always considered the vampire a creature of myth or a mental aberration. Any mention of such things, even in his family history, he'd chalked up to imagination, metaphor, or medieval superstition. But now, in the light of Roger's story, it seemed he had better rethink this.

His own family tradition claimed that several millennia ago, the Ring had fallen into the hands of the master vampire (which maybe wasn't a metaphor, after all!). It was not until the tenth or eleventh century that the Guardian monk Praetorius had finally retrieved the Ring once more. Though unable to destroy the master vampire, he'd managed to bind him underground with a hedge of light. A temporary measure only, to keep the lid on his power until the time of the Consecrated One (referred to in prophecy as The Hammer), who was supposedly destined to shed his blood on the altar of sacrifice to destroy this one who called himself Charon, along with his vile brood.

Father Paul suggested that Roger be wary of his friend Lee. Something was not right in whatever had happened to him. If only the whereabouts of the cave hadn't been lost, he could have confronted that ancient monster in its lair as his ancestor had. Or, he conceded, it may very well be that he wasn't the one meant to do that. So, where was that royal family? To his knowledge, they hadn't been heard of for centuries, so why was the Ring here, then? With a sigh, he left Roger to his work.

He resumed his busy schedule, relegating the puzzle to the back burner once more. All that was in the past; God knew he had enough on his plate. Still, he couldn't seem to stop thinking about it. Apparently, God was not about to let him off the hook. The mystery had taken on a life of its own, and he was caught in the middle, like it or not.

Just when he thought everything was back to normal and would continue on that way indefinitely (by now, he should have known better, of course), the whole thing exploded like a mine on the battlefield, right in his face.

The Hammer blasted into his life like a bolt from the blue (literally!), changing everything in an instant. The royal family had clearly not been extinguished, after all, no matter that they'd vanished from the face of the Earth for five centuries.

The message was clear, he could ignore it no longer; now it was his turn. Now he was called, as certain as his ancestors had been, to honor the long-ago oath and serve.

One fateful night, as he was driving down a country road thinking of other, more mundane things—anything but that—the prince of the blood walked into his life. Or fell into it, would perhaps be more accurate.

Who would have guessed that a backwoods boy sprung from the foothills of the Ozarks was a prince? And yet, there was a certain regal dignity about him, like some exotic flower growing delicate and lovely among dandelions and thistles. He was completely unaware of who he really was, as it turned out, or of his pre-ordained role in wresting the fate of the world from the clutches of the vampire Charon and his rout.

Father Paul's responsibility was clear and unmistakable. Struck in an instant by something beyond the natural, he'd sensed the importance of this apparent happenstance meeting. He was the Guardian, perhaps the only one who had any inkling of what this was about. Though somewhat in the dark himself, he realized that this was not something he could ignore.

Gradually he came to understand that this boy was indeed the key to the whole mystery. It was up to him to break the news to him—gently, of course. One slip of the tongue and all would be lost—but he'd always had a way with people.

By treading carefully each step of the way, he began to instruct his student and to give him direction. He'd never expected to accomplish his task overnight. In truth, it was an arduous process, with many worries and praying late into the sleepless nights. Yet the time came when his patience was rewarded, so easily that he wondered (with a rueful glance up to heaven) why he'd been so worried.

He did at last gain the boy's trust. Lo and behold, this hope of the world began to confide in him! And soon, all those other hard-won bits of information, like pieces of a jigsaw puzzle, began to fall into place too. How it finally happened was a marvel and a miracle. Then again, what about this whole story wasn't?

The Mark

April 2014

The monk thought back to the sequence of events that had brought him to this point. First, the reappearance of the Ring in the hands of a student who had no idea of the significance of the treasure he'd found while he himself, who did know, had so blithely shoved it to the back burner. Nearly a year had passed since, but coincidentally, the monk was working over the puzzle in his mind once again as he drove to the abbey.

He hadn't planned to go on retreat at that particular time. He'd meant to wait until the end of the month, then come back rejuvenated for the winding up of the school year and preparing for summer classes. But the bishop had stepped in and told him to go at once (he had a sense for when people needed a break). Obedient to the bishop, he went, though not without a regretful glance at the mound of papers on his desk. Only later did he see God's hand in this; one slip could have meant disaster.

The retreat was just half over when a call came from the bishop's office; His Excellency urgently required his presence at lunchtime the next day. At this interruption, Father Paul grew anxious to get back to his regular duties; he decided not to wait until the next morning to drive back to the city. He filled his thermos with strong coffee, and thus fortified, bade his Brothers farewell and set out for Tulsa. He enjoyed nighttime driving, and the weather was perfect—the stars were out, and the sky was clear. Singing and black coffee would keep him awake.

He was well into his first song when that blue flash of light ahead startled him into silence. Lightning? He peered around and upward. Strange, there wasn't a cloud in the sky. Two more flashes in quick succession streaked upward and along the tops of the trees. An electrical disturbance? A tree fallen across a power line? He slowed the car and proceeded cautiously, eyes peeled for a broken line or pole. There was no wind; an accident, then?

That was when he topped the final rise and saw at a glance that it was none of these things.

A car was parked in the road, its motor running, doors open, headlights blazing. The monk squinted to see past the glare. Dark figures were moving this way and that, what appeared to be men scuffling beside the car. Amidst the moving shadows, two spots of light suddenly appeared. Oddly, almost like deer eyes glowing in the dark. But then blue flame streaked from them, and with an explosion of sparks, a wooden fence post across the road burst into flame.

The monk stared in disbelief as the post crackled and burned. *Dear God, those weren't deer eyes! Did I just see what I thought I saw?* He quickly made the Sign of the Cross and pulled over to the side of the road, not far from the scuffle. He might have been invisible for all the notice he attracted.

Several men were trying to force a resisting young man into the car. He seemed to be giving them a bit of trouble even with his hands tied behind his back, but it was a losing battle. They pushed his head down, and for an instant, his hair shone bright like a flame in the light of the car's interior. Three grown men against a mere stripling?

Outraged, the monk had leaped from his car and waded into the melee. A few well-placed kicks and punches, and it was over. There were four men, actually. They piled into the car and fled in a spray of gravel.

As the dust settled, the monk caught sight of something gleaming on the ground at his feet. *A needle! So that was what this was about.* He turned to the boy with the thought of checking his pulse but hesitated as those eyes opened and tried to focus.

"Don't be afraid. The men are gone," he said quickly, breathing a prayer of thanksgiving as the eyes closed (he didn't care to have them focus on him, after what he'd seen — or thought he'd seen). He set about cutting the cord that bound the boy's wrists, administered first aid, and drove him home.

Without a second thought, he'd invited him to join his classes. He'd seen at a glance that the boy was a natural; he just needed direction and training. If he'd met that boy six months earlier, the thugs wouldn't have made it to first base. Anyway, he knew he had to get to know him, and class was a start. For this was no ordinary boy; there was more to him than met the eye. Something told him this might be one of that royal family.

And the fact that others were interested in him too — the wrong kind — spoke volumes. It couldn't be mere coincidence that he'd come along just at the right moment to foil the designs of the evil one. Like his ancestor Praetorius, he was the Guardian, bound by the oath. He had to look into the matter; it wasn't an option. He now knew where his duty lay, saw the handwriting on the wall, heard the Voice calling. Like Samuel, he could only say, Here I am, Lord, come to do Thy will.

That changed everything. This was his mission; now, he burned to accomplish it. His mind went into overdrive, planning, accessing various avenues of research and Roger Lewis. Classes would resume on schedule, opening the path. The boy would have to come to him, which didn't look too promising, he feared. His mother was very protective and wary of strangers. *Well, all in God's time*, he told himself.

It was a harrowing four weeks of waiting; time seemed to pass at a snail's pace. The monk was on edge the whole time, wondering if the boy would come to him before it was too late (whatever that meant, but he had a feeling).

Then it happened.

That Wednesday, the monk's class of "misfits" had already finished the mandatory opening prayer and was well into the warm-up exercises, when he noticed the boy standing in the open doorway. He'd come! The monk called to him to remove his shoes and join in. He did so but took his place rather conspicuously as a newcomer, in T-shirt and faded jeans. The veterans wore tank tops and shorts.

The rest of the class eyed him askance at first, some with superior grins, until they realized what he could do. The grins faded and turned to admiration. His lean build was deceptive, gave the impression that he was slight and delicate, but in truth, he was like a cat, with every movement revealing a latent power. Yet, for all his natural talent, he needed the confidence and discipline that comes with proper training and practice.

The monk meant to provide that.

Before long, the boy surpassed the other students, but this evoked no envy. The combination of toughness and his sweet disposition disarmed them all. This popularity seemed to surprise the boy. At times he seemed to withdraw into himself for no apparent reason. It was, the monk eventually learned, due to unfortunate experiences at school, his fear of revealing what he referred to as his "oddities," and being called a freak. Or worse, the Goblin King. However, most of those in the class either came with the monk from the inner city or from the outer reaches of the community; few had known him before.

The monk had rules and enforced them. There was to be no harassment, no hazing, for this was a brotherhood. All took an oath of loyalty to one another. Like the knights of old, the purpose of developing fighting skills was to protect and defend the weak. Chivalry was the order of the day, the ideal to cultivate virtue and practice charity.

In the beginning, the boy had had no idea what to do with his powers or how to control them. They just happened. The monk gave him the means to deal with them and helped him grow in self-knowledge, self-discipline, and above all, faith in God.

A daunting task. But I must do this. I am the Guardian. He, the prince of the blood. I am certain of it.

The martial arts class was step one of his training. When the boy came to trust him as a friend, the monk arranged to teach him one-on-one. No easy task; his mother seemed apprehensive. Was it because he was a stranger, an authority figure, a priest, or all of the above? With the monastery so close, it was unfortunate, and untenable, that she (a teacher!) hadn't taken advantage of its treasures. It appeared to him that she must have become disenchanted with the Church at one time, for she avoided attending, though seemed never to have lost her faith entirely; she'd obviously passed it on to her son. But perhaps some of the shadows as well, the monk decided, when the boy resisted his invitation to attend a retreat at the monastery, and even Mass, when he first invited him (though later he found that it was another reason altogether).

The regular classes worked wonders. He blossomed and gradually came to confide in the monk, revealing one thing and another about his life. All the old stories, about the fireball falling from the sky that dawn, the recurring nightmares, the Lady in Blue (as he referred to her), and his oddities.

The monk made notes and conducted some research. He soon saw that this boy wasn't who, or even what, he seemed. There were discrepancies. For one thing, he looked nothing like his mother or father, and there wasn't one person in his ancestry who could account for his looks, at least not in any of the photographs the monk saw when he was finally invited for dinner.

Here the monk proceeded with caution. He feared that if the boy's mother got the idea that there was more to this than just a casual interest in mentoring a fatherless teenage boy, she'd stop his plans cold. The woman shied away from anyone who showed an interest in her son. *Why?*

Did she know of his destiny, or — *aha!* Did she have no clue about it?

The monk suddenly recalled her husband's dying words and tried everything short of asking outright if the boy was her natural child, but she was a regular Houdini — impossible to pin down. The boy himself clearly had no idea.

The monk checked the court records; they backed up her claim that the boy was born at home. The record at a nearby church noted in the margin that his mother had baptized him herself. The priest was not entirely approving since the baby was not in imminent danger of dying, and she herself rarely attended church.

So. Back to other resources. The answers had to be somewhere. Thinking back, he wondered that he had not known at once who the boy was. He'd heard of him through the grapevine. But he was more than a local legend; he was sure of it.

A thought struck him — that scroll Roger had found in the cave, with its so-called prophetic poem! He'd been so focused on the Ring that he'd dismissed the scroll as of little account. Now he wondered if he had been too hasty. What if the scroll with its poem was the key to solving this riddle? The boy had to be the One! Everything added up; no, it couldn't be just wishful thinking on his part.

How many humans had eyes that glowed and the strength of this boy?

He certainly had never expected to find the hero just up the road from the abbey, but he should have; God's plan is always perfect.

That name should have been a clue, though it wasn't the name he'd expected. His name should be Sperling. That had stopped him in his tracks, but only for a moment. There had to be an explanation for that, and he'd figure it out. There was that certain something about him.

The Testament

Soon after, the monk discovered the manuscript that confirmed his theories and changed everything.

The monastery was always open to the monk when he was disinclined to drive back to the city after class. The boys who rode out with him were welcome to stay in a guest cabin. The peaceful atmosphere was more than beneficial; not often did the inner city boys get to breathe serenity, but they also enjoyed the monks' homemade raisin cookies, pound cakes, bread, and cheese. Hospitality is part of the Benedictine tradition; when Brother Pascal learned that the boys were mostly from poor families, he prepared packages for them to take home when they were ready to start back the next morning.

The monk had dropped Jude off at his home on the way to the abbey, as usual. After settling the other boys in one of the guest cabins for the night, he made a beeline for the library, which was extensive; in all the time he'd spent perusing the books, he'd not nearly plumbed its depths. He was sure he would find what he was looking for, a clue or something, urged on by the feeling that time was running out.

Corroboration of the tales passed down from his own family was what he needed—some small hint that they weren't just legends. *I mean, vampires? Royalty? Give me a break, Lord. How medieval do You think I am?*

Medieval. Ah, yes, there was that book he'd noted before—odd how it had somehow slipped his mind. The devil is hard at work, here—*I must be onto something!* And there, at last, he found an unexpected treasure. To think he'd nearly missed it!

The book on Solesmes that had seemed so promising turned out to merely point the way to the real treasure—a slim volume that slid out with it as he plucked it from the shelf, a leather-bound book with faded gilt lettering. He was about to return it to its place with no more than a passing glance at the front cover, until the author's name caught his eye. *Sperling.*

Sperling was the name taken by the family he was sworn to serve!

It was as if the book was placed in his hand! Literally. Ah, but wasn't that how everything had been going in this matter of the Ring? *Whatever You say, Lord.*

He returned the other book to the shelf and, heart beating fast, opened the old manuscript. Age had taken its toll, but the leaves were of the finest quality vellum, beautifully hand-stitched. It was written in Latin in an elegant hand. Watermarks blurred the words on some of the pages. Tears? He glanced again at the title. *Yes, I'd say so.* He found an armchair and sat down to read:

Theodor Sperling's Account of the Dolors of Engelsburg (1573)

To the loving Reader.

Since I must, I now set down this testament of the tragic events that took place this past year. Abbot Robert has charged me with this task, that the truth be not lost. Thus I sit down to write. It is for me an arduous work, and one of unfathomable sorrow. I humbly ask your forbearance, dear Reader. The tale I tell, however difficult to believe, is the truth. To this I solemnly swear before God and upon my family's honor.

At the foot of this holy mountain lie the remains of the village of Engelsburg, a once-peaceful paradise amidst our strife-torn lands.

My story begins with the arrival of Father Ludger, pastor of the village of Engelsburg, at our gate one dark night. The hour was late. We had just finished Compline when the bell rang. The old priest was spent after his trek up the mountain, his face ghastly white. Brother Porter hastened to open the gate, fearing wolves were at the traveler's heels, so frightening was his visage. He brought our visitor to the warmth of the hearth, round which we gathered to take the chill off before retiring to our cells.

How the old priest had braved the night to come to us, I do not know, for evil was abroad in the darkness, an evil more ancient and ravenous than wolves. We welcomed our weary guest with customary hospitality and revived him with bread, cheese, and a cup of heated wine. He implored us to bear with him should we find his tale beyond belief. With that, he gave utterance to the unspeakable: vampires had come to the village of Engelsburg.

We glanced at one another, shifted our feet uneasily, and murmured amongst ourselves. Some shook their heads. He could not have meant vampires. No, they are not real. Such tales arose from vestiges of ancient pagan beliefs still clung to by certain of the lower classes, mere superstition. The educated no longer believed in them. We murmured in sympathy, but our skepticism was impossible to conceal. Even those of us who knew him best and loved him most wondered. This holy man of God had served for many years. The suggestion was untenable. Had age taken its toll?

Father Ludger hastened to explain that he would have referred to them as demons, had Herr Mond not insisted that he specify. Mathias Mond! The good doctor was renowned as a grave and sober man of science, not given to superstition. Abbot Robert quieted us with a stern look and assured the venerable

Father that we would help him in any way we could. And so in troubled silence, we listened to his tragic tale.

This very evening he was called to the house of a highly esteemed family, to the deathbed of a young man whom he could vouch for as beyond reproach. He had baptized him, taught him his catechism, trained him as an altar boy, and watched him grow to virtuous manhood.

Sweat beaded his brow, and his face grew pale in the telling of his story. His eyes lifted to the concerned faces around him. When his gaze met mine, he broke off in mid-sentence as though his voice failed him just then, and he quickly glanced away. The silence grew long before he finally resumed speaking.

As he neared the house to attend the dying youth, the night seemed unnaturally dark and still. There were no clouds, yet a creeping black mist obscured the stars. The rising moon had a sinister red cast to it, and he felt the taint of evil. He shivered, but not from the cold. Nor wolves, for none were howling in the nearby forest. Only utter silence and a strange chill in the air that seemed not natural. He arrived at the stately home and was led to the youth lying on a bed, still and pale as death. He prepared to administer the last rites in the event that there was a spark of life there still.

As his shadow fell across the bed, a shudder racked the body lying there. He saw that the young man still drew breath, though very slow and shallow. He commenced the ritual. When he signed the cross on the forehead with holy oil, the young man's countenance expressed unimaginable agony. Concerned now that this was of the devil, though he did not wish to unduly alarm the family standing around, he held a crucifix to the young man's lips for a kiss. The boy's eyes flew open to glow red with sheer hatred, and he gnashed his teeth. Father Ludger snatched the crucifix back to prevent desecration. The boy's eyes and mouth closed, and his face returned once more to its accustomed angelic beauty. The priest would have doubted the horror he had seen but for the heartrending groan that followed. Someone began weeping quietly.

The priest recited prayers of exorcism while sprinkling holy water copiously about. He managed to conceal his anxiety as he offered words of comfort to the mother and father and turned to leave. Surely a Christian burial in hallowed ground would end this.

But as he passed through the kitchen, the doctor, Mathias Mond, spoke to him. The esteemed physician held a cup of wine. His hand shook as he lifted it to his lips. The priest, with heart sorely troubled, saw that he would not make good his retreat just yet, though he longed to go to the church to plead Our Lady's counsel. The doctor poured another cup and pressed it into the priest's hand.

"Here. Have some wine, Father. You look as though you need it." The doctor emptied his own glass in one gulp.

"No. No, thank you, Mathias." The old pastor raised his eyes from the trembling hand to the perspiring face.

"What do you think?" The doctor nodded toward the other room as he refilled his own cup. "Your pallor betrays you, Father. I know you, too, have seen something."

"Ah, you are disturbed, Mathias." The priest was not yet prepared to affirm the doctor's suspicion. "What is your diagnosis?"

Mond shook his head. "Is this not more your area of expertise?" He took not his eyes off the priest as he tossed back the wine.

"I administered Extreme Unction," said the good Father. "Prayer and holy water have by the grace of God ousted the devil. Let us hope we see no more of him."

"I don't think it's enough this time," said the doctor slowly, crossing himself. He leaned closer. "You don't think so either, do you? The boy's father perhaps has his suspicions. He was frantic when he came to me. And you know Franziscus. He remains always calm, whatever the provocation."

I felt a chill. That was my father's name! Had I heard him aright? But to pursue that angle was madness. Maybe he meant someone else. The old priest continued.

"He said the boy was listless all day," the doctor went on. "Then, when he went out to secure the outbuildings for the night, he did not return to the house. Franziscus found him lying unconscious on the ground. Aside from a bit of blood on his mouth, nothing seemed amiss, yet clearly, something was very wrong. He begged me to hurry.

"Franziscus, anxious? I said to myself. I grabbed my bag and rushed over here at once. You know what I found. The boy was that pale because he had almost bled out! There was no cause that I could see, at first. The cut lip would not account for it. There was no blood on the ground, his father said, nor on his clothing.

"I then examined him more thoroughly..." He gulped more wine. "Then I saw them. Two small puncture marks at his throat." The doctor stared at the priest as though waiting for a comment.

"And that accounted for the loss of blood?" said the priest uneasily.

"What do you think?" whispered the doctor harshly. "Bite marks, Father! Not animal, nor human. It could only have been the work of — no, I dare not say it! But I must! Father, it goes against all that I believe, but this is the work of a vampire! There, I have said it. Call me mad if you wish, superstitious if you must. Or tell me it is not that. You are the expert on these matters. I am only a physician."

Father Ludger was silent. He was not prepared for this. He did not believe in vampires. Demons, yes, but vampires? That foul superstition of the peasantry? "Are you certain?" He searched Herr Mond's face. This he had never thought to encounter.

"No, of course not! Do you think I actually believe in such things?" He shook his head. "But what else could it be? Tell me. I want to know that I am wrong, or I am a fool — anything but that!"

"I agree; it is preposterous. Show me the wounds." The priest knew the doctor would not make this up. And after what he himself had seen —

Quietly they reentered the room where the young man lay. The distraught family members stood or sat, waiting. The mother sadly glanced at the priest and doctor, then urged the children to kiss their dying brother before taking them off to bed.

Only then did the doctor speak softly to the father. He nodded, and the priest went over to the young man. Herr Mond drew back the bedclothes, exposing two barely noticeable marks on the white throat. He pressed the waxen skin, and they oozed red.

"See these puncture wounds, caused by the same razor-sharp instrument as those on the lip. No tearing or bruising, which rules out any tool that comes to mind. Tell me this was not caused by a vampire's teeth!"

The old priest stood silent. A young life struck down in so hideous a manner chilled his blood and his soul.

"He must be told." Herr Mond nodded in the father's direction.

Mechanically the priest agreed. They drew the young man's father to the kitchen and told him of their suspicions. Delicately they suggested that precautions be taken. The father, in his grief and shock, denied the obvious. The doctor left shaking his head; the priest had not much hope that the man would oblige.

Father Ludger was asked to stay. It was not long. He led the prayer for the dying until finally, the young man breathed his last. The moment of death was stark and terrible; there was one final, convulsive movement, so utterly, unnaturally silent, almost as though his soul was wrenched from his body, rather than passing peacefully from this world to the next. The priest regarded with compassion and wonder that terrible image of the devil gnashing his teeth as the weeping mother tried to comfort her son. Finally, the boy was still, the illusion faded as though it had never been, and he lay like a sleeping angel in his mother's arms.

As Father Ludger left the house, he wanted to turn the other way; to pretend he had not seen what he had seen. He went to the church and poured out his heart before the tabernacle. There he felt the urging of Our Blessed Lady; he must hurry to the monks on the mountain to plead with them to storm heaven for mercy. He had no other recourse. The father was not amenable to staking or beheading his son, which, even after all he had witnessed, seemed a gruesome measure. Even now, it was difficult to believe in the existence of vampires. He kept seeking some other, more credible explanation. But he had felt the evil there, seen it, and could not shake the feeling that the funeral would likely not be the end of the matter, after all.

These terrible tidings wrenched at all our hearts. I myself felt a growing dread, but even so, when the old pastor revealed the name of the unfortunate boy, I was stunned. It was my own brother, Niklaus. With permission, I retired to the chapel to pray.

I was awakened for Lauds at dawn by the monks, my Brothers. I had fallen asleep on the floor of the chapel and had missed Matins. In charity, they had let me sleep. By that time, our visitor was well on his way down the mountain. The good monks had persuaded him to stay until dawn, as they feared for his safety. But he was anxious for his flock and hurried away at first light.

I could not dispel the image in my mind's eye, of hell opening up to swallow our village. Vampires! Had Father imagined it? No, he was not prone to fits of imagination, and the respected doctor had verified it. Of course, my father would deny it. Such a thing was too horrible to contemplate about one's own child. The only solution unthinkable.

Abbot Robert set us to storming heaven at once. Day and night, we lifted our pleas to God and chanted the prayers of exorcism. In the end, I could not but believe. Though I myself was not allowed to leave the monastery, a contingent of our Brothers attended the funeral, to scout the battlefield, some said. From my aerie, the abbey on the mountaintop, I gazed down upon the valley and turned my heart to Jesus, my Savior. How else can I bear this anguish?

Even when I had renounced all I loved in the world by entering the monastery, it was not like this sense of abandonment. God had called me to this life, and His love was ever my consolation, though I missed my family then, as well. No, this was not the same. I grieved as I gazed down at the pine forests falling away into the morning mist. Beyond was the patchwork quilt of beech groves and vineyards stretching down to the village.

It was not over. Even from the mountaintop, we heard the eerie wail that chilled our blood as the coffin was lowered into the ground. We prayed, but that did not stop what happened after. My God, my God, what had Niki done to so draw divine wrath down upon his head? Ah, but who am I to doubt God's infinite wisdom? I resign myself to His Holy Will. Everything He does is for love of us. We continued to pray.

Evil lay like a dark cloud over what had once been a land of light and peace. After they buried my brother, he came back a slavering beast, and the killing began. When he tried to go into the house and was unable to enter, all doubt vanished as to what he had become. He was a vampire. Villagers raided the cemetery and opened his coffin. It was badly scored and empty but for a broken rosary. We could not but believe, then.

Word from the village had it that my brother was seen in the company of a woman in black. A vampire, some said. Together they ravaged the land. For a fortnight, terror and madness reigned as my brother slew all of our family, and others as well. That woman was wearing the Ring! Had she beguiled our Niki into giving her that precious heirloom? Woe betide us, a Judas in our midst! His betrayal tears my heart asunder, yet I pray the Lord to be merciful, to save his soul from eternal damnation.

But the Ring, fallen into the hands of evil, is a catastrophe of the highest order. May God save us! Alas, where was the Guardian?

It is said that the Ring was passed down from the king, our ancestor since ancient times, to belong to those of our lineage forever. Both blessing and curse are attached. He who possesses the Ring by right shall rule, but should it depart from him and fall into the wrong hands, dire consequences to the entire world shall follow. Thus was a Guardian assigned to the Ring. Beyond that, a cloak of secrecy veiled this tradition, and only the heirs were privileged to have knowledge of it, for one day, it would pass to them.

Woe to those of evil intent; claim it at your peril! The fate of your soul hangs in the balance, and perhaps that of the entire world.

It should come as no surprise, then, that the Ring has ever been regarded with a certain amount of fear in this age of superstition. Only in our family, or in the care of the Guardian, is it safe.

The Ring's appearance is no secret. It is designed of gold filigree, intertwined leaves, crown, scepter. One large, perfect red carbuncle is set with three small blue sapphires. Red for the Blood of the Lamb and blue for Our Lady. Beneath the stone is a symbol by which the Consecrated One shall be recognized: A tau cross hammer with a loop signifying eternity.

It is said that whosoever possesses it shall hold the world in his hand. But he must be of our royal blood. That is, the Consecrated One, chosen by God to defeat the lord of the night. Fair and mighty, he shall be known as Our Lady's Hammer, by virtue carrying her favor into battle. A mark on his body will reveal him, the same as on the Ring. He bears a cross on his shoulder and is destined for suffering and sacrifice. Woe to whosoever holds the Ring without right, for he shall bring destruction upon all.

Now the Ring is lost. Where is the Guardian in this, our time of need?

Father Ludger worked untiringly to administer Extreme Unction conditionally even where all hope seemed lost, sadly burying many of his dear flock. We at the abbey join them in spirit, begging God's mercy and Our Lady's intercession. Between Abbot Robert and the Prince-Archbishop, a solemn exorcism is now initiated.

Our line dies here. I am the only one left. Is this the end of the world? I know not. Why spare me only, Lord, unworthy servant that I am? The answer comes from the depths of my dark night. I must offer all I have, myself, my life, for my family, for the salvation of the soul of my forsaken brother and for his victims. Blessed Lady, let him not be lost forever. For my mother's sake, if not for his own. Lord, have mercy on his soul.

Now, at last, the Earth and sky shine bright and clear. The beasts are gone, swept away at last by God's Holy Will. Alas, how soon the world forgets. But the tattered remnant of our once thriving village of Engelsburg will never forget how death rode out from the jaws of hell to harrow the length and breadth of our valley, sowing destruction and desolation. No family was left untouched by sorrow.

In this village riven by tragedy, some blame our family and would exact vengeance if they could. But all are dead except me, and I am beyond their reach. The Ring is gone. No Guardian has come forward to remedy matters. Perhaps none are left alive. I myself have renounced all worldly possessions, so I must let it go. Its disappearance remains a mystery. All else that once belonged to my family has come to me, and thus to my Order, which will use it for the good of all.

Afterward, some said that the plague had come to Engelsburg, but they were wrong. When my brothers the monks emerged from the monastery like a swarm of bees, a heavenly army to rally the villagers, it was with spiritual weapons that they at last routed the enemy. This was no plague. Not of the earthly kind.

Once he'd started reading, the monk couldn't put the book down. Impossible to read it and not weep. *Oh, bitter sorrow!* This Brother was, of course, long dead and gone to his eternal reward; his hand had penned this missive nearly five centuries ago.

If only I'd been there, the monk said to himself. *Why didn't those of my blood save them?* The Guardian failed in his sworn duty! *Dear God, the whole royal family wiped out in one fell swoop! What now will be the fate of the world?*

He brushed away a tear and quickly glanced around to make sure no one had seen. Then he remembered, this was the monastery library. And it was three o'clock in the morning! Of course, there was no one to see.

He rose from the chair, the book in his hand. Lost, all lost. But…what about the prophecies? And the boy? He'd been so certain. That boy must be the Hammer. Had to be. His name was Martel, wasn't it? That couldn't just be coincidence. Martel was the French word for Hammer. *I haven't forgotten my history lesson — Charles Martel, or Charles the Hammer, was the great hero who beat back the infidels in the Pyrenees way back when and was the father of Charlemagne.*

So where had the boy come from if the line was destroyed back in 1573?

Lord, help me find the answer. It can't have ended there. The monk crept from the library and into the chapel, where he fell on his knees to pray.

The answer came sooner than he expected. At the next class, Jude arrived in "uniform" for the first time—tank top and shorts like the other boys. When he turned his back, the monk saw it, a birthmark on his shoulder. *The birthmark.* It rocked him back on his heels, but—no doubt about it. It was the mark, the ankh symbol, golden, perfect, just as on the Ring. Just as the manuscript described, just as the so-called prophecies said.

And that scroll! Ah, the sight of the Ring had bewitched him, it seemed. How could he have so blithely dismissed the scroll that Roger had stolen from the vampires' cave and the theories the young student had developed? It was clear to him now that the poem held the secret: the prophecy of the hero, that destroyer of vampires; the Consecrated One destined to crush the master vampire's power and ruin his plot to rule the Earth. The meaning was right there in front of him all the time!

It was all he could do to control his excitement, but he made it through class without anyone asking him if he was feeling all right, though he felt eyes on him occasionally, Jude's included.

He went to see Roger again. This time with the borrowed book, determined to compare notes and solve this puzzle before it was too late. For as time passed, that sense of urgency increased.

The scroll, Roger. He pounded on the door without thinking that it was much too early in the morning for such a night owl. Impatiently he paced the floor, waiting for the young man to answer his door. Finally, Roger peered out, bleary-eyed, glasses askew, and a series of lines crisscrossing one side of his face. Apparently, he'd once again fallen asleep in the wee hours, slumped over his books.

The monk apologized hastily. Then, declining the offer of instant coffee, he asked to examine the scroll again and Roger's notes on the interpretation of it. The young man produced them without hesitation. The monk settled into the ancient wooden swivel chair at Roger's desk and shoved a stack of papers to one side. Carefully, he opened the scroll, conscious of the student's watchful eye (as he prepared a cup of instant for himself), and began making quick comparisons between it and the notes.

Since reading the manuscript from the monastery library, the monk was electrified by the possibility of the two corroborating each other. Upon perusal, Roger's notes appeared useful for his purposes, so he asked if he could have a copy of both the scroll and notes. Roger gladly photocopied them, and the monk took the copies home where he could study them thoroughly and have them handy for reference.

Jude had to be the One, he told himself. All the details were right, though Roger's notes concerning a red star or comet and a solar eclipse had yet to be realized. Of course, there was the one hitch—the hero had to be of the Sperling family line, and they'd apparently been wiped out back in the sixteenth century.

So, where had Jude come from? Unless…

Roger's interpretation of a half-human, half-vampire was difficult to countenance, but as he said, what else would "spawn of day and night" mean, and those other suggestive phrases? And he could see no other way.

He thought of the legends that had grown up around the idea. Some said that the half-vampire had preternatural powers: Among other things, it was able to sense vampires and kill them with ordinary weapons—it didn't need silver bullets or wooden stakes.

Yet there was also a generally held opposing view that vampires could not reproduce, which would, of course, void the entire theory.

But according to Theodor's writings in the old book, his brother Niki had become a vampire. Was that the answer, after all?

The monk considered this in the light of his feeling that Mrs. Martel was hiding something and that Mr. Martel's dying words were significant. He'd mentioned "taking the child of another." *Ah. So that was it! But then, where had the boy come from?*

Whatever his origins, the monk decided, they weren't of primary importance at the moment; he must first be prepared for what was to come. The mystery of his existence, his origins, would, no doubt, be resolved eventually.

That was when he decided that he must get Jude to talk to him, to confide all that he knew or suspected.

As it turned out, the opportunity came about almost by accident, certainly with much less difficulty than he'd anticipated. He'd arranged a private session with Jude one Saturday afternoon at Coon Hollow. Mrs. Martel insisted they have lunch first, then she left them to it while she drove away to take care of some errands in town.

The monk was satisfied with Jude's progress; he was a quick learner. But the day was sunny and hot, even in the shade. When they were at last ready to call it quits, Jude poured them each a tall glass of iced tea, and they sat in the shade to relax after their workout. After a bit, at the monk's request, he brought out his violin and played a few songs.

Jude Confides

"This is important," the monk said to Jude when the boy had finished playing and laid aside the violin. The fragrance of flowers filled the air in the warmth of the midday sun. Tree shadows dappled the lawn, softly stirring in the breeze. "Just tell it all from the beginning. Whatever you can remember. No, don't worry, I'm recording it. I can sort it out later. With all that I myself have learned—okay, never mind that. Just begin when you're ready." He pressed a button on a small, hand-held device.

Jude took a deep breath and began his tale. "I knew I was different. All my life, I knew, though I didn't know why. Mama and Daddy said I should keep my oddities hidden from other people, who wouldn't understand. What the heck—even I didn't understand! Maybe Mama and Daddy didn't either; at least they never explained. I mean, who else heals so fast and never gets even a little bit sick—ever? Nobody I ever heard of. I can see farther and clearer than anyone else I know—even in the dark. I've always been stronger and faster. It wasn't easy pretending, but mostly I managed. Anyhow, we didn't get out much. Daisy knew, but she never told. And she helped. A lot. Dear Daisy.

"And I remember things, or maybe they're just dreams. But they seem so real. Yeah, and 'episodes' (that's what Mama calls them)—sometimes when I play my violin." He shot a glance at the monk, then went on. "It's kind of weird, really, like being in some other place or time. Like a dream, but I was awake. Together with my actual dreams, they tell a story, I finally figured out." Jude paused.

"Go on," the monk said when the silence grew long. "I'd like to hear them."

"Um, sure, if you like—if I can. It's hard, you know? They seem so real."

"I understand. But they too may be important."

"I reckon," Jude said, rather dubiously. He wasn't looking forward to this—didn't really see how dreams and those episodes could be important. Or maybe he was just afraid of getting pulled into them again. But he was convinced of the monk's wisdom; knew he could trust the man, even if Mama didn't, but she didn't trust most people. Still, he needed someone to help him deal with all this, and it was starting to look as though the monk was the one. He absently picked up the violin and stroked its shining wood, a beautiful instrument and very special, made just for him, his Daddy had said.

"I know this sounds crazy, but sometimes when I play this violin, I feel like it's… enchanted, somehow. Its music is like… from heaven — you've heard me play. Anyhow, at times I feel myself transported somewhere else. You know about my heightened senses — not just the five, but the sixth too. As soon as I'd set the bow to the strings — sometimes, not always — there I'd be, smack in the middle of *Grimm's Fairy Tales*, or *Ali Baba,* or something like that. Like watching a movie, except I'm in it — though the other players don't usually seem aware of me.

"Yeah. Oftentimes, I'd see this big, black-bearded old man in front of one of those half-timbered houses, like in fairy tales or pictures of old Europe. The ones with vineyards and dark forests and a village with a church… Okay, the dream.

"The old man would be carving a piece of wood, and a tall boy would come up the path with a little girl by the hand. Brother and sister. The boy was rather like a colt, long-legged, with a thin face and black hair; the little girl was rosy-cheeked with blond braids, pretty as a doll. She'd sing a song for the grandfather, sweet as a nightingale. Then they'd sit and listen while he told them a tale. When the story ended, he'd hand a violin he'd made to the boy — *my* violin! The boy would play while the old man kept time with his foot, and the girl listened with a dreamy look. The boy's face was transfigured while he played, beautiful as an angel's, as though there was something magical between him and the violin. Like me, and — and this one. 'Course, this is the one."

He paused to look down at the treasured instrument in his hands. The monk stirred, and Jude hastened on with his story. "While he played, long shadows would reach out as the sun set and night fell. It would get dark and kind of spooky; then the boy's eyes all of a sudden would glow red and — and there was blood on his mouth! Just for a second or two. I almost thought I imagined it; none of them seemed to notice.

"The scene would fade, and I'd come to myself, still playing my violin in our little cabin right here at home, like I hadn't been anywhere else. Of course, I hadn't, but it always seemed so real to me. No one else, other than Mama and maybe Daisy, ever noticed, that I know of. I didn't even pause, just played my song through. Sometimes these came as actual dreams at night while I was asleep. Yeah, this happened quite a lot.

"There were other scenarios. Like the one with an ancient city under a blood-red moon. A beautiful city with hanging gardens, white stone houses, golden temples and palaces, wonderful bronze gates, high shining walls painted with lions, bulls, and gazelles. Like something out of *Arabian Nights*, maybe. But even longer ago, the temple was kind of like a pyramid with about a million steps to its peak and terraces at different levels along the way. One of those ziggurats you see in the ancient history book, I reckon. It towered above the city, reaching right up to the sky, almost."

Jude paused. The monk nodded encouragement, so he took a deep breath and went on.

"At first, it was like a vision of heaven in the middle of this great desert. But after the sun set, it turned into a nightmare. On every street of the wealthiest part of the city; inside palaces, temples, and splendid houses, people were lying dead. With blood everywhere. The wailing of those left alive was like Egypt after the Angel of Death passed through, in that old movie. There was a chill in the air, of—I don't know what—something not natural. I was so terrified I wanted to get out, but I couldn't; I had to see it through. I knew it was a dream, and yet…

"I followed two sets of hoofprints from the palace stables, out the back way, through the narrow streets, down to a small secret gate, and out of the city. Two riders were fleeing on horseback; they galloped across the bridge and out into the desert, long dark robes flowing behind them. Once away from the city, they took a well-traveled road used by traders and merchants, but at first, it was a long, terrifying ride through the dark night. The rider in the lead, a young man, was constantly glancing over his shoulder and scanning the skies, even as he urged the horses to greater speed.

"At last the sky began to lighten in the east, but they didn't slacken their pace until at last dawn broke, and the sun rose, painting the rocks and ridges and dunes all shades of red and orange and gold. Only then did the lead rider call a halt; he drew out a flask and offered the other a drink of water. A delicate hand reached out from beneath the dark cloak, and I realized—the second rider was a woman. I glimpsed a flash of gold and a sparkle of jewels—and a face delicate and beautiful, eyes dark and shaped like almonds, like that picture in my book, of Scheherazade. She had to be a queen; *but where was her court?* I wondered. Then I recalled the bodies strewn around the palace, and I knew.

"As the young man scanned the area, always on the alert, I noticed how unusual was the color of his eyes. They were kind of a murky green, like the water in Tremaynes' slough where we sometimes hunt bullfrogs. The Guardian sprang to my mind, like that's who he was—and the image of a ruby ring." Jude shrugged, then went on.

"Already heat waves were shimmering above the rocks and dunes. They resumed their journey, more at ease now that the sun was high. Yet, the queen once or twice pulled her horse to a halt, to gaze longingly back toward the city. 'O, my king,' she mourned. 'My children.' I think maybe her family was back there… dead."

The monk nodded, and Jude continued.

"The Guardian was hardly much older than I am, but he was wiry and strong. He turned those green eyes to her and said, 'We cannot go back, my queen. Have hope; we know not yet the king's fate. If he lives, he shall find us.'

"'But what of the Ring?' she said sadly. 'Must we fail him there too?' At that, the young man bowed apologetically. 'We can do no more now. One day I, or someone of my blood, shall recover it. Now you must flee far from the city where Death stalks the night, for the sake of the king's child you carry. Our duty lies ahead, with this, his only heir yet living—if we would save the future from destruction.' He took the reins and drew her horse around to face west again.

"The queen turned tragic eyes upon him, then lowered them in resignation. After a time, they joined a caravan protected by armed guards, a group led by a noble who meant to settle in some faraway land. The two of them never told anyone who they were, or what they were fleeing, only followed the sun with the caravan until they came to a wild, mountainous land of dark, dense, sighing trees.

"There, the queen's time came. Some women of the group attended her in a tent set up in the deep dark forest, while the Guardian stood watch outside, his lean, strong hands gripping his gleaming brass blade, green eyes ever vigilant. Nearby, the hobbled horses snorted and stamped nervously at every hoot of an owl, every creak of a branch. The sound of wolves howling in the distance sent shivers up my spine and made the travelers nervous, but the Guardian didn't seem disturbed by the wolves so much as by something else. I didn't know what, just saw how he tensely scanned the overhead branches and the barely visible night sky.

"Finally, the queen held a newborn child in her arms; both were wrapped in fur robes against the chill of the mountain air. The Guardian continued to watch over them as they slept—he never seemed to sleep.

"This was the king's child—the royal line was not cut off, after all! It seemed a cause for great rejoicing. I started to wonder if this was about some important person of the future, who would save the world or something?" Jude shrugged, his face red.

"Go on," said the monk. "You're doing fine."

"All this stuff came to me in bits and pieces; I'm trying to make a more or less smooth story out of it, to make sense of it. If it's a message, I don't know where it came from, or why to me."

Jude paused again and glanced at the monk. His face was impassive, but his eyes were kind, and Jude felt encouraged. "Maybe you can help me figure it out."

"Possibly, son. Continue."

(Why did it seem as though the monk knew something about all this?)

Jude shifted his gaze from the monk's face to concentrate on the pictures in his mind. "Other times I'd see a castle on a hill overlooking a village beside a river. It was the same story continuing on, I knew; from one episode or dream to the next, time kept jumping ahead. The baby born in the forest had become a young man and was the ruler of the people there. Never mind that his black hair and eyes, bronze skin, and lean physique were nothing like the blond, blue-eyed, giant natives of that wild forestland—there was no mistaking he was the son of a king. He had that aura of majesty about him, I reckon you'd call it.

"And, as always, the family of the Guardian continued to serve the royal family. Those with the green eyes were called Guardians of the Ring."

"Ah," the monk said, his own green eyes piercing all of a sudden.

Jude was a little disconcerted, but even then, he didn't get it. "Hey, I'm just telling you what I saw, and felt, and..." he said, a little defensively. The monk gestured for him to continue, so he took a deep breath and went on. "Um, I'd, of course, wake up from my dream, halfway through, sometimes. If it was an episode, I'd return in the blink of an eye from long-ago foreign places, right into the twenty-first century, and our cozy little cabin in the foothills of the Ozarks. Boom! And there I'd be—playing my violin. Sometimes to a little audience that never noticed anything out of the ordinary, though for me it was—well, kind of a shock; took me a bit to get back to real life afterward.

"I never forgot them—the dreams and episodes—couldn't, even if I wanted to. Mama says I have a photographic memory. The terror in the nightmarish parts felt so real. Though for the longest time I never knew what we were so afraid of. Not until centuries later— The prince at that time was blue-eyed and blond. The young Guardian was tall, lean, red-haired—and had the green eyes, of course. Instead of jewels and the silken courtier's clothing of his ancestor, he wore the woolen robes of a monk. He, too, was armed. Along with the usual long blade, he also had a silver crucifix. Praetorius was his name."

"Ah, yes, Praetorius. Of course," murmured the monk.

Jude glanced over, but the monk did not elaborate, only signaled him to continue.

"A silver crucifix," Jude went on. "I first thought it was because he was a Christian, a monk, but there was more. When I finally saw the thing, I understood. One night, the prince was on the walkway atop the castle, studying the stars. All was serene and beautiful under the glittering sky, or so I thought, until my skin prickled and a shiver crept up my spine as though something evil approached. I knew that feeling. Then I saw a dark figure gliding in on the night mist. Its white face and outstretched claws gleamed in the moonlight against the black of its cloak. As it crept over the edge of the parapet, a brilliant red flash on its finger nearly blinded me—a ruby! *So that's who took the Ring!* I thought to myself.

"It reached out long skeletal hands and drew the prince to itself with terrible ease. Though a strong young man, he seemed unable to resist as it sank its fangs into his throat. I gaped in shocked disbelief as it began to drift upward with him in its arms. It was carrying him off! Not only did I feel certain that this was a catastrophe, but I now identified this ancient peril: vampire! But vampires aren't real, I told myself, unconvincingly.

"I wanted to shout a warning, or call for help, but couldn't make a sound. The thing turned glowing eyes toward me and—oh, man! It saw me. I kept telling myself this was just a dream; it wasn't real. Still, I was petrified. Maybe mesmerized by those demon eyes, I couldn't look away. I was falling, falling into those burning coals, black and deep as hell's pit. Its long hair and cloak fluttered in the breeze as it reached out to me with that terrible smile. *Mama, help!* It had fangs! And blood on its mouth.

"I sank down, down, into a nice soft featherbed—no! I knew it wasn't— but oh, it was so fine. Maybe that's how a bird feels in the jaws of a snake. I felt, saw, pictures passing from my mind, as though it was feeding upon my deepest self, my memories, drawing them from my very soul, out and away. And I was afraid. The name Charon sprang to my mind, not as the Boatman of the Styx, but as something even more horrible. Ever since, that name makes me shiver every time I hear it or read it.

"Then I was free, and it was writhing on the stone floor of the parapet, its eyes flashing fire and its mouth wide and shrieking. The monk Praetorius stood over it, one hand gripping its cloak while the other seared its face with the silver crucifix. The prince was lying as though dead on the stone floor. Dead? No! For some reason, I knew that would be a very bad thing— the dashing of all hope; chaos and worldwide desolation.

"In the next instant, the thing whipped over the edge of the parapet. The monk still had a death grip on its cloak and went with it. I ran to the edge, but they'd vanished. Anxiously I scanned the ground far below, but there was no broken body of the monk lying there. Could he have survived somehow? At any rate, there was nothing I could do. I turned to the royal heir lying so still on the cold stone. My breath stopped when I saw the wound on his throat. Then I sensed a faint pulse. He was alive! I breathed again.

"I heard the sound of flapping wings somewhere in the night and glanced up in terror. There was nothing visible against the clear sky with its glittering stars, nothing silhouetted against the full moon. Presently I heard faint sounds of chanting in the distance. The monk! I recognized his voice. I was jubilant at this evidence that he still lived, though other sounds chilled my blood: snarls, shrieks, roars, curses. Thunder and lightning, clashes and booms, a hideous clamor as of a terrible battle.

"A faint rustling nearby startled me. My head whipped around. My heart pounded. But it was only the prince, as he sat up, his face pasty white, one hand pressing the wound at his throat. He leaned wearily against the stone wall and closed his eyes. Servants came and carried him into the castle. I followed them, down the stone steps, into a candlelit bedchamber. The prince was put to bed and covered in furs. He looked like the heck, but he was alive.

"I got the feeling that his death would have meant the end of the world. Or, maybe the end of me, though how that would be, I have no idea. Kind of an unsettling feeling. *Who is he?* I wondered. Or maybe more to the point, *who am I?* Or, forget I said that. I don't know what that would have to do with anything."

"It certainly may have more to do with all this than you think," murmured the monk.

Jude sent him a sharp glance, but again the monk waved at him to continue.

"We watched and waited through the night," Jude went on. "At last, I sensed a bustle of activity as the day dawned, and town and castle awakened. A fine thing, I was thinking, after that hideous storm of battle and the eerie silence that followed. The sun was already high in the sky when Praetorius returned. Footfalls echoed through the outer passage, and everyone glanced toward the door in anticipation. Even the prince revived somewhat. With white, claw-like fingers, he clutched the edge of the fur robe covering him. His hollow eyes burned as he fixed them on the heavy wooden door.

"The door opened, and there stood the monk. Like an Old Testament prophet, he gripped his crucifix and stared at the prince with righteous fire in his green eyes, now red-rimmed, in a face black with soot. His robe was in a sad state, his red hair singed and dusted with ash. A faint odor of charred flesh and sulfur wafted from him. His cheeks were sunken, and he seemed to have aged ten years but stood straight and tall.

"'My lord, you still live!' he croaked. 'I feared for you. Here, I have the Ring! The honor of my family is salvaged at last!' He opened his hand. Everyone gasped as a flash of azure and crimson leaped from the palm of his hand to dance across walls and ceiling.

"'Well done, my faithful Guardian,' whispered the prince, his fingers fluttering against the coverlet. 'The beast. Is it slain?'

"The monk fell to his knees at the prince's bedside. He bowed his head. 'A thousand pardons, Majesty. It has the strength of a demon from hell. Until dawn broke, I prayed and fought, but kill it, I could not. The accomplishment of its final defeat is to be the privilege of another one day, I am given to understand. But for now, a Hedge of Light surrounds the netherworld so that the beast is bound there by all celestial light; not only the sun, but the moon and stars, as well.'

"The prince put the Ring on his finger and declared a festival to celebrate. There was rejoicing throughout the land.

"But the peril was not over. Though the great beast was trapped underground, others yet roamed free, doing its bidding. There were mortal minions at its beck and call, as well, as it plotted to recover the Ring and destroy the royal line. Never would they be free of this immortal being that pursued them through the ages, not until the prophecy of the monk Praetorius should come to pass. Meanwhile, those of the royal blood must be guarded for the future, or all would be lost.

"A council gathered. There was much discussion, but in the end, they agreed: The royal heirs must be hidden. But how, and where? Royalty, by its very nature, reveals itself. It was the humble court jester who stepped forward with an unexpected solution: Hide the royal family in plain sight, he explained. All were astonished. How could that be done? Sprung from fourteen generations of entertainers, he quickly warmed to his subject. Optical illusion and sleight-of-hand were their stock in trade. Create a smokescreen, he said, and while the audience is distracted, have the two families switch roles. Not until some future time when it is deemed safe, or necessary, might they reveal their identity.

"Unthinkable; pride would not allow it—and yet, no price was too high, the council decided, to this end. And it was done. The royal family and that of the Guardian traded masks; the evil ones were deceived for fourteen generations. Not long enough, I am given to believe. The fall of the young violinist of the glowing red eyes unveiled the truth, the Ring was lost once more, and the royal bloodline was wiped off the face of the Earth."

The monk was suddenly alert. "The young violinist? So he fell! Of course, he did — the glowing red eyes. Hmm, fourteen generations," the monk mused, nodding, while Jude frowned, deep in thought. "Ah, I see now. That would be the tale told in the manuscript written by the monk Theodor Sperling. He spoke of his brother — the young man turned vampire who wiped out his entire family."

Jude felt the monk's eyes on him speculatively.

"Let me get back to you on this," the monk said. "I'll have to do a bit more research. You're frowning…"

"All that stuff I saw in those episodes," Jude said slowly. "And in actual dreams — seems like it should mean something important, but I don't know what."

"Yes, very important indeed," the monk said slowly. "I believe the king and queen were your ancestors. It would seem that back then, the ancient enemy did very nearly extinguish the line, but it was saved through that one child born after the queen fled the city; everyone else was killed. That prince went on to perpetuate the line in their new country, where they seemed to have remained in comparative safety down through the ages." The monk paused. "Well, to a certain point, at least. The vampires would not have been idle; no doubt, they continued to search. As immortals, they had all the time in the world, and they were still determined to prevent the so-called Consecrated One — who was destined to confront them at some future date — from ever coming into existence by annihilating his entire family beforehand. A perilous undertaking, no doubt, but apparently it seemed a more feasible plan than to actually face him." The monk glanced over, speculatively.

Jude seemed not to hear; he was caught up in his own thoughts at the moment. "A time came," he continued, "when I saw — or experienced, rather — something else. An episode, I reckon — it had to be, I was awake! — but I wasn't even playing my violin. I hadn't taken it with me to the Mile Zero City. So I don't know. I—" A sob escaped him.

"I've never told anyone. Ever. Not to this day. Even now — no, I have to do this. It's time; I can't put it off any longer. Maybe if I tell you, you can help me sort it out. Okay."

Jude took a deep breath, then began in a great rush of words. "It all started in the museum. One minute I was there, and the next — I don't know, it was like I fell into a — a — another place or time, maybe. I think that was it. Or both. Yeah. I don't know how it happened, but I just fell into this abyss, down and down, until finally, I found myself in a cave or a kind of winding passage. All was cold, dark stone — I somehow knew it was deep underground." He lifted haunted eyes to the monk's face.

"Yes, go on," the monk encouraged.

"Right in front of me was a girl with long dark curls. Or… no." He shivered, then with a quick glance around, went on. "It appeared to be a girl, but it was a vampire. I don't know how I knew, I just did. She looked exactly like that Little Lulu in the old comic strips. I'm not kidding — she really did! A scary Little Lulu.

"What was even more scary was that I seemed to be seeing all this through other eyes — someone else's, not my own. I don't know how. Like sometimes happens in dreams, I reckon. Though not in my dreams or episodes, either. I've always been myself, before this." He stifled a sob. "I — I — don't know if I can — " Here he choked up.

After the silence grew long, the monk spoke gently. "It's okay. Go on with your story. No one will condemn you."

"It was awful. I was so scared, I think I… yelled. But Mama didn't come. She wasn't there. No one I knew was there. Oh, I was so alone… and lost, and — there were all these vampires! The master's terrible… eyes! I was afraid he'd see me — I didn't belong there; I thought he'd kill me or turn me into one of them. But he didn't seem to notice me at all."

Jude closed his eyes and took several deep breaths before he finally managed to continue. "But the other one — oh, even worse. Those eyes, and fangs, and — and he — " Jude lifted horrified eyes, unable to find his voice for a long moment. Finally, he forced himself to speak. "They screamed like all the devils in hell and — all that blood! I was sick on the grass in front of the museum, and Grandpa thought it was just my imagination. But it wasn't. It wasn't…"

Premonition

Clayhurst Crossing, BC. August 1869

Bella had never seen a Huntress taken down before. Nor had most of the others. Now they watched in fascination the Prince's eyes aglow like wind-blown embers as he drank deep. Their craving drew them near, though none dared interrupt him as he fed. They sensed the power, the ecstasy, and leaned in, trying to take a bit for their own.

Suddenly the Prince threw the Huntress to the ground. Bella and the others leaped back. None wished to be the target of his fiery glare. But his eyes were again black, with only sparks to reveal the presence of that coveted blood, and Bella wondered, was that fear that flashed across his face? (Surely not—this was the *Prince*!)

He stood gazing down at the Huntress. Now that she was weakened from loss of blood, the other vampires dared to creep closer, gloating. Their Prince had dealt with her. Oh, yes, how the tables had turned! She, who had thought to wipe them off the face of the Earth, was just another foolish mortal, after all. Now it was her face that was pale and colorless, her lips bloodless, while he was beautiful, his skin fairly glowing and his lips blood red. She was the one ashen and wasted now, while he was beautiful as a god!

As he stood over the Huntress, Nyx was demanding that he dishonor her. That was her delight, to destroy innocence, to crush the enemy to dust. The Prince had, on occasion, indulged her whim, so it was said. Though now abuzz with the effects of the blood, he seemed half-sobered by whatever had happened and ignored Nyx; he just stared down at the Huntress with a strange mix of astonishment and anger. He seemed not eager to touch her again.

"You see what I have done to you," he said finally.

"But what has happened to you?" she cut in, panting between every few words. "That was no memory of mine."

He seemed disconcerted for a moment—or would have, if he'd been anyone but the ever self-assured Prince. "Memory, was it? I think not. And I take what I please."

She continued as though he hadn't spoken. "I felt the abomination of your foul embrace, your beastly mouth, and your demon fangs, but more than that—" She paused to catch her breath.

He watched her with an enigmatic expression. Nyx was muttering behind him, but he seemed not to notice.

"I see a far country across the great water. A mountain," she murmured, as though sleep-talking, her eyes far away, "and a village, with stone fences and rows upon rows of... vines. And a house of stone, tall, with flowers at the windows."

Bella thought he'd shut her up, but he only stood as though entranced. Can the Huntress mesmerize a vampire? *Of course, not!*

After another short pause to catch her breath, the Huntress went on. "A woman, beautiful as the Madonna, smiles as a small boy runs to her. He was innocent, then." (*What was she talking about, and why did he just stare?*) "She catches him up in her arms and kisses him." The Huntress turned her eyes away in distress. "Oh, my dear Jesus, You loved him then and love him still." She lifted her gaze to the Prince's face once more and opened her mouth to speak again.

"Shut up!" Nyx snarled. "Prince!"

He waved her away impatiently; his eyes narrowed, still fixed on the Huntress. "It means nothing," he growled. "The power of your blood, only." Still, he listened.

"My blood, but not my memory." A deep sadness filled those dark eyes. "There's more. I see the woman much later, sorrowing as a young man dies in her arms." She lifted up her gaze to the Prince once more. "You know this. I only received it unasked. For the sake of Jesus and a mother who loves you still, prays for you still, I grieve for your innocence lost and the demon you have become."

Nyx kicked her in the face. A red welt rose up on her cheekbone, but the Huntress did not take her eyes from the Prince's, as though by sheer force of will she would finish. Bella shuddered at the feeling of horror in the pit of her stomach. Was this an omen? *No!*

"Not another word!" Nyx barked and turned to the Prince. "Why do you listen to this drivel? Dishonor her and be done with it!"

He motioned her sharply to silence, but the expression in his eyes as he turned to her was almost tender. "You know you are everything to me, Nyx," he said softly.

Bella shivered. How unlike the Prince to so display his feelings.

Nyx seemed somewhat mollified but narrowed her eyes as she turned again to the Huntress. "Open your mouth to my Prince again, and I'll cut your tongue out!"

The Huntress closed her eyes for a moment; her lips moved. Bella was fixated on the blood and wouldn't have bothered listening, except that the Prince seemed so strangely interested.

It seemed she was praying, "O, my Lord Jesus, it is as You say. The power of a mother's tears softens Your Heart and draws forth Your mercy, though justice must be served." Her expression was resigned when she opened her eyes; she ignored Nyx and the ring of hungry vampires as though they weren't there. As though no one was there but the Prince.

His eyes hardened. "You are dreaming, woman. I have no such memory." He glanced around at the other vampires and beckoned with a graceful hand. "Come. As I promised, a taste."

Nyx growled. "Prince, I don't like this. Crush her spirit, now!" She took up the Huntress's unresisting hand. "Know this! You will not die easily, Huntress!" she hissed. "First, you will endure our foulness, as you refer to it. We will taste your blood. All of us. And my Prince will defile your virtuous body before you die. You will not be so fine then, will you?" With that, she bit the slender wrist.

When at last she tore herself away and nodded to the others, they descended upon the Huntress like a horde of mosquitoes, biting whatever part they could reach first. Bella guided China Boy to the jugular, deeming that he needed more than just a taste for his first feed. His gaze was caught at once by the bright ribbon of blood at her throat; he quivered in anticipation but hesitated, uncertain.

"That's right." Nyx's smile was cruel at the sight of tears welling up in the eyes of the Huntress as she recognized her kinsman. "Yes, we do have one of yours, forever. Bella, show him to the feast."

"Jimmy," whispered the Huntress, with a sob.

He hesitated and glanced up at Bella with confusion written on his face—and horror, dread, and reproach…? *No, can't have that.* She ruffled his hair, then crouched over the Huntress, bent to her throat, and promptly forgot Nyx's warning. *Oh, to be lost in this wild red sea forever, forever, so sweet. Ecstasy —*

There was an explosion of stars, of silver and black spots. She found herself lying face down on the grass. She sprang up, snarling.

"I said just a taste!" Nyx snarled.

Bella cowered. But it was so wonderful. She glanced around; others were cringing. No doubt Nyx had backhanded them as well.

"China Boy?" She despised her own pleading tone.

Nyx gave a quick nod. The pleasure of watching the Huntress mauled by her own cousin was too tempting, even to spite Bella.

"Come here, *niño!*" Bella beckoned to China Boy. *Oh, how she wanted — !* *No.* She had to get hold of herself. The Huntress was already pale as death. "This is what you want." Still, he held back; his eyes sadly turned to those of the Huntress Marie. A quick remedy was needed, Bella saw at once. She kissed him on the mouth. The taste of blood set him on fire; his eyes flared with unholy flame as that eternal hunger gripped him. He sprang at the Huntress, clumsily biting her throat. Bella laughed. "Easy. This is not your little turtledove. Show your cousin what fangs are for."

The Huntress Marie's brow creased in her distress. Tears welled from beneath closed eyelids to slide slowly down her cheeks. Not so much from the physical pain, Bella somehow realized, as from the knowledge of what this boy had become.

Bella was so lost in that odd thought that she was startled when Nyx said, "Enough!" quite sharply.

Bella realized that the Huntress was lying almost too still and quickly yanked China Boy back by the hair. He fell to whimpering at her feet, blood running down his chin and glimmering on his shirtfront; he lifted up pleading eyes.

"That's enough," Bella soothed. "She has very powerful blood. Here, let me help." She licked the blood from his face.

"She's just fainted," Nyx was saying as she crouched beside the Huntress, while the Prince stared down at the still form, frowning a little. Nyx slapped her across the face. "Wake up! We're not finished with you yet!" The Huntress shivered; her eyelids fluttered. "That's better. Finish this now, Prince." She got up and stepped aside.

He stood in silence until the Huntress raised her eyes to his, heavy-lidded and slow. "It has come down to this, Huntress," he said, finally. "We have tasted you, and you have had a taste of us. You heard Nyx, what she wants. But I promise you this: give us back our Josie-girl, and I will not touch you again."

"Do your worst," the Huntress replied faintly. "Josie is far away, out of your reach. You will never have her."

"Never means nothing to us," the Prince said in a flat tone. "We are immortal."

At this, she smiled slightly, but with sadness in her eyes. "That is your sorrow. Today I will be with my Master in Paradise. Where will you be with yours?"

His black eyes blazed with sudden fury. "This I do promise," he hissed. "Charon will have her. If not her, then her daughter, or her granddaughter. Sooner or later, one of her blood will come to us, drawn by the immortal bond he has created. Time is something we do have, and you—you have no more time!"

Nyx was still going on about dishonor, but the Prince's attention was on the foe at his feet.

The Huntress closed her eyes for a moment; the small wrinkle of concern on her brow smoothed out so that when she opened them again, she met his cold gaze with her usual composure. "You will not be rid of me so easily. From heaven, I will watch over them. And there is nothing you can do, because then I will be immortal, with God on my side."

With one long step, he stood astride her, reached down to grasp her hair. Her face twisted with pain, but her eyes were calm as she met his gaze. His lip curled. "I have tasted the blood of many innocents, but that of Josie was the sweetest. I shall not forget it; nor will she forget me, ever. Think of that as you go to your death."

"As God is my witness," the Huntress said slowly, "you will regret the evil you have done this day."

Nyx gnashed her teeth. The others stirred apprehensively at what sounded like a curse.

The Prince barked a laugh. "That's impossible. Vampires never regret." Roughly he released her hair and let her head fall back. He finally seemed to hear Nyx yelling behind him and was about to turn when the Huntress spoke again.

"No," she whispered. "Not them. You." With an indefinable expression, she searched his eyes. "Just you."

The Prince seemed disturbed now by those eyes steady on his face; he shifted his gaze, unable to meet them.

Bella decided she wouldn't want those eyes on her like that. In fact, they were all disturbed by it in some way that none of them could explain. But this was the Prince. He wouldn't be daunted.

He seemed not to hear Nyx screaming as he caught up the knife from the grass and turned to the Huntress again. He shifted his gaze to the long blade in his hand and ran his claws the length of it.

"This blade has served you well, Huntress, cutting off vampires' heads. Let us see if it serves as well to behead a Huntress." At that, he leaned down to entwine his fingers in her hair once more, and his eyes met hers, "Your head will serve as an ornament atop the master's throne. One of many."

"No, Prince, stop!" wailed Nyx.

With one quick slash, he cut off the Huntress's head and held it high. Flame shot from his eyes; all shrank back, even Nyx, as he planted his feet wide and lifted his face to the sky. His shriek of victory and defiance echoed along the river, bounced from the cliffs, and finally died to a deep growl.

Set afire, all raised their fists and screamed as one in reply. He swept them with his piercing gaze, eyes glowing red as blood ran down his arm, and he turned for all to see his trophy. The blood! How it drew them, even then.

That sweet, strong face, so pale and serene in death, just as it had been in life. Odd, how peaceful it was; there was no grimace of pain and terror, as one so often saw.

And Bella wanted to vomit, for some unaccountable reason. She staggered off to the trees, trying to get hold of herself. *What is wrong with me? Compassion, desolation, sorrow. Human feelings!* Where had they come from? With a supreme effort, she crushed them down into the black core of her being. *Get down! There is no place. For. You. Here!* She had an uncontrollable urge to weep. But that was impossible; vampires have no tears.

"We are finished here," she heard the Prince say as he lowered his arm. "We go south at once."

In that instant, a blinding flash of light transfixed Bella for an instant and then was gone. In that brief moment, it seemed as though she once more looked upon that unforgettable angel child. Or, was it an angel? Something had glowed with an unearthly light, but it had no wings, so — not an angel. A boy, perhaps twelve years old, and so beautiful... Then she saw: this was not an abyss, but the vault of the sky. How had things got so turned around? What heavenly creature has descended to our realm? He turned his eyes upon her, but she could not abide that pure blue fire illuminating the tarnished core of her being; interiorly, she fell on her face before him and would have kissed his foot, but something prevented her. She knew she was not worthy to touch him and despaired. Oh, to throw herself into oblivion. And yet, and yet...

Somehow she managed to avoid the blue fire of his gaze and with all the bitterness of lost hope, lifted her eyes and reached out a trembling hand toward his. But it slipped away as many wings not his own surrounded him with a protective light. Dazzled by its brightness, she had to shield her eyes as he was carried upward, arms outstretched, his face radiant with joy. Yet in her mind's eye, she seemed to see him reach out once more to touch her brow. A flame shot from his finger and seared him from her memory.

Another mystery. Her memory, like the rest of her, was immortal. All that remained was a shadow, a vague impression, a terrible longing. She searched the skies in vain; he had vanished from her sight. She now felt truly forsaken. She moaned with longing for she knew not what, in this blackness of utter despair.

She swept the clearing with a puzzled glance. All was as it had been, as it ought to be. But she had seen, had felt something, for an instant—or an age. She reached up to touch her brow, certain she'd find a wound or burn; her skin was smooth and silken as ever.

The clamor of cheering vampires and preparations for departure pierced the desolate alien world in which Bella languished. She pulled herself together and went to find Rojo and China Boy. To her relief, they seemed to notice nothing amiss. She crushed the unaccountable feelings until they faded into nothingness. Rid of them at last. So why that sense of loss and not one of freedom?

What just happened?

Even Bella could see that Nyx wasn't happy that the Prince had ended this so abruptly without satisfying her demands. He took no notice, however; his mind seemed to be elsewhere. It was unsettling, the way he seemed so preoccupied with the enigmatic words that the Huntress Marie had spoken. And he hadn't retrieved Josie for the master, but one day he would, as he'd promised the Huntress. One day.

He wrapped her head in the cloak of a staked vampire. A fitting end for a Huntress, a fitting shroud.

And Charon accepted the Huntress Marie's head with pleasure, another trophy to crown his throne, and a reminder, a promise, that Josie would also be his, at some future date.

The Monk Considers

Throughout the telling, which took some days of hours-long sessions of recording, the monk had sat enthralled, trying to grasp all that Jude was saying. He had to admit he was a bit startled at times, to say the least. A horrific experience at the Mile Zero Museum for a youngster of that age; it must have been quite traumatic. Now that he knew more about the boy, he could see the effects. They weren't pretty, but he was handling it quite well, under the circumstances. And the dreams, too…

Some of it was unreal, fantastic—yet his research tended to verify many of the details: There was the scroll Roger had found, containing the prophetic poem. The young monk's manuscript recounting the events of 1573, in which he told the story of his brother becoming a vampire and the loss of the Ring. Well, the Ring had been found—irrefutable proof of its existence. It wasn't a stretch to imagine the origin of the boy's oddities, if one could accept the idea of a half-vampire.

Well. If vampires were real, why not half-vampires? An abhorrent thought, but it was the one way to account for that five-century gap in the royal family tree and still allow for the existence of a prince of the blood, Charon's prophesied nemesis of the future.

Despite that ancient enemy's attempts throughout the ages to blot out this family from the face of the Earth, it seemed he had failed each time. If, as Father Paul was beginning to believe, this boy was the Consecrated One.

The monk could not dismiss the theory of the half-vampire out of hand. He kept an open mind but wasn't one to accept the fantastic without due consideration. Yet if Theodor Sperling's brother had indeed become a vampire—supposedly immortal, he could still roam the Earth—and perhaps have produced a child half-human, half-vampire.

Theodor had survived, of course, but there was no evidence that he had broken his vows. Father Paul was quite certain that his own family would have recorded any skeleton in the royal closet that hinted at an erring churchman and his progeny, had that been the case.

There was no getting around it; the boy might not be happy to hear it, but Father Paul realized he must seriously entertain the idea suggested by the manuscript and by Roger's notes. Especially since his own family history and the boy's dreams and visions filled in the blanks. They fit very nicely, in fact.

Ah. The thought struck him that this might also explain why the boy dreaded approaching the monastery. It did repel that vampire known locally as the phantom…

Each evening after he left the boy's home or other setting of interview, he'd returned to the abbey, and solitude, where he could ponder it all more fully.

At first, he was tempted to dismiss these crazy theories as impossible, or at least improbable, but again, there were those oddities the boy had been taught to suppress. And the monk himself had recently observed little things not normal for a human, things that fit into the context of, say, a vampire. For example, during exercises and forms, the youngster had shown a fluidity of motion unnatural to a human, at times so quick as to be a blur to human vision, and often he had to concentrate hard to slow himself down so as to appear natural. And there was the power of his eyes, a frightening thing, even to himself (he'd recently expressed gratitude for the discipline of the monk's training in helping him learn to control it).

Too much power. Fortunately, from a young age, he'd been taught to avoid inflicting hurt, no matter how he was trod upon. His heart was both gentle and courageous. The monk noted how he'd expressed concern for hurting the man who had attacked him. However, he had soon learned the difference between self-defense and the use of excessive force.

Yes, he had the potential to become the hero the monk was convinced he was meant to be.

And Roger had found the Ring in the hands of vampires. The monk had the fleeting thought that he should have tried harder to get Roger to hand over the Ring. Should have realized the importance of it being in the possession of the Guardian. *Uh-oh.*

Now the monk asked himself, if Jude's father was a vampire, where was he? And who was Jude's mother? Not Mamie Martel, he was certain. How and why the boy came to be raised by the Martels—well, for now, that would have to remain a mystery.

Jude's experience at the Mile Zero museum was another enigma. He'd only managed to recount it in bits and pieces, so painful was the endeavor. From the hours of recordings that resulted, the monk had managed to sort them into a rather more flowing narrative. He'd spent weeks going over all the documents and sorting through the mass of information compiled of the dreams and episodes—and now the story he'd constructed from that somewhat disjointed telling of that traumatic experience at the museum—until he was sure, and then he decided.

The boy had to know.

One day, shortly after, he arranged to speak to him alone. Preliminaries out of the way, he sprung his news.

"Jude, I have come to believe that you are the Consecrated One spoken of in the prophecy. You have a Mission. You are the one destined to destroy the master vampire and all his followers. No, just listen a minute. They thought they had rid the world of your line and the possibility of you ever seeing the light of day when they massacred your family in ancient times and again in 1573. And possibly, more times through the ages, that we know nothing about. Yet here you are. For a reason. I believe the time is coming when you must confront them."

Jude blinked, then stared. "No," he said finally, shaking his head. "I can't. It can't be me. I'm only fourteen, and—and I'm no hero."

"You can do this. I'll train you, and when the time comes, you'll be ready."

"No. You said yourself that they wiped out the whole family in 1573. So, where do I come in? No, this can't be about me. It's impossible. You've got it wrong."

"No. I haven't. That monk's brother—" He saw the sudden light of terror and anguish in those eyes and quickly backtracked. "Never mind. Don't worry about all that now. We'll take it slowly. Just keep coming to class." The monk studied him with compassion. *No, he's not ready to hear that he may be half-vampire.* "No pressure, son. Never fear, I'll not force you."

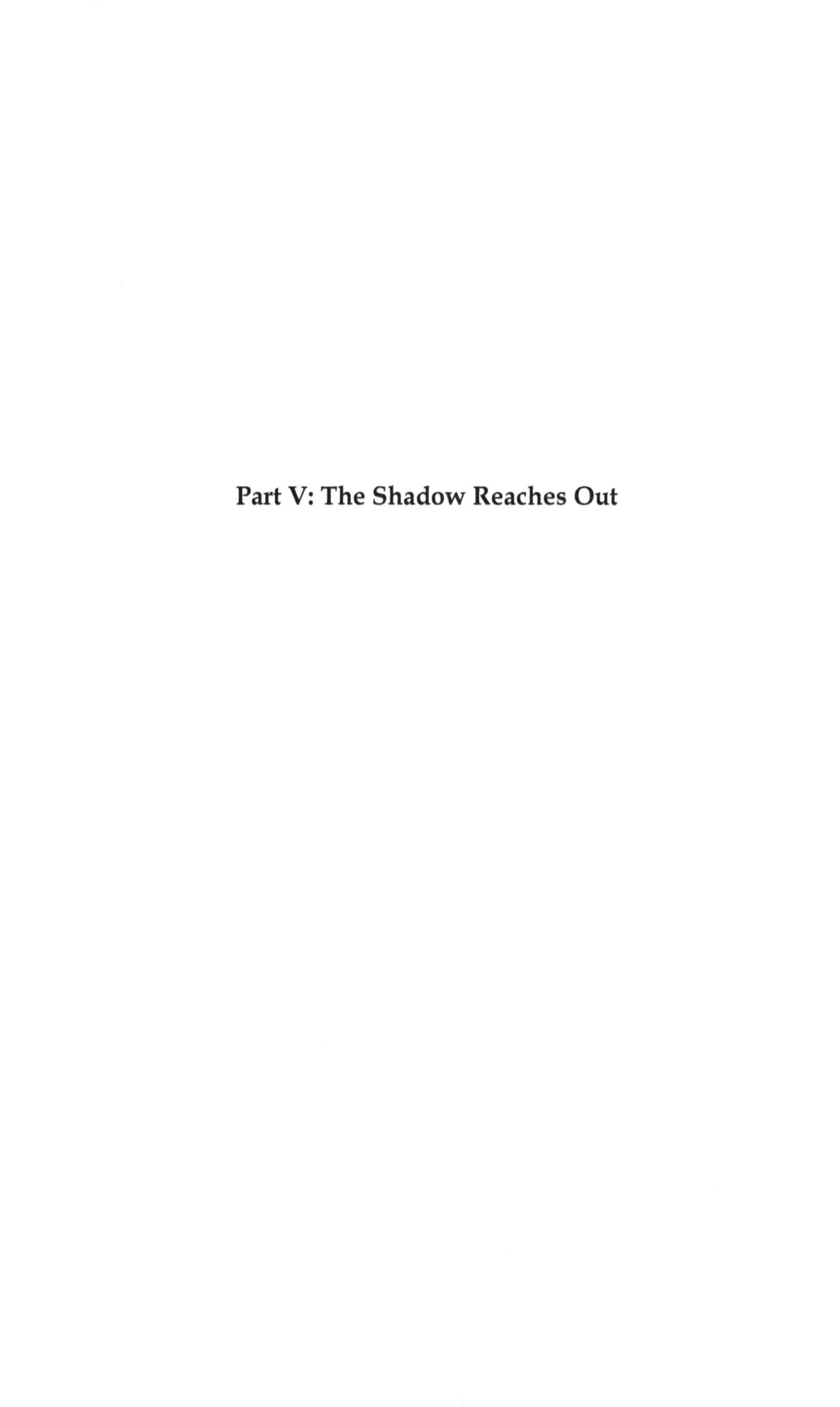

Part V: The Shadow Reaches Out

Return of the Rocket

Southern Illinois, 2017

The sky was dark, the stars obscured by gray, wispy gauze, and the moon but a sharp sliver as Bella emerged from the mausoleum. The sun was long set, and she was anticipating the hunt; it was time to prowl the night.

Bella!

She stopped short and listened. Had someone whispered her name? It seemed to have come from a patch of brush at the edge of the graveyard. *Bella!* it said again (she was almost certain that time). The voice, the presence, seemed familiar, but no—it couldn't be the Rocket! He was dead, gone. Or was he? Wait a minute. Hadn't Letha the witch said he was still alive (undead, technically)? Ah yes, she'd promised to draw them back with her magic. So it was true, after all. And the moonchild…? She glanced around a little apprehensively.

Rojo and China Boy had gone on ahead but would be circling back soon. Tonight she'd already had other things on her mind besides hunting. As she'd passed Charon's study on her way out, a glimmer of light at the half-open door had brought her to a halt. She'd lingered for a moment to listen to the sound of his pen scritch-scratching on paper (though who knew better than she the futility of pining?).

She'd moved on (silently lamenting her loss of favor so long ago), and none too soon. For just then, Styx and her "dogs" had rounded the corner. Bella quickly feigned adjusting the shining hoop at her ear, but a fleeting glance caught their exchange of knowing looks. How she hated Styx—her pathetic smirk and tragic blue eyes. No doubt, the Prince deemed himself well rid of her. Sure, Styx needed to console herself after losing the Prince, but why choose two so lacking in refinement or culture?

"Bella!" This time it wasn't a whisper but a rasping voice.

At first, the only movement she saw was the stirring of trees in the night breeze. Then she heard a slight rustling close by, amongst the dead grass and weeds. *Ah, there!* A pale smudge of a face, a dark shape; how oddly they blended with their surroundings.

A little disconcerted, she hissed, "Show yourself!"

A grotesque figure shuffled into view, and Bella jerked back at the hideous sight. Like a skull—a dead thing!—yet eyes burned in the sockets. Scraps of flesh and skin, and a few strands of dark hair, clung to bare bone blackened in places (charred?). There was no nose; the lips were severely damaged, but oddly, the teeth were perfect.

"Shhh. Not so loud. We need to talk."

"Rocket?" Bella said tentatively, trying to recover from her shock.

"Of course! Who else?" he snarled.

"Well, sorry! I didn't recognize you!" She was taken aback. *¡Ay de mi!* He was in worse shape than Sweet William after the Huntress Mara'd hacked off half his face in that big battle some years back.

"Fine, be that way!" He sulked and turned away.

¡Ay! It's the same old Rocket, all right. "I said I was sorry." She held onto her temper. "What happened to you? You look, um, I know you cannot see yourself, but—"

"Don't you ever shut up?"

She drew herself up to her full height and dignity, and he wilted. "Explain, *por favor*," she said haughtily.

"It was the dawn."

She repressed a shudder. The dawn, a vampire's worst nightmare! *What kind of a fool would let himself get caught by the dawn? Well.* And to think he had been quite handsome at one time. Seventeen years, and he had not yet regenerated to his original form! Maybe it was better to avoid commenting on his appearance.

"So. *Amigo*. What happened to the child?"

His eyes darted around nervously; he lowered his voice. "I lost him when the dawn took me and—"

Bella gave him a glance almost of sympathy. "I hate to break it to you, but you are in big trouble, *muchacho*."

"I know that!"

"And you dare to come back without the baby? Charon will—" She saw the dangerous glow in his eyes and decided, after all, not to mention anything about Charon frying him where he stood. He'd had enough of that sort of thing, from the look of it. "—he will not be pleased."

His gaze wavered. "I know where the child is, but I can't take him by myself. I don't know if it's possible to take him at all. You can't imagine. I must tell Charon; he'll know what to do. But—but he'll burn me on the spot. I need a, er, a buffer."

"Hey, *muchacho*. Whoa there. Uh-uh." Bella shivered under that pleading gaze. Then she thought about it. The possibilities were intriguing, actually.

"What if I helped you catch him first, then we take him to the master and — ?"

"You don't get it, do you? He is a child no longer. Even when he was, well —" He choked on the words. "I — I —"

"Yes, I understand. You have had a bad scare." Bella managed a bit of sympathy, then leaned toward him conspiratorially. "You know, it will be quite different if we bring it in; better than going to the master empty-handed. He was not pleased when — okay, calm down." She tried another tack. "Remember when we used to rip through crowds of mortals, even mobs out for our heads! And this — this is only one. One! So he is dangerous? We laugh at danger! Where is your sense of adventure? Come on, Charon wants this more than anything else in the world. We will be his favorites again!" (*Not that the Rocket ever was, but no matter.*) "This is the big one. It's worth the risk, hey?"

She drew back, a little shaken by that horrible whimpering sound. Whatever had happened had obviously destroyed his nerve.

"I — I — are you going to help me, or not?" he managed, finally.

"Fine! I will see what I can do." She suppressed her contempt with difficulty. "After I feed. You know how much fun I am when I am ravenous!"

He jerked back.

She turned away; she needed time to think. It was no small thing to go to Charon and bring up that topic with nothing to show for it.

Just as she was about to launch herself into the night, she sensed the approach of Rojo and China Boy. Of course, they'd wonder what had delayed her. She signaled sharply to the Rocket, and he scuttled into the undergrowth. Rojo and China Boy descended from the sky just then, cloaks fluttering like black banners behind them.

"Coming, Bella?" Rojo's foxy face was creased by a pointy-toothed smile. "Breakfast awaits, out along the highway."

"Perfect prey," said China Boy. "A lone traveler. No one will miss him."

Just one glimpse of that beautiful face, and Bella nearly forgot breakfast, the Rocket, and even Rojo. After all these years, sweet-faced China Boy still held her in the palm of his hand, though she'd never have let on. It wouldn't do to give him an inflated opinion of himself. And if she showed favoritism, Rojo would never forgive her. He was her first, after all, but beautiful he was not. Or maybe it was just a matter of taste. She preferred the Latin type. China Boy was tall, dark-haired, and — *well, close enough.*

It had taken both of them to console her after the Prince had left them and she saw her chance at him gone forever. No one, not even Charon, wanted to see that Huntress Mara's head on a spike more than she did. And to think he was nearly hers. So close. How did the Huntress lure him from the master? It had to be some dark magic to ensnare him; to light his fire. Cold? *Ay*, the moonchild certainly put the lie to that theory.

"What the hell?" Rojo's exclamation brought her to her senses. She glanced up; his grin had faded. "Who's there?"

China Boy's black eyes went hard and flat as they fixed on the brush where the Rocket was hidden.

"Time to go," Bella said. "I'm hungry." She took each by an arm and started off across the graveyard. "Where did you see breakfast walking, my darlings?"

They darted suspicious glances back toward the mausoleum, but Bella quickly diverted them. They had their fun and their feed. The man never reached the town, where he could have lain down and slept in safety. By the time a passerby found him in the ditch, it was too late.

The scritch-scritch of the pen sounded loud as Bella paused outside the door of Charon's study. Dared she disturb him? From where she stood in the corridor, she could see shadows dancing across the walls. She could feel the Rocket's presence behind her, his tension, and his eyes like augers drilling holes in her back from his vantage point at the far curve of the passage. She'd told him to stay outside, but he'd followed her. She steeled herself at last to step into the doorway.

"Enter," Charon growled, without pause in his writing.

Of course, he'd known all along she was there. She glanced back to see the Rocket quivering, his eyes wide. He ought to be frightened. She was a little anxious herself.

She hurried inside, maintaining her dignity with an effort. Charon frowned in concentration and didn't interrupt his writing or even glance up. Handwritten notes and papers filled with equations were strewn across the table, lit by the flickering glow of the oil lamp. Maps and charts were tacked on one wall, weapons hung on the others; shelves were cluttered with ancient leather-bound books, scientific instruments, and skulls.

Charon turned to her with his piercing gaze that filled her with dread, yet she couldn't help pausing to admire the pale, angular face that had ever entranced her. At his peremptory gesture, she snapped out of it, rushed to him, and bowed. "Master!"

"Yes?" His eyes flicked to the doorway; his face darkened. He sprang to his feet, knocking the chair to the floor with a crash.

Bella fell to her knees and clutched the hem of his cloak as it swirled around him. "My lord, let me explain." Of course, he'd sense the Rocket's presence. She threw caution to the winds. "Good news, master. The child is found! Hear me out, *por favor!*"

He snarled, his face like a thundercloud. Her nose to the floor, she fully expected to feel the hot blast of his fury directly between her shoulder blades.

"Rise, my sweet," he said softly, instead. She stood, gathered her tattered dignity around her, and lifted her eyes. He wasn't smiling, but at least his eyes weren't glowing — yet. "The moonchild is found, you say?" His gaze snared hers.

"The Rocket has returned," she hastened to explain. "He was unable to come sooner, due to an accident. He begs your forbearance, that you listen to his tale."

"Ah, the moonchild at last," he mused, stroking her hair. "Bellatrix, my heart, you bring me good news." Would he kiss her or bite her? She trembled with anticipation, but he let his hand drop and growled, "Bring the scoundrel here. At once."

No kiss, but — he'd touched her! Elated, she bowed and withdrew to summon the Rocket. "He will see you now, *amigo.*"

"Bella, I'm afraid." His voice shook.

"You should be! But he is very pleased. ¡*Ay de mi!* So do not dwell on your stupidity. Apologize, certainly. Do tell him that you will lead us to the child, *por favor.*"

"But — but —"

"Get in there now! Stop stalling!" she hissed. "My head is on the block too. I do not intend to lose it for you. Stop whining and make it good, you ugly piece of — !"

"I'm going, I'm going," he sulked.

"You will be fine, *niño,*" she said in a softened tone.

He gave her a glance that could have been grateful, though it was difficult to tell on that face. "Would you please come with me, Bella?"

How could she refuse? She was drawn to Charon like a moth to a flame. And there would be glory to be gained in the capture of the moonchild, surely. She began scheming. With her irresistible charm and —

Charon was bent over the table again, scribbling madly as his gaze moved from map, to star chart, to scroll, and back again. The flickering light of the lamp highlighted the pale marble planes of his face with an orange glimmer and turned his dark hair to a rich brown. Bella gazed with deep longing. They waited.

"So, you have come to lead us to the moonchild," he said finally, his voice dangerously soft.

"Yes, Master, if you will but listen to my unworthy tale." The Rocket threw himself face down.

Charon finally deigned to look upon the groveling creature at his feet. And Bella stood admiring. How like an eagle he was, with piercing eyes fixed on his prey.

"Speak."

"Yes, Master. I did my best to bring the child to you with all good speed. As you know, I am very fast. But I miscalculated and, and the dawn caught me." He nearly choked at that. "And I burned. Burned! I thought it was the end and was grieved that I had not completed my mission. Perhaps that is what sustained me." He lifted pleading eyes.

Charon gestured impatiently. "Rise. Stand while you speak."

The Rocket lurched to his feet and bowed. "As you say, Master." The fitful flame of the lamp cast orange lights across his skull-like head, emphasizing the ludicrous ears bereft of their natural points. The face gleamed white, its features ill-defined with no nose or lips or eyebrows. *Ugly!* Bella had to avert her eyes. The Rocket didn't seem aware of her distaste; he couldn't see himself, of course. And he was a little preoccupied at the moment, talking for his life.

"I was set afire and fell from the sky. But as luck would have it, I landed in a deep snowdrift. When I recovered my senses, I found that the flames had not consumed me entirely; the snow must have extinguished the fire. But I had to find shelter, as the sun was rising. I also feared the flare might have attracted unwanted attention. I gathered my tattered remains and found my way to a cave. It wasn't easy. There was little left of me; only charred bone and bits of smoking flesh. What you see before you now may not look like much, but compared to then—" He flinched at the master's impatient gesture and rushed on. "I resolved that when I awakened at sunset, I'd retrieve the child and complete my mission with all due haste. Alas, I did not awaken for—well, for five years, according to my best calculations. By then, I was regenerated somewhat, but still very weak." He paused to draw his cloak more closely about him.

"And the twelve additional years?"

"I had to feed, of course. At first, I could only manage small domestic animals, chickens and the like. It wasn't easy. Farmers set dogs on my trail. You have no idea. Anyway, the child. I could sense its presence in the vicinity, but the atmosphere in that area was somehow oppressive, not only impeding my regeneration, but also dimming my powers, so that I had trouble even pinpointing the child's location." He paused, his eyes darting around. "Like, like it was a holy place! Yet each night, I bravely emerged from hiding to continue my search.

"When I finally found the child—alas, he was an infant no longer! I remember it well. I'd just sunk my teeth into a sheep in a barnyard—" (At this, Bella snickered; he cast a reproachful glance.) "Don't laugh. Even the blood of an animal was elixir, so starved was I. Alas, I was somewhat clumsy; my victim's struggle awoke the rest of the flock. The animals stirred and grew noisy, alerting their owner.

"I heard a door creak and the approach of footsteps. How I longed to feed on a human but dared not chance it. I began to flow from the corral when the scent hit me! A sledgehammer blow, instantaneous, powerful, affecting my body before my mind could take it in. I was drawn to it like a magnet. Oh, it was the sweetest thing. I was nearly overcome by ecstasy, and I hadn't even tasted! I did not understand then yet, why.

"Before I knew, I was at the garden fence, so close to the mortals that I could almost touch them. And they, unsuspecting. *A child should not be difficult to snatch and make off with under cover of darkness*, I said to myself. I'd pounce as they came through the gate. But there they paused; I saw a glint of metal in the moonlight. *A shotgun!* I dared not face a mere mortal man, much less an armed one. I remained still as a shadow.

"Then the boy tugged frantically at the man's sleeve. 'That smell, what is it? Daddy, there's something evil. There!' The child stared right at me and, I swear, his eyes glowed! Bright blue. Then he turned away. I felt such dreadful loss then that I very nearly threw myself at him—to devour him, or kiss his feet, or—I hardly knew. Crazy, but—"

"Yes, yes, get on with it!" Charon growled.

The Rocket ducked his head, words now issuing from that ludicrous lipless mouth in a torrent. "Then it hit me. This was the very child I had dropped so long ago! No longer an infant, but a boy. Yet unlike just any boy, he could sense my presence. This was the moonchild. The one you wanted. I could have reached out and grabbed him, he was so close, but before I could see how to manage it in the face of a man with a shotgun and me with my unreliable reflexes, they were away. Back inside the house.

"Still, I was cheered. I had at last located the child. After that, I haunted the farm, wild to capture him, but I had to be cautious. I dared not let them guess my intent. One glimpse of my ruined form would set any mortal to screaming flight, and my powers of mesmerization are weak at the best of times. I lurked in the shadows, waiting for my chance. At last, one night, I came across him riding in a pickup with the man out on the highway. I ran them off the road, but just as I was about to carry off the boy, a monk happened along and warded him with holy water. Rotten luck! But the man died in that accident, and I consoled myself with the thought that now my task should be easier.

"One night sometime later, I emerged from my cave, hungry as usual, and was heading for a nearby farm to raid the chicken house, when I sensed the child. That stopped me in my tracks. I was jubilant. He'd played right into my hands, for there he was, sitting in the meadow, alone. Well, there was a girl with him, but she was nothing. Of course, he sensed my presence at once, and they fled for the trees. I let them run. I was in no hurry. It was fun. I was the cat, they the mice.

"They held hands as they crashed headlong down the trail, the girl blundering and tripping. The boy was not so clumsy. It was only later when I had time to think that I realized. He could see in the dark and moved with the grace of a vampire! At the time, I was too busy laughing at my good fortune, playing the fool.

"Finally, the girl's clothing snagged on a branch, and she was caught fast. Oh, I had them now! I was so sure, as I watched the child madly trying to free her. How sweet was my anticipation of the kill! I could already taste the girl's blood and feel the warmth of the child in my embrace — and, of course, I anticipated placing him in your hands.

"The girl stared, petrified, as the boy tried to unsnag her; he had his back to me. She wrapped her arms around him protectively, as if that would help. Hah! Pathetic. I reached out to snatch him from her arms. Just then, he turned, and his eyes widened in stark terror." The Rocket shook his head grimly.

"And that is all I remember about that. The next thing I knew, I was back in my cave, with no idea of how I'd got there. It took me a while to recall. My chest hurt abominably, as though stuck with a red-hot poker. I found a burn mark; the stench of my scorched flesh brought back the terror of that fateful dawn. Then it struck me — the boy had done this. He'd burned me with the power of his eyes! Glowing eyes. I recalled that a terrible flash like blue lightning had shot out from his eyes! It burned me; knocked me to the ground. Then I knew. He has that power like yours, Master."

Charon at first seemed displeased with the comparison. Then interested, and finally thoughtful. "Of course. Let us not forget that this child is half-vampire. Continue."

The Rocket shook. "Yes, Master. After that, I watched and waited, but it was as though all of nature conspired to foil my designs. As the child grew, so did his powers. He appears so naturally mortal that once or twice, I ventured close enough to be singed, but he never pursued me. I think he was confused by his own powers, which seemed to manifest spontaneously when he was frightened and such."

"And you? Did you pursue him?"

The Rocket ducked his head. "Yes, though I had been burned so badly, and all my nature screamed at me to shy away, I did once have him in my grasp. But he is very strong; he threw me off and ran to the monastery grounds. I could not touch him there."

"Blundering fool, you should have been more careful with the child in the beginning." Charon turned to Bella. "Call everyone to the Hall. We must deal with this at once."

Covert Mission

Bella hurried to do Charon's bidding. Her spirits soared. The master had deigned to notice her again. Would he appoint her to lead this mission? She hardly dared hope.

She rounded up the others; no mean task, but quite a number were already in the vicinity of the mansion and the labyrinth. Those out hunting and feeding returned just as dawn was approaching. Finally, all were assembled.

Bella silently watched as Charon sat upon his throne, deep in thought. The Rocket was the object of much curiosity and horror and exclamation, which he suffered as meekly as he was able, knowing well enough that the master's forbearance would last only as long as his usefulness in this endeavor.

Bella waited impatiently as he was obliged to tell his story again, for the others. Reactions varied. Though excited by the news he brought, they mocked him for drinking the blood of animals and jeered at his stupidity in being caught by the dawn (a measure of their own fears, Bella decided, like a mortal whistling in the dark). When they stopped laughing, some averred that he'd overstated the peril; his tales of the danger posed by the moonchild gross exaggeration. Bella tended to agree that the experience had shattered his nerve; they dismissed his warnings out of hand, fools that they were.

But how could they have known? A creature half-human half-vampire was something quite beyond belief. An abomination. How was it that they forgot, when it came down to the crunch, that he was not just any mortal? When Bella thought about it later, with the clarity of hindsight, she cursed herself for being the biggest fool of all.

How rash they were! Those who tasted the moonchild's power and survived were not so quick to condemn their poor brother afterward.

They couldn't say he hadn't warned them. He tried. "Listen! He's no longer a child — by now nearly grown. And his powers — you have no idea. He can mesmerize you with his eyes, his voice, his face." The softening of the Rocket's tone at the last elicited a flurry of ribald comments. Their contempt of this ruined shell of the pretty thing he'd once been seemed to make them deaf. "Listen!" he shrilled, then muttered, "Listen to me if you want to live. He is like his father — "

"What did you say?" Bella gripped his cloak and jerked him close.

He snatched the brittle fabric from her grasp and gathered the tatters around him to preserve the remains of his dignity. She glared. He tried to speak, and finally managed, "Like his father, his face is so dazzling, so wonderful, you never dream how terrible — "

Of course. Why did she keep forgetting that this was the Prince's child?

An image formed in her mind (a memory?) of a boy with the face of an angel… but…what did that have to do with anything?

¡Ay de mi! The Prince's child! The Rocket's warnings scattered, and all common sense took flight. "You will point him out to us, of course!" she burst out eagerly.

"Bella! Did you hear me, Bella?" The Rocket's eyes were wild. "He — it — this thing can kill you with a look."

In her little dream world, she had already figured it all out and was scheming, not yet quite grasping, the fact that this was something quite outside of her experience.

Charon spoke from his vantage point high upon the throne. "Listen well." The raucous laughter and din of competing voices died away. Every face turned toward him. "The Rocket's fears are not without cause. Recall Lee Davis's failed attempts; caution is imperative, to be sure. But time is running out. The moonchild must not interfere with our destiny. I will have him. Alive if possible; dead, if necessary. Just bring him to me."

They were all aware of the date of the upcoming solar eclipse. Murmurs rose from the crowd. Who would be chosen? Was the moonchild a terror beyond imagination, as the Rocket would have them believe? They'd laughed, but…

Nyx leaned close to Charon. "Let me take him."

Bella gave a hiss of outrage. To her surprise, Charon dismissed Nyx with a wave of his hand and nodded to Bella. She glanced behind her, but no, his gaze was on her, not someone else. Exultant, she bowed. His smile shone upon her, and her heart sang.

"Bella, choose your band." His lips twitched. "He's a seventeen-year-old boy. You know what to do." Then, more seriously, "But note, he is no ordinary mortal."

Her head in the clouds, Bella nodded.

"No!" Nyx's shriek pierced the din. "I won't have it! Charon, you promised the child to me — not her! I will not be cheated of my heart's desire — Charon?"

"True, I did promise to let you have the babe, but your Rocket failed to bring him in, did he not? Time has passed; now, he is grown, and all has changed."

Bella drew herself up to her full height and stared Nyx in the eye. "I can do this. You know no man can resist me."

"But he's mine!" Had her eyes been wooden stakes, they would have annihilated Bella. "Not her, Charon. Anyone but her."

His face darkened. "I have spoken. And if I want a pretty boy dead, why would I send you? If you had carried out my directive last time, there would be no problem now."

"What about your deal with Lee Davis?" Nyx spat.

"He had his chance. Twice he tried and blew it. I want the world. No one stands in my way. Bella, bring me the child, alive, or his head on a platter, I care not which."

Bella shrugged off Nyx's furious glares like rainwater from a leaf. As soon as Charon turned aside his glance, Nyx was in her face, black eyes flashing fury. "You take the child to yourself, and I'll—"

"You'll what?" Bella dared to sneer.

"I should have left you in the shaman's trap!" Nyx hissed.

The shaman! Bella shuddered. She owed Nyx. She was about to assure her that she wouldn't take what was by rights hers, but Nyx had already turned away.

Bella's spirits couldn't be dampened for long. This coveted assignment was hers! The Rocket's repeated warnings that the moonchild could smell a vampire a mile away daunted her not at all. Her beauty could dazzle the eyes of any man, making him forget what his nose or any other of his senses told him. No man was invincible. None.

She chose as her team Rojo and China Boy, Pinkie and Blue Boy, and some others whose names were lost to her memory as though they'd been burned to ash with their bodies. Pinkie nervously chewed at a blond curl and clung to Blue Boy's arm, not sure she was up for it, but he steadied her; he was his usual easygoing self, game for anything.

The Rocket balked, now that he'd tasted freedom from that oppressive atmosphere, but he had no choice. Only he could point out the target. He dared beg Charon leave to be excused from accompanying the party, to wait until he was more fully regenerated before facing the moonchild. Charon's face darkened. The Rocket got the point. He ceased his protest and slunk from the throne room.

He is afraid of this thing, this child, Bella and her crew told each other. *Chicken.* And they laughed.

The Rocket quivered like a leaf in the wind, jumping at every little sound and movement in the night. They had caught some beneficial air currents and traveled fast, following him as he guided them to the home of the moonchild. When they arrived, the August moon had risen. Stars glittered in the black velvet Oklahoma sky. A bank of clouds along the eastern horizon sent a smudge of dirty fingers upward.

They sensed the oppression of which the Rocket had warned, but as it seemed to pose no overt threat, they brushed it off. A log house soon came into view, in a small clearing of neatly trimmed grass bordered by poppies, nasturtiums, and marigolds. Beyond a grape arbor were a fenced garden, a chicken coop, and a barn. Hollyhocks bloomed along the garden fence. In the corral adjacent to the barn, sheep and goats stirred uneasily. A mist rose from the creek winding through the meadow and into the woods.

In utter silence, Bella and her crew drifted down out of the night sky. An old blue Ford pickup truck sat in the driveway. Light shone from a window of the house. Tense as drawn bows, they watched. Foremost in their minds were the Rocket's wild-eyed tales of a fantastic monster. Though afraid beyond all reason, and cringing at every shadow, the Rocket had no choice but to be there; the master had spoken.

"There, smell that?" he blurted out.

The others shook their heads. Had he addled his brain? Then, between one moment and the next, they too caught the scent. Of mortals, and something else. Bella shivered with delight; all of them did—except the Rocket — he stood petrified.

"*¡Ay!* What is that?" Bella burst out.

"Don't pretend you don't know. The place reeks of him."

Reeks! A strange word for a scent so tantalizing.

By then, the crew had landed in the yard, silent as a shadow. The glimmering window attracted them, and when a silhouette advanced across the shade, they crowded in for a better view. Only the Rocket hung back.

Those furtive glances—he meant to sneak away! Bella snatched the front of his cloak and dragged him up close, nose to nose.

"You sniveling coward!" she snarled. "You'd better stick around long enough to identify him for us. After that, you can go to hell for all I care!"

His eyes were wild with terror. "Bella, please! I promise, this is the place; when you see him, you'll know." He feared her temper, as they all did. "Okay. I get it."

She flung him away, scowling, and scanned the yard. There, something moved, near the barn.

"*¡Oye!*" she hissed, instantly alert. "Listen!"

The stamping of small hoofs and baaing of sheep drifted to them in the clear night air, but that was not what caused the sudden excitement among them. Two-legged footsteps and a man-voice soothing the animals did. The mortal must have emerged from the house while they were distracted by their little squabble. Bella drifted toward the solitary human as he walked to the corral. Her small band cautiously followed.

A scrabbling of claws and a loud roar brought her to her senses as a large black dog leaped the corral fence and charged into their midst, its teeth gleaming white in the moonlight. They sprang up out of reach to drift easily above as it ran to and fro, barking and snarling. The dog posed little danger, but they didn't particularly want it drawing its master's attention to them. They scattered like young spiders floating on a summer breeze and continued to survey the area. The dog stood stiff-legged with raised hackles in the center of the yard, growling, every now and then erupting into a fury of barking.

"What's the matter with you, Li'l Scorpion?" exclaimed the young man. "Pipe down over there."

At once, the watchers hovering above went absolutely motionless. They weren't about to chance being targets of a lethal gaze. To their relief, the young man shrugged and turned back to his work, humming to himself.

The Rocket was gibbering with fear after that sudden, unexpected noise.

"Is he the One?" Bella snarled.

A low wailing sound escaped him; he did not seem aware of it.

"Shut up!" Bella hissed. She wanted to smack him.

They drifted like shadows toward the barnyard where the tall young man leaned down to scratch the head of a lamb that had come to the fence. Cautiously they approached, ever on the alert for him to sense or smell them as the Rocket had claimed he could, but he seemed oblivious to their presence.

"Okay, let me take him," Bella said softly. "Rojo, China Boy, watch my back. We want no surprises. You, you, you, all of you spread out and keep watch for anything amiss! Be ready. Got that? No mistakes now."

They all scattered to take up their posts, while Bella whirled about to concentrate her efforts on the moonchild. She alighted on the ground just behind him and stood for a moment in rising excitement, admiring the muscular shoulders and back. Her hand reached out almost of its own accord, to touch. Then she realized what was happening and jerked her hand back.

He straightened and turned, beginning to whistle a cheerful tune, but halted with a sharp intake of breath at the sight of her, surprise in his pale blue eyes. "Wha — ?"

His voice was pleasant, his smell tempting, but his eyes weren't glowing. Yet. He seemed an ordinary young man; his tall frame lanky, big hands and bony wrists protruding from rolled-up, plaid flannel sleeves. A slight breeze ruffled his hair; the fine feathery ends gleamed platinum in the moonlight. Within the angular planes of that open and honest face were a strong nose and a generous mouth. A nice face, but not that of an angel or, as the Rocket claimed, a paragon of beauty.

Was the Rocket high on something? He did seem a little messed up. She should have known then that they had the wrong one, but with the hunger upon her, she tended to ignore such details. And sometimes common sense flew out the window. She was careful not to let down her guard, though he didn't seem very dangerous, so naturally mortal did he appear. She decided that the best strategy was to go on the offensive.

"Hello, there," she said, her sultry smile and intonation calculated to knock any mortal male off his feet. Or, was this fabled creature like ordinary mortals? Still, a challenge always intrigued her. A little batting of eyelashes wouldn't hurt.

"What, er — howdy, Miss," the young man stammered, put off balance, no doubt, at the sudden appearance of a mysterious lady in his humble yard.

He seemed quite a peasant boy, upon closer observation. *Noble blood? Hmm.*

"I didn't even hear you. I mean, where did you come from?"

He was surprisingly easy to mesmerize. His eyes gave him away, startled at first, then glazed with rapture. Their glow appeared to be no more than the reflection of moonlight – anything but lethal. In the next instant, her fingers were tangled in his hair.

"You don't want to know. All that matters is that I'm here, and I'm all yours."

With an effort, he gave himself a shake. He tore his gaze from hers to cast a quick glance up toward the house. "Oh, Miss, what are you doing?"

So someone there mattered to him. Well. She'd soon make him forget. She turned his face so that his eyes met hers.

And he was caught. "You — you're gorgeous. Your eyes are so, who, what — ?"

She stopped his words with her trademark kiss; tasted blood. And he was putty in her hands, like any other mortal man. To hell with Nyx's first dibs!

The dog roared out of nowhere. Its swift attack froze her where she stood for a moment. It could have torn her limb from limb with those savage fangs but merely latched onto her cloak, so deceptive to mortal senses—even those of a dog. Her terrible shriek gave him pause, and she tore herself away to escape into the sky.

It took a bit to gather her wits after that scare, as Rojo and China Boy and the others watched apprehensively, clustered together. She realized that they'd all drawn near, instead of keeping a lookout for danger as she'd commanded.

"What the hell were you doing, Rojo, Blue Boy, all of you?" she shrieked. "You were supposed to be on guard!"

They muttered hasty apologies.

"Well? Speak up! What do you have to say for yourselves?" She was still trembling at her narrow escape.

Rojo cringed. "Sorry, Bella. We, I was watching—"

"Watching what? Me? This is a mission, not a peep show! You were supposed to keep watch so I may do my job! There is a difference, you know."

Rojo ducked his head, and only then did she realize she'd raised her hand to him. She let her hand drop and swung around to confront the others. "And you? What about the rest of you?"

"But you're so beautiful, Bella, when you, when you—" China Boy faltered and burst out with, "You're so good at it!"

"True," said Pinkie, gripping Blue Boy's arm possessively. "I wish I had your technique."

"Fine," Bella said impatiently. "Enough with the flattery."

"Actually," said Blue Boy. "I was just hungry, and I really wanted to bite him too." Everyone stared at him for a moment, and then there was a chorus of agreement.

"Well," Bella growled. "Remember why we are here. We feed later. Later, *comprende*?" She directed her attention once more to her intended victim and saw that the dog was nudging him with its nose and whining, no doubt to warn him of their presence. They hung back, not quite certain he wouldn't yet come alive to blast them out of the sky with his lightning eyes.

Finally, the dog succeeded in stirring the confused young man into action. He slowly made his way up the path toward the house. Whenever he paused as though not certain of what he was supposed to be doing, the dog nudged him on his way.

As he approached the garden gate, he ran a hand through his hair and shook a little, coming to himself again. The trance-like effect tended to wear off after a while, but now that Bella had bitten him, there was a connection that would always lead her to him and make him more susceptible to the power of her will. If all went as usual.

The whistling began again. He appeared to have forgotten the incident, though he seemed a little puzzled. He entered the garden path, latched the gate behind him, and vanished beneath the canopy of grapevines. Presently he emerged, and with a more confident stride, continued toward the house.

The dog had not forgotten them. It trotted in ever-widening circles around the young man, growling, and gave a sharp woof every now and then.

"What's the matter, boy?"

The dog whined and ran to him, nuzzling his hand anxiously. He patted it on the head, and it followed him up the steps. He staggered a bit. A shaft of light streaked out as the door opened.

A slender shadow fell upon the patch of light, though the person who produced it wasn't visible. "Oh good, you're back; we still have time to finish the game before we go. My, are you okay, Beau? What happened?"

Even Bella's head spun around at the sound of the girl's voice, so sweet and clear. Now that was the voice of an angel. She gestured sharply to restrain her boys; they seemed about to swoop in and make a real mess of things.

Beau! So that's his name: beautiful, the same as mine. No, she had to keep calm; nothing must endanger the mission. *But—a girl, here? He'd tasted innocent...*

"I, I'm not sure," he said slowly. "I must have tripped or something."

"Tripped?" The girl sounded doubtful and concerned. "But your lip is bleeding. How did you manage that?"

The boy lifted his hand to his face, as though noticing for the first time. "Ow. You're right. I, um—I may have run into something. Funny, I don't recollect."

"Here. Come inside. I'll fix it up for you."

The shaft of light vanished as they withdrew inside and closed the door. The dog flopped down on the porch; its ears laid back. It growled occasionally.

"What now, Bella?" said Rojo. "Will the moonchild come out again, or are you going in after him?"

He was always so curious, so eager. That from anyone else would have drawn a frown, but Bella gave him a fond glance, which was as near as she ever came to an apology. She hadn't meant to strike him. He knew that, of course.

"Just wait; we will see. They're playing a game; I think she said. Maybe he'll come out after. Let's peek in the windows, but mind the dog. Do not rouse it."

They crept near, noiselessly, so that the dog didn't so much as twitch an ear, and peered in through a lit-up pane with its shade drawn up. After a short investigation, they met again at the edge of the yard to confer.

"Did you see the girl in there?" said China Boy, an eager light in his obsidian eyes. "She's beautiful."

"Yes," said Blue Boy, ignoring a sharp glance from Pinkie (she was so jealous!). "Maybe this is the girl the Rocket mentioned," he hurried on, as though that were his real reason for casting his eyes upon a beauty other than Pinkie. "Is it?" He glanced around. They all did. The Rocket was nowhere to be seen.

"What the hell?" someone said. "The Rocket's gone!"

"Curse him for a coward!" snarled Bella. "Find him!"

Everyone scattered to search the area. Bella rose above the trees and tried to catch some sense of him in the night breezes that rustled through the leaves. Nothing. She rejoined the others at the edge of the yard; they shrugged and shook their heads. Not a trace. No one had seen him leave.

Bella expressed her displeasure with a string of epithets. *The coward abandoned us!* Well, he'd led them to the moonchild. Though it wouldn't have been amiss for him to remain until they had it in hand. *Good riddance,* she thought sourly.

"So. What about the girl?" said China Boy, always with the one-track mind.

"Please, can we have her, Bella?" rasped Rojo over China Boy's softer voice, his tongue hanging out.

"Cool it. First things first."

"I think she's too young," said Blue Boy. Everyone stared. Abashed at having all eyes upon him, he shrugged. "I mean, to be the girl with the moonchild when..."

Bella gave him a level stare. "Right. Let's get on with it."

After a short discussion, all spread out around the yard, silent and watchful. Time dragged. Bella cast an anxious glance at the sky, but the night was young. Would the young man ever come out? A light still burned; there was a murmur of voices and laughter. She considered going to the door, maybe draw him out, but— No, she'd give him a bit more time; let him come to her.

The dog lay on the porch, with an occasional twitch of the ears and a low rumble in its throat. They paid it no heed.

Suddenly the kitchen light went out, and the porch light came on. A ripple of excitement went through the group of watchers. The mortals were coming to them at last.

A Date with Death

They waited, tense and watchful, as the dog got to its feet and faced the door, tail wagging. Presently the door opened. The dog whined, then growled and yipped to warn of the peril lurking in the night.

The young man emerged, followed by a girl with long blond hair that shone like spun gold in the moonlight. Bella's boys quivered with eagerness, but her sharp gesture quelled them.

"And they'll be back tonight?" the girl was saying.

"Or tomorrow at the latest," the young man replied. "You'll meet them Sunday afternoon. Mama's inviting them over for a barbecue. You'll love that. Miz Martel makes a mean peach pie."

The girl glanced up at him with a sweet chime of laughter. "It totally sounds like fun. I can't wait."

His eyes twinkled. "Just be ready, Rachel. Mama loves your singing. She'll ask you to give us a song, for sure."

Again the tinkling laugh. "Oh my, what will they say?"

"They'll fall under your spell, too. Jude will give us a tune on his violin, maybe even sing a duet with you. Try 'Come What May.' That'll be something, the two of you."

"I don't know," she said doubtfully. "It's our song. Yours and mine. I love singing it with you."

"But I'm always off-key. Not Jude. You got to sing it with him. His voice is like yours, so fine. You'll never want to sing with me again." He noted her scowl and grinned. "Okay, maybe you better not. You'll fall in love with him, and then where will I be?"

"You've got yourself a deal, Mr. Funny Man. Just promise me right now you won't get jealous."

"Of my little bro? Not a chance." Beau laughed and gave her a squeeze. "It'll still be our song, just—" He turned to the dog, which was anxiously trying to get his attention. "It's okay, boy." He patted the dog on the head, but it wouldn't calm down. "It's not like Li'l Scorpion to get riled about nothing. I wonder what, maybe a bear or cat passing through. Reckon the sheep ought to be safe in the pen, though." He glanced around, frowning.

The girl took his arm and gazed out into the night. "Are you sure? You wouldn't want anything to—" She broke off with a gasp as the dog exploded off the porch in a mad storm of barking to scatter Bella and her band once more.

Without thinking, they'd moved closer. The scent of mortals drew them, but it was the girl's voice that was irresistible beyond all reason. Luckily for them, the light from the porch blinded the two humans, and they weren't discovered. They couldn't stay away. Their natures, their appetites, drove them. Rojo and China Boy were squabbling about the girl, while the others hovered in anticipation.

Bella itched to get her hands on the boy—even if he was the One, she could take him easily, if she kept her wits about her and watched out for the eyes. She tensed as those eyes warily searched the night. It didn't appear as though he'd sensed them yet.

"We better get crackin' if we want to make that movie, honeybunch," he was saying. They descended the steps and started toward the pickup. He walked with calm assurance, but the vampires could feel the acceleration of his heartbeat as the girl clung to his arm. "Heck, the dog can keep an eye out for the sheep. He knows his job."

"Whatever you say, Beau, honey," said the girl, her cornflower blue eyes adoring as she lifted them to his face. "But maybe we shouldn't go to the movie tonight. You don't look so good."

"Well, I like that." He smiled ruefully, and with a tender glance, patted her fingers where they rested in the crook of his elbow.

It was all Bella could do to keep from springing at them. She gestured sharply to her boys to cool it, to disguise the strain of keeping her own impulses in check.

"I only meant—" the girl began.

He laughed. "Fine by me if you'd rather wait. It's playing tomorrow night too. Maybe by then, I'll be more presentable."

"Alyssa did ask us to watch *The Hobbit* with her. We could do that instead."

Their footfalls were soft on the grass as they walked down the slope of lawn to the driveway, unaware of the vampires hovering above. The young man gazed up at the sky. "The stars are right pretty tonight. Like sparkling diamonds."

"Diamonds," China Boy said softly in a tone of awe. "'Diamonds are shadows of the sun... shine, shine, sweet lady, make me thy shadow still.' Oh, Bella, I want her. She does so slay my dark!" Caught up in a frenzy of romantic feeling, and heedless of Bella's sharp gesture for him to be silent, he leaped from MacDonald to Keats, "'Yet do not grieve; She cannot fade, though thou hast not thy bliss, for ever wilt thou love, and she be fair!' Ah, diamond girl—"

"Quiet!" hissed Bella. His fits would be the death of her yet. She had only herself to blame, of course. How many hours had she spent trying to instill in her boys an appreciation of literature? While Rojo fidgeted and yawned, preferring timewasters like dice and cards, her wild Indian boy took to poetry with a fervor matching her own.

"I can't believe how totally bright they are." The girl's sweet voice jerked Bella from her reverie. "It's awesome."

"Yeah, city lights got nothing on our country sky," the boy said, "and would you look at that moon?"

"Oh, it's so big and round," exclaimed the girl. "Is it a full moon tonight?"

"Not quite. See that shadow on one side? Looks like the clouds'll be covering it before long, anyhow." He pointed to a streamer of dirty gray reaching for the shining orb.

The girl shivered; glanced around. "What was that? I thought I heard something."

The boy scanned the yard but didn't think of searching the sky. Not that he could see them (*or could he?*). "Nothing to worry about, hon," he said with a tense laugh.

He put his arm around the girl, opened the door of the pickup, and glanced around anxiously as he gave her a hand up. Then his back was turned, and Bella could not help herself. Here was her chance to take him without danger from those eyes.

She sprang.

With a snarl, the dog launched itself at her. She cursed and flung herself aside. Even as the dog snagged her cloak with one of its fangs, she tore loose and melted into the shadows. The dog was hard on her heels, roaring. She could have killed it but dared not risk losing her intended victim.

"What the heck's the matter with that dog tonight?" said the boy, shaking his head as he peered into the darkness.

He seemed to be staring right at Bella, yet his eyes didn't glow. After a bit, he turned away. By the time she recovered her self-possession, the pickup was halfway down the drive. The dog continued to bark sporadically.

The vampires drifted from the shadows. Two pairs of eyes stared at Bella until they saw that she had come away unscathed. Those of Rojo and

China Boy. The others varied between casting impatient glances after the departing vehicle and apprehensive ones toward Bella, unsure if she would blame them again.

"After them!" Bella snarled to cover her ill-advised move. She rapped out several names. "Don't let them out of your sight. We lose the moonchild, we lose our hides." She caught up to Pinkie. "You were eyeing the boy. Did his eyes glow when I attacked?"

Pinkie's blond curls bounced as she shook her head. "No, he seemed surprised at the dog, but I don't think he saw you. No glowing eyes at all. Just a shiver, maybe."

"That's right," Blue Boy put in. "He glanced around while he started the pickup, but his eyes didn't glow."

"She, she was looking out the back window," moaned China Boy. "Her eyes, they were afraid. I want her!"

Bella scowled. They were so close. They dared not make a wrong move now. "Come on, let's catch up with the others."

They drifted easily, their movement much swifter than that of the pickup bouncing down the lane, over washouts, ruts, and potholes. The air currents lifted them above the trees as they followed the rumbling of the motor below.

"Can we have the girl, Bella?" Rojo dared to ask, cautiously. China Boy's eyes gleamed with an unholy light, but he kept his mouth shut for once.

Bella glanced upward. The clouds had partly obscured the moon. "Wait, I must think. Charon might like her if she can sing. Okay, let's see where they go."

The pickup turned out of the drive and onto the road. The vampires drifted in its wake. After a mile or so at a snail's pace, they turned into another driveway and bounced along until they arrived at another farmyard. The stalking vampires watched them park the pickup and enter the house.

Through the night, Bella and her crew lurked there, hungry, but reluctant to abandon their watch. They dared not make their presence known. Not yet. The approach of dawn put an end to their vigil. Perplexed and disappointed at the young man's failure to reappear, they made for the hill where the Rocket had pointed out his old lair.

"Tomorrow night, my pretty," said Bella, her eyes hard. "We have a date, you and I."

"A date with death," said Rojo eagerly.

They flowed into the crevice in the hillside just ahead of the dawn and settled in to sleep away the day.

It wasn't difficult to find the young man the next night. Bella and her crew emerged just after sunset, itching to feed, but they dared not let him give them the slip again. With only days left until the eclipse, they were running out of time.

Bella had a plan. This time there would be no dog to interfere. She concentrated on her connection to seek out the target. They first checked out the home place and found it empty. They sensed that Beau had indeed been there but was now gone. Bella and her crew followed the faint sense of him toward the farmhouse where they'd left him at dawn and soon spotted the old blue pickup on the road, outward bound.

Elated, Bella issued orders. They followed the vehicle along the gravel road, their excitement increasing as they drew near Bella's chosen point of interception. Its mortal occupants had no notion that they wouldn't see that movie, and that they'd lose each other – and perhaps their very lives – before the night was over.

The vampires quivered with anticipation as they took up their stations, shadowing the pickup as it followed winding ups and downs and jolted through potholes. Bella hovered just above the circle of light. From there, she could feast her eyes on the driver through the windshield. A little frown of concentration creased his brow as he negotiated the ruts caused by spring flooding, where the road dipped beneath the high-water mark. He and the girl appeared to be carrying on a lively conversation, unaware that evil stalked them. Every now and then, Beau took his eyes off the road long enough to give his girl a tender glance and an easy grin. She sat next to him, but her face was mostly obscured by the rearview mirror, from Bella's perspective.

"Okay. Soon," Bella said. "I'll take him. Rojo, China Boy, don't let the girl interfere or escape. The rest of you, keep watch. I am not sure what we are up against, here, so be ready."

They nodded. That little fox Rojo had his tongue hanging out already. China Boy's perfect white teeth flashed in the night. There were growls of assent from the others. They knew better than to grumble, whether or not they were miffed that Bella should favor her boys. And besides, all were a bit anxious.

She flew ahead, just out of sight over the rise. In the blink of an eye, she'd whipped off her telltale cloak and folded it into a convenient handkerchief-size that tucked easily into the pocket of her long, elegant black dress. They couldn't be too careful, even if he was hers from that first bite. Anyway, a little playacting made the game more fun. She stepped out onto the road.

The pickup topped the rise just then and caught her in the beam of its headlights, setting the gems on her dress asparkle. The driver cranked the wheel hard to the left, but the bumper caught her. She went sprawling in a whirl of skirts and lay in the middle of the road, still as death. She didn't flinch as the pickup skidded to a stop inches from her.

Beau flung his door wide. "My Lord, I've hit someone!" The yellowish headlights shone full upon her. She watched through half-closed eyes as big shoes and long, jeans-clad legs approached. The young man bent down and peered into her face. "No. Please don't be dead." She felt a tug at her skirt as he covered her exposed legs. "Sorry, miss."

She felt him blush and just managed to suppress a hiss. Touching. Maybe he was innocent. *Too bad, Nyx, he's mine.*

"Is everything okay, Beau?" the girl called out, her voice shaking. "Can I help?"

He didn't answer immediately but whispered something that could have been a prayer and reached out tentatively to touch Bella's shoulder. She let her eyelids flicker.

"Oh, thank God. She's still alive."

His racing heart set her afire. How she wanted to bite him but dared not make a move with those eyes looking into her face.

The girl climbed out of the pickup and came over. Her hand flew to her mouth. "Is she going to be all right?"

"I don't know. She seems awful cold. We should get her to a doc." He rubbed a hand across his eyes. "Dear God, I didn't even see her, before — gosh, we just come over the hill, and there she was, right smack in the middle of the road. I tried to dodge, but—"

"It's not your fault. Can you lift her? Or, you don't want to move her wrong, in case her back…. Should I call the ambulance or someone? I'll get my cellphone."

"Wait. I think she's coming to. Miss, I need to move you. Are you hurting anywhere?"

Bella lifted her eyes to meet his. He didn't appear any more threatening this time than before. Had the Rocket exaggerated his powers? Was this the moonchild? The Rocket had pointed him out. *Sort of.*

"We need to get you to a doctor, Miss."

His voice pulled her out of her dream world, and she quickly closed her mouth (hoping he hadn't noticed she was tasting the air).

"It's okay; don't try to talk," he said.

She could have kicked herself for allowing herself to be distracted. But he was so lovely. It seemed he couldn't resist staring at her. So even he wasn't immune to her charms. She hadn't imagined it. He was just a boy, after all. She captured his gaze once more, with the usual devastating effect.

He swallowed hard. "You're so beautiful. I reckon the doc can wait." With a low laugh, he leaned down. Just as she thought he'd kiss her, he tore his gaze from hers and ran a hand through his hair. He muttered in a distraught tone. "Sorry, miss."

"What are you doing, darling?" said the girl anxiously. "Beau, honey?"

At the sound of her voice, he would have turned his head, but Bella touched his cheek, and he glanced back. Her eyes once more ensnared his, and he leaned down slowly to kiss her, though she could feel him resisting the pull. (So this was why Nyx liked them innocent!) Well, he wouldn't resist her for long. No man ever had. She reached up to tangle her fingers in his hair and caught him to herself. His strong arms went around her, and all at once, he was kissing her desperately. (Her boys didn't call her Spanish Fly for nothing, though she would have preferred a pretty name, like Butterfly, or some such.)

The girl began to voice an outraged protest, but with a snap of his cape, Rojo flitted to her and held her fast. Her eyes went wide with shock and fright as she struggled uselessly against his wiry strength. China Boy flew in and clapped a hand over her mouth, delighted at the excuse to touch her.

Bella didn't care, as long as they kept the girl from distracting Beau.

Greater Love Hath No Man

Was he the One? *No, this was too easy.* Doubts nagged at her. She so wanted to turn him, to keep him forever, whoever — whatever — he was. It had been nearly a hundred and fifty years since China Boy. She was due for a new playmate. But alas, Charon might take issue with that, if this was the moonchild. Still, he wouldn't begrudge her some fun. She slipped out of Beau's embrace and left him kneeling on the ground, bewildered, while she stood over him.

Flushed and breathing hard, he got to his feet. "Sorry, miss," he managed. "I don't know what come over me. I, er, I didn't mean to do that."

"Not your fault," Bella murmured as she rearranged her hair. Just then, a muffled cry came from the girl. The boy turned his head at the sound. Bella caught his arm to distract him. "Ay, what muscle! Do you work out at the gym?"

He avoided eye contact with her; his voice was a little tight, but he seemed unable to rudely ignore her question. "Huh? Gym? Er, no, miss. Just, um, hard work, like chopping wood and wrestling calves and hay bales and such."

"Lovely." She stroked his arm; his muscle tensed. He politely tried to extricate himself, once more distracted from the plight of his girl.

"Um, are you sure you're not hurt, miss?"

"I'll be okay in a minute." Bella clutched at his arm, and with difficulty, resisted the mad urge to bite. *Calm. Must not rush this. Have to get hold of myself.* She quivered with the effort, and he misunderstood.

"Don't worry." His voice was strained as he fought to keep his head above water, not knowing yet that he was in quicksand. "I'll get you home safe." As Bella recaptured his gaze, he was reduced to stammering, "You're so, I mean, your eyes, they're gorgeous. Like a deer. Dear God, what am I saying?" He tore his gaze from hers. His eyes darted around, searching.

Bella was ensnared by that heartbeat. "Never mind, it's not important," she said, feigning breathlessness.

He gazed down from his height, that sweet face so unspoiled and unsuspecting, yet so strong and manly. With the ease of long practice, she drew him in. So much for those vaunted legendary powers. Or, if he was *not* the One, she was beyond caring.

"I, I—" He couldn't tear his eyes from hers. "I, er, what about—oh, hell." With that, he crushed her to him. (Hell it was, all right, much closer to the truth than he knew.)

The girl called out his name. Bella bit him on the mouth, stopping his last feeble attempt to pull away. He fell into rapture and she wanted it all. *Now. No.* Must entice him to the master. She pulled away and studied that face. His mouth was bleeding, his eyes reproachful.

"Come, be one of us."

He grimaced faintly. Blood welled from the razor-fine cuts at his mouth. She licked it off.

He jerked back and gingerly felt his lips as though just realizing something was wrong with them. "What have you done?"

Ay. Here it comes. Now the eyes will glow. And the blue lightning will strike. Nothing happened. Was this just a mortal man, after all? But hadn't the Rocket said—? Or, no, he didn't, but—ah, the moon. She glanced up. There was no moon; it was now behind the dirty gray clouds. Maybe he depended on it for his powers. Was that why the master called him moonchild? If so, best to take him down while the moon was hidden.

"I have given you a taste of heaven, *niño.*" Bella moved toward him; he flinched. "None of that, now. You know you want this. And the master wants you, so let's just—"

"The master? Who—what are you?"

As if on cue, eyes glowed in the dark, and the others emerged from the shadows outside the circle of light, mouths hanging open in hunger. Beau jerked back, his heart pounding in a wild, irresistible rhythm that set them all afire.

Bella restrained herself with difficulty. "More to the point—who, and what, are *you*? On a winter dawn seventeen years ago, a child fell from the sky. Are you that One?"

He frowned. "Fell from the sky?" He shook his head a little and dropped his gaze.

He was hiding something, she could tell, but she had no idea of the meaning of self-sacrifice, or that Beau had guessed whom she was seeking and would protect his "little bro" as he always had.

So, he is the one! she said to herself and went for his throat.

The beat of his heart echoed through her in a grand kaleidoscope of emotion and memory and life experience as his blood poured down her gullet. Nyx claimed that the innocents were sweetest; she had no doubt of it now. *How did I not know?* Of course, it was because she avoided difficulty whenever she could. Those in the state of sin were easy. This one was frustrating, but so inexpressibly sweet in his resistance—unlike Rojo and China Boy, and even they were wonderful! They were nothing to this! At the moment, they were scrapping over which of them would taste the moonchild next, and the girl.

If only she could persuade him to drink of her blood. Then she'd have her heart's desire, and ay, what a sweet companion he'd make! But no, he turned his face aside; tried to push her away. She let go of him, and he fell back heavily, his eyes dull. Cautiously the others approached, now that he was down on the ground and appeared to be somewhat incapacitated. He didn't seem aware of them.

"Who are you people?" said the girl anxiously. No one answered. China Boy ducked his head guiltily and clapped his hand over her mouth. She tore it loose. "My dad will pay whatever you want!" she cried, her eyes swimming with tears at the sight of her sweetheart lying helpless at their feet. "Let him go, please. Please?"

Rojo slapped her. "Shut up, stupid girl, if you want your beau alive," he mocked. Of course, that would never happen, but she didn't know that. She subsided, and Rojo held her easily with one arm. The light died out of her eyes, and she watched dully. "Do we get to taste now, Bella?" His foxy face split into a pointed-toothed grin; he squeezed the girl meaningfully.

"I get the girl," said China Boy. His tongue whipped out to taste her cheek, her throat. "Pretty diamond girl." His voice was husky, and his smile strained. "Bella, I'm hungry. Give."

"Wait your turn, you jackals!" Bella snarled as she turned back to her victim. A ribbon of scarlet streamed down the side of his throat, staining his shirt collar. To turn this one would be her ultimate triumph. How she hated to be denied.

"Just a little taste," whined Rojo. He'd let go of the girl without realizing, but China Boy held her easily.

"Stop pestering! I'm trying to think."

They shrank back, muttering, and cast hungry glances at her victim. The rest of the crew stirred but were careful not to provoke Bella's notorious temper. She stared down at Beau. His face was ashen, his breath shallow, his eyes heavy. Very near death.

Rojo edged closer. China Boy's eyes were glassy as he pressed the girl to himself. She had ceased her struggle, desolate as she watched her Beau being heartlessly destroyed before her eyes.

Bella turned inward to search the memories she had ingested. "A falling star," she said. Rojo jerked back, but she paid him no heed. "A ball of fire dropped out of the sky. You know; you were there. You saw the Rocket burn!" She frowned down at Beau. "Was that you? Are you the One?"

He lay as if dead, but he wasn't; she could hear the faint beat of his heart. She stroked his hair and kissed his face. His eyes slid away to avoid her gaze. He knew now, at last, what she was and what was happening to him. So, where were his fantastic powers? Oh, right, the moon was still hidden. That had to be it. She refused to think what it would mean otherwise.

Rojo spoke up. "What is it, Bella? Is he the One?"

"I cannot be certain," she admitted reluctantly and leaned down to study his face. He feebly raised a hand to push her away; his strength was gone. He closed his eyes, his only defense. "His innocence shields him, and yet it almost certainly proclaims him the One. I ask you, how often do we find a young man of his years so untainted?" She gave him a sharp slap across the cheek. "Wake up, *mi querido*, and answer my question."

At the shock of the slap, his eyes opened halfway. "Yeah. I saw the fire falling, falling from the sky, so cold..." he panted. "Water. Please."

"So, you were the child that fell from the sky?" Bella coaxed. "Come, the master has a plan for that child. For you, if you are he."

"The sky, I was... just a baby, yeah, I—I'm so...thirsty. Water."

How Bella hated this run-around. "Answer me straight, *niño*," she said petulantly. "You were there, you saw. I can taste it. Are you the one, or must we seek another?"

He closed his eyes and was silent.

"Is he dead, Bella?" cried China Boy in despair.

Rojo whined, "You've killed him!"

She kept her eyes on her victim, who feebly clung to life; she sensed a war within him. "Well? The truth now."

He opened his eyes and stared past her. "Jesus, save me."

She leaped back, snarling. "He will not help you!" she hissed. "Only I can, so answer me now!"

"You know... so much about it. Why... ask... me?" he panted with the effort of speaking and closed his eyes.

Bella sat back on her heels. "You are thirsty? Drink, then." She lifted him, held him in her arms, and spoke softly. "Become one of us. If you are the One, it is you the master has chosen to sit at his right hand forever, a very great honor. Come now, be wise. Give me your answer."

"Or I'll tear it out of your head," snarled Rojo, ever on a short fuse.

Bella peered into the tired, gray face. "It's not in your head, is it? It's in your heart."

He sighed, bone-weary to the point of death, but under the electrifying scrutiny of her vampire eyes, roused enough to faintly slur, "I'm not, why do you, uh, mm..."

She leaned closer, trying to catch all his words, in vain.

"Fire...falling from the sky...and they found mm...um, I—" His lips still moved, even as his voice faded out. He sagged against her arm, trying to catch his breath.

She smiled down into that face so pale and drawn. "That was not difficult, was it?" He didn't respond. Maybe he really didn't have any power without the moon. She glanced up at the sky a bit anxiously, but there was no sign of that dark mist lifting. "You don't have to die," she said softly. His eyes remained closed. "I offer you immortality, youth, and beauty forever. No more pain, weakness, or death, ever again." He was silent. "Here, you are thirsty." With a razor-sharp claw, Bella slashed her breast; lifted him up. "Drink now, if you wish to live. Accept my offer. You are too young to die."

The vampires stirred, unconsciously drawing near. China Boy held the girl securely, but she was too overcome by horror to put up a struggle. She stared straight ahead, her eyes dull.

With one great heave, Beau flung himself from Bella's arms, as though to run, but his legs gave way, and he fell to his hands and knees in the gravel. A pity. A short time ago, he was strong and perfect, happy and full of life. Now he swayed, head hanging.

"Go back to hell where you come from," he panted but did not taste of the black that smeared his mouth. "I make no deals with the devil."

Rojo was beside him in an instant, yanking him by the hair to glare into those tired eyes. "You ungrateful piece of—!" he hissed. "You spit on her gift? Let me bite him, Bella. Please." He fixed her with hot, outraged eyes. Little Rojo, burning to avenge her.

He was right. It was a slap in the face. She imagined Nyx's scorn; fury blinded her. Charon would get his head on a platter, then. She would not fail her mission.

"Bite him," she snarled.

Rojo sprang. The others surged in to overwhelm the stricken young man, biting, clinging, sucking the lifeblood from him.

"Bella, Bella," whined China Boy, left holding the girl. Much as he would have preferred the girl, the victim on the ground seemed more a sure thing.

"Go," Bella growled, slipping her folded cloak out of her pocket. With a practiced flick of her wrist, she snapped it into its full size, donned it, and fastened the clasp at her throat. Vampires' cloaks were a large part of what made them invisible to mortal eyes. "She will not get far if she thinks to run."

With one parting caress, China Boy rushed to join the others at the feast.

The girl stood forlorn, her cornflower eyes tragic. "What are they doing to him? Please don't let them —"

"Don't let them what?" Bella sneered, her own mouth smeared with his blood. *What was the silly girl thinking?*

The girl stared, dazed, as though unable to understand what they were doing. *Like a bunch of magpies picking at a piece of garbage, that's all*, Bella thought sourly.

Beau was barely visible beneath the fluttering dark cloaks just outside the beam of headlights. He had collapsed beneath the cluster of noisily feeding vampires. The girl finally seemed to realize what was happening, and with a loud cry, ran toward them. To do what, Bella could not imagine. For the sake of Charon getting her intact, she dared not let her disturb them in their frenzy. She snagged the girl's long golden hair and yanked her back.

"Where do you think you're going?" she growled. The girl trembled, her tear-filled eyes turned toward the obscene sight. She seemed unaware of her own danger, thinking only of him. Was that love? The image of a sweet face came to Bella's mind, of a boy, long ago. Furious, she crushed the sensation. *Leave me alone!* She tried to think of something else, anything else, and one of Beau's thoughts sprang to mind, one of those she had collected within her. "So. You sing? Give us a song, then."

The girl's lips quivered, her glance flicking from Bella to the others in a futile search for her sweetheart, and back to Bella. "Beau. Please help him. I can't—"

"Sing!" Bella shrieked. "A song for his life. Now!"

The girl shrank back, shivering, but then realization kicked in, and she sang. It was beautiful. The others, too, were ensnared by the power of that lovely voice. They halted in the midst of their feeding and drifted close around her, Beau's blood smearing their faces. She had mesmerized them all, it seemed. Little did she realize the power she had over them. She only sang, desperately, for her sweetheart's life. A sad song, a lament so mournful that if vampires had tears, even they would have wept.

When the girl at last finished her song, her audience stood like statues, struck dumb with awe. China Boy dropped to his knees as though to worship. Bella gave him a boot in the ribs.

"A fine gift for Charon," she said coldly. "He'll love the nightingale."

The girl turned her head toward the boy lying on his face in the grass beside the road. Her eyes filled with tears and her lips quivered. "Beau? Darling, are you okay?"

She stumbled toward him, oblivious of the vampires standing in her way. At Bella's nod, they let her pass. She watched the girl with narrowed eyes. *Curious thing, love.*

Beau lay still, cheek pressed to the ground, tatters of his clothing lifting in the night breeze, his platinum hair fluttering. The girl almost fell at the shoulder of the road, not seeing the slight drop-off because of the glare of headlights. With a sob, she threw herself down to crouch beside him, reaching out to touch, hesitantly.

"Beau? Can you hear me? Please get up." He didn't move. She tugged at his shoulder, trying to see his face or to turn him over. He was a big boy, a dead weight now, and she was just a slender little thing, so she couldn't lift him. She burst into tears of frustration and settled for gazing into his face, trying to brush the dirt and grass from it. "Please, God, don't let him die," she wept aloud.

Impatiently Bella went and stood over him. "I have no time for this. Your sweetheart? Not anymore, *niña.*" Reaching down, she tangled her fingers in his hair and yanked his head up. "Here, have a look."

Surely she could see how his half-closed eyes were glazed over, the bite marks, the blood soaking his clothes. Grass and dirt stuck to the side of his face and his mauled throat. The girl threw herself at him, weeping loudly and raining kisses on the tortured face. He didn't respond. *She must know he'd never light up her life again,* Bella thought cynically, as the girl wailed, crying out to her God. Maybe she thought that would wake the dead. She made enough noise for it. Ay, good luck with that, *niña.* A fine lot of good that will do.

China Boy had come over to shadow her but was curious and a little confused by her actions, so did not touch her. Or dared not, seeing Bella's foul mood at having her plan go awry.

She tore the boy away from his girl by the grip she had on his hair and peered into his face. "Well. He had his chance."

Rojo crept over to lick at the blood that bubbled from the wound at his throat. Beau's arm flopped so that it fell into the girl's lap. Still wailing and calling his name, she picked it up and held it tenderly in her hands, tears raining down on the pale, limp fingers. She lifted it to her lips and kissed it, then held it to her cheek and rocked back and forth, moaning disconsolately.

China Boy stroked her hair, but she seemed oblivious.

"Someone's coming down the road," Blue Boy announced.

Pinkie repeated it and a murmur rippled through the ranks. The rumble of a motor was growing louder as a vehicle approached, fading out as it eased down a grade and picking up again as it climbed a rise.

"I'm still hungry," said Rojo, coming alive. "Do you think they'll stop?"

"Of course," someone else said. "Or we'll make them stop." That comment caused some laughter. Now that their appetites had been whetted, not much could deter them.

"Come on, Blue Boy," giggled Pinkie. "I'll bet you get the first one."

She is so silly, thought Bella darkly, *it's a wonder she has survived this long*. "Time to finish this," she growled, pulling a long sharp knife from her belt, still with a grip on Beau's hair. Regretfully she stared down at him. Too bad he hadn't co-operated. He could have been beautiful forever. Now the pale blue eyes were fixed and fading, no more to cast a tender glance. The damaged mouth hung open, smeared with her dark blood; those straight white teeth would no more flash a friendly grin.

But he'd made his choice. He'd spurned her gift of immortality and refused to taste. How she hated not getting what she wanted. She glanced at the girl and felt a surge of jealousy. Her eyes narrowed. Fine. *If I cannot have him, neither will she*. His head will be atop Charon's throne where she may look upon it as she performs for the master and know what she has lost.

With two swift strokes of the knife, Bella separated the head from its body. She held it up to study the face once more. The body flopped down beside the girl; the hand was pulled from hers. With a sharp cry, the girl fell to the ground in a faint.

China Boy rushed to pick her up. She was limp in his arms, her face pale as death with blue shadows beneath her closed eyes. "Ah, diamond girl," he moaned softly. Bella couldn't help but stare with a mix of cynicism and admiration and fondness. But he didn't stop there. He was spouting Keats' *Ode to Fanny* now. Overcome by feeling, he faltered at the last. His fangs glinted between parted red lips; his black eyes fixed with great longing upon the pulse in the girl's white throat.

"No," Bella said. "The nightingale is for Charon."

China Boy's head jerked up as though he'd forgotten she was there. It was a good thing she'd reminded him. He might have bitten the girl. Now he pressed her to his chest and closed his eyes. She was so fragile. Would she survive to reach the master?

The others had drifted into shadow, lying in wait for the approaching vehicle. Bella had no doubt its occupants would stop to investigate, but they'd not stand a chance against her troop of hungry vampires.

The beam of headlights flickered on the trees above them and skittered further and further past until the pickup came into full view with its lights glaring right at them for a moment before it started downward again.

Bella lifted up her trophy for a cursory examination. Charon had asked for the head; he wouldn't quibble about the platter. How disappointing that the boy had proved intransigent, though. It wasn't often that one she chose refused her. That was why she preferred the bad boys.

Gravel crunched, and Bella turned, just as a dark green late-model Dodge came up the rise and eased to a stop at the side of the road. The door on the driver's side opened. Oddly, every vampire sprang back, hissing. An instinctive defensive reaction, perhaps?

Out stepped a tall young man, beautiful as a god, his hair like burnished gold in the blaze of headlights. They gaped in awe. This one had the face of an angel! Bella stared as he turned to speak to the woman sitting in the pickup. Where had she seen that profile before?

"It is Beau's pickup, Mama," he was saying. "I wonder what he's doing out here?"

That voice. It was a sound to melt the heart, if such a phenomenon were possible for a vampire. That face turned her way again, and she was stunned anew. And those eyes. She wanted nothing more than to drown in them.

Pinkie stood gaping. Bella was about to tell her to shut her mouth when she realized she had better pick her own jaw up off the ground. She closed her mouth with a snap and shook her head, trying to gather her scattered wits. Not since she first saw the Prince had such a thing happened to her. (Oddly enough, she didn't at once make the connection.)

He was well-muscled, yet almost delicate, as though somehow not of this world. Had not the Rocket said—

¡*Ay de mi! This was the One!* Bella let go of Beau's hair; the head dropped beside the body with a soft thud. She stood staring, unable to move as the young man walked toward them.

The Moonchild Strikes Back

"Beau? Where are you, Beau?" the young man called. His shoes crunched on the gravel as he squinted past the headlights.

All at once, he turned, his sweeping gaze passing over the lot of them to finally come to a halt at the exact spot where Bella stood in the shadow of the old blue pickup. Her crew had spread out in a semicircle, crouching on the ground, or clinging to tree branches just outside the light. Surely, he couldn't see them!

Bella felt his heartbeat change pace and recalled what the Rocket had said about this one's ability to sense vampires. He knew they were there! His face hardened, and his eyes became piercing points of blue as they searched the shadows.

Alarm bells rang in Bella's head. She knew, knew without a doubt, not a one of them could take him alone. The Rocket was right, after all. It wouldn't be easy, even for all of them. In fact, she wondered if it was even possible. A terrifying thought struck her: before this night was ended, they might very well be, too.

She had thought to work her wiles on him to bring him in alive, but now, for the first time, she doubted herself. Could she even approach him without falling into a witless swoon at his feet? They should have listened to the Rocket. But then her pride kicked in. She had to try. *I am beautiful. No man can resist me.*

She remembered to wipe the blood off her face. She gestured to her team to hold off, steeled herself against the great cold lump of fear inside, and went out to meet him.

Her cloak swirled with her movement, creating an aura of mystery about her, she knew. Her dark eyes smoldered with a look calculated to slay any mortal man. "Good evening to you, sir," she greeted him in a sultry tone. She watched those purported dangerous eyes and turned on the full power of her own. *Overkill was not an issue here,* she feared.

And found that she'd guessed right. Those blue eyes turned to gaze into her vampire eyes and were not mesmerized, shielded as only the Huntress's would be. Very daunting. But at least they hadn't started to glow yet.

"You," he said suddenly, as though in recognition, with an unconscious little grimace.

It came to her that there was something familiar about him. "Have we met?" she said inanely, feeling somehow off balance. Had she seen him before? Or was he mesmerizing her? *But no, that wasn't possible!*

He shook a little, as though to rouse himself. Was he feeling the effects of her eyes, after all? She regained some measure of her natural confidence.

"Where is Beau? His pickup—" He gestured toward it.

"Oh, he, um," (she smiled in her best imitation of embarrassment.) "He had to go into the bushes. He'll be out in a minute. Are you his friend?"

"That's right," he affirmed, with a quick glance around. Then his eyes were on her again, hawk-like. "And you? You're with Beau? Why?" For a moment, he seemed disconcerted, as though realizing that his remark was impolite.

"He brought me home to meet his family." She scrambled for the bits of information gleaned from the conversations and her ingesting of Beau's blood. "We just came from feeding, er, feeding the neighbor's animals. We're on our way to a movie."

"My, or rather, our animals," he said, gesturing toward his pickup, in which the woman sat peering through the windshield with an anxious little frown. "But why you?" His eyes narrowed.

She wasn't sure who he thought she was. Maybe he was, like any man, captivated by her beauty. She turned inward to her store of Beau's memories. "We met at college. He maybe told you."

He didn't comment but continued to watch her with an expression none too pleased. Whatever that meant. He was so handsome. It was all she could do to keep her head. To stand there, speaking to him. (Why did her throat tighten up so?) She could understand that irresistible urge to sink her teeth into him. But why did she want to throw herself at his feet and kiss them?

Or, wasn't that what the Rocket had said?

Now his eyes narrowed, and he scanned the area once more. Had one of her team made a move or a sound? No, they hadn't; she would have noticed. "There's evil here," he said, frowning. "Beau?" he called out again. There was no answer, of course.

If she didn't take him while he was yet unsure, he'd finish them all. She had to make a move. Oh, why did she feel so sluggish? *He's only a man,* she argued with herself. *No, a mere seventeen-year-old boy. I can do this.* She put on her most captivating smile and touched his arm. He jerked back as though burned. She swiftly withdrew her hand beneath her cloak. Had he noticed the claws, or—? She could not interpret his expression. Horror? Nostalgia? No, that couldn't be.

"I'm sorry," she said quickly. The thought struck her that her survival perhaps depended on him not guessing what she was. "Did I shock you? Sorry, it must be the static in my cape." She gave a little laugh. He seemed to be trying to figure something out; it would be better to act before he did, she decided. "I should introduce myself," she went on, as though everything was normal (one touch and she was tingling!). "My name is Rachel." She extended a hand.

She was a bit surprised when he clasped it. *Oops.* To him, her hand would be ice cold. She tensed, prepared for anything; anything except what he did.

He slowly turned her hand over and studied it. She was intensely aware of his warmth, heartbeat, breath, and innocence. It was all she could do not to reach up and tangle her fingers in that lovely hair, which in the yellow light seemed to throw out beams of its own.

"It's so cold." A little line of puzzlement creased his brow. "I remember you." A tear glinted on his cheek, though he didn't seem aware of it. Then his voice and his expression changed. "That museum up north… That was you at the Peace River. 1869. I, uh, don't understand. How can this be?"

"I—I don't know what you mean," Bella stammered, shocked. She should have fled right then and there. But without thinking, she brushed the tear from his cheek. And then she knew: he was that wingless angel child that had descended into Charon's realm long ago and disturbed her very existence, even to this day.

He caught the wrist of her outstretched hand. He maybe hadn't realized the tear was there. But his eyes! They were dark blue with a shimmering overlay of sun-bright turquoise like the waters off Barcelona. They were like the sky, night into day, and she wanted nothing more than to fall into them, though that sun-bright sky would be the end of her.

She couldn't tear her gaze from his; didn't want to. *¡Ay! It was supposed to be the other way around, wasn't it?* What could make her lose all sense of time and space, forget her mission, her team, Beau, and even Charon? She had to get hold of herself, had to mesmerize him, or she'd never get him to kiss her. If she could once bite him, that would be it (at least, that was how it worked with ordinary mortals). She hesitated (he was not ordinary!) and recalled a harsh lesson learned — at the very time of which he spoke, in fact. And quaked. No, this was no time to falter. She tried to put some human feeling into her expression, to perhaps draw him to herself by that route.

He suddenly seemed to realize he was holding her wrist and quickly released it. "Sorry, miss. I don't know why I said that." He glanced around and shivered, then seemed to collect himself. "Beau? Watch out, a bear's going to get you," he called out; his face reddened as he glanced at her. "Pardon me. We josh each other that way sometimes."

Bella nodded but managed a worried expression. "Beau, honey," she called (in a perfect imitation of the real Rachel), "Are you okay?" She clutched at his arm. "Bears? Oh, dear. Do you think —?"

He tensed but didn't shrug her off. As he glanced around, she realized he could see in the dark! And her team was hidden there. Fortunately, the pickup sat between him and Rojo crouched over the corpse, and China Boy holding the real Rachel.

"I'm a city girl," Bella said anxiously. "Are there bears?"

"Not bears," he said, tensely listening. A breeze stirred the treetops; otherwise, dead silence (aside from the low rumble of motors). "Something evil," he muttered, and then barked, "What have you done with Beau? Show yourself!"

Bella flinched before she realized he wasn't addressing her. She was all but undone by his touch and his heartbeat, frantic to bite, but afraid to; yet she could not flee. She slipped her arms around him and clung to him as though terrified of whatever had taken Beau (playing her role to the hilt). She felt his hand gentle at her back (not a stake through the heart), and a sob of relief escaped her.

"It'll be okay, don't worry," he said softly.

She could feel his eyes on her now, though her face was pressed against his shirt. She trembled with anticipation. *No, it would be suicide to attempt a bite.* But his heart, beating so close to her ear, was entrancing; it set her afire like nothing she had ever known.

A pitiful moan from the darkness whipped his head around. The girl! It was now or never. Bella glanced up to see the sweet pulse in his throat exposed now above the collar of his shirt. Teeth bared, she went for it.

His reaction was instantaneous. She didn't get a taste of him or even break the skin before he flung her away. The next thing she knew, she was lying on the ground, staring up at him. Those eyes. Blue Boy sprang out of the darkness, to her rescue, maybe, but the moonchild's fist laid him out on the ground.

Pinkie's shriek brought Bella to her senses; she sprang to her feet. "¡Adelante! Attack, *hermanos*!" *It was their only chance*, she thought, not knowing that it was already too late. Pinkie flew to Blue Boy. The others sprang at Bella's command, thinking, as she did, that together they could take the thing.

His eyes glowed, and a blue flash shot from them like a bolt of lightning. With no time even for a shriek, one attacker burst into flame, burned white-hot for mere seconds, and drifted to the ground as ash. Bella stared in shock; the others' momentum carried them on. The moonchild kicked out with a long leg, laying another out on the ground. His fist caught Rojo's jaw and flipped him into the bushes, red hair flying. While the moonchild was thus preoccupied, Bella streaked around to avoid those lethal eyes, to spring at him from behind. As she gripped his hair to drag his head back, two more vampires burst into flame and were gone without a shriek. Next, he took out the one on the ground, burning him to ash in a heartbeat. He turned to zero in on Blue Boy, but Pinkie had already dragged him back to the bushes; only the edge of the blast caught him.

If Bella hadn't seen it with her own eyes, she wouldn't have believed. They were fast (they were vampires), but he'd just blasted them with his eyes, methodically, like shooting clay pigeons. She could only watch in horror and disbelief as the tragedy unfolded. Everything happened so fast; it was as though the world had stopped. *No mortal could do this! Or, what had the Rocket said?*

She got hold of his hair, but not soon enough to save her team. She pulled his head back and went for his exposed throat. Again, just as her teeth were about to graze the skin, she found herself lying on the ground at his feet.

She thought that was the end for her. All it would take was a look. Unbelievably, he only stared, his eyes filled with profound sadness and questioning. They did not glow.

She abandoned every scrap of dignity and hurled herself into the shadows. "*Flee, hermanos!*" she shrieked as she flew from the scene. It was but a tattered remnant of her cocky little band that escaped that night.

Blue Boy was the only one to taste of the blue fire and survive. Rojo had scuttled away under cover of the bushes, pausing just long enough to see that Bella had made it. China Boy flung himself into the shelter of the woods with the girl clasped to his chest and soon joined the others for the journey home without relinquishing his precious burden. Bella carried Blue Boy all the way, while Pinkie hovered, aghast at the seared flesh and charred exposed bones of his right arm and shoulder. A narrow escape; he would regenerate. The thing did not pursue them. But she had lost half her team!

Charon was furious that they hadn't brought the moonchild back or killed him. Once more, his Black Sun ritual was performed as planned during the solar eclipse, though without the expected interference from the moonchild. Still, it was to no avail. Again. They were unable to walk in daylight, and Charon remained imprisoned underground.

All was not lost, however, though the mission had failed. They had the measure of the One now and knew where he was. And Charon was pleased with the gift of the nightingale, now known as Diamond. He did not turn her but kept her for his own, by his dark magic, it was said, indefinitely. She spoke to none of them, but with her gaze cast down, existed as though in a world of her own. Sometimes it seemed she talked to someone no one else could see. But she sang when she was told and otherwise found favor with the master. That was what mattered.

After everything settled down, it was back to the drawing board for Charon. And then one night, a new possibility struck him, like a bolt of lightning: What if the moonchild was somehow necessary to the ritual? *Aha! Now to find the connection.*

And to draw him in.

Child of Destiny

Hanna, Oklahoma. August 2017

It didn't seem right that the sun was shining, or that white cloud-sheep grazed in the blue sky-meadow, placid and serene, as though nothing had happened. How could this be, how could the world not be filled with gloom, with the light of Beau's pleasant, smiling face gone forever? Dark, threatening clouds would be more fitting, it seemed to Jude, and rain, falling from a black sky like the tears of weeping angels.

A small gathering of family and friends stood around the grave in the little cemetery next to the small white Baptist church, while the minister intoned some prayers. The scent of new-mown grass filled the air, and a few stray daisies the mower had missed near the fence swayed in the soft breeze. After the sound of the words died away, silence hung heavy and oppressive while members of the family dropped roses, fragrant and lovely in red and white and yellow, into the open grave. Tears flowed once more as clods thumped hollowly on the coffin.

Jude had no tears but stood dry-eyed on the close-cropped turf next to Mama and the Aldens. Yet somehow, he felt far from them, as though a great stone wall had arisen between them.

How could I have done this to them? Why didn't I stop this from happening? I could have saved him, if only I'd been there.

How he got through it, he never knew, amidst what seemed to him meaningless words of comfort and sympathy, tears and weeping all around. No, not meaningless, though he spoke them as if by rote, and could feel nothing, nor shed any tears. As soon as everyone headed to the hall for refreshments and chatter, he fled the scene.

Got to get out of here.

He walked home and climbed the hill, as he usually did when he needed time alone. There he sat, on the big rock at the very peak, contemplating all that had happened. Alone at last, he could mourn his dear friend, the nearest to a brother he'd ever had — oh, how could he have let this happen?

Of course, he knew who had really killed Beau. Or what, rather.

Why? Why did You let them? They wanted me. They mistook him for me. No, I'm sorry, God, forgive me. It was I who let them. I should have been there. I could have saved him, but I — I was too late. Too late.

He bowed his head and wept.

He knew what no one else did: vampires had caused Beau's death. Well, he'd dealt with them — with a vengeance. It wasn't enough, though, never enough. But now he knew that he could. He'd managed to get that much out of the monk's instruction, at least. It was the first opportunity he'd had to actually test it "in the field," and had rather shocked himself at how easily he'd controlled the power that had always seemed so unmanageable and frightening. And yet...

He thought of all, all that the monk had said, that only he could do this. So was the monk right, after all, when he said that he really was the One who must prevent the master vampire taking over the world? Doubts rose. *No, who am I to do this?*

But the monk believed that he was the only one who could stop them, that this was his destiny. That he was born for this, whatever the cost.

With a sigh, he bowed his head in resignation.

After a moment, he got to his feet and set off down the hill, heedless of the beauty of wildflowers lining the path and fragrant breezes sighing through the pines. He didn't notice the crunch of gravel under his feet or the dust of the road wafting away behind him. He didn't hear the birds singing in the trees or the gurgling of the creek under the stone bridge as he ran down the road to the abbey. All seemed so far away, as though in another world, one that he had left far behind.

There, the great doors of the basilica whispered open at his touch. He entered, and they closed softly behind him as he dipped his fingers in the font and crossed himself. Smelled the faint scent of incense and burning beeswax. He caught sight of a black-robed figure kneeling before the tabernacle and froze. Panic threatened.

No, I can't do this! he wailed inside himself.

The red sanctuary lamp burned steadily, calming him somewhat, while his glance took in the depictions of the fourteen Stations of the Cross lining the walls, and finally, the great crucifix above the high altar. He exhaled slowly, only then realizing that he'd been holding his breath. *God, help me know what to do.*

In that moment, he recalled the words of Jesus in the garden: *Father, not my will, but Thine be done.*

He went to the monk, tall, rigid almost, and delivered this line: "I am ready."

Mina Ambrose was born in Oregon, a cradle Catholic, and grew up on a farm. Along with taking care of animals, she enjoyed reading, drawing and painting, playing music (mainly accordion, but a smidgen of piano, organ and guitar), and of course, writing. She began with stories and poems, as well as jotting down pages of notes—ideas for novels that never went anywhere due to the distractions of her many other interests. But she kept them on file and took them out occasionally to dream.

At age twenty-one, she moved to British Columbia with her family. There she married, and for a number of years was raising children and running a busy household, her other interests relegated to the back burner (though she took them out and dusted them off occasionally). During this time she found new interest in sewing, gardening, and baking dozens of cookies and muffins for her growing family.

After her five sons and three daughters were grown, she returned to college, determined to at least get her Bachelor of Arts degree. (And did.) Meanwhile, she had a short story and poems published, and reawakened that lifelong dream of writing a novel. As she wrote, it grew and grew, until the novel became a series: *Shadows of the Sun*. *Child of Destiny* is Mina's second novel, Book Two of the series.

Mina is a member of the local art society, Catholic Writers Guild, and the American Chesterton Society (as well as volunteer typist for their online project) and has also been involved in the pro-life movement for many years. Mina has recently begun playing violin, and, since her retirement, once more finds herself baking cookies, in order to have some on hand for when her grandchildren come to visit. She lives surrounded by her eight adult children, eighteen grandchildren and one great granddaughter.

Published by
Full Quiver Publishing
PO Box 244
Pakenham ON K0A2X0
Canada
www.fullquiverpublishing.com

9 781987 970258